the legend of the son of man

A novel by
Jonathan Richard Cring
www.imsonofman.com

Life with Style - Publisher

ISBN 0-9704361-2-2
LWS PUBLISHERS
227 Bayshore Drive.
Hendersonville, TN. 37075
(800) 643-4718 A.C. 74

www.imsonofman.com

dastardly dissension. I remembered running into Mekel. With all the morning's excitement, I had forgotten all about it. How strange he had not recalled who I was. He certainly was in a hurry. I thought about Marius, a just man, now dead and deserted on a muddy shore. Could Mekel possibly be connected with Marius's death? I shook my head, dismissing the thought as ridiculous.

"I hope you don't mind."

I was summoned back to reality by the sound of a most musical female voice. I looked up to see a beautiful fair-skinned woman, carried on a purple bed by two men wearing gold-braided crowns. I must have appeared comically surprised, because she laughed at me.

"I didn't intend to alarm you," she said. "You were certainly in a world of your own."

"Not at all. It's just that this is my first visit from royalty today."

She laughed again, a full-bodied, joyful peal.

"Please do join me, I've dangled my feet in this water for so long I'm all wrinkled from the ankles down."

"And to think I just thought you had old feet," she chided, as the servants eased the couch to the river's edge. She extended her hand and said, "My name's Joanna."

I wiped my hand on my robe and stretched to take hers. "I'm Jesus. Pleased to know you."

She caught me glancing at her couch and smiled. "I'm not trying to flaunt my wealth or anything. I'm crippled." She wasn't apologetic, just informational. Her voice did not have the customary drop in tone, or her eyes the common downcast expression associated with one emotionally debilitated by their infirmity.

"Then I will never complain of wrinkled toes again," I said, bowing my head.

"And I won't complain about the quality of my robe," she commented dryly, rolling her eyes at the tattered state of my frock.

I peeked down at my robe--a disgrace, soiled and torn. We both giggled. Barriers alleviated, we spent the afternoon sharing freely.

Joanna was the wife of Chusa, who worked in Herod's palace, in charge of the household affairs. She had spent her childhood in Athens, but her family moved to Jerusalem when she was ten so her father could oversee the and tugging at the body.

"Let me help you," I said, grabbing hold of a leg.

"No need. I wouldn't know what to do with it anyway. Yes, there's always danger," he continued. "But the work goes on. And it seems to draw bigger crowds. You have the faithful and a whole bunch of assassins to fill the ranks."

"What next?"

He shrugged. "Now there's a question I can truly avoid. Why don't you start off with something easy, like the color of God's skin?"

This time we both laughed.

"Seriously," Alphaeus inserted. "This will be a day with no people to baptize. This place will be deserted, like it was attacked by man-eating locusts."

I grimaced at the terrifying image.

Alphaeus grinned and continued, "But note I said man-eating. I'm going to my station because I figure the women will be spared."

He strolled away, leaving the body for other less involved persons to care for.

"Can I join you, brother?" I caught up with him.

"Aren't you frightened of the Romans?"

"Actually, I'm more afraid of the women."

"Wise," said Alphaeus. "The Romans might kill you and leave you to rot, but a woman is prepared to nag you through eternity."

We had another good laugh, this time, I'm sorry to report, at the expense of the female of the species; false bravado to mask our real trepidation over a dead Marius, angry zealots, and lingering assassins.

Alphaeus was right about the women. Their numbers had diminished, but not greatly. There were still many who were undaunted by the death of Marius, and determined to see their missions fulfilled and their sins washed away. Alphaeus wasted no time, baptizing one after another. I sat on the bank of the river, dangling my feet in the murky water. I let my mind wander. Occasionally a victorious cry from the scene interrupted my speculations. The day, which had started out overcast, was delightfully clear and warm. It seemed incredible this peaceful spot could be the stage of murder plots. I thought about the events at the campfire the previous evening, complete with heavenly dimensions and

Table of Contents

SITTING 1
A Stable Decision

There is nothing quite so satisfying as the warm afterglow of thoughts that accompany time well spent.

It is good to be back. Dying was not much fun, take it from me. A painful loss of control. The pain is predictable, I guess. Crucifixion is a great deterrent to life.

Losing control. The body likes to breathe, and becomes quite agitated when you suggest otherwise.

Killed. Murder, the greatest insult to the mind; forced to die at someone else's whim. I didn't like it at all. I searched for some sense of nobility, and ended up--really upset.

People wanted me dead, and stood around to watch it. My last performance, and I couldn't select the stage or costuming. I was accustomed to sparking my own fire. Of the two great liberators, money and freedom, I prefer the latter. Money buys convenience, but freedom allows choice.

I choose to live, I said in my mind a hundred times. I liked living, especially when assaulted with the alternative.

Who likes death? It is a hell of an idea.

Decreation.

The most difficult task was getting alone to come here. My friends were not willing to lose sight of me again. I can't blame them--they are justifiably suspicious. You can't really call it paranoia when it happened before without your permission. Consider their perspective of the recent events: they watched a friend die. I keep telling them, "Hey, I'm here" But old memories die hard. It's no wonder they are on edge. Truthfully, it is astounding we all aren't jumping at the sound of the slightest creak.

I reassured them I would return. They requested Peter accompany me on this jaunt so I wouldn't get killed again. A nice gesture.

I am standing at the door of the Inn containing the stable where I was born. My intention? To see the place before moving on. So it is the memory of my birth and the trouble it caused which brings me to the City of David (although hardly a city and David claimed so many locales the title lacks individuality.)

Nevertheless, it is where I began and where I desire to plop down for a good look before I go on.

Of course, there may be a problem in explaining to this aged innkeeper the nature of my business. Would he remember two frightened, country kids arriving at his gate, the girl brimming with child? Dear Lord, I can see them now. My father frantically demanding a room for his pregnant bride, the seasoned innkeeper smirking, and the hapless lad desperately trying to keep the squeak of adolescence out of his voice. Perhaps my mother could only muster a few grunts and groans, but I am sure her limited communication had its measure of effect. Women can intimidate on many levels. In hard labor would have to be primary amongst the ways.

Anyway, they got the stable. It was clean, had a bucket of water, and a tonnage of furry companions. I can assure you, it is a child's dream to be born into a world filled with pets.

SITTING 2
Overshadowed

I certainly was not the first child born before provision was made, but this most recent inconvenience had followed a bizarre pregnancy.

Mary saw an angel, or so it goes. I do not know which was more difficult for my mother to explain, the premarital conception of a child, or the heavenly intervention promoting the idea.

Joseph stepped forward and protected her, a bold move by a simple man; one that ended up having eternal consequences. Considering the fragile nature of the male ego and the flamboyant imagination common to us all, he was probably greatly tempted to believe Mary was unfaithful and involved in a clandestine relationship. Word has it he had a vision, too. Yet even an angel might find it difficult to convince a virile male his betrothed was still in her predisposed virginal state.

I think it is important to note he was determined to stand by the woman he loved even before he was given the supernal advice. I am sure Gabriel's confirmation was greatly appreciated, but the decision to remain was his.

Of course, every noble overture is condemned to its day of persecution. Nazareth became a fiery pit of gossip for the perplexed duo. In the midst of the haranguing, Mary went to visit a relative named Elizabeth, who also claimed to have seen an angel and was carrying a promised child of her own. Just think of it! Two supernatural visitations within the boundaries of one family. Seems more odd than God. Yet it did create a simple sisterhood, granting strength in a most oppressive time.

Mary concluded her visit and returned to Nazareth, daintily showing the firstfruits of three month's worth of child. Slut or saint, she was pregnant and a baby would be the result.

Actually, people were already becoming bored with their own vindictive chatter. The gossips were eagerly hunting for their next victim. Matter of fact, the only eyebrows raised at all were when Joseph decided to take his full-term wife to Bethlehem to pay a new tax levied by Augustus. He wasn't about to leave her at home to encounter undue scrutiny--or miss the birth of his son.

So Caesar thought he was going to get rich on the meager sustenance of poor Bedouin peasants. As things turned out, more noble causes were being unveiled in the shadowy confines of a hay-strewn manger.

SITTING 3
Relah

I knocked on the door, expecting a grizzled chap, since it had been over thirty years. Knowing I would be dealing with a suspicion factor, I had brought some coins to sweeten his will.

Suddenly, the door was flung open as if propelled by a strong gust of wind. There before me stood a young girl in her flowering years, foot planted, hand on her hip, and a foreboding snarl curling around the lip. I was a little surprised; I seemed to be an unwelcome interruption.

"Is the good man of the house about?" I asked cautiously, eyeing her cemented features.

"There ain't no good man in this house."

"Might your grandfather be here?" I requested, gauging her age.

"Hope not. He's dead."

"I'm sorry."

"Oh, don't be. Not even grandma cared much. The old geezer was so stingy his heart stopped pumping blood."

"Then might I speak to the new innkeeper? It is really quite important."

"I guess you are. Ain't nobody left but me and my older brother . . ."

"Well, then. Might I. . .?"

She interrupted, anticipating my request. "He's as crazy as a loon! He thinks he's a fig tree blooming by the desert oasis."

We stared at each other. Then she began to shut the door. As far as she was concerned the conversation was over. I gently, but purposefully, placed my hand out to prevent closure.

"Who are you and what do you want?" she demanded, gawking at my extended arm.

"Jesus of Nazareth in Galilee. I preached in these areas. Perhaps you have heard of me?"

"Preacher, huh?"

"Not in the conventional sense."

"What could be worse than an unconventional preacher? Do you owe me money?"

"I have money."

She smiled. "I don't like religious people."

"Me either."

"Why are you one?"

"Did I mention that the money was for you?"

"Do you eat snakes?"

"I was wondering if I might see your stable?"

"Need a new home for your flock?"

"Very good," I laughed. "No, much more personal reasons."

"You got something personal goi.ig on in my stables?"

I considered myself a fine communicator, but on this day, I couldn't have been arrested for stealing a clever phrase.

"I was born there." She waited for me to continue. "During the Caesar census."

"Before my time."

"You have heard of it?"

"Caesar or a census?" she directed with a playful smile.

"You aren't going to make this easy, are you?" Her grin grew as she shook her head. "Your grandfather rented the stable to my mother and father because the Inn was full."

She burst into a husky roar of laughter. "Now that makes sense. My grandpa would have taken great pleasure in relieving some hill country Galilean of his hard-earned money for the promise of lodging in a stable."

"Might I have a few moments in there?"

"To do what?"

"Five denarii," I stated quietly.

"You can have the whole damn place for ten."

"Let me start with the stable."

"It's small, it stinks, I'm closed, good day."

She was shutting the door. I stuck my foot in. She stared at me in disbelief.

"I don't want to be overbearing, but if you could just give me some time."

"Because you were born there?" she asked with a fresh dose of sarcasm.

"Yeah, that's right."

"What kind of parents let their kid be born in a stable?"

"I suppose surprised ones," I said as I pulled the coins from my leather pouch and placed each one into her hand.

She giggled, squeezed tightly and held them near her breast. "You will need a light," she said with a smirk.

"I suppose so."

"How long?"

"Till I am done."

"There is nothing down there worth five denarii."

"Not until I arrive."

She winced at my strange answer. "I will have to lead you."

"That's appreciated."

"Don't try nothing funny. I got a dagger."

"I won't make you use it."

The deal was done.

I was back in Bethlehem--nearly as welcome as the first time.

SITTING 4
Mangerial Skills

W e made our way down the stairs into the darkness, a bleak presence of black perpetuating its own chilling force, the candle only illuminating a small patch of fluttering glow directly in front of us.

At the bottom step we discovered a barricade constructed across the entrance to the stable--clumps of moldy hay, old clothing, pieces of stone, and broken pottery.

The young lady turned the candle toward me, exasperation on her face. "Have you seen enough?" she snapped, trying to over-compensate for her lack of vision.

"What is your name?"

"Relah." A hybrid name, probably chosen not to offend Jew or Greek.

"Listen Relah, I can take it from here."

"Take what?"

"I can find my way."

"There ain't nothing to find, cause there ain't nothing to see."

"I am here to reminisce."

"You must not need much to entertain you," she smiled, greatly relieved, handing me the candle.

"I will come and tell you when I am done."

"I will check on you."

"No need."

"My job. By the way, neither the Inn nor me are responsible for anything that might gnaw or chew on you."

"My project, my risk."

"Suit yourself." She shuffled up the steps, then paused at the top, turning back. "By the way, Nazarene. I would have let you see the hole for nothing." She opened the door and escaped within. I thought I heard the residue of a nasty chuckle but it could have just been her sandals rubbing against the stones.

I was alone. Now what? I wondered what Relah was thinking from her warm, well-lit perch up above. Probably sympathy, like she feels when her brother insists he is a tree sprouting leaves. Come to think of it, some foliage might be nice about now. Deserted stables do tend to chill the body.

SITTING 5
Be Careful What You Ask For

I lifted my candle expectantly. Lying before me were the remains of the life of the innkeeper--discarded, barely recognizable fragments of formerly meaningful possessions, now totally encased in mold.

Then an intrusion by an existing tenant--not a living thing, even though its presence was undeniable. The place really stinks. I don't know why I hadn't notice it before--a reeking cloud of decaying everything. The once noble idea of coming to this place is losing its gleam. Yet I am stubborn--one of my more endearing qualities.

I pushed at the barrier. A shuffle and squeaky retreat let me know I was not alone. Poor rat; thought he found a private hideaway and then I show up.

I continued my labor, pulling at the heap. Part of the blockade toppled, providing a small hole directly above my head. I established a foothold and climbed up the stuff, wiggling my shoulders through the top. Suddenly, the whole mess gave way and I tumbled head first, landing unceremoniously on my backside. I laughed. It wasn't much different from my first arrival in this same room. Then, too, I had been in the dark, trying to squeeze through a tiny entrance, to be dropped out on my butt.

"Welcome back, Jesus of Nazareth," the walls seemed to echo the resonance of my fall.

I was able to retrieve my candle, which I had fortunately hidden away.

I was here! Four walls with some stone partitions, I assume used for stalls. I whirled around, looking for treasure--just animal dung and a small woven basket. Some mother might have used the container as a tiny cradle for a newborn package. Closer look--a feedbag for some hungry beast.

I continued snooping. The stench was lessening, or worse, I was getting used to it. Isn't that the way it is? What hangs around eventually gets accepted. In other words, there was still stink, but now I liked it. . . Dark places do tend to bring out the philosopher in the common man.

Speaking of philosophy, what was I really trying to uncover in this dump? Or was it something I needed to *recover*? I guess I wanted to live it all again; needed to find the place within this corral where I began.

It certainly would not have been near the entrance. People would have been coming in and out all night, checking their livestock. Privacy would have been impossible for the modest virgin and her terrified spouse. The wall nearest the street would have been too noisy due to the milling, drunken souls who were trying to drown their sorrows over Caesar's latest taxing.

As I turned the candle about the room, my eyes focused on a small ledge, actually more like an indentation on the east wall, near the stalls, and as secluded as possible. Could this be the spot where the Nazarene couple huddled together to shroud some privacy for their first-born? I couldn't be sure, but it seemed right. I walked across the room and sat down on a lump of stone that had surrendered its position in the nearby wall. Of course, there was no proof, but it worked for me. I was on a mission to dream, not confirm.

As far as I was concerned, this was my first home-- a simple structure buried away in a common inn, surrounded by a tiny village of forgotten people, more closely resembling a tomb than a nursery. But Mary and Joseph made it a castle for their little king.

I sat and let the time slip away. The settled silence and sacred solitude provided the shrine for my sweetest memories to find a sanctified release; sheer joy at just being alive. The tears came freely.

It was time to celebrate my life.

SITTING 6
Birthing a Notion

There was no rest for our new family. A stable is a place where animals find shelter--people must take their chances.

The young mama and papa couldn't have fathomed the forces at work that night, being quite content to see me born safely with all digits intact.

Privacy was interrupted by the arrival of excited shepherds; herders claiming to have seen a vision of angels. They said these heavenly messengers had sent them to see a newborn king in a manger. One might be impressed by this, but there were two logical explanations. Shepherding was a lonely profession--the lamb watchmen were often known to partake of the fruit of the vine during the creeping night hours when conversation was only "sheepish." A drunken shepherd was likely to see anything in the night sky.

The second possibility involved the spiritual and political climate of the times. The Jewish race was so desperate for something to happen, so frantic for the arrival of a *Deliverer* to free them from the Romans, that prophets and visions were being conjured at an alarming rate. So the intellectuals of the day had begun to disregard erroneous reports, while the fervently religious were growing exhausted and somewhat faithless attempting to verify the latest Messianic rumor. You can understand why these common laborers might have been ignored by their neighbors the morning after.

I don't bring this up to water down the story. There *were* forces at work--the planets, stars, and angels were busy, continuing a vigil long past the initial birthing eve, beckoning a select few to come see what had been accomplished by a young maiden's willingness to be touched by the Spirit in a unique way. The saga unfolded. For some fourteen months a star persevered in the sky--more to come.

My parents stayed in the stable until Mary gained strength. Giving birth was a great shock to her frail frame. She hadn't eaten enough during the pregnancy. Excitement, worry, persecution, and lack of funds had hindered proper nourishment. She was a little girl with adequate fortitude to sustain me, but her body was startled. I was a large baby, too. They say I weighed two stones, quite a strain for the young lady.

But by the eighth day, strength was returning, so my father gathered us and made the short journey into Jerusalem to have me circumcised-- the Jewish law. They were glad to get out of the manger, and the trip was the perfect length to enable Mary to get exercise without becoming exhausted.

Jerusalem--a symbol of Moses in a Caesar-controlled land. Temple business was carried on reverently by a people acting as if they were still free. Deep within their hearts, though, they all knew, from chief priest to common slave, that the ruler of Jerusalem was not Moses or his god. Their present master was in Rome, languishing on a lavish throne funded by the coinage and sweat of the once-chosen people; all an inglorious facade. The Jews pretended to be independent, self-sufficient superior beings; the Romans just kept building roads, aqueducts, and palaces--all of which continued to cement the reality that the seed of Sinai was an occupied people. Meanwhile the common folk were absorbing gentile culture, demanding a golden miracle while peddling a worthless trinket.

Small wonder they didn't even turn their heads to see a young peasant couple enter the gates of the city. The supervising priest felt no stirring in his heart as he circumcised their child. Even when an old man and woman came forward to prophesy about the young baby, no one was awakened from the mundanity of their duties. Anna and Simeon were part of the aging vanguard of the temple, considered more "tetched" than touched by God. As usual, answers were ignored because men were too busy practicing their prayers.

My father decided to keep his little family in Bethlehem. Nazareth seemed far away, lacking promise. After all, a child with any future should be near the City of David.

Joseph hired on as an apprentice craftsman. Wages were bread to eat and room to sleep. It made no difference. We were together and all seemed destined toward a quiet, uneventful life in the little town.

SITTING 7
A Word from the Wise Is . . .

One year passed, filled with the simplicity of settling into the normalcy of our surroundings. I started to walk shortly before my first birthday. Joseph called all the neighbors together and bored them with each detail of my stumbling extravaganza, then wore me out making me repeat the activity in front of each bystander.

My birthday was graced by a visit from Zacharias and Elizabeth, who were traveling to Jerusalem and stopped in Bethlehem to secure lodging. They were accompanied by their son, John, eighteen months old. He was a brute of a kid, and didn't care much for me. He took a pot of water and dumped it over my head, leaving me drenched and whining, my first of two baptisms from the little rascal. They brought news from home. Relatives were fine, but uprisings from the rebels were riddling the ranks of all the families in Galilee. The Romans were suspicious of any ritual resembling Judaism. Zacharias had been accosted and questioned by a soldier concerning the whereabouts of ardent zealots in the region. The times were tense with the inflexibility of men's desires.

The visit from home folks did a world of good for our family. Joseph had grown weary of his work. Labor without friends is most tedious. I had become his life; his source of hope and strength. We were close. People commented, "wherever you find the carpenter, the son was a mere toddle behind". My first words were "Pa-Pa."

Mary was somewhat perturbed by my choice. After all, she was the feeder, changer, and carrier. "Mama is as easy to say as Papa," she protested.

I had a closeness with Joseph, who let me be a young, energetic, rambunctious boy. Mary was more careful, faulted with the dubious attribute of foresight. I loved them both, being granted the two most glorious people alive as parents.

When I was nearly two years old something happened that changed my life forever. It was hot, and I was napping. Mary awakened me, cleaned my hands and face, and changed my clothes, dressing me in my synagogue robe. I never wore it except on the Sabbath. Had I overslept three days? Her face was aglow with excitement; deeply absorbed in the labor of trying to make a hot little boy look proper and dignified.

I might have been frightened, but she was singing. I loved to hear her sing, assured everything must be all right if Mama was making melody.

Joseph appeared in the doorway, bellowing, "Is he ready?"

Now I was worried! He was always on the job. Why was Papa at home? Perhaps it was the Sabbath!

Joseph was bustling around, straightening up the room. My Papa doing housework? Something was truly amiss. Mary finished her task, and stood me to my feet, stepping back to admire her labors. She grimaced, then fussed and fretted some more. My hair seemed her greatest preoccupation--just enough wavy curl to have a rebellious nature.

Joseph was growing impatient. "Hurry, Mary."

"I am trying to make your son presentable for our guests."

Guests? We never had guests. There was barely room in our abode for abiding, let alone inviting. Well, there was one very brief visit from the senior carpenter, more an inspection than a social call. Visitors were rare. Who would be coming to see us? Granted, we were not lepers, but had similar social invisibility.

"Mary, he looks fine. Can I show them in?"

"Tell them the place is very messy."

"It looks fine, I'll get them." He was out the door. Them?

Joseph reappeared. "This way, your Excellency." He bowed with the ease and grace of a man who works with wood and stone.

In walked the tallest man I had ever seen--a beard, funny eyes, and a tail coming out of the back of his head, dressed in a golden robe that shimmered even in the faint light of our dwelling.

He turned to my father, pointing down at me. "This is the boy?"

I thought he was going to eat me. I know it sounds ridiculous, but he definitely embodied the power to devour. I grabbed my mother's leg and clenched it tightly.

"This is Jesus, your Excellency." Joseph bowed again, improving with each dip

"Come to me."

I looked at Joseph, who nodded his approval.

Mary pulled my hands away from her robe. "It's fine," she coaxed.

I was not certain of the stranger's intentions, but I relented. Better to be eaten in obedience than remain defiantly intact. I shuffled my way in dangerous proximity to his massive grasp. He knelt down and stroked my hair, laughing. He smelled of animal and sweat. "So this is the king? They do make them small."

"I am not a king," I said impudently.

"We have come very far, little one. We have followed a star, a star which led us to your home. You are a king." He must have seen my confused expression because he continued. "You don't need to think of it now. This is the time for you to be a lad--young, playful, and alive. There will be time later for royal demands."

Then he ushered in his companions, six in all, another as big as the giant, two dressed in purple, one with a long nose and earrings. a beautiful woman with hair to her knees, and a little boy.

"How old are you?" I asked the smallest. I was drawn to him because I could see his face. All the guests laughed.

"He is not a boy," said the giant. "He is a dwarf."

I was confused. He looked like a child and grinned like a boy. I liked him. "I don't understand." It pretty much summed up my feelings. Yet something did rise in my spirit as the giant spoke, chilling my spine while warming my heart.

"Would you like to ride my camel?" asked the giant.

"Yes," I screeched.

The next three days, our guests expanded my mind with stories of their world to the east, feeding us delicacies from their homeland. I was exhausted by camel rides and playtime with the dwarf, who consented to be a little boy during the visit.

The morning of the fourth day they came into our house carrying large boxes.

The giant spoke. "My name is Santere, leader of these wise few, who have sought you out, my King." (He said the big name slowly enough I could understand it.) "We have brought gifts for you, and before we depart, we leave them in your care."

My heart sank--our guests were going to leave. I was losing my playmate.

"We bring gold," Santere continued, turning to Joseph. "Use this to fund the child's needs but save enough for him to establish His kingdom."

The beautiful woman stepped forward. "I am Chenaul, precious soul," she smiled, leaning down to my face. "I bring the King frankincense, the sweetness of life, to fragrance his every move."

Then my dwarf. "My name is Beloit." He had such a wee voice. "This is myrrh, the bitterness of responsibility that faces this king as he lives, and even in his death."

They stepped back, bowing.

Mary was weeping. Joseph moved forward and embraced Santere, who whispered something in his ear. Joseph looked scared. I found out much later Santere had warned my father about King Herod. Having sought counsel from the potentate upon arriving in Judea, he naively trusted Herod for help, but in a dream was warned to avoid further contact with the ruthless ruler. All the wizened souls believed I was in danger from the jealous despot.

Farewells were uttered and beasts mounted, as the itinerant givers made their way across the burning sand. We solemnly watched as the caravan disappeared into the desert. They were gone, but the excitement of their visit would remain.

We were all exhausted; Mary, quiet--Joseph, distant.

I was ready for bed, to sleep and dream of wise seekers from the East, forever my friends.

SITTING 8

Run and Not Be Weary

Time wound its way in an endless crawl, nothing to compare with the experience of Santere and the wise ones from the East. I lost the tiny man who introduced me to such wonderful games.

There was one little boy living near the carpenter shop, about three years old, but small for his age. Mama said it was due to all the sickness he had. I didn't care; he was the right size and made a well timed replacement for my playmate. His name was Jeremiah; he taught me new words and I taught him how to run fast. His parents, Rachel and Jamon, let us play at their house all the time. Then we moved into our new home. We finally got a real dwelling place instead of just a space. My Papa received news from the senior carpenter about a house available on the outskirts of Bethlehem, so Joseph seized the opportunity to be relieved of the cramped quarters above the shop.

Moving--an exciting day for Papa, as he carried me on his shoulders all the way through town to the doorstep of our little abode, Mary walking alongside, trying desperately to keep up with the rapid pace set by her exuberant husband.

"Here it is!" said Joseph, with the fervor and reverence of a priest revealing the Ark of the Covenant.

"It is beautiful, and so big!" Mama knew exactly what to say to make my father's chest puff out.

"As long as we live, me and my house shall serve the Lord. This shall be our home. May God smile on what is done within its walls."

A time for speeches. What my father lacked in eloquence he more then compensated for in enthusiasm, sweeping Mary off her feet and carrying her through the door to her awaiting palace, where an appropriate amount of "ooh's" and "aah's" were graciously poured forth from the lips of the adoring wife.

Out popped my father and whisked me up into the air, catching me before I plummeted to the ground. "Let's go, Jesus, we're home."

The house was much bigger, actual areas to sleep and room to play. I could even run inside as long as I didn't make Mama scream. I could hardly wait to have Jeremiah over to see it.

The first week was spent cleaning and arranging, Mama attempting to make the dirt floors as tidy as possible. I kept asking when Jeremiah could come.

"Soon." (Don't parents understand, "soon" is an unacceptable answer?)

We were making progress, the house beginning to resemble a place where a family lived. My mother placed mats down for eating and sleeping, carefully distinguishing between them.

I was very proud of my new residence.

The day before Sabbath, Papa stayed home from the shop to do some "man" things about the house. He had me bustling about, carrying pieces of stone and skins of water. I was so exhausted I didn't eat, crawled up on a mat and went fast asleep--dreams came easily; visions of friends and play.

I saw Jeremiah in these passing flashes, searching for something, or maybe somebody. I called to him, but he didn't answer--he couldn't hear me. Then I sensed a beckoning voice. I thought it was my own cries for Jeremiah. Then I realized it was the deeper pitch of a man's speech.

"Jesus, wake up, Jesus." Somebody was stirring me--Papa. "Please son, wake up."

My eyes blinked and I saw the crouched figure of my father kneeling over me. Was this still a dream?

"Jesus, we must leave, please be quiet about it!"

"What's going on? Mama?"

"She is fine, don't be afraid."

"Why are we leaving? This is home!"

"Son, please, Papa has had a dream."

"I had a dream, too."

"Please tell me later. Now, get dressed."

Could it be more friends with presents? Something was different. The voice of my father quivered as he spoke, the assurance gone.

I listened for singing. Mama please sing, then I will know everything is fine. She busied herself in silence. Had I done something wrong? Why were we leaving our home?

Suddenly Joseph reappeared. "Mary, the animal is ready."

She picked things up with a sullen, abstract detachment, weeping.

Joseph grabbed her hands. "Stop it! Please, you are scaring the boy. Leave it all, we can't carry it."

Mama obediently dropped all she had gathered, picked me up in her arms and scurried out the door. I could feel her trembling. She climbed up on the donkey.

I shivered. "Papa?"

"Jesus, please be silent."

Joseph lifted me up and handed me to Mary, and turned, busying himself scouting for an exit. Mama trembled. Joseph pulled on the rope and the donkey trudged into the darkness, a bleak cold of a foreboding wilderness. I wept against my mother's breast, bitter tears; tentative sobs of a little boy snatched from the security of night dreams, my world without definition.

I thought about Jeremiah. He never saw my house. What was Papa thinking? A family needed a home.

My thoughts were ever-so-mercifully overcome by a fit of sleep. My last recollection was my Papa mentioning something about an angel and King Herod. I went to sleep believing either King Herod or God had evicted us from our new lovely quarters.

I didn't like either one.

Living on the Cutting Edge

I awoke shuddering, heart racing. The shock not worn off. The sun was in my face and the glare hurt my eyes. The air was hot and heavy and very hard to breathe. We were still moving; inching our way through the tan sea of sand in the throes of a repressive gloom. It must be Sabbath. Mama told me yesterday Sabbath was near. Why would we journey on Sabbath? I had been warned of fierce punishments for such evil doings. Why were we in this desolate domain, rejecting the laws of God? It was a troublesome burden to my frail thinking.

As my eyes adjusted I made out the figure of my father--deliberate, determined, perspiration streaming down his face, eyes moist and hollow. Mama stared at the horizon, occasionally glancing at the struggling, beleaguered form of her melting mate.

I tried to remain quiet, but hunger pangs won the day. "Mama."

"Joseph, he's awake," said Mary apprehensively. It startled me so much I started to cry.

"I'm hungry," I whined. "Where are we going?" A drizzle of tears nearly engulfed my question.

"It's all right, Jesus, everything is fine."

Joseph's words were properly placed but lacked the tenderness of consolation.

"Mama is here. We will eat soon." There was that dastardly word "soon", again.

"Where are we going?" I persisted.

Joseph brought the donkey to a halt, picked me up in his arms squeezing me tightly, uttering a light whimper. "We must go away for awhile."

"From our house?"

"Son, you must trust me. There is danger in Bethlehem right now."

Danger. I thought of monsters or maybe a giant like Goliath. I had decided never to be afraid of any of those things. "We can fight."

"This is not the time for a fight. You must learn when to stand and when to move."

"Is it a monster?" I wanted detail on size, color, and variety.

"The worst monster of all. A man who feels no conscience toward God or his fellows."

I didn't understand. The words were not meant for me, not phrased for my comprehension. Joseph's thoughts were concealed deeply in his treasure of responsibility. I looked toward Mama, who was weeping. I wanted her to stop. So not knowing what to do, I released a fresh river of tears.

"Silence now, it is time to eat. Mary, make ready some of the bread and I will open a skin of wine."

I recognized the tone. There would be no more discussion. It was time to listen and obey. My father was in control.

We sat on a mat and quietly began to eat, the bread salty from my tears. I looked out over the glistening sand, some granules reflecting the gleam of gold and the polish of silver. There was nothing else in sight. My father ate while watching the hills. Mama nibbled, peeking at Joseph. Suddenly my father rose to his knees, peering in the distance. I looked, too. I couldn't see anything but a great mountain of sand. I watched him closely. He squinted and shaded his eyes, straining to distinguish the distant sight. I looked again. There was something, very small, more or less a tiny black speck on the horizon, so far away I could not determine if it was coming or going.

Joseph eased to his feet. "Mary, prepare the boy."

It was now certain. The darkened splotch was moving our way, closing quickly. Joseph threw the mat on the donkey, picked Mary up and placed her upon its back, then lifted me, gently handing me to Mary.

"What is it, Joseph?"

"Perhaps nothing, let us all pray so. Yes pray, that is good to do."

Mama obediently bowed her head. I didn't know any prayers, especially not about black specks chasing us from across the range. I was terrified, but decided to look back. I could see more now. It was not just a speck, it was a man on a beast. Yes, there could be two of them. Joseph pulled on the donkey's rope trying to coax the best effort from the over-burdened animal. He attempted to initiate a run. The donkey saw no need, given the morning heat, to be quite so active; escape was futile. I could now view two men, one old and large, the other young and small. They were riding a four-legged creature I had never seen before.

"We must hurry and hide," Joseph said with an uncharacteristic panic in his voice. This presented a problem. Where do you hide in the desert? If we could see, so could they. We had been spotted. They were heading our way.

"They will take him," Joseph spoke to Mary.

Who, me? Why would they want me? I was little and not good for much but bouts of play. I took another peek. Now they were so close I could see the outline of their faces; skin nearly as burned and black as their robes, the smaller one, a boy.

"What are they riding, Papa?"

"Horses, Jesus. Roman horses."

He drew out his staff, wanting to appear the warrior prepared for battle, but resembling more a terrified, young carpenter quite out of his element.

The twosome was now upon us, the animals snorting sand and heat from their nostrils.

"You need no weapon, my brother. We are your countrymen," said the larger.

Joseph gripped the staff. "You ride horses." Joseph was careful, agitated, moving his feet, shifting his body weight from side to side.

"A gift from some Roman soldiers who were not practiced on the use of the sword. I am Jehu, of the tribe of Benjamin. My son, Simon," said the horseman, with a disconcerting flurry of friendliness.

"You are thieves, we have nothing."

"We are not thieves. We are Zealots. We only steal Roman gold. We only kill the ones who stand in the way of our freedom."

"We are just a family on a journey," my mother spoke for the first time.

"On the Sabbath? Where?" Jehu dismounted.

"Stand back, it is no concern to you."   Joseph moved toward the Zealot.

"Easy, my brother, we mean you no harm. We are just watching out for our countrymen; even degraded souls, such as yourselves, who ignore the Sabbath."

He helped his son down from the well-lathered beast, a very skinny boy about ten years old.

"We are journeying to Egypt," Joseph said nervously.

"Egypt? No place for a fine kosher family to go. What business have you with the heathen?" Jehu asked, taking on the mannerisms of a priest.

Joseph didn't respond. Mary started to speak, but father raised his hand, commanding her to remain silent.

Jehu walked over to our donkey. "You were pushing this donkey quite unmercifully. Were you trying to elude us?" Jehu's eyes met the ferocity of Papa's burning glare. The disquieting calm was long and labored. "What burdens this animal so?" Jehu looked through the basket carrying our few possessions.

Joseph pulled him away. "What is it that we can do to aid you?"

A smile inched it's way across the aging fighter's lips. "Oh I see, now you wish to aid us. You yearn to be of use to the cause. Do you desire to provide comfort for your battling brethren?"

"I just wish to be on my way." Joseph stepped closer to the donkey.

"As well you should," said Jehu with a smile. "With such a fine family, you wouldn't want to be delayed for too long. I doubt if this dazzling maiden would wait patiently for pleasure to arrive, she seems ready now. And this boy. . ." The black robed warrior reached down and stroked my cheek with the back of his hand.

"Leave the boy alone!" My father wailed furiously.

"How about this lovely one?" Jehu grabbed Mary by the hair and brought her lips close to his own. Joseph leaped onto his back, casting Jehu to the side in a fit of rage. The zealot stumbled to his feet, unsheathing a sword twice my height, covered with dried blood.

"Damn you, filthy swine. Don't you ever touch her again!"

"I don't want the woman, I need money for supplies and food. The boy is hungry."

The little boy drew his sword in anticipation of combat, also coated with blood, an alarming indication of how quickly the boy had lost any semblance of childhood, and been forced into a survival struggle in death and despair.

Joseph gritted his teeth, his attention riveted on Jehu. I had never seen him this angry.

Suddenly the young man raised his sword and slashed my Papa across the right side of his face. Mary lunged forward and pushed the boy to the sand, as my father sank to his knees, blood streaming to the ground. Jehu stood motionless, eyeing the treachery of his offspring.

Simon leaped to his feet. "Kill them, Papa!" Tears were in his eyes. It was a weeping of humiliation from being overtaken by a woman and a frenzied outpouring brought on by the fresh sight of human blood. "They are bastards, kill them!" The language was harsh and out of character for such a young man.

Jehu watched in a strange sense of awe with an unmistakable admiration for the intensity of his son's reaction. He had trained the boy well. Jehu carried the disposition of the fulfilled instructor, evaluating the student's latest performance.

My father slumped to the ground. Mary covered his motionless body with her own and screamed, a primal agonized outcry of a vanquished entrapped beast. "Haven't you done enough? He is dead! Do you brave Jewish warriors also kill women and children?"

The intensity of the volume nearly shattered my ears and rattled my heart in it's cage. She grabbed me and hid me under her robe. It was dark and I laid my head on her breast. Was Papa dead? I heard her heart thumping.

Jehu finally spoke. "Leave them. We don't kill the innocent." He rummaged through the basket. The first thing he happened upon was the flask of frankincense. "I knew this animal was burdened. Look, my son, this will buy us the provisions that we need."

Jehu was an impatient man for had he looked further he would have found the gold and myrrh. But like many men ardently absorbed in a cause, he lost the good common sense that brings ultimate opportunity.

Simon was still panting, eyes darting, like a predator possessed with the taste from the recent kill.

"Come son, we have business to attend to." Jehu placed the flask on his horse, mounted the animal and turned to his son. "The battle is over, we have our spoils." Jehu motioned for the boy to mount but he remained frozen, eyes fixed on the devastated family before him.

"They should die, they are Gentile bastards."

"One bastard a day. God will be pleased with that, Simon. Do not overwork yourself. You have years to kill all the remaining slime." Jehu spoke in soothing tones. Part of the weary teacher already feared the dementia of his own son. He had created a killing force, one he would have to sleep beside tonight.

"We are not Gentiles," Mama spoke through tears with teeth clenched

"Then you are just bastards." Jehu's flippant attitude brought a smile to young Simon's face. "Come son, the rebellion will not be won by sluggards."

The boy leaped on his horse with the grace of youth and a condescending disregard for the mutilation he was leaving behind.

"My lady, we appreciate your donation to the Zealot cause," Jehu nodded, as his horse reared and snorted in anticipation of the ride.

"I would not donate my dung to your damned cause." My Mama was strong. I liked that even though it scared me. The boy was one leap and reach from finishing off the lineage of Joseph. I kept watching for a sword to pierce her cloak and kill both of us.

"The frankincense will be sufficient. You may keep your dung. There is an oasis over the next hill, an adequate burial spot for your lover." He pulled on the rope and the diabolical pair prepared to ride away. I dared to take a peek out of the robe.

The boy turned on his steed and delivered one last warning. "You, little boy. I will see you again, far from your mother's breast. When I do, I will kill you!" He turned, digging his heels deeply into the horse's side, and raced into the desert.

Jehu laughed, approval of a mere thief in sadistic admiration of his murderous comrade. He pulled on the reins and made a more controlled escape.

"Is Papa dead?" I spoke, beneath her garments. She embraced me. The warmth of her skin and touch brought peace to my soul.

"No, but we must reach water. Your Papa is hurt badly."

I will never know how she did it. Somehow the young girl got that huge man on to the donkey. Sheer determination pulled us up over the next hill to a small oasis with water and slight sprinkling of perseverant greenery.

Joseph's face was still bleeding. He came in and out of consciousness.

"Jesus, get me some of the myrrh," Mama requested. I scurried to the donkey, excited to do anything to help my Papa. She mixed it with water and forced it into his mouth, then poured some directly into the gash.

"His eye is still intact," she mused. "We will just have to wait." She placed his head in her lap, rocking back and forth like a mother with an ailing baby. "Please, God, save my Joseph."

He lay very still, death trying to make its home in his features. We waited. Hours passed. My Mama prayed. She attempted a song, which diminished to a hum by the middle. Eventually, sleep overtook us both, a slumber promising rest, delivering the re-living of the horror. I awakened, shuddering with a hellish vision of Papa's assassin striking the blow. I saw my mother place cool water on my father's brow. Then the fatigue of sadness would blur my eyes and seduce me into a fretful heated hibernation. The night arrived to relieve the stark sameness of the unchanging day. Night, with its cooling breezes, mercifully encompassed the desert sands. Joseph's body, gripped with a tremendous fever, tossed from side to side upon the mat, as he cried in his delirium to the God of Moses to free his soul. Perhaps he spoke directly to the Lawgiver, for he was more of the heavens than of us. My mother would pray, and then release great sighs as if no solace could be found. It seemed the God she sought had granted Himself leave from such minute and tragic dealings. Heaven had closed for a day, without warning the needy of the vacation.

The sun rose with its normal determination to broil the sand a deeper brown. Still the fever persisted. The wound was deep, exposing the bone in my Papa's head. I was afraid: of the heat, death, life, and most of all, that ugly slice in my father's face.

He cried again and again. "I have been faithful, don't kill me."

Arbitration was being conducted on the highest levels. Somewhere, God was considering the plight of a misplaced Nazarene. Mary cradled his crushed face in her arms and comforted his ramblings.

Another day passed. The fever was unbearable. The heat of the sun made it worse. Mary would carry water in her robe and heave it on Joseph's body, causing steam to rise from his molten flesh. He was incinerating from within. She persisted.

On the third day a small caravan happened upon the oasis. Mother sought food and assistance from the leader, a young, slight man identifying himself as a Mongol, slid down from his perch high upon the laden camel, reached in a bag and pulled out some herbs and seeds, crushed them into a fine powder and moistened them in the waters of the oasis, wrapping them in a leaf garnered from a nearby palm. He took a knife from his girdle and moved towards my Papa.

My mother lunged forward and caught him by the arm.

He gently removed her hand and said, "When we are bruised, it is difficult to trust being touched again. Please, let me help your husband."

His words were filled with warmth and compassion. Such tenderness had exited our lives and left behind the recounting of tragedy and the maintenance of frustration.

Mary stepped back wearily and said, "Please don't hurt him."

The young man smiled. "If the medicine is good, what may hurt now will heal later." He took the knife and cut open the wound.

"Oh, Joseph," she whimpered.

Darkened blood and a thickened, watery, yellow discharge spurted from the sides of the incision. He took his hands and spread the wound to make room for the leaf filled with medicine. As the leaf was inserted, Joseph's body convulsed in pain.

"Leave the poultice in for one day and night. Keep it moist. After that time remove it, and with the help of the Spirit One your man will live."

These angels of mercy filled their skins with water and were on their way.

My mother was obedient and bathed the wound in the cool water of the oasis. The added nursing duties decreased her times of introspection, and lessened the need for tears. Perhaps it was only wishful thinking, but the fever seemed to be receding. The wound was uglier then ever, but Joseph was leaving the point of crisis.

"Mama, why is Papa hurt?"

"He was in the way of men doomed to destroy others."

"Where was God?"

"Trying to find a Mongol with a fast camel," she smiled and then stroked my lips to discourage further inquiries.

At the end of one day she removed the leaf of medicine, the foulest looking mess I had ever seen. She buried it in the sand. Another day passed. She continued to heave water on the carpenter's body--no more steam.

The middle of the night on the fifth day my Papa opened his eyes. He performed this miraculous feat with the ease and normalcy of one arising from an exhausting sleep. "Mary?" The voice was only a shadowy remnant of the original booming timbre, but nonetheless, the carpenter.

"Joseph, my God, Joseph." Mary fell on his chest and released the tears reserved in respect to the movement of faith.

"I have," he said and paused.

"Don't speak."

"I. . . . have . . . failed you."

"No," said Mary. "We just misunderstood the angel."

What angel? This was the first I had heard of an angel.

"I'm sorry."   His voice was stronger but still fragmented by pain.

"You will get strong. We will return to our home and forget this devilish nightmare."

"I'm sorry," he insisted.   He closed his eyes and went to sleep.

"You rest, my love, then in a few days we can get out of this oven, and go back to Bethlehem."

The next five days passed quickly, because Papa was getting better. Soon we would be going home. I could finally let Jeremiah see my new house.

SITTING 10
Because They Are Not

M y Papa was up very early. The sun was beginning to creep over the darkened hills, a chill in the air, and just enough light to make out his form--a shadow lumbering about our small campsite. I was glad it was still dark, because I was squeamish about looking at his face, smashed and crusted. I wondered if he had noticed my hesitation. I tried not to be afraid, but it was just so unnatural.

And so was he for that matter. Something was missing. Papa possessed a certain robust determination his critics called conceit, which his friends graciously dubbed confidence. Now that had changed. There was a certain carefree assurance absent from his presence. More than frankincense was poached from our family treasure. A timidity had found its way into Papa's mannerisms. He clung to Mary with the apprehension of a child, instead of the burning desire of a passionate man.

I asked Mama, "Why is Papa so scared?"

"I didn't notice he was."

"His hands shake when he touches me."

"Oh?"

"And his eyes are always wet."

"He is a man glad to be alive," she said, reaching out and patting my arm.

"Didn't he always like being alive?"

"He just has a better idea of its worth."

The conversations of the last few days had revealed our plight. It seems Joseph had been visited by an angel warning him of danger, and telling him to take his family from Bethlehem. Normal questioning of such an apparition was dismissed, because my Papa had remembered Santere's warning about Herod's intentions. Hastily, we abandoned our pursuit of normal living. Now in the light of all that had befallen us, my mother and father felt the interpretation of the dream was reactionary, and our exit premature, if not unnecessary.

"Perhaps just caution." Joseph conceded.

"If we break no law, why would a king be concerned with us?" reasoned Mary.

"We will return and rebuild our lives. My scar will remind me not to be too hasty to chase dreams in the middle of the night." It was a decision absent the conviction to ignite a great notion.

The sun was beginning to win the battle over the desert darkness. Mary busied herself preparing a small meal for our threesome. We would be journeying. Joseph prepared the donkey, placing each article neatly on the animal's back; work conducted efficiently, cloaked in the silence of unsettling doubt. Why were they so quiet? Perhaps it was an attempt to maintain solitude in vigilance. Perhaps, puzzlement over an unresolved quandary, feeling foolhardy to deny the visitation of a spirit. If this angel were merely conjured in Papa's mind, how could they ever be assured of divine direction again? Or worse, how could they be certain it was the hand of God leading thus far? No one spoke because words might confirm the true dilemma.

It was time for me to interrupt the silence. "Is it morning?" They rushed to my side.

"Good morning, son." My father hugged and kissed me, careful to keep the gash from my view, obviously aware of my aversion.

"We are going home, Jesus." Mama bubbled the words and tickled me. I obligingly giggled.

"Papa took us on a trip, but now it is time to return to our home."

"Did we plan this trip?" I asked, squinting into the morning sun.

Mama and Papa glanced at each other, conferring on an appropriate answer.

"Yes, Jesus. Why do you ask?" Mary posed cautiously.

"Did you want to be cut, Papa?"

"No, that was a surprise," he said, looking to Mama for help.

"I thought surprises were good," I persisted.

"They are." Mary glanced to Joseph for aid.

"God sometimes gives things we don't understand," replied Joseph, ill-prepared for this theological discussion.

"God wanted you cut?" I interrogated.

"Mary?" pleaded Papa anxiously.

"First we eat, then we journey," said Mary as she handed me a piece of bread, the theory being that chewing jaws don't speak.

"What about the angel?" I continued my probe, not intending to annoy.

"Let's not talk about angels," said Mary evasively.

"No, the boy needs to know. Papa thought he heard an angel tell him to leave Bethlehem. I was wrong and now, by the goodness of God, I have the opportunity to correct my mistake. You don't get many chances to change a decision. I am grateful."

"But what about the king?" I did not want to quarrel with a king.

Mary spoke first. "You are in no danger from King Herod."

"Why would he want me?" Mama and Papa stared at each other.

Joseph shook his head in disapproval. "This conversation is much too deep for a meal of bread and water. Perhaps a more suitable. . . " He stopped in mid-sentence, peering off in the distance.

I tried to see where he was looking. I couldn't be sure. They were so very small. But yes, there were more specks coming our way.

"Prepare the boy." Joseph tried to speak with authority but there was a wavering in his voice. Memories of past desert visitors still tormented his mind.

"No God, please no more!" Mary feverishly picked up our remaining things and hoisted me on the donkey's back. "We can't outrun them."

"They are on foot. It is a good sign," said Papa, sighing in relief. His words were comforting but didn't keep us from fixing our eyes on the people moving our way.

"Two of them," said Papa. "Man and a woman."

This greatly relieved Mama. She relaxed the tightened grip on my arm. "A woman can mean us no harm."

It was clear that the two travelers had spotted us. Their pace had slowed. They were exhibiting great caution. They were as leery of us as we were of them.

"Thank God! Relax! It's fine," exclaimed Joseph. "We're safe."

"It's Rachel," Mary said exultantly.

"Jamon?" Joseph called as he ran.

The two familiar travelers hastened their pace as they gained view of friendly faces. I looked for a third. Where was the lean and somber countenance of my friend, Jeremiah?

At this moment of pending reunion with dear hearts from home,. a cool breeze blew up and sprinkled a light, chilling shower over me. As quickly as it came, it left. The rain water was so cold it collected in icy droplets on my skin. I felt an inner refreshing and cleansing as if the burdens of all circumstance were lifted from my young heart, my spine tingling with excitement as I panted, gasping for air. I looked for a reaction from Mama, but she

*had run on ahead to greet our friends. It was my own
private misting; brief and personal.*
  I trotted toward the four of them. They were
meshed in sweet fellowship on the sand.
  Rachel caught a glimpse of me out of the corner of
her eye. "It's Jeremiah," she shrieked, and collapsed into the
muscular and ever-ready arms of my Papa.
  "Rachel? Rachel?" Jamon fanned her with his
hands.
  Why did she call me Jeremiah? Where was my
little language coach? I ambled up just as she was regaining
awareness.
  "Is it Jeremiah?" she said breathlessly. Her voice
was distant; her demeanor deranged.
  "No, Rachel, it's little Jesus." Joseph was
comforting, but confused with the mistaken identity.
  "Jesus . . . Jesus?" She squalled, waving her arms.
  "Yes, Rachel, it is Mary and Joseph's little boy,
Jesus." Jamon embraced her to subdue the flailing arms.
Papa motioned for Mary to assist.
  "It can't be Jesus. How?" Rachel babbled to
Mama.
  "Where is Jeremiah?" My boyish voice pierced the
rhetoric.
  "If the boy is lost, we can help you find him," said
Joseph confidently.
  "He's lost, but cannot be found." Jamon dropped
to his knees.
  "Don't give up hope, Jamon." Joseph supported
the older man to prohibit his total collapse. "I don't
understand."
  No explanation was offered. Rachel just stared at
me.
  "Where is Jeremiah?" My insistence sprouted some
impudence.
  "He's dead." With this utterance Jamon fell on
Joseph's chest, weeping deep, aching sobs.
  "No, I don't believe you!" Tears rushed to the
corners of my eyes, ready to flood down my cheeks.
  "The soldiers came . . . " Rachel regained speech,
punctuated with sullen, haunting tones.
  "Soldiers?" Mary grabbed Rachel by the shoulders,
interrogating her.
  "King Herod's men, with a proclamation sealed
with the king's ring."
  Jamon interrupted. "We told them he was three but
they would not listen."

"I don't understand! What proclamation?" Mama's inquisition continued.

Papa calmly pulled her away from the grieving mother. "Mary please, give them time."

Jamon sighed deeply and tried to explain. "All men children aged two and under were to be killed, immediately."

"Killed? Why?" Joseph conducted his own cross-examination.

Jamon took a deep breath and continued. "The soldiers said Herod's seers had foretold that these children were cursed with a plague, and if not slain while young, would spread their disease throughout all Judea."

"That's ridiculous. There were no sick children in Bethlehem." Mary addressed her comment to Joseph, glancing towards me.

"Jeremiah was three . . . three years old . . . I know. We talked about it," I blurted.

"But he was small . . . so small for his age," shuddered Rachel.

"I begged the soldiers to check with the priest who circumcised him," said Jamon. "They had no time. They said the boys must be disposed of in one night's span."

"I offered myself," said Rachel frantically. "They said, 'what would we do with a dried-up old woman'?"

"They took all the children into the middle of town, slit their throats," Jamon began to crumple like a dried leaf in the noonday sun.

"Don't, my brother." Joseph placed his hand over Jamon's mouth.

Jamon flung his arm to the side and said, "Don't you try to silence me! I want to tell it over and over again so I will never forget!" Spittle foamed at his mouth and splattered on the ground in tiny puddles. "Then those bastards took daggers and cut into each boy's body, removing his heart," he whimpered, pounding his fist into his hand.

"I ran to the soldiers, and asked them why they must desecrate the bodies of our babies." Rachel was sitting with a transfixed gaze, rocking back and forth on the shifting sand. "The soldier nearest to me turned and said, 'it is proof to his majesty that the job is done'."

"It was a counting of hearts," Jamon gasped, looking to Joseph for some purpose to the madness.

Joseph and Mary sat in disbelief, frightened to breathe, Mama absentmindedly groping for my hand, needing some contact with her living son. Jamon and

Rachel squatted on the sand, shivering and pale, in a distraught union.

She wept.

He festered the memory.

Rachel interrupted the silence. "Where were you?" she asked pensively.

"On a. . . a journey." Joseph was choking back tears.

"Stay on it."

Mary replied, "We will . . . and you?"

Jamon answered. "For now, we just move. Jeremiah was the child of our later years. He was the promise of the loving warmth of a son in the face of death. We will journey until we can find that hope in each other." He squeezed Rachel's hand; she attempted a smile.

Mama and Papa begged them to stay, but they were refreshed with water and on their way. Not once had they noticed the ugly slash in Joseph's face. The victims of tragedy are permitted a season of blind indulgence.

We did not travel that day. We cuddled and caressed. We had heard an angel. We were to go on.

"God forgive my doubt," said Joseph with resurrected vigor.

I really tried to envision Jeremiah lying in the street, his body ripped open. I couldn't. All I could see was the little, melancholy smile of a boy who could not run well, but knew lots of words.

We left in the morning, saddened but refreshed, broken and revived, relieved; older yet reborn. We were bound for the unknown, exiled to the mysterious land of Egypt.

SITTING 11
The King of Egypt

Alexandria, Egypt. The people in the streets scurried around us like a sea of swarming ants. It seemed no matter how fast we walked, we just stood still in comparison with the merchants of the city. Alexandria was Egypt in it's most elite form, culture in it's most flamboyant disguise, and knowledge at it's most fastidious conceit, much like its namesake, Alexander the Great--intense, overbearing, incisive, youthful, tenacious, and intoxicated on its own sense of power.

We were swallowed up by a community's ferocious, ravenous appetite for achievement. We were truly invisible. The populous seemed unwilling to grant us the simple dignity of maintaining human space. So many faces, everyone motioning and debating with one another as they raced down the streets; so much speed and no apparent destination.

Two soldiers, in their gala haste, nearly stepped on top of me, their crimson capes fluttering like a nomad's tent in a desert storm. Mama quickly retrieved me from the red cloth and scurried me on my way.

Then I heard a cackling sound. I turned to find its source. Was it man? Certainly none I had ever heard. Animal? Definitely not one I wished to encounter. I peeked around a corner of the street, and eyed a man gawking at me, unleashing his laugh, the origin of the mysterious sounds. He was the oldest man I had ever seen, skin browned and wrinkled like a late-season fig, smile playful, partially revealing a speckled row of alternating blackened and yellowed teeth. His hair was white, and his beard gray, with a body so slight it appeared he could lie flat and slide under a door.

The cackling chortle continued as he spoke. "I thought we had lost you, little seed. Please beware of Romans bearing capes. For you see, everything to a Roman is a weapon in the making." He burst into trebled wheezes of laughter, holding his stomach and sides as if anticipating a breech.

Mary was not amused. "He is just fine," she said, tugging me away.

"Why did you call me Little Seed?" I escaped, inching my way closer to the stranger, keeping a careful eye on the proximity of Mama's robe.

"Meant no offense. Your father had the plow, and your mother had the rich soil. You are the seed. It will take time to see what you will sprout."

"Jesus, come along." Joseph was in no mood for a marketplace philosopher.

"Please, please, let me introduce myself. My name is Xantrippe of Alexandria. They call me King Xantrippe."

"You are not a king," my mother mocked.

"Not by birth my lady. But he who knows Alexandria, rules Alexandria. I have lived here all my life. She is my mother, my wife, and my harlot."

This last word was new to me. How I missed Jeremiah's verbal tutelage. I would ask Mama for the meaning later.

"We are honored, King." A wry smile came across my father's face as he simulated a centurion bowing to nobility.

Undaunted by my father's sarcasm, Xantrippe continued. "You be Hebrews. A fine race, as well they know it."

"House of David," Joseph touted proudly.

"Oooh, you know good people. What brings you to Alexandria?"

"Visiting for a time." Mary attempted cordiality.

"Now that's a lie," said the old man abruptly. "Hebrews don't visit Egyptians. You be needing something. You see, some people come to Alexandria to learn, and some to forget. Some forget to learn, and some learn to forget. I would say you Hebrews are here to escape the wrath of some unfriendly reality."

"I need work," Joseph stated, changing the subject.

"Have you a trade?"

"Carpenter, stone mason by training."

"Training? What training?"

"Apprentice to senior carpenter, village of Bethlehem, Judea." Joseph spewed the information with efficiency and expectation.

"All that we build, carpenter, is pagan."

"A building is a building. I needn't worship there to put stone in its place."

"Go on the morrow, and speak to Bantar the Stonehead."

"What?" my Papa said, puzzled.

"It is a joke. Seriously, talk to the head stone mason on the job of building the statue of Caesar. His name is Bantar. Tell him the King sent you." A huge grin came across the old man's face, unveiling the full host of rotting teeth.

"The King? I am sure he will be impressed that I come on the recommendation of the king. Come on Mary, I must find work." Joseph was about to leave in a huff of disgust when Xantrippe grabbed his arm.

"Hold on, Hebrew."

"My name is Joseph!"

"A good name for a Hebrew in Egypt. The last circumcised Joseph through here did quite well for himself. I will make you a deal."

"To deal with a fool is to become his latest victim."

"You talk too much, Hebrew. Proverbs don't satisfy the growling belly. Listen, if you get the job on my word, you must allow me some time with your Little Seed."

"To what end?" Mama was back, claws extended.

"To the end he learn all there is of Alexandria. You followers of Moses have a terrible reputation for staying in a country you know nothing about, claiming it's your own by divine right, and then moving on, never the wiser. The boy has a chance to learn, while he forgets. Don't cheat him."

"And what is your reward?" Papa posed, suspiciously.

"My reward is the knowledge that there will be one Abrahamite who will grow up with an appreciation for something in life besides shew bread and alters of stone."

"I will speak to Bantar and then we will discuss my son's further involvement with the pagan," said Joseph with all the nationalistic pride he could muster.

"Spoken like a true bigot. It's a deal." With this the self-proclaimed monarch stuck out a bony hand as a gesture of friendship. My Papa clumsily shook it, made his farewell, and we were on our way.

We resided at the home of the rabbi of the local synagogue. The city took great pride in having representations from all known religions. The Jewish contingency, though small, was well housed in a finely-constructed little temple. When we related our story to the priest, he warned us to avoid dealings with street rabble. "We Israelites must keep our true flavor even when forced to be boiled in a pot of heathen stew."

The next morning Papa left very early to see Bantar, as the old man had advised. Several hours later he returned, his beaming countenance lighting the dim, drab room; the confidant glow of a man who felt he possessed it all. "I have work!" he exclaimed, exhibiting the boyhood exuberance of a man exactly his age.

Mama danced across the room, leaping in the air, wrapping her spindly legs around papa's well-nourished middle. "We're going to eat!"

"I start tomorrow. We are building a statue."

Papa was prepared to continue, but was interrupted by the arrival of the rabbi, who had come to see what frivolity had invaded his somber surroundings.

"A statue, my son? We do not believe in graven images." His brows receded, covering his eyes, and it looked so funny, I giggled.

"There is no humor in the law of God, little boy," he thundered.

My father moved swiftly to the holy man's side. "Master, the boy means no harm, nor do I for that matter. I love the law of God, but I must work to support my family. It is a pagan land; not much call for a carpenter to build temples to our One God."

"What statue will you be building?" The aging one peered out of dark, cave-like sockets.

"Caesar. It is very large and will give much work for a long time. Bantar said . . . "

"Bantar is a cursed idolater. He is a mockery to all that is holy."

"Our benefactor is correct," proclaimed Mary. "We should not eat meat provided by the adoration to uncivilized gods."

"Mary?" Joseph objected, irately.

"Your wife speaks with the eloquence of Deborah, the great judge of Israel," praised the rabbi.

Mary continued her explanation. "Yes, truly we should abstain from this ungodly occupation, and how blessed we are, my beloved Joseph, that we have a fine Jewish brother here, seed of Abraham, to feed and clothe us so we may be able to make this noble stand for the dignity and the integrity of the Chosen People." She turned and winked at Papa.

Joseph caught on to Mary's ploy. "Thank you, master! You are most assuredly a great teacher of Israel, who would support our little family as we stubbornly refuse to succumb to the temptation of working for the uncircumcised. There are not many like you, sir!"

Joseph embraced the astonished scribe, who pulled away as if suddenly touched by a leper. "There is much to be said for peaceful co-existence," he inserted quickly. "This is not Judea. We must make adjustments for the fact we are

God's representatives in a strange land. Perhaps I was too rigid."

Mama and Papa feigned shock and disappointment.

Finally Joseph spoke. "Are you saying, father, that I should accept this damnable employment?"

"Times are changing, young man, you can't live off the hospitality of others. You must execute this work, and in so doing perhaps bring destruction to the irreverent cause."

"I don't understand." Mama protested.

"Your husband should work, but as he lays each stone he should breathe this prayer." The rabbi cleared his throat. "By the power of the Most High, may this idol never stand."

"But wouldn't it be better if we just stayed with you, Master?" Papa pursued, making sure there would be no future interference.

"No, no, you mustn't. Not that I wouldn't be happy to help those of David's lineage, but you would not respect yourselves. You must work, but simultaneously, rebuke the product of your labors."

My father relented, took my mother's hand and said, "May we be found worthy."

The hosting holy man bustled from the room to attend to his priestly duties before the young couple could change their minds. As soon as Mama and Papa knew he was gone, they burst into laughter.

"Dear God," said Papa, when the joviality resided, "we mean no harm or disrespect to this, your servant, or your law. This is what we know to do, and we will do it until you show us more."

"Amen," said Mama with a whisper of sudden reverence.

Papa did well on the job even though there was great risk working with the heavy stone. I overheard him tell Mama horror stories; large stones slipping and crushing slave workers to death, bodies sometimes removed, but more often cemented into place to speed the project along. Caesar's statue was built, like Rome itself, upon the bone and blood of innocent men.

King Xantrippe persisted in his quest to borrow me for cultural instruction. At first Papa resisted, and then, mostly out of a deep sense of appreciation, he allowed the old street ruler to educate me.

Xantrippe showed me the spectrum of Egyptian culture. He taught me everything, from the elegant and dignified to the more treacherous and seamy sides of life.

The old man tutored me with the fervor of a dying missionary. We made frequent visits to the great library of Alexandria, reading the poets and orators of times past, and those contemporary thinkers of the day who managed to convey their messages, despite the obstacles of men's misconceptions and miles of endless terrain. There was even a time he instructed me on the technique of the pick-pockets of Alexandria, explaining how they selected their victims. He noted the shrewd chicanery applied to relieve traveling merchants of the contents of their fattened purses, while explaining the wages of their deeds. Being an impressionable young lad, and he a responsible teacher, I was shown the end result of this kind of thievery, as we observed these purveyors of the sleight of hand would eventually get caught by a more observant fellow. The King made me watch as the trickster would lose his life at the end of a sword, a vivid reminder to avoid any kind of charlatan activity.

"You never will develop the skill to fool everyone you meet," said Xantrippe with a stern glare, bringing his face close to mine. "If it is a thief you select to be, you will eventually meet your match. Then you will pay for your evil in one swift blow." He accentuated his point by poking me in the ribs.

The point was received and registered from this aging vagrant; my mentor in this gentile world. I was a little alien boy and he was my patron in discovery. Though just five years old, he took me on an odyssey through Egyptian life, made me consider the differences and similarities in people, and refreshed me at a time when I was thirsty for acceptance and needful of challenge.

I would also say he sustained me through some very worrisome times with Mama and Papa. We had acquired living quarters in the heart of the city. We were comfortable, but still feeling the alienation of foreign habitation. Mama was still adjusting to her newly found neighbors. I think she expected the Egyptians to be a race that devoured their children, while praising gods belched from the depths of degradation. Instead, she discovered a genuine folk, loving their offspring, and spending most of their time trying to get a better price on dates and barley.

We were assimilating. Still, I sensed some tension between my parents. Gone was the gaiety gracing my first years with joyous diversion. Papa was austere and Mama brooding. I assumed I was the source of their conflict. Our family had become a simmering pot threatening to boil over in an emotional volcanic eruption.

It did, on the eve of my sixth birthday. My parents sent me off to be with Xantrippe, who was nowhere to be found. I searched for awhile, and finally decided to return home. As I neared my door, I heard the angry voices of Mama and Papa, yelling at each other. Don't get me wrong. They did have arguments. This was much different. No one was listening; just the entangled exchange of two speakers at war. I wanted to run or sing, to cover up the noise. Unfortunately, it was just too prevalent to ignore.

"You are a cold woman, Mary," said Papa bitterly.

"I'm cold? You have not touched me for months, and I'm cold? A woman needs to know a man is aroused by her presence."

"Don't talk that way! You are special. Stop raving like some common street whore!"

"Why? Because I want my husband to caress me, and hold me, and make love to me?"

"You needn't be vulgar. I love you Mary, but it just isn't right. I mean I just can't look on you as another wife."

"I live to be the wife of Joseph the carpenter."

"But you are also the mother of a miracle baby. I mean, God has been inside you. I can't . . ."

"Joseph, he brought us together. We have made love. Why the sudden concern?"

"Why can't you conceive? It is as if we are unable to be together for any other purpose than to raise this child."

A jolt went through me. So it was true. I was the problem. I was bringing pain to Mama and Papa; six years old and already I was destroying lives.

Mama continued, "I don't know why, but I can't believe this is the end for me. I love Jesus, but I want to make a child with you."

My curious nature drew me closer and closer to the source of the confusion. Just then, the door flung open, and out walked Papa, flushed with anger, and surprised to see his birthday son. "Jesus!" he exclaimed in horror.

I didn't know what to do, so I turned and ran. I heard Papa calling for me, so I ran harder and faster. I could feel my heart beating in my throat, and my tears turning cold as the passing breeze froze them onto my face. Then there was Mama's voice, frantic. I couldn't stop. I couldn't see them right now. They would lie to me and tell me everything was fine. Everything wasn't fine. I was ruining the love they had for each other. I must find Xantrippe. If I was to be orphaned in this foreign land, I would need a contact. I could get a job. Maybe the King would let me live with him until I could find a house of my own. Could a boy own a house? I scanned the marketplace for my friend, praying he would let me stay with him. He was old, but I thought he would probably live long enough for me to become a man. I needed to go. I would have to leave so Mama and Papa could regain their love. I heard their voices again. They sounded close. They must not find me. I hid behind a large basket filled with dates, panting and perspiring, listening for any sound of those people who used to be my family, eyes stinging with tears at the thought of being separated from them. Then an eerie silence. I could not hear them anymore. Had they stopped looking for me? Maybe they knew it was best I leave.

"If you are hiding, I have bad news for you. Because if an old man can find you, truly you have done a terrible job." Xantrippe. Never had I been so glad to hear his voice. "What is wrong with the little Jewish boy?"

I told him as much as my six-year-old mind could understand; about Mama and Papa, and their terrible, venomous words. He listened faithfully, as if he had never heard any tale more intriguing, or any woe more saddening, so kind I wanted to keep talking just to feel the warmth of his eyes soothe my aching soul. "What should I do, King?"

He scratched his head, spreading the few strands of hair remaining. He spoke slowly and deliberately. "Go home, son. They need you now. Nature will take it's course, and when it does they will feel very foolish. Mother Earth always catches up with Father Demand. Don't try to hurry her, or she will procrastinate just to permit you time to birth some patience. She will always have her day. And those unfortunate souls who try to slow her down, end up crushed by the weight of her task."

I didn't understand a word he said, except 'go home'. So that's what I did. I went to my little room. I didn't want to talk to them. I didn't know if I was angry or just sad. It all felt the same.

The time passed. King Xantrippe was right. Several months later, my Mama began to get a fat tummy. Shortly before my seventh birthday, she gave birth to a plump blob of pink legs, stomach, cheeks, and bottom. I called him ugly. They called him James. They told me I had a brother. I sniffed competition.

SITTING 12
Pyramids, Promises and Places to Go

"Do you believe in God?" My eyes squinted in the noonday sun, giving the illusion of a smidgen of impudence.

"Well now," said Xantrippe with a heavy sigh, "I think we have the question turned around. The question should be, 'Does God believe in me'?"

This was typical Xantrippe evasion. As always, he was answering one of my deciphers with a question of his own. He posed thoughtfully, and continued in his normal philosophical way. "Since this being, God, has been ruling for so long, and has made everything, I would think, Little Stone, it would be more interesting to hear what he thinks about me."

Little Stone was one of his favorite pet names for me. He dubbed me this because of my father's masonry work, saying 'I was like gravel off the big rock'. I remember once he convinced some of the street people of Alexandria I was Moses come back from the dead, explaining God had sent me to bring more plagues upon Egypt, unless they let all the Phoenicians go. King Xantrippe laughed heartily when one of his street cohorts lamented not being aware there were any Phoenicians in Egypt.

"Come on King, I just want to know if you believe in God."

Xantrippe scratched his face, the sound of a sharp knife scraping against a rock. I sat quietly waiting for his wise reply. After several minutes he responded. "I know there must be a God of some sort, but I have found this personage was not there when I needed him. Yet, when I did not need him, he would suddenly appear."

I leaned forward, putting my hands on my knees, to listen even closer. "I don't understand."

"Oh, I'm just rambling," said Xantrippe, waving me off with his hand.

"No, please tell me what you mean."

"I mean," he said, feigning annoyance, "the times in my life I needed a god, I found myself very alone. The times I felt I could handle things on my own, there was god, right in front of my nose, usually disguising himself as my conscience."

"Why would God do that?"

"He doesn't plan it that way, just the way life is. For instance, I don't want god around when I meet some beautiful woman, or run across a large flask of wine, or have an opportunity to relieve some merchant of his burdensome purse, but god always seems to arrive on the scene in the form of an angry husband, a horrendous hangover, or a scurried chase through narrow streets. I guess he is always there reminding me there is something better, but never convincing me I should pursue it." He looked down into my face, and could tell I had bypassed bewildered. I think that was one of the reasons Xantrippe liked me so much. I kept him fresh, young, and thinking. To me he was a hero-god with wrinkled human skin, my informational source. He was an Egyptian guru, tour guide, playmate, and ornery influence, all rolled into one pleasant aggravation. To him, I was a pair of virgin ears for all his frustrated, unfulfilled visions of grandeur floating loose and free in his mind, but never escaping the snare of creeping senility.

"I believe in Him."

"Who's him?"

"God."

"You call God, Him?"

"Of course."

"You know the Almighty well enough to address his majesty as Him?"

"Well, I don't know, I never really thought of it that way."

He loved to confound the kid, fueling his untiring fetish for teasing me. "I thought it was the Jews' style never to utter the name of The Reverent One," challenged Xantrippe with a hint of a smile curling around his lips.

"I don't know about that. All I know is the God I feel inside me is one that wants to be warm, fresh, and alive."

"Then never lose Him," said Xantrippe with a note of cold finality in his tone--time to move on to other territory.

Subject after topic after question after answer had come up during our trip. It had taken the King almost two weeks to convince my Mama and Papa to permit me to come with him. He had told them the trek would take ten days. They were apprehensive. It was a long time for their boy to be away. He told them I would see the great treasures of the land of Egypt, even the glory of the pyramids. Permission was finally granted. I will say this, Mama and Papa always strove to give me as much as they could, without overwhelming me with too much freedom.

We walked for three days through the hottest desert sands, occasionally passing a fellow traveler. Conversations were always easy.

An Ethiopian merchant would say, "Would you desire it to be any hotter?"

A Syrian would trudge by and note, "The gods must have planned this heat especially for us sorry souls."

I would assume, when you are in the desert, the heat is the easiest way to create rapport, but it was the last thing I wanted to talk about. I had to be careful staying out in the sun too long, because my skin would burn, leaving large reddened splotches on my legs and arms, seeping, making quite the mess.

Many times I wondered if all the oppressive heat, long walks, and aching feet were worth the trouble, just to see some buildings constructed for dead pharaohs. Xantrippe, gauging my mood, would lighten the load with a joke or story. What a precious gift he was to me.

On the fourth day, Xantrippe awakened me very early, his eyes gleaming with excitement, voice squeaking with delight. "My little Jewish wonder boy, I am about to show you the mysteries of Egypt. Come on now! It's just over that rise."

"What?" I was grumpy.

He looked at me and frowned, greatly annoyed with my lack of enthusiasm. "Perhaps I should scour the sands to find a lad with enough energy to see the tombs of the Pharaohs."

I scurried to my feet, mostly to regain Xantrippe's favor. Also, part of me did want to see the gravesites--a very small part of me.

"They point to heaven, arrogantly displaying the remains of the greatest men of Egypt," Xantrippe elaborated.

I knew he wanted me to be enthralled, so I didn't disappoint him. "Can we hurry? Can we go now?"

My eagerness satisfied the old man's need to be appreciated. He shouted, "Yes, let's go now!"

The sun was just rising as we made our way over the crest, a rapturous moment. We walked through the early morning mist. A slight breeze stirred, and the rising sun contributed its fresh new brilliance in the distance, dispelling the haze, unveiling the spectacle of the pyramids on the horizon. They emerged from the earth beneath them, as if the sand had funnelled to form a peak rising defiantly toward the sky.

I looked at my old friend, the morning sun reflecting the glint in his eyes. This was Xanthippe's synagogue.

He glanced down at me, then countered to the sight. "Aren't they beautiful?"

"I never knew anything could be so beautiful." I expected mortar and stone. Before me was a living treasure.

"Are you ready to go? Would you like a closer look?"

"That would be great."

We started off at a break-neck clip across the shimmering terrain. It took us most of the morning to reach them. We really didn't mind. We had the vision of glory to inspire us. As we trodded along, they grew and we shrank. Finally, we arrived at the base of the closest stone triangle.

I looked over at Xantrippe, who read my mind. "I suppose you wonder, now what do we do?" Exactly. As beautiful and elegant as they were, they did seem to lack any practical application. "You see," he said, "that's the problem. Leave it to the Egyptians to build something that when you gather the energy to climb it, and get to the top, there is no place to stand!" He threw back his head and laughed, slapping his knee, my knee, the desert sand, and everything nearby. I didn't totally understand, but I joined the frivolity, giggling in my child-like manner, throwing handfuls of sand into the air.

For a season we sat and stared. The King had great respect for these tombs, and I had a great respect for the King. We marveled at the labor involved in mounting these edifices to death.

At length Xantrippe spoke. "Little Stone, when my body finally gives up the responsibility of carrying my mind around, I want to be buried in the sand near these pyramids."

"Please don't talk like that!" The realization of the toll the aging process was taking on my closest friend had already begun to haunt me, anyway. I couldn't imagine life without Xantrippe. He was my family, my link to reality. I loved Mama and Papa, but there were times when they were busy with James and the new little baby. (I now had a sister named Ruth. It seemed that the fertility factor no longer threatened the lineage of Joseph.) New babies might be wonderful for Mama and Papa, but I needed answers to the batch of fresh questions springing forth in my mind daily. I needed someone to dry my eyes while they were still damp with tears; too old to be Mama's focus and too young to be without someone to embrace me while the fester was aggravating my soul. Xantrippe was the grandfather I never knew, and I, the son he never allowed himself place to create. I couldn't lose him.

I think he realized the turmoil of my thoughts, because he interjected, "I am not saying, little one, I am going to leave tomorrow. Someday we all must go. If we stay too long, people will grow weary of looking at our face. Just, when I finally do pass, I want my body to be buried right here." He took a finger, extended it in the air, then plunged it deep into the desert sand.

"I will remember."

"So," said Xantrippe standing to his feet, "you must be hungry. Let's eat."

We set up camp near the pyramids and spent a day there, talking, sharing, laughing, and crying; fellowship defining the action, a treasure chest of warm feelings, that even when you experience them, you think to yourself how much you will enjoy remembering them later.

True to his word, Xantrippe delivered me home, ten days after our departure. Little did Mama and Papa know I was not the same eight-year-old boy. I had seen the pyramids of Egypt, but more importantly, for the first time in my life, I had foraged deeply into the heart of another human traveler, discovering what was important to him, and what brought him joy. (*Every man needs, not only a single dream in his life, but many oases on the way to the destiny. These garden spots refresh the soul, stir the conscience, and awaken the senses to the temporal nature of existence, and the sheer joy of being alive.*)

I was back home in a living space infested with the activity of two babies. I loved King Xantrippe, because he became a companion Mary and Joseph could never be. Still, they were the portion he could not fulfill, my touchstone with a particular reality; a Jewish heritage actuated by the circumstances of my birth. They were my parents, the ones who loved me because I lived and breathed, not merely for what good I might accomplish.

Remembering back to our trip, Xantrippe had shared with me, shortly before we reached Alexandria, a very strange exchange. "My son." He had never called me that before. It seemed foreign, but I liked it very much. He continued, "You will not be with me much longer. I feel your family's time of departure is soon." (I do not know if Xantrippe had knowledge of my father's plans, or if he possessed some prophetic insight, but he spoke with certainty.) "Your father grows weary of building the loins of Caesar." He smiled as he always did when he felt he had a uttered a particularly clever saying. "Do not taint the memories of our time together by resenting your family for leaving Egypt. This God you call 'Him' has planned it. We must move by faith, it will make us whole. Only in obedience can we gain the purpose of His glorious conclusion."

I nodded, not knowing the full magnitude of the commitment.

Soon after I arrived home, my father called the family together for a meeting. He informed us of the death of King Herod.

"Must we return?" I asked

Joseph paused and then spoke slowly. "I am not sure what path wisdom will select."

Not long after that meeting, my father was awakened by an angelic visitor. It had been eight years since the last dream. The message was clear. It was time to return to Israel.

When Papa informed us, I felt a quick flash of rebellion well up in my soul. Alexandria was my home. I was not a little Jewish boy, deposed in a foreign land. I was Egyptian. I recalled Xantrippe's words. The frustration subsided. I knew no matter what happened, I wanted to be with my family.

Plans were finalized. There was another new development. It seemed Mary would be traveling with child again. I thought the timing was really bad. They should have planned better. But other than that, all seemed destined toward a smooth and quick departure. We had even made tentative plans for Xantrippe to visit us in Bethlehem.

One morning I arrived at the marketplace, looking for the King. I was informed he had fallen ill and taken to a tent just outside Alexandria. I rushed along the cramped streets. I located the tent where my friend lay, dying. I entered, a strange sensation overtaking me. I barely recognized my tutor. He was lying in the corner, on a bed of mats. I eased my way to his side.

He opened his eyes, smiled, and spoke feebly. "Little Stone, I have not given you a very good going away present."

I wanted to be brave and strong; to honor my friend with hope, instead of despair. "What's wrong with you?"

"My young friend, it is not always so easy to tell at my age. Often it is not that something is wrong, just nothing is quite so right anymore. You will have to ask your God to explain why we get old. Seems ridiculous to give health to the stupid, while cursing the intelligent with aching bodies."

It seemed so senseless for such a man to die.

(From that day on I developed a hatred of death, vowing to remain the enemy of such a foul concept; my life given in the pursuit of its defeat)

I pickcd up his hand and said, "I love you, King." How thin my voice, how vacant of comfort.

He smiled, as if he had lived his whole life to hear those words. "I know, and I love you too." His eyes closed, and his hand slipped from mine, tenderly squeezing for just a moment, one last time. He was on his way to discover the mystery of *Him,* once and for all.

I ran home, tears flowing down my cheeks, a determination in my soul to honor the request I had pledged to this dear heart.

I asked permission of Mama to go see Papa on the job. She was saddened by the news of Xantrippe. He had become surrogate family to all of us. She quickly granted me leave, and I was on my way. Running through the streets of Alexandria, toward the construction site of the statue of Caesar, I diligently sought the face of my papa.

He found me. "Jesus, what are you doing here?"

"Papa, Xantrippe is dead."

Quietness settled on my father, as tears trickled down his cheeks, moistening his soiled tunic.

"Papa," I said, garnering as much courage and deliberation as possible, "I promised the King I would bury him near the pyramids."

He interrupted me. "No, Jesus. We could not possibly make such a journey. We're on our way back to Judea. We can not delay our departure." He sensed my disappointment. "Son, the King would not expect you to be held to such a promise."

"He is not holding me to the promise. I want to do this for him. There was so little I was able to do because I was just a child. If I could do this, I could feel in some small way that I had paid back this fine man."

The words were passionate and eloquent beyond my years, because they were laced with the depth of true love. Papa looked at me.

I continued my case, "Papa, where would we be without Xanthippe's help? He got you this job."

Joseph was moved by my pleading, but indignant over my tone. "Jesus, you must realize life is not always as simple as a little boy sees it. Sometimes we must weigh our commitments and feelings, then do those things we can. Often that leaves things undone."

I interrupted Papa again, "There is nothing more important than granting a friend his last wish." My lips quivered as I struggled to fight back bitter tears. "I want to do this, Papa."

My eyes fixed on my father's perplexed face. He was battling between anger over my impudence and admiration for a son's integrity.

I risked another challenge. "I don't want to disobey you, but I must do this for the King!"

My Papa looked at me for a long moment, surveying me, gauging the depth of my conviction, determining whether this was just a childish desire to revisit the pyramids, or the legitimate mission of a blooming man, wanting to honor a friend at all reasonable cost. He placed his hand on my shoulder and said, "I am leaving this job as of today, anyway. We could take this honorable vigil together. On the way you can tell me all about your first trip. I think he would like that." He held me close, and we wept without shame for a friend we both loved.

The next day my Papa and I departed on the journey, and made our way to the pyramids. We dug in the sand together, until we had made a hole large enough to contain the body of our friend.

My father lifted his eyes to heaven and said, "We do not know if he knew you, God of Israel, but we do know he was kind to your children. Please reward that kindness. Cover any lack of holiness with your mercy that endures forever."

We both shared stories about the King, reciting incident after incident over the his grave. We left quietly.

Xantrippe lived his life with great dignity. Now he was bequeathed a place of rest, as he desired, next to his fellow Kings--the less noble monarchs of Egypt.

We returned to Alexandria. Mama had made all the necessary arrangements for the exodus. We departed into the deserts of Egypt. We had passed this way before; now, seven years later, we traveled again--still alone but united. We had learned much from this foreign land. We had grown up here and started a family, made friends, worked, and loved. Egypt had granted Joseph and Mary the confirmation every young couple needs: affirming their love was strong, and they could sustain in a very real world. It was time to duplicate what we had in Egypt, back in Bethlehem amongst friends and our own people.

Mama was very busy with the younger ones. I had grown up fast, yet I still required the tenderness of her touch. Now I was the oldest, and her attention was focused on James and Ruth. Papa wisely stepped in and filled the gaps left by Mary's schedule.

The passage was long, but uneventful. No interruptions from zealots or caravans along the way. Papa and Mama had no real desire to go back to Nazareth, which was but a faint memory of a very confusing time. They felt it would be better to raise the children closer to the source of our religion and culture.

Upon arriving in Judea, we discovered Herod's son had assumed the throne; a feeling of unrest was prevalent in the area. Joseph was concerned by rumors of violence and rebellion against the Roman Imperialists. It was a difficult time to make a decision. A family without a home is in a most vulnerable position. So Joseph headed to Galilee, settling in Nazareth. It was here the Egyptian family of five, with one pending, would attempt once again to begin a new life.

Relah Returns

"I hope I'm not disturbing you. It sure is dark. Hello. Where are you? I can't see. Remember me, Relah? I thought you could use another candle."

"Thank you, I'm over here in the corner."

"Oh, I think I see you. Finding what you need? I thought we might talk."

"Talk? Sure, I can talk."

"I brought some food."

"I am not very hungry."

"The last man who said that to me ended up eating the whole backside of a broiled lamb, right before my eyes."

"I really am not hungry--actually, kinda busy."

"It's warm bread with sweet honey from the comb. Any man can eat that when he is full to the jowls."

"I do like my honey comb, even though I pick flecks of the comb out of my beard for weeks after. Thank you for thinking of me."

"I have been."

"Oh, I see. Well, I have been doing some thinking of my own--quite busy--of course, I said that. This is so kind of you."

"Are you a married man?"

"No."

"Don't like women?"

"No. You misunderstood. I mean, yes, I like them--women."

"Would you consider me?"

"Would I consider you what?"

"As your lady?"

"Well, we are leaping a few camels from 'Hey, here's your candle.'"

"You may find me a little pushy, but I've learned not to play the girl by the fire when love comes howling. You seem to be a fine enough man, body smells more like trees than dung; a hint of sweat but that has its way. You were angry but did me no violence. I could use such a man."

"I was not angry, just a trifle distracted. I have had a busy month; well, too much to share there."

"A good male, sometimes clean, is difficult to find. I have grown accustomed to the warmth of a man in my bed, and the feelings following."

"You have a man?"

"I don't want to talk about it."

"I didn't mean to probe."

"No, it's all right. What's done is done, if you know what I mean. Hell, who cares? It's over anyway."

"Listen, I have troubled you enough, no need to tell. . ."

"His name was Danyon, a soldier, stationed here in Judea, from an outpost in a land called Gaul, just north of Rome, wherever Rome is. He said he loved me. Sounded good to me. I gave myself to him. I will never forget that feeling, the sensation of freedom--total release, like little ants crawling up and down your body as someone poured cool water over your head. Too many duties for a young girl, that's me. It was amazing, for a few moments, to be lost in the arms of a lover pleasuring me. Well, I became a believer. Have you had your way with a lady, I mean in a loving sort?"

"I shared love with many women, certainly a loving sort."

"He was so strong, and so experienced for his age. I thought we would be married. He was transferred, and never said good-bye. I sent a message once to his new assignment, but never heard."

"I am sure he thinks about you everyday."

"Are you married?"

"Me? No."

"A guy like you? You aren't fiercely handsome, but you sure are the best-looking religious man I've ever seen."

"Thank you, the holy often miss out on the sun."

"Much to be said for walking about."

"Too many scrolls."

"And not enough rolls, if you know what I mean?"

"I do enjoy a clever phrase."

"No lady, huh? Is that normal? I mean you got needs, right? I know some of you fanatics hate women, but you better believe that a lady is far more enjoyable than some old piece of parchment."

"I like women."

"Then you have a lady, your own special breed?"

"Nobody special, Relah. I have dedicated my life to a mission. It wouldn't be fair to ask a woman to share it.

"I think any woman would be honored."

"I have loved many women, but possessed none."

"What do you mean?"

"Yes, what do I mean? How can I explain--I certainly don't want to mislead you. I have walked among their fragrance, enjoyed their intelligent sparkle, and watched them emerge from dark clouds of despair. I was there to love them, in my way. Sometimes I wanted more, but usually I was full."

"Oh, you are probably just waiting for the right girl."

"And when she comes I hope she'll be as lovely as you."

"Last chance."

"You don't know how right you are."

"Well, I must go."

"Please leave the food. I will make good use of it."

"How much longer will you be?"

"A little while, not trying to be a bother."

"No, it's fine. Keep thinking and while you do, consider this lady."

"A prize indeed."

"I may check in later, if you wouldn't mind. So long."

****

Well, cold dark manger walls, she's gone. I have remained faithful once again, so future generations of boring scholars may note my celibacy and misinterpret it as a "God Obsession" by a frigid, unromantic prophet. Not so, slimy stone. I fought it all the way and it may be one of my only regrets. I have questions when I reach The Glory.

SITTING 14

Father Hagabus

Some towns are small due to their lack of resources or obscurity. Others are depleted by the disappearance of adequate economic stability. Then there are some villages remaining tiny because they promote a shortsighted, shrunken vision, denying the compelling need for expansion and the aching cry for human compassion. The latter is the status and epitaph of Nazareth. Perhaps I sound a trifle jaded, for we all may decry our town of upbringing. Let me share my dilemma.

Mine was a love-hate relationship with my home. I loved the location. Nazareth was on the caravan routes where travelers from the east would make connection with the south. All nationalities, races, religions, and tribes of humanity drank at the wells of Nazareth, sharing tales of homes, family, and philosophies of life. Anyone from Nazareth could come and guzzle from a gusher of human culture; a fresh well-spring of planetary information. Few did. Most Nazarenes sold supplies, made repairs, and sheltered men and beasts as strangers, the Galilean profile being independence. Having rejected orthodox Judaism years ago, they weren't about to be drawn into new ideas from other nations which they deemed pagan. They believed just enough of the Torah to make them bigots toward any diversity of approach to the divine. I also loved the rolling hills, the uncompromising heat, and the merciful frosty shroud cooling our wilderness by night.

I hated the emotional and intellectual isolation, a narrow-mindedness propagated in mass; an unwritten, unspoken, predetermined edict, which declared life spawned, was maintained, and should conclude within the confines our rigid borders. I hated being considered the dreamer because I yearned for a fresh concept.

I loved being with my family, but I hated how quickly we surrendered the openness and creativity of Egypt for the mundanity of Nazareth. I loved the people, but hated the stagnation of thought. I loved the new language, but hated how it was vandalized by gossip.

Gossip--didn't take long for that to begin. Ten years of conspicuous absence had not eliminated erroneous memories. Time never closes the book on stories embellished in the minds of bored malcontents, often taking decades of ignoring to silence the ignorant. I am referring to the rumors and innuendo surrounding my conception and birth.   Most relatives and sympathetic friends chose to recreate the circumstances of Joseph and Mary's wedding. But there were those who saw the arrival of our family as the opportunity for fanning the dying embers of a once roaring controversy.   Nazareth, like most small villages of the time, had a town father and mother.   The patriarch of our community was the rabbi, Hagabus.   The matriarch was a prematurely-aging seller of cloth named Chiolita.   She worked at her loom all day, weaving the fabric of her craft and tales of scorn for the alarm and amusement of her customers.   These sister cronies would sit, watch, and listen to her, as she postured and preached on the latest plight threatening the tranquillity of Nazareth.   Her cloth was beautiful.   The tales she told were ugly, tearing into the fiber of truth.   People were anxious to hear, desiring to be titillated while distancing themselves from personal responsibility. Chiolita delivered a polished discourse, complete with vile accusation, judgmental conclusion, and adequate piety for any unseemly doings in the   village domain.   She was a gossip.   Her home sat on the edge of town at the foot of a slight rise, above us, transcendent of human frailty, always watching.

She wasted no time beginning her venomous campaign against our family.   Gossip, by design and function, is a two-headed viper--a rhetorical question followed by a vicious observation.   It might unfold as follows:

"Why do they let little Jesus wear foreign clothing?"

"If you ask me, I think they are just trying to stir up trouble."

"If you ask me, I think there should be more repentance in her attitude."

I have found the question, 'Why do they?' and the statement, 'If you ask me', have done more to destroy lives than any vice the devils have conjured.

I became known as the 'Carpenter's Bastard'.   I didn't know what any of it meant.   No one explained the circumstances of my birth.   I was also referred to as the 'heathen idiot', because I was ten years old and had not learned the Letters of Moses.   Other children had been instructed years before. If it had not been for the kindness of Master Hagabus, I might have opted for a rebel's path.

He was caught in the middle of a melee of accusation, rabbi both to giver and receiver of the platter of rancored gossip. The problem was further complicated because we were guests in his home while my father established business. We crammed into the little cubicle of his life to sleep, and escaped outside during the day to live and breathe. If that were not enough, my mother was pregnant with the latest child.

The rumors were rampant:

"They are pagan."

"They are lazy."

"Isn't it strange that none of the children look alike?"

"They are taking advantage of the rabbi."

"They don't follow the Law of Moses."

I despised attending synagogue, people staring and whispering. The rabbi said to smile at them. I tried. Unfortunately, it resembled more of a sneer, so this started more chatter--the oldest boy, Jesus, impudent. Now, it seemed, I was a snotty bastard. I was ready to explode.

I went to talk with Hagabus. "Why do they call me a bastard?"

The venerable priest fidgeted in his chair, as if suddenly perched on a prickly plant, surveyed me, determining how much he could share with this fragile, blossoming youngster. "It is a word," he began, "which means much to the person who speaks it, and hopefully little to the one who hears." I opened my mouth to object, and was silenced by his raised hand. "I know, I know, that didn't exactly answer your question," he replied, scratching his beard; a growth layered like a gently blown sand dune in the desert hills, each ridge sporting a different color--first red, another laced with white, one streaked with gray, and a fourth tawny; all cascading in noble curls upon the scribe's chest. "There are people who have very strong contentions about your family. I do not believe they mean to be vindictive."

"You mean that old witch, Chiolita? You don't think she means harm to us?"

"You are an impetuous lad, Jesus. Chiolita is not a witch. Actually, if she were, then our solutions would be easier." For a moment the teacher stared wistfully into the distance, and then continued his thought. "She is a woman with strong conviction. It is a thinking that has placed your family in her disfavor."

"What have we done to her?"

"You have crossed the lines of what she deems sacred. In the court of her conscience, you are judged unacceptable. She feels she does God service by exposing this proposed error."

"I don't understand what you mean. I haven't done anything."

"Chiolita is not your problem. There will always be people like her wherever you go. They will damn you, and if you have the audacity to believe otherwise, they will curse you. If you accept their verdict of damnation, they will bury you in a pit of condemnation and piously walk from your freshly dug grave, content in the righteousness of their mission." The priest's ambiguity had kindled heat. This was not an insight from a counsellor sharing from a scroll, but rather the testimony of one seared by the fire of burning prejudice. Remembering he was nurturing a little one, he continued, softening his tone. "The important thing is not what they think of you, nor what I feel about you. To be honest, what you think of yourself will also burn away with the chaff of useless ideals. Someday the Great Judge will evaluate the truth of what each of us really was. He who has seen in secret, will proclaim in the open. When all the fat is boiled away, the lean loin of revealed reality will survive the furnace of scrutiny. I believe this to be true, even though everyday events cause me to question the veracity of such optimism. You must dare to risk self-inspection, to avoid the ravenous hypocrisy that constantly threatens to devour our identity."

Once again Father Hagabus was over-estimating the retention of his young audience. But I welcomed it. Even though I could only make out a word here and there, I felt mature having a brilliant holy man talk so grown-up to me. He was right. I was trying to slay the dragon of gossip with my feeble tantrum. Not today.

Hagabus sat quietly, with his head bowed, a weary warrior too shattered by the battle to gather the spoils of the war.

He slowly lifted his face, revealing eyes glistening with tears. "I have been too harsh. You are just a boy. Learning should be slower, easier, and laced with the fun of life."

I reached out my hand and patted his soft beard. "I do not understand the words, but I can feel their meaning."

"Jesus, if you can really feel, you will always learn." He took my hand and kissed my palm, stood to his feet and said, "I will teach you."

"Teach me what?"

"There is a rumor, pardon the expression, that you have not learned the law and prophets."

He was right. In Egypt, there was no organized study for the Hebrew boys. Joseph told me many tales of historic splendor, but I had never learned the law and prophets from a master.

"I can not place you with the little boys, but I will tutor you at night."

"Just you and me?"

"Of course. It will be our secret. Right after the twelfth hour each evening, except Sabbath. Not long, now. I am an old man, and need my rest."

I reached up and hugged him.

He embraced me, pulled back and warned, "Now we must not aggravate Chiolita and her consorts at the loom. Wisdom is to leave the snake to escape the heat and find the coolest nearby rock." He smiled.

I giggled. I liked snake stories.

"I have said too much." Hagabus smiled, covering his mouth with a wrinkled hand to disguise the quivering lips, primed and ready to laugh.

I ran all the way home, barely feeling the need to inhale the air. Hagabus had not answered any of my questions, but I felt fresh. Not since Egypt had I possessed a sense of belonging. The gentle soul of Xantrippe had been resurrected just in time to aid one displaced Jewish boy. The King had returned to my life in the form of a village priest named Hagabus.

SITTING 15
Mother Chiolita

One year eased away, my time divided three ways. During the day I tried to learn the carpenter's trade. and by night reconstructed the history of the Jewish people with Hagabus. The third part of my time was spent adjusting to family with my two brothers and two sisters. That's right, Mama had a girl, Elizabeth, in honor of her cousin and friend. I had lost motherly attention and concern, and was given more freedom than I was prepared to manage; a breeding ground for disaster, unless someone was prepared to channel my energy.

As Hagabus requested, I told no one of my evening adventures, except Mama and Papa, who were reticent over the whole learning-by-night concept, arguing I was going to exhaust myself in all the varied pursuits. After a few sighs, a gruff warning, and a tender hug or two, they relented to my enthusiasm.

I was captivated with each of the sessions--so many wonderful stories about such diversified people. The rabbi, tired by the time I arrived, tried to be grumpy, yet when we were through, he would embrace me and tell me how the visit had refreshed him from the daily routine of the priesthood.

I was brimming with questions, so much information available about God, and so few souls desiring to know Him personally. "It seems that people don't really want to get too close to God."

"Why do you say that? The synagogue is always full," Hagabus objected.

"That is a safe place to meet Him. You can talk to your friends, and recite some words, and be gone before He has time to speak to you."

"Some things were not meant to be known, little Jesus."

"But why would God want to be so mysterious? What would He have to gain?"

"Well," the master paused to reflect. "If you knew too much, then you would soon take all the blessing for granted. Yes, that is the way of man. What he possesses soon bores him."

"But the more I learn, the more excited I become, like pursuing a lizard across the desert sand. You may catch him once, but that does not mean he will not entertain you with a merry chase next time."

He shook his head, not appreciating likening the quest for God to a childhood scamper for a lizard. "Why must you know everything? Where is your trust in God?"

"I don't want to know everything, but if I am close to the truth I become restless to find out all I can about it. Is there anything wrong with that, Master Hagabus?"

"It is not a moral question of rights and wrongs. Too much knowledge is not proper for a man to attain. It brings the pride of Beelzebub into his bosom."

"He fell because he wanted to be god. I just want to know God. I want more than the fantasy. Don't you yearn for more than bowing and praying? I would like to talk to Him."

"Only Moses and Abraham and the great prophets did that, Jesus. We are just men. We live and die. What we learn, we pass along to our children. What we don't know remains our legacy of ignorance."

"Why would God make so many wonderful things if he didn't want us to get them?"

Hagabus smiled with his lips while frowning with his eyes. I have never known anyone else who could do both at the same time. "We will continue tomorrow. That is, if you think your quest for the truth can be held off that long."

Thus would end most evening sessions: me with questions bouncing through my mind, and Hagabus dehydrated of answers and energy, ready to retire for the night.

As I walked home, I felt the stars sparkling their approving gleam upon my head. The evening's cool would invigorate me and keep the questions growing in my mind. I would arrive home wide awake, as if splashed in the face with cold water, give a brief summary (Papa's request) of my lesson, nibble a bite, and prepare for bed.

Sleep was a fruitless endeavor. I lay awake for hours, staring into the darkness, mulling over the unresolved.

Perhaps this is where I developed my strange sleep habits, night certainly not my favorite time to slumber. It is precious solitude, lending itself to glorious indulgence in thought. I grew fond of taking short naps. I grabbed sleep when things were the most unruly all around me. My friends say I can sleep through a storm, which I proved one night on the Sea of Galilee.

I was overjoyed to be alive. Everything seemed in order. Some normalcy had settled into our little home. The

rumors had stopped.   Even Chiolita was civil to us at
synagogue. I asked Papa why they stopped talking.
    He smiled, a twinkle in his eye. "I guess they just
grew tired of us, Jesus."
    I knew there was more to the story.
    A few weeks later I discovered the real reason for
the reprieve. I was in the marketplace purchasing some
items for Mama, when I heard a familiar voice. I crept and
hid behind a large pile of mats next to a huge clay pot. I
craned to listen. Standing, gaining the ear of Rabbi
Hagabus, was Chiolita. She shook her finger at him, and
swung her hip from side to side as she related her story. I
leaned forward as far as balance would permit.
    "I hope you are satisfied. You have defended the
heathen and they have taken over," Chiolita rebuked, waving
her arms. "That Mary and Joseph have done nothing but stir
up trouble since they arrived from the pagan lands."
    I checked Hagabus' reaction--diplomatic interest
disguising terminal boredom. "What is it now, Chiolita?
What have they done?"
    "I'll tell you what she did, that Mary, she came into
my home and chased all my customers away."
    "How did she do that?" Hagabus seemed more
interested. I couldn't blame him. I was stretching so far I
was beginning to get cramps in my legs.
    Chiolita continued, "She told them if they didn't
leave she was going to pull their hair out by the roots. They
all ran out like sheep scattered before the wolf. Then she
grabbed me by the arm. See the mark she left?" She lifted
the sleeve on her robe to reveal her fleshy member. It
looked unharmed at my distance, though I did chuckle as
she wiggled the flap of skin. Hagabus nodded as if
accustomed to viewing invisible injury. Chiolita continued
her tirade. "She sat me down and threatened me."
    "How did she threaten you?"
    "She said, and I quote, 'If you don't stop talking
about my family, and cursing us, you old devil, I am going
to rip your clothes off and drive you down the main street of
Nazareth with a palm switch at your butt.' What do you
think of that, rabbi?"
    "I would rather not think about that at all, Mother
Chiolita. It is too gruesome for mortal man to visualize."
    "You better know it is gruesome. These are the
people you permit in our community. What do you plan on
doing about this? You are the patriarch of this village."
    "Indeed," he said, "something shall be done. But,
my dear, we must be sensible to the timing of the

Almighty. This kind of deed will not go unnoticed before His all-seeing eyes. There are rewards for such actions."

She glared at him for a moment, not certain of his meaning, but figured rhetoric was the confirmation of a man's calling to the ministry. She stomped away, justified, having said her piece.

I skipped home, totally enthralled by Chiolita's story of my Mama's grit and growl. Chiolita may have still been infuriated, but decided to maintain a silent rage instead of tempting Mama's patience any further.

We never heard another word of gossip.

As a boy of nearly twelve years, many mysteries teased my mind, not the least among them was my teacher and friend, Hagabus. He was not a native of Nazareth. I had overheard some of the town elders discussing his past. They said he used to be a priest in a village near Jerusalem, called Bethany. I did not know how long he had stayed there, or the circumstances of his departure. Nazareth had been his home and work for over twenty-five years. Still, my curiosity was getting the better of me, so much I didn't know about him.

At one of our evening sessions, I had been asking many questions and had repeatedly stumped my teacher.

He spoke, "I know your family attends Passover each year. Why don't you ask the priests of Jerusalem some of these questions you have?"

I seized the moment. "Who should I see? Who do you know I can ask?"

He was surprised by my question. After a moment's delay he suggested, "I have a brother who is a priest there of the Pharisee's order. His name is . . ."

I rudely interrupted him, "Why did you leave Jerusalem? Couldn't you do more there?"

"Doing is not dependent on a place. There is just as much need in Galilee as in Judea."

"You know what I mean."

"Yes," he said, "I know what you mean and I know what I mean." His face twinged in crimson, and he folded his arms across his chest. "Let us just say when you are close to the fire, the heat no longer warms--it burns. I backed away from the embers to feel warm again, and to let the charred areas of my life heal." He loved to give me answers in parables, smirking as I squinted and twisted my face in confusion. He paused to weigh the heaviness of his response. I remained silent, fearing I had tread into a private area.

"Would you like to know my brother's name, so you can interrogate him?" Hagabus asked, offering a peaceful resolution to the impasse--a gracious gesture from a spirited gentleman.

"I do have questions. You would honor me with the name," I said with my head bowed, humbled but invigorated over the possibility of firing my inquiries at a Jerusalem pharisee.

Hagabus sat quietly. I think he knew I was determined to discover the story of his life. There was a sadness in his features. What was he thinking? "He is a fine man. You will find him at the Temple during the hours of prayer. You will recognize him, because he is a taller, younger, better-looking me. He knows things I have long ago forgotten."

"And I should address him as?"

"Master or rabbi should be fine," he said, chuckling, probing my stern features.

I knelt down at his feet.

He drew a deep breath, and lifted himself slowly to his feet, and walked a few paces to the farthest corner of the room. His turmoil was visible, his anguish palatable. Whatever happened so many years ago still haunted his soul. He lifted me to my feet and led me to the door. I was leaving without the needed information. I was disappointed, but also ashamed of myself. This was not my business. If Hagabus chose to maintain his solitude, it was not my right to interfere.

I started down the path leading home, deciding to be satisfied.

"Jesus," spoke the quiet voice from my rear.

"Yes, Master." I said, turning back.

"His name is. . . . Nicodemus."

SITTING 16
Jerusalem-Part 1

In the distant fog lay the great source of my curiosity. My stomach was tied in knots and ached--hunger or fear--I had plenty of both. The excitement of the journey had kept me from eating like I should. Apprehension accompanied each step of the path. What awaited me in Jerusalem? What if I could not find Nicodemus? Of course, there was one additional dread. How horrible would the story turn out to be; obviously ghastly enough to keep Hagabus in exile these twenty-five years. Accordingly, I had almost decided to forget trying to pursue the secrets of the private priest's past. I was feeling guilty about my curiosity. I might be resurrecting a memory Hagabus assumed was healed. After all, if he wanted me to know, he certainly could have shared some of the details with me. Nevertheless, I was resolute in my mission, my precocious nature winning the day. It was better to know. Maybe I could help him forget the pain.

I had enjoyed the journey. We had made the pilgrimage once before, the Passover following our return from Egypt. I was very small, both in size and comprehension, finding the experience boring and tedious. Mama and Papa were captivated. To me, it possessed the two deadliest demons to the mind of an energetic boy: first, we listened to a whole bunch of speeches, and secondly, we stood around doing nothing. Needless to say, I was not impressed. Fidgety and fussy to a fault would be more accurate. So in the years following they journeyed alone, leaving me and the smaller children with relatives

This was my first "trip of knowledge" to the Holy City. Never had I seen so many people converging on one point--all races, colors, and forms of dress, a giant vat of humanity simmered and stewed in the springtime sun. Caravans of pilgrims streamed along narrow roads. Conversation rumbled like a low, growling thunder, the atmosphere aromatic with the sweating scent of spice and grain permeating from every pore. There were sellers courting their buyers, and artists hawking their well-rehearsed talents for the delight of the shuffling hordes. Merchants were meshed together in dangerous proximity to thieves, and children ran frantically in all directions, trying desperately to derive enjoyment amidst the repetition of movement.

Holding Papa's hand, I became engulfed in this surging tide, my grip tightening to a frantic clutch, feeling like a single fig fallen to earth in a giant oasis filled with towering palms. My Papa looked down at my terrified grimace and burst into laughter. I must have been quite a sight, with my fevered red cheeks, furrowed brow, and bulging eyes. I kept trying to swallow my heart back into my chest, but it continued to creep up my throat.

I whispered to myself, "This is where you will learn the truth." Not very reassuring, given the present surrounding danger--a mere misstep from being squashed underfoot.

All at once we stopped, Mama and Papa staring intensely into the distance. What was up ahead?

"What is it, Papa? What do you see?" I asked, standing on my toes.

"It is the temple, Little Jesus," he responded, maintaining his affixed gaze at the vision before him. Neither of them moved, eyes sparkling with the glory of the spectacle. I leaped to gain height for viewing. Joseph looked down and smiled, and with one giant scoop, swooped me up and placed me on his shoulder. It took a moment for my eyes to adjust to the sudden burst of sunlight. And then I took my first glance at the showpiece of Judaism: the Temple. Someone had meticulously molded a large chunk of the sun into the form of a shimmering edifice of stone, gleaming, glossy, and glimmering. This seemed proper and right for the dwelling place of the Most High. It was aflame with luscious color and iridescent, dancing sprinkles of light. God's home. We Jews not only knew God's address, we had rented Him a house in one of our finer neighborhoods of a most Holy City.

"Papa, let me run ahead. I want to see more." It was an unreasonable request, which he chose to ignore, smiling. If I launched out alone, I would soon drown in a river of tumult.

"Soon," he replied, giving place to my desire, but direction to my inexperience. "Let's secure lodging." He lowered me to the sand, and I hugged him. He touseled my hair, and I felt a wiggle of excited contentment trickle down my spine. No need to hurry. I was in God's backyard, and soon I would be asking his servants the questions entangling my thoughts.

It took the rest of the day to secure our sleeping quarters. Jerusalem had planned a celebration without allotting space for the celebrants. When we finally found a corner, bedded with hay, I excused myself from dinner and collapsed into a deep, restful sleep, snoozing in the town where the Most High never slumbers.

Two days passed. We had been back and forth to the temple, but I had not been able to get away long enough to ask the priests and caretakers any of my burning questions. I had seen many religious leaders pass by. Scribes, priests, pharisees--each one in gala robe with widened borders to distinguish rank and spiritual prominence. I had even reached out and touched the hem of one of the passing dignitaries, expecting some sort of blessed exhilaration. Just cloth.

Mama and Papa were always too close for me to squirm away and ask anybody for anything.

On my third day in the city, I devised a plan. Hagabus had told me to look for Nicodemus in the Temple during one of the hours of prayer. I decided to leave our lodge very early and sneak into the city under the cover of darkness. Mine was a two-fold mission--to get the answers I needed from the religious overseers and return safely to carry on my duties with the family before they noticed I was gone. My youthful mind saw no conflict. Nothing could go wrong.

I embarked on my early morning vigil to the Temple. It seemed larger, activity everywhere. The beggars had already arrived and were scouting out the best location to receive alms consideration. I asked several pilgrims where a priest or Levite might be found that could answer some questions. Most of them laughed at me.

"Priests are everywhere," was the most common reply, followed by a stern warning. "But they're too busy for little boys."

As I shivered and mused, a bit overwhelmed, a man scurried along and bumped me, knocking me to the ground. His robes were long and flowing and carried the dark, austere coloring of the great men of the temple.

"Pardon me, my boy," his voice thundered with resonant command, "I didn't see you there." He helped me to my feet. My head whirled as my eyes struggled to focus. My tongue lay limp in my mouth and my lips were frozen shut.

"Are you all right, lad?" He brushed at my robe to remove unseen dust and dirt. Was this a priest? This was my chance. Questions burst the seams of my mind, intercepted just short of my tongue. I managed one word: "Nicodemus."

The man peered at me, shrugged his shoulders, and replied, "He will be here shortly. Here, go down by that gate." He pointed to an entrance just across the courtyard. "Tell the gatesman you are not a vagrant or offspring of a leper. Inform him you are waiting for Master Nicodemus."

"Thank you sir," I replied, displaying my best Galilean manners even with the addition of an awkward bow.

This elicited a chuckle from the stern scribe. "Quite alright, and tell the gatesman Master Annas said it was fine for you to wait there."

"Thank you, Master Annas." His eyes narrowed and darkened. I suspect he was filled with questions. What is a boy doing in the Temple? What is his business with Nicodemus? He chose to move on. As he walked away my tongue released from its prison at the roof of my mouth. "Father Annas, why can't we all experience God like Abraham or Moses?" I was shocked at the defiance in my tone. Maybe a shred of disarming sincerity. Sincerely defiant. A dubious partnership.

The old teacher wheeled about as if confronted with an enemy in battle. "What is your name?"

"Jesus of Nazareth, Galilee. Son of the carpenter Joseph, Mother Mary, House of David . . . "

I would have continued my whole lineage, but the disgruntled priest stopped me. "I am not a synagogue school teacher for a backwoods chatterbox."

He didn't like me; I was too forward. "My deepest apologies sir, I am just a boy filled with wonder."

"Wondering boys grow into lazy men who beg in the street."

A horrific thought. I did not want to be a beggar. I would starve as one. "I don't want to be a beggar, sir."

"No one wants to be a begging sluggard, carpenter's son. It is the curse of God on nosy little boys." He stood over me, staring down on the top of my head. I had greater empathy for David's plight with Goliath.

"Pray, dear sir, that I not be a beggar or a sluggard, for that matter." I fell to my knees, weeping.

He scoffed at me. "It may be too late. I just hope for your sake we don't meet again when you are in need of gracious favor from me."

"May it never happen."

"Why? Because you think I'm selfish?"

I was not going to escape unless I convinced my mouth to retire to its original dormant state. I shook my head. He fastened his eyes on me until his glare forced my glance to the ground.

As he started to walk away my tongue escaped its quarantine. "Does this mean you don't know the answer?" I queried, obviously insane.

Annas waved his hands in the air and moved along his way, mumbling in Hebrew as he swished.

My first encounter with a priest had ended in disaster. I scurried to the gate and told the keeper all that Annas had instructed me. I even asked for a description of the master.

A young boy came up and spoke, "Are you looking for Master Nicodemus?"

"Yes," I replied.

"He will be here soon." He anticipated my next question, "I know because he is my father."

I was flabbergasted with this burst of good fortune. The master's son! A fantastic blessing!

"My name is Madez." He extended his left hand to me.

"Jesus." I noticed his right hand was hidden, perhaps missing; I was not sure. I was apparently too obvious because he pulled his right hand from its resting place.

He held it up and said matter-of-factly, "It is withered."

God forgive me, I stared at it. The hand was tiny, almost infant-size, and covered with gray flesh, peeling away in white flakes. I was apparently very typical in my curiosity.

"Since birth," he said, anticipating my question once again.

"Looks like it gave up on growing." I was appalled at how my innocent insight came bumbling off my lips.

Madez laughed and laughed. "You are refreshing. Usually people just say I'm sorry." His giggling was infectious; we both just sat and laughed at my crude observation. The gatesman scowled, as if we were both tetched in the head.

When the glee subsided, I patted Madez on the shoulder and said, "I'm sorry."

He mocked disappointment, saying, "Oh, see, now you are typical."

This created a fresh outburst. The gatesman took a step our way and thought better of trying to discipline young boys for silliness.

Madez was the first to manage speech. "What do you seek from my father?" A good question. I didn't know exactly how much to share with my new companion. I didn't want to be evasive. "I am from Nazareth," I cited. I was hoping the mention would bring some recognition. He didn't acknowledge. I continued, "I have come on the request of a friend to deliver a message to Master Nicodemus."

Madez was satisfied with my sketchiness, his question more polite than interested. We were just thrilled to meet another boy; nice to have a playmate.

"Would you like to meet some other friends?" It sounded terrific. The ceremonies of Passover were very dull and had left me somewhat in need of amusement. But. . . I was here on a mission. No time for play, at least not yet.

"No, I must wait for your father."

Madez slapped me on the back and said, "Come on, loosen your loincloth, let's have some fun. Anyway, my father will track us down. He is going to show me around the temple during the closing presentation."

It made sense. If Nicodemus was going to find Madez, and I was with Madez, I would find Nicodemus--a glorious plan.

I jumped to my feet and we were off. Madez could run like the wind. Running had never been my greatest strength, but now I felt like I was wearing stone sandals, barely able to keep him in sight. We rounded a corner and, before my eyes, was a whole circle of children my age and younger, busying themselves frolicking. Quite bizarre. Here, within the walls of this austere spiritual sanctuary, children reveled, totally oblivious to any concern over the Holy of Holies.

"Let me introduce you to everyone." Madez pulled me forward from my retreated position. "Hey everybody, this is Jesus of Nazareth."

They all looked up, stared momentarily, and then, as if on cue, burst into laughter. I was shocked, wounded, and perplexed. What had brought on this ridicule? The source of their amusement was my tattered, grimy, homespun robe. They were dressed in the finest. I was a tiny mite in the coffer with gold coins. My mind said to run. The message was intercepted by my uncooperative, trembling knees. Even Madez was smiling, eyeing my apparel. Finally one of the circle, a young boy perhaps thirteen, stepped out, larger then the rest, a good cubit taller than the youngest. I was ready to be shoved, but instead the boy grabbed me by the shoulders and said, "Welcome, Jesus, what do you want to play?" All the circle closed in on me, patting and gently punching me into a sense of inclusion. Apparently this tall guy carried a lot of influence.

So, to his question--what did I want to play?   I didn't know many games.   "Whatever you are playing, teach me."

Teach me they did.   On into the morning I learned game after game.   I also learned name after name.   The young comrade who came to my aid was   Caiaphas.   A beautiful girl quickly garnered my full attention.   I finally worked up the courage to ask her name.

"Veronica," she replied with a soft voice dribbling from her moist lips, floating like a cloud in the desert.

Madez grabbed my arm and warned,   "Be careful, hill boy, that girl is already betrothed."

I frowned and shook my head in disbelief.   "She is so young. What? About nine or ten years?"

"I don't care," he said, "she is already claimed territory."

"By whom?"

Madez motioned in the direction of my tall rescuer, Caiaphas.   I had no desire to tangle with him on any level, especially for the affections of the young Veronica.   Wisely, I pursued other companionship.

I discovered each one of these children had a father who was a priest or a wealthy merchant.   Some were the children of local Roman officials.   Such was the case with a short, cute girl named Joanna.   Her father was commissioned by Caesar to build roads in the Judean province.

Roman, Greek, or Jew made no difference to our gathering.   They were even willing to accept a Galilean.

I became so absorbed in activity I almost forgot the reason for my temple visit.   The sun was in the noonday position. I had hoped to be back at the inn with my family by now.   But I couldn't leave.   I was so close to meeting Nicodemus and getting the answers.   I was about to ask Madez why his father was so late when I looked up to see a familiar face bearing down on our playground--the priest I had offended, Annas, in full regal apparel, with another man standing next to him.   I tried to catch Madez's eye, but he had already run up to the second man.

"Papa," he said. "We have a new friend."

So this was Nicodemus. He did slightly resemble Hagabus; a Hagabus not being nagged and gnawed on by the treachery of aging.

"Who is your new friend, my son?"   His voice was soft and mellow, almost cheering, quite unlike the vocal thunder found in the throat of Father Annas.

"That is the boy, my brother--the rude lad looking for you."   Annas motioned toward me.   Every head turned, this time, no giggles; instead, a silent empathy given to a condemned soul.

Nicodemus sensed my plight. "Doesn't look rude to me, Brother Annas. A bit soiled, but not rude." Everyone chuckled, partly out of respect for Nicodemus, but mostly due to my physical appearance. "Come here, lad, let me see you." He turned my head around, and my body followed, completing a circle of inspection. "Well, Brother Annas, he is not a beggar. No beggar would be caught dead in that tattered robe." More obedient laughter. "What can I do for you?" Nicodemus stood back, putting a hand on his bearded chin, as if mulling the correct price to pay for an ass.

Finally, my turn. I cleared my throat. "I have a message." My voice squeaked like a baby mouse.

"Speak up, boy!" commanded the amused scribe.

I tried again. There were giggles to the right of me and chuckles to the left. "I have a message from your brother, Rabbi Hagabus."

The playful brow of Nicodemus, raised in amusement, now lowered in a deep furrow of deliberation. "Now there is a name I haven't heard for some time." His eyes darted toward Annas as if seeking insight. The older priest quickly shook his head and turned away.

"He is your brother?" I piped.

"Little boy, I have many brothers. Annas is my brother." With this Nicodemus reached over and patted his cohort on the shoulder. I started to speak, but was interrupted. "So, we can talk of these things later. Now, what is this I hear about your question to Brother Annas?" His eyes were ablaze with pent up anger. What was he trying to hide? Why would anyone deny he had a brother, especially one as kind as Hagabus? I was angry at this pharisee. What was his ploy?

The delay must have been uncomfortable, because Annas decided to relieve the tension. "I'll tell you what he asked. This little dropling wanted to know why we couldn't hear from God like Abraham or Moses." He released a sarcastic chortle. The children obediently joined in, mimicking the tone and volume of the priestly example. "Can you imagine that?" he continued. "I knew he was just a boy and therefore could not be held accountable for comparing himself to our great fathers."

I was tired, angry, hurt and very much alone, a particular combination of feelings not lending itself to logic. "Why not? The Father loves me as much as Abraham."

Nicodemus anticipated Annas's volatile reaction and tried to step in, but it was too late. "See here, lad," said Annas with fury. "We do not compare ourselves to the likes of Father Abraham, and we certainly do not call the Most High our personal begetter."

I didn't understand everything he said, but I didn't like his attitude. I was ready for a fight, enraged at Nicodemus for denying Hagabus, and frustrated at the children for deserting me in the presence of these grown-ups. I was also furious with Annas for dismissing my inquiry as some improper boyish ramble. I continued, "Why did God make us then? Is it just to worship He and Abraham? We must have more purpose than that. I believe . . ."

With this Annas threw his hands up in the air. "You believe? You believe? No one cares what you believe. You are just fruit from loins. It is the Law and Prophets which must be believed."

A crowd was gathering; common passers-by and priestly sorts popped in all around us to catch the specifics of the debate.

One of the faces blurted, "Do not dismiss the boy, brother. Why don't you answer the question?"

"I do not explain to a thief why he can't steal, nor will I tell a child why he can't be Abraham." A snarl and a hiss rose from the amassed.

I determined it was my turn to speak. "I mean no disrespect. I want to know what my life means. Isn't it to discover everything I can about my creating Father?"

Annas tugged on his robe for dramatic effect. "We don't call him Father!" He directed his last statement at me and all the surrounding spectators; shouts, cheers, laughter, and some jeers. The people were grateful for the diversion from the temple tedium--a sideshow of burgeoning proportions.

I was about to speak again when Madez tugged on my robe. "Slow down, this is serious stuff to him. It's no game."

Nicodemus had positioned himself between us.

Suddenly young Veronica ran up, in tears, and grabbed Annas' legs and pleaded, "Papa please, you will cause yourself another spell."

Caiaphas followed his young betrothed to Annas's side. Veronica was Annas' daughter. A sick feeling gurgled in the pit of my stomach. I was attacking the father of a friend. I had not known them long, but they had been kind to me. Now I was returning her warmth by attacking her papa. I just wanted out of there.

I think Nicodemus sensed my dilemma. "Well, this has been exciting."

Annas stared at me, panting. Nicodemus grabbed Madez's arm and he mine, and we wriggled out of the circle.

My tongue would not lay still. "I will be back with more questions."

The crowd cheered my proclamation.

"Come the day following the morrow, and Brother Annas will have a whole roomful of priests gathered to answer you," chimed the same man who had spoken before.

Annas frowned at him as the crowd taunted the aged priest.

"Are you afraid of the lad, brother?"

"Don't you know your letters, rabbi?"

"I can answer any questions a Galilean whelp could ever devise." Annas chest swelled with pride.

"I will be there," I hollered. "You can count on that."

Nicodemus was scurrying us off and away. As I left, I heard cheers and laughter, as the crowd dispersed with a collective sigh and a grunt of disappointment that the confrontation had ended so soon.

Nicodemus was running, dragging Madez and myself along like a bandit escaping with dry goods. He did not stop until he had taken us safely out of the gates of the temple and far from the frothing anger of a most perturbed priest.

Feeling safely withdrawn, he stopped to regain breath. After a few moments of sucking in air he turned to me and spoke between great huffs. "You are either . . . the bravest lad I have ever met . . . or the craziest." He drew a deep long breath and concluded, "Forget that, you are just insane. Father Annas does not make a good enemy."

"I don't want an enemy. I just want information."

He squinted at me, probing for a semblance of common sense, or some innocence to rationalize my presumption. "To get answers, you must first make sure, Little One, that you are permitted the honor of inquiry."

I considered his point. Was questioning a privilege or a necessity?

Before I could decide he continued, "Now, where are your parents?"

"They are back at our Inn."

"Alright, now where is that?"

"I will show you," I replied, and started off down the street.

Fifteen minutes passed, then half-an-hour. Down the streets we tramped, everything blending into the same tan or gray background. The obvious conclusion--someone had hidden my house. A very sick joke was being perpetrated on this young man from Nazareth. An hour slipped away and still I could not locate my dwelling. I had lost a whole building and a set of parents, too.

Nicodemus spoke "You are lost, Jesus, and before we join you, let's go to my home. The hour is getting late. We will not find anything in the dark."

Where was my family? I could not stay away. They didn't even know where I was. I wanted to cry, but fatigue had made me tearless, and I was with strangers. I obediently followed Nicodemus and his son to their abode. My heart was broken, mood sullen, stomach and soul empty. I ate a few morsels of the portion provided, and then humbly asked for a mat where I might sleep.

Nicodemus looked down with sympathetic eyes, "It will be fine. We will find your parents on the morrow."

Made sense. They would certainly come and look for me. Through bleary eyes and achy head, I examined, "Do you really not know Hagabus?"

The rabbi laughed. "You are the most persistent boy I have ever met. Yes, I know Hagabus. We will talk of him when it is morning. Now sleep, if you can ever turn your brain off." He walked away. His chuckle is my last remembrance. Sleep won over persistence.

I awoke to Madez's face peering into mine, as he anxiously shook my arm. Where was I and what had brought me to this strange location?

"You Galileans certainly know how to sleep. The day is nearly half-spent. Get up before you miss it all," he scoffed, squeezing my nose.

It suddenly came back to me; all the strange occurrences of the previous day peppered my mind with contorted visions of children at play and a crazed pharisee at bay. "Have you heard from my Mama and Papa?" This was primal in my sleepy mind--first things first. Priority two would be to beg their forgiveness for my indiscretion. Then, if time permitted, I would still try to find out about Master Hagabus. How ironic; these three priorities had directly reversed from yesterday's adventuresome crusade.

Nicodemus came into the room and stated he thought it best for us to stay around the house today. He had left word at the temple that anyone inquiring about a missing child should be sent to his cottage immediately. I think he was trying to keep adequate distance between Annas and myself.

I welcomed the day of rest, giving me time to get to know Madez and Nicodemus. I discovered there was no Mama Nicodemus. She had passed away from a fever three years ago during a blistering heat spell. I was astonished how openly they shared with me, treating me as family: adult family at that. I felt so comfortable I asked Madez more about his dried and shrunken hand.

"That is the way it has always been," he said. "I wouldn't recognize it any other way." He mustered a tiny smile, radiating a candor which only partially disguised disappointment.

"Have you prayed maybe God would do something with it, like heal it, as he did Naaman the leper?"

Nicodemus jumped in, using his characteristic wit. "Naaman had to dunk seven times in the Jordan River. I can't even get Madez to bathe once every seven days."

They both laughed, but I continued. "No, I'm serious. What about God the Healer? Is that not part of the nature of the Father?"

"It is a part he has not chosen to shine on us, my friend, so for now we love each other and accept each other as we are--Madez with his withered hand, and me with my ever-withering body."

I laughed heartily with them, temporarily escaping my pre-adult leaning to the dark and somber. We munched on some bread and sipped some wine. Each of us knew the next topic of discussion. Each, for his own reason, was stalling.

Finally Nicodemus looked up and said, "Hagabus, is he well?"

It was finally here. I was going to learn the truth. Part of me was frightened by the prospect of total revelation. Hagabus was my friend. I wanted it to stay that way. "Yes," I replied slowly, "He is very well. You do love him?"

The question was awkward, but one I needed answered before chatting further. I did not want to analyze a friend, unless it was with another friend.

"Love him? Hagabus was my god. As a lad I mimicked every move he made. I tried to walk like him and talk like him. I am probably in the priesthood because of him, God forgive me. It has taken me years to discover myself in the massive shadow of his presence. Yes, I love him."

"I misunderstood your statements at the temple yesterday." Nicodemus claimed love for his brother but seemed aggravated the affection existed.

He continued, "You must understand, Jesus, when something dies you must bury it, hastily, before the passing of time causes disease to spread from the decaying carcass. In a way, Hagabus is dead to me. I still love him, but he is a dark spot on the memories of many of my brethren here about Jerusalem. If I try to keep his memory alive I will just be guilty of continuing to spread the pain and disease." He paused. "Just tell him Nicodemus said nothing could ever keep me from loving him, but time has not healed the wounded." He stood to his feet. "I do not wish to be an ungracious host, but it is the hour of prayer and I must go to the temple."

"But Master," I jumped to my feet, "What happened to Hagabus? Why do you feel this way?"

He turned and spoke sharply, "If it was meant for you to know, young sir, Hagabus would have told you. I am not going to be his confessor or his judge. I can tell you no more. Why can't you just be satisfied to be a child and play with something besides people's painful pasts?" He stormed out the door.

I sat in the devastation of one rebuffed, frustrated, and perturbed by the lack of opportunity to respond.

Madez was shocked. "My father is not a mean man, Jesus. There are things he cannot say, or he will be cast from the order."

I quickly turned toward Madez. He knew more than he was sharing. "What is it? What is so terrible no man can speak of it?"

"I should not say. I am not supposed to know anything."

"Hagabus is my friend, I must know."

He wept, and I felt terrible. I had brought sorrow to his home. "I overheard my father, two or three years ago, speaking to Father Annas. Papa wanted to make an overture of peace to Uncle Hagabus. He said time had passed, no man should suffer this long for his sins. I was hidden away and continued to listen. Annas forbade any reconciliation. He went on to recount to Papa the 'iniquity' as he put it, of his brother. This is the story. Hagabus was teaching in the synagogue in Bethany when he became close friends with a merchant named Trinius and his wife, Shira. They were both Gentiles, converted to our faith, very loyal. Trinius loved and trusted Hagabus and asked him to keep an eye over his household and wife while he traveled on his buying trips. Jesus, I don't know, I shouldn't be saying these things. It is gossip."

"I want to know, Madez!"

"Alright, well, Hagabus fell in love with Shira and they did things old people do, if you know what I mean. They were both shocked by their deeds and decided never to see each other again. But a neighbor named Simon told Trinius about Hagabus and his wife. Trinius went crazy. He came to the temple and threatened everybody. He said he would kill Hagabus. My uncle confessed it all and agreed to leave, but before he could go Trinius fell on his sword and killed himself. There was an investigation. The Romans cleared Hagabus of any involvement, but the temple was stained with the scandal. Hagabus left, Trinius was buried, and a few years later Simon, the next door neighbor, contracted leprosy and died."

Silent. I had prayed he would stop sooner, wishing I had never heard.

Madez engrossed by his own tale, continued. "Shira never married again. They say she never leaves her home except under the cover of darkness."

A horror story. I could not go back and pretend I was ignorant of Hagabus' past. I wanted to see some healing. I wanted my friend to know God could forgive all of this. Where to start?

Madez spoke again, "You mustn't tell anyone I told you. No one knows I know. They would kill me if they knew I let you in on the secret."

"I won't, don't worry. The story is over as far as I am concerned. I just want to go home and let Master Hagabus know I love him and try to help replace the spot left vacant in his life by this disaster."

I couldn't sleep that night, partly because of Nicodemus' anger; partly because of my silly insistence on digging up what I deemed the truth. There was also my status as a temporary orphan, and Shira, who felt she could never leave her house in the light of day. I knew on the morrow I would have to go to the temple and confront Hagabus' prosecutor. I had many questions for Master Annas.

Father's Business

I arose determined to complete my mission. Nicodemus reasoned with me to stay away from the temple. Madez slipped and informed me that a group of rabbis and holy fellows met each week to discuss temple business and mull over the universal. I insisted we attend.

The official ceremonies of Passover were over. Most of the thousands of pilgrims had already returned to their homes. This was most perplexing. Where were my Mama and Papa? Certainly they would not have left Jerusalem without me. I was worried, yet still committed to have my time in the temple with Annas. There was business to be done; what I considered business for the Father.

Nicodemus knew I was a boy possessed; right or wrong, I was going to do it. He agreed to permit me to go to the temple as long as he could accompany me. Madez pleaded to come, too. I think he shared my desire to justify his uncle. I was not angry--more should have been done to restore the ravaged souls involved in the Hagabus-Shira fiasco. I had questions. Did I expect answers? Maybe not, but I wanted my inquiries acknowledged by this huddle of esteemed theologians.

The streets of Jerusalem were nearly deserted in comparison to the pandemonium of a few days earlier. I tried to banish the thought of abandonment from my head. If orphaned here, then let my life begin in the temple doing what I believed was right. Mama and Papa would have to find me. I didn't know where they were. But let them discover me doing something which would make them proud of me.

Arriving, Nicodemus led me into a large hall, much deeper in the heart of the temple. Each step drew us closer to the throne of God. We opened a huge cedar door and walked into a room filled with wall-to-wall beards, long hair, robes, dark, musty, rumbling with subdued growls emanating from the depths of melancholy spirits.

Annas looked up, squinting in our direction, and crinkled his brow to accentuate his displeasure. "Brother Nicodemus, this meeting is not open to children," he said aloud, to bring focus to the proposed indiscretion. The assemblage fell silent. Nicodemus stopped in mid-step.

Madez and I nearly ran into his backside. The three of us stood motionless, scores of eyes glaring our way. Finally a voice; the familiar ally in the quest to get answers to my questions.

"Now, now, Father Annas, this young man is hardly a child. Anyone who can construct a question a Master of Israel must ponder, certainly is not a youngster. Unless you are willing to admit you have been bettered by the inquest of a babe." There was no great affection between the two men. Somewhat odd for the gruff and fearless Annas to be intimidated by anyone.

Annas spoke, "Ruler Jairus, it is not a question of my desire, rather a matter of propriety. Are we to turn the great hall of the Sanhedrin into a synagogue school for little boys? Nay, no matter how good his question may be, for the sake of maintaining a holy order, Nicodemus, we must ask you to take the boys away from these chambers."

Nicodemus, speechless, remained paralyzed by fear. Murmurings ensued, the hall humming and hissing with the basal tones of pious debaters--difficult to make out content. The general consensus was disagreement with Annas. The issue was far past propriety. Evidently ancient aggravations and ongoing feuds were bewitching this gathering of the darkened priestly. The men sitting before me in this theological dungeon were creatures facing pending extinction. For if they did not construct a theology to challenge the young hotheads of Judea, while still appeasing the Pax Roma of the Emperor, they would soon find their great "Sinai Experiment" relegated to the status of folklore. This had become the great source of their consternation. Although I did not realize it, mine was a trial case. If they dismissed two boys from the temple because they had questions, the negative publicity would haunt them for months to come. They didn't want to ignore a future generation of taxable temple tenants.

Annas, sensing the dissension amongst his brethren, spoke with greater finality. "Get those rascals out of here, brother."

Nicodemus finally enlivened his tongue. "With all due respect, Father Annas, knowing you are the Master of masters throughout Israel, I believe if you search your faultless memory you will recall, without error, it was your bidding and wish that this Jesus of Nazareth have audience with you on this day. This is not to imply you had forgotten or that age has taken its toll on your faculties. Perhaps it was my fault in bringing the lad prematurely to his appointed time. Please forgive the early hour. As for my son, he merely wanted to accompany us here to feel the presence of the Almighty as the great men deliberate the finer points of the law."

Spineless diplomacy. I had no stomach for verbose, twisted logic. Nicodemus appeared to be a plucked, stuffed bird trying desperately to avoid inevitable consumption. To connote Annas had forgotten our meeting was pure hog dung. Annas was evasive, condescending, and self-righteous, a particular trio of attitudes stirring me to rage. I was ready to speak and angry--angry about the way these pious hounds had chased Hagabus from Jerusalem, that my questions were being summarily dismissed by ignorant judges, and at Nicodemus for compromising our new-found friendship. I was even angry at my Mama and Papa for leaving Passover without me. Most of all I was angry for placing myself in this dubious situation. Was this my day of rebellion?

I looked for an ally. Jairus sat quietly, smiling. Annas turned and consorted with several nearby robed cohorts.

After a few moments, he turned to Jairus and spoke, "As I stated, Lord Jairus, we are always more than happy to answer any of your questions, even if you choose they be uttered from the mouth of this suckling."

This elicited a flurry of response: Jairus bowed, Madez cheered, the gathering rumbled, Nicodemus sighed with relief, and I fumed.

"We will see who is the suckling, Master Annas." I punctuated each word of my response, not appreciating being dismissed as too immature to think.

"Impudence is an attribute best worn by a peasant. Ask on, my son." Annas smirked, seeking the favor of silent supporters.

Jairus placed his hand on my shoulder and leaned down to whisper in my ear. "Choose your words wisely, my son. Opportunity is rare in this life. Do not squander it on the foolish rhetoric of hostility."

He was right. It was a regal moment--one I had dreamed about many times. Now here, soon to pass. I offered my apology, "Please forgive my attitude and tone, Father Annas. I am grateful for this forum to quell my confusion concerning insights on the law and prophets."

Annas sat up straight and peered about the room, assuring himself each one had heard my concession and conciliatory words. "Proceed, young man, but limit your comments and questions to those that also ponder the mind of our dear brother, Jairus. As an ass carries water from the well, you are to obediently ask only that which your master demands."

Jairus patted my head, anticipating a fresh eruption of childish rage. I was calm, already learning a war of words is won in a battle for control of one's own emotions. No longer entangled by my anger, I was curious if this priest could help me in my pursuit of the Father. "Let us begin with my, I mean, the, original question. Why can't we experience God by faith like Abraham of old?"

Annas didn't hesitate, launching into his dissertation. "Some men are born to rule and some are born to serve. When rule is established, the monarch steps away and all become servants to the standard. Moses, Abraham, and the prophets gave us the holy law as attained from the mind of God. They passed it on, having fulfilled their unique mission. Now all men are subservient to their experience and bound by the law they delivered. When the truth has been revealed, to question further, or to seek deeper revelation, is to dig away at the foundation of the needful mystery of holiness. We, as priests, have been granted the humbling and often arduous task of discerning the more practical will and purposes of the law for the general distribution to the beloved, but uninformed, masses. They are subject to us, we to Moses, and Moses, alone, to God."

This brought a chorus of "Ayes" from the surrounding committee. I leaned toward Jairus, who had stationed himself at my side. "Ask away, little Nazarene," he whispered in my ear.

"Then why do we seek a Messiah?"

Annas glanced at Jairus. "The Messiah will bring to pass all that Moses promised. He will restore the House of David and give us Abraham's land of promise."

"And the Romans will allow him to do this?"

"When The Deliverer comes," said Annas, gruffly, "then we will know."

"Then will all men be able to experience for themselves?" I was firing the questions from my soul, only pausing long enough to simulate receiving them from Jairus.

"I do not know," said Annas.

On into the morning the interrogation continued, eventually becoming a predictable round of questions followed by, "I don't know," or "It is not good for man to know," or "These are questions that were not intended to have answers."

A stalemate--my questions versus his evasion. I felt it was time to bring up the treatment the Sanhedrin had given my friend, Hagabus. I knew, out of deference to

Nicodemus and especially Madez's confidence,   I mustn't allude to any specifics. I phrased the question in my mind. "What value is the law if it only produces condemnation and doesn't afford the true impact of redemption and restitution?"

Annas blurted,   "It   does   through   the   blood sacrifice."

"So if a man confesses and repents and is blood-atoned, he is forgiven?"

"We believe so," said Annas, "but there is only surety of forgiveness in the mind of God. Man can only assume."

"Then what is the purpose of living if you can't assure your conscience all is well and that repentance has brought restitution?"

Eye to eye, a pause, another stalemate.   Then an interruption to our   deadlock--a sudden release of light in the room. startling me,   my eyes   accustomed to the darkened quarters. The door opened and a stream of brilliant sunshine flowed into the room, forming a beam so intensely vibrant one would be tempted to walk on it.   I was not able to make out the features of the arriving guests; gradually, two forms in the haze of the brilliance.

A voice came from the sunlit doorway, "My son, why did you leave us?   We have looked everywhere for you."

The second figure spoke soft and low, sadly.   "Why have you treated us this way?"

Papa and Mama.   "You knew where I would be.   I had business for my Father."   I didn't mean the words to be sharp, but the edge was there.

Joseph   spoke.   "Forgive   me,   gentlemen,   for intruding. I have come for my son--time we journey."

Annas smiled, relieved, possessing a gloat of victory.   "No trouble, my son, just take your boy and be gone."

I squeezed Jairus' hand, stopped and hugged Nicodemus, and kissed Madez.   I told Nicodemus and Madez I would see them again, then quickly joined my Mama and Papa at the door of the chamber.

It was over, my temple journey completed.   I took one last look back into the circle of faces.   My eyes met those of Master Annas. He stared,   looked away,   whispered something to a nearby colleague, and they both chuckled. There was something extraordinary about the moment.   I would be back.

Joseph slammed the door, twirled me around and said, "Your Papa's business is carpentry, and your Papa's business is to take care of his son."

Mary grabbed his arm and said, "Joseph, stop it. He's scared. Leave him alone."

I had caused them pain. I would never do it again. I had learned my lesson. I must stay close to Mama and Papa. I had also learned much about human nature. The piety of Annas was a rude awakening to my spirit. The handicap Madez had and the ongoing cloud of guilt festering around Hagabus, made me more aware then ever how personal suffering is to all of us. I also learned the Sanhedrin didn't have answers to my questions, but kind men like Jairus would encourage me in my quest.

My search for truth and personal worth would have to continue back in Nazareth at the home of Joseph the carpenter. Nazareth seemed more inviting than ever. I would submit and learn, and maybe, in doing so, I would find out once and for all who Jesus of Nazareth is, and why he feels so strongly there is something he must do.

SITTING 18
Inn-stability

I hear a scratching.

No, perhaps better described as a scraping sound, a noise one might expect from an animal's claw digging at loose stone; an intensity to set the teeth on edge, yet muffled enough to make it difficult to determine direction. I sit still. Curious. Alarmed souls always select a profile in silence. Perhaps flamboyance or a loud clanging might be a better protection.

Anyway, my ears strain to hear. There it is again, coming from my right. No, perhaps the left. The echo of the stable makes the origin of the commotion uncertain. I remain silent. The moments pass slowly. My head begins to throb, and my hand shakes as I hold the candle aloft in the darkness, creating eerie shadows, further creeping my soul.

I reach down into the loose stones and rub my fingernails across a jagged rock. Silence, then suddenly I hear more scraping in the foreground. I repeat my endeavor, once, twice, and a third time. Each time, the other scraping stops when mine begins. Then it begins again, momentarily after mine stops. Obviously, whatever lies in the darkness is now aware of my presence. I stop scraping, my hands raw and burning from the attempts at communication. How wise is it to pinpoint my location to some trapped beast with keener senses than mine?

The scraping continues. It could be my imagination, but it seems to increase, as if frustrated mine had ceased.

I listen.

A growl.

Wait. . . Not really a growl--higher in pitch, a bit softer in timbre, but very brief. My heart pounds. Silence. Everything is so still I can hear a slight wheeze in my breathing. I am ready to dismiss the whole affair, amused at how quickly I have terrified myself--time to get back to the bliss of reminisce.

There it is again! Longer this time; still what I would call a whining or growling sound, yet different, not guttural, in two parts connected together. A very brief groan-word, "grrt". Then a pause, followed by an elongated "ooot".

It does not sound animal. Missing is the hiss or raspiness of a rodent. Present is what appears to be a mongroled attempt at human speech. I feel a trifle ridiculous trying to discern the articulation of a common howl, yet there is something unique in this tone, like no other beast I am accustomed to hearing. Silence persists, then the utterance repeats, exactly the same sound, duplicated flawlessly. Even the pause between syllables is identical. Perhaps syllables is a bit overstated, but this is certainly a purposeful grunt. Is this creature trying to communicate with me? First the scraping and now an attempt at conversation? I am intrigued. I choose to imitate, hoping this overture will be perceived as friendly.

I mimic the speech. "Grrt-oot," I yelp into the bleak environs. Nothing. Then, a response, quicker, as if the being is excited at the prospect of connection. Gone is the pause. It now seems to be some primitive word.

"Grrt-oooot," I elongate and wait for reply. I am rewarded with like response. This friend is imitating my variation. I decide to change the sound and pitch and create a new expression. "Brrt-ooot," I offer into the darkness.

No response. Have I frightened the beast away by my presumptuous introduction of a new sound?

Then "Bruta-oot-a."

There it is. Not the same, but close enough to prove my suspicions. This was not a beast--human. In my haste to establish contact, I speak, "Don't be afraid, come here."

The stillness proves the folly of my outburst. I was communicating, but got in too big a hurry to succeed. I begin to scrape and then moan. I fill the air with attempts to re-establish contact with my fellow stable-dweller. No success. Beads of sweat burst on my forehead, partly from nerves, but mostly from the exertion of scraping and growling.

Perhaps he is gone. He? Yes, I am quite positive it is a he.

An hour passes. I am talking softly under my breath, trying desperately not to scare my colleague. This is becoming an absurd pursuit.

Then I hear some movement in the shadows. He is still there. Thank God for the human grunter's faithfulness. I glance about me. Verbal communication appears to be faltering. I need a new method. I see some small pebbles in a corner. I pitch one into the darkness. I wait. What am I anticipating? I pitch a second, then a third. I keep up the vigil. One pebble after another I throw into the blackness.

Nothing. I am about to give up when I spot a larger rock. Call it desperation, aggravation or total insanity, I pick it up and heave it into the shadowy surroundings. An overwhelming sense of foolishness taunts my mind. I laugh at myself. While shifting to adjust my buttocks to a more comfortable position, a large rock flies out of the darkness, striking me in the chest, producing quite an audible thud, and propels me back on my hands.

"Grrt-oot--Brrt-oot," squeals my friend, gleefully.

I laugh. Most assuredly I have made my first steps towards fellowship with Relah's brother---the fig tree.

SITTING 19
Anisa, the Princess of Treoli

I was not born to be a carpenter. It took me many years to accept this reality. Throughout my adolescence I struggled to pursue the trade in an attempt to derive a livelihood. Being the firstborn son of Joseph of Nazareth, the carpenter, it was assumed I would follow in his footsteps. Actually, assume may be too passive a word to cover the intensity of the predestination--pretty well a sacred trust.

So I learned the trade. Learning, for me, was the easy part. As far as comprehending the work or demonstrating the tools, I had no match in proficiency. Mentally I was a topnotch carpenter. On the strength of an interview I could have been hired to rebuild Jericho.

Each day I absorbed Joseph's instruction like desert sand gulping infrequent rain. Yet when the tool was in my grasp, and my mentor of wood and stone walked away, I'd fumble and falter to accomplish my usual adequate job. When Joseph would return I could see the look of disappointment--a forced smile and encouragement on his lips--but I knew my labor had fallen well short of the standards set for the shop.

I don't want you to get the wrong idea. Joseph wasn't an unrelenting perfectionist. It was me. I was seventeen years old and unmotivated in an occupation supposed to provide me food and shelter for the rest of my life. It was becoming evident if I continued in carpentry I would starve, not due to laziness, even though ineptness appears to resemble that vice. Stone just left me cold. Trying to be enthralled with the subtle differences between jobs wasn't fooling anyone. The enthusiasm lasted a day or two, then I would return to the musings in my heart; obvious to me if I continued, I would die a pauper who had just completed his latest barely acceptable job. After all, mediocrity is a profile most souls accept in themselves and denounce in everybody else.

Joseph despised competence. He once told me, "Jesus, there is nothing worse than almost good. Half the people demand to know why you didn't do more. The other half will ask why you even bothered to begin in the first place." Not the words of a compromising craftsman.

Coming home at the end of the work day was the worst part of it. Mary wanted to be supportive of her "manly providers," and sensed all had not gone smoothly. She would try to involve herself by being cheery, saying things like, "You mean you have to lift those big rocks?" Or, "Did you build something really important today?"

We sat and stared at her, Joseph too exhausted from working to answer, and me too frustrated from the work to carry on idle conversation about the details. Mary perceived our reluctance and quietly gathered the remains of the meal while humming some unfamiliar tune. Joseph excused himself to go and tickle the youngest offspring, while I made the rounds of the faces in the room to see if any of the little ones were oblivious to my ineptitude. Finding a friendly face, I chased the tyke out the door and into the fading light of the day. I ran until my aching legs relieved my troubled mind of its cumbersome worry. I was positive I would never be a carpenter. I just didn't know how to tell Papa.

Some relief came that summer when James became old enough to join us on the jobs. Of course, in no time at all the little runt showed me up. Still, it was very good to have some easing of the pressure, giving me some time to consider my plight. My problem was trying to please three very different parts of myself. There was the me--a young man linked to this Jewish family. There was another segment, a seventeen-year-old ready to explode from every fiber of his being. The third portion was the most confusing of the three, repressed at this point, having a will to become the strongest, buried deeply under the other two dominant forces. Yet that didn't stop it from being annoying, always trying to wiggle to the surface and gain breath. This "me" didn't resemble anything I was trained to be or experienced from the other folks around me; unrevealed, but desirous of manifestation. I am like everybody else, imbalanced, considering wild and demented thoughts, but prudent enough not to share them with anybody. Every young man my age sails through the raging waters of insanity enroute to a safe port of awareness. It just appeared my three waves were drowning me in a sea of uncertainty.

Papa became concerned, convinced I needed a woman. Nothing was ever verbalized. Daughters of his friends would just happen along to the work site, bringing water to us on a hot day, dressed and smelling like synagogue. Joseph would wink at me and motion for me to talk with the young and willing damsels. I didn't know what he wanted me to do. Married people always think it is so easy to start something up with a complete stranger. They have forgotten the utter bungling associated with the whole process of meeting someone. I didn't need help finding girls, they do frequent the path. I was not oblivious to the attributes of the opposite sex, very normal, in that way. Everything manly in me had bloomed and sprouted with the same equity granted Brother Adam. I had urges at times digressing to violent, ransom demands: *do something or we will kill you.* I just didn't want to get married for a lack of something better to do, my life a muddled accident, culminating in my untimely death. I know it sounds gloomy, but remember, I was seventeen. Gloomy is a lifestyle.

I needed to know the meaning of life before I started procreating more of it--the value of my life. If I had a son, and he asked me to explain things to him, I wanted a real answer--my own conviction. I didn't want my reply to be the frustrated misgivings of an aging carpenter of Nazareth, who should have at least tried something else.

Thoughts much like these were twirling in my mind one very hot summer afternoon, when our work was interrupted. We were building a wall. Papa was perspiring so profusely I thought he was going to drain the last drop of life from his body--the kind of heat that sucked all energy, leaving a sense of dread at the prospect of movement.

Our sweat to the death was postponed by the arrival of a runner. He was a stranger to our town. In Nazareth, you knew every soul down to the proximity of all warts and moles. I was sure this panting racer was not from our village. He gasped, attempting to retrieve lost air, tried to speak, but was overcome from his endeavor. Papa leaned down and gently poured some cool water into his mouth. He snorted and then guzzled. "Easy, my friend," said Papa, in soothing tones.

The man babbled, but we were unable to understand his language. He tried again, using primitive, broken Aramaic. "She . . . die. You . . . come."

"Where?"

"Man . . . of herbs?"

"He needs a doctor," said Joseph to himself as he inspected the horizon.

"Herbs," the recovering runner repeated.

"I understand," said Papa, patting his shoulder.

"Princess," he said frantically.

Princess? There were no princesses in Nazareth. Perhaps he was deranged from the desert heat. I think Papa suspected the same because he probed again, "Where?"

The man pointed in the direction of the oasis. "Princess . . . sick. Give herbs!" he said, grasping my father's robe to accentuate his plea. Joseph stood to his feet and stared off into the distance, his gaze set and rigid, brow furrowed, joining the two sections of hairy humps into a singular line of fur. I knew he wasn't trying to see the oasis--too far. He knelt down and scribbled in the sand with his finger. Now I understood. Papa was thinking; the posture he selected before he would decide anything of importance.

I once asked him why he took the time to do all that scrawling and scratching. "Better," he said, "to take a few moments planning what to do, than to end up taking the whole day correcting what was done poorly."

I reviewed the situation myself. If what the runner said was true, there might be a princess in danger for her life. The next move would be crucial.

Joseph lifted himself up and began to bark orders. It was a marvelous sight. Papa was in charge. Whatever was ailing the princess would soon be resolved. "James, run to the village and get Hagabus and tell him to meet us at the oasis."

James leaped to his feet, scattering sand like a billowing cloud in all directions, scurrying away. Papa turned to the recovering visitor and said, "Man of herbs . . . come." The exhausted fellow smiled.

Hagabus was a wise choice. Though the local rabbi, he enjoyed making potions from herbs and roots. He really didn't use them to nurse others, but often treated his own aches and pains with a specially concocted remedy.

"Jesus," Papa said deliberately, "I want you to run on ahead to the oasis and tell them their messenger has arrived and help is on its way."

"What if they don't understand me?"

"You will find a way to communicate."

I nodded and was off, no longer noticing the heat. This was an authentic adventure, not the tedium of prolonged carpentry. I was on my way to an oasis to meet people from far away. One of them might be a princess. As I ran, my mind tried to access every piece of information I had on the subject of princesses. The extent of my experience was paltry, to say the least. I remember, as a boy in Egypt, seeing a parade of people on the streets of Alexandria. I asked Papa what was going on. He told me it was a princess and her admirers. She was very beautiful. I wondered if the princess at our oasis would be just as attractive. Some prerequisite of comeliness was required to even be called a princess, I guess.

I continued my run through the scorching sand, my heart trying to climb up my throat, the air so hot and heavy my body objected each time I inhaled. I thought back to the original objection I had voiced to Papa. How would I get them to understand me? If they all talked like the messenger, the princess could die before we figured out a way to exchange greetings.

On and on I raced. I came up a small rise, the oasis in sight. I could see some tents and camels. I reached deep within myself for some unused reservoir of strength and ran the remaining distance, stumbling into the camp, collapsing to my knees. I understood why the runner was so depleted of energy and incoherent when he arrived.

There were six or seven men and women who rose to their feet and strolled to my side.

"Help . . . is . . . on its way," I wheezed.

They stared at me quizzically. Just as I feared, they couldn't understand me. Would I have to jaunt and leap about, making sounds and faces to get them to comprehend? How humiliating!

"Who are you?" asked a young man with long, yellow hair, clad in the trappings of a warrior.

"You understand me?"

"Who are you?" he repeated.

"There is a man of herbs coming," I spoke, having regained a swallow of breath.

"A man of herbs?"

"Your messenger arrived," I began, sipping on a bit of cool water one of the gracious hosts brought to me, "and my Papa sent me ahead. He is coming with the priest."

"A priest? I thought you said he was a man of herbs. We need medicine, not prayers," spat the rugged soldier.

"Bandi, please have some respect for our guest and his noble efforts." The second spokesman was aged, with long, glistening, white hair falling in layers down his side and back. Chains of gold dangled from his neck, shimmering, with a jeweled earring in each ear.

The one he called Bandi, about my age, bowed to the authority of the elder and apologized. "I guess it is better to have a priest than a gravedigger."

The old man smiled at me and said, "I am Tabuli Manta--teacher, seer and protector of this caravan for Princess Anisa of Treoli. What is wrong? You seem shocked."

"It's just that you don't talk funny. Your messenger spoke like a baby learning his first words."

Tabuli Manta frowned and glared around the circle of onlookers. "I told all of you to learn the language. If we are to travel as pilgrims amongst these people, we at least should know how to speak to them."

One of the entourage spoke to the elder in a dialect I did not understand.

"Who else?" demanded the protector. "Who else has failed to learn their Aramaic?" He looked around with the scowl of a schoolmaster correcting the naughty. Two hands raised, very slowly. "Young man, what is your name?" he asked, whirling, maintaining his rebuking profile.

"Jesus of Nazareth!" I blurted obediently.

He smiled, noting my alarmed and subservient posture. "I am sorry. I didn't mean to speak in harshness to you," he said, as he bowed down on one knee and then rose again. I imitated his bow but failed to rise, still fatigued from my run and quite overwhelmed by the authoritarian. "Your priest is a healer?" he asked, helping me to my feet.

"His name is Hagabus. He likes to mingle plants to make dripping messes and strange-colored drinks."

Bandi rolled his eyes and stepped away, turning his back. Tabuli Manta just smiled.

"He will heal the girl," I insisted.

A lady, veiled in fine silk, stepped forward and interjected, "She is not a girl, peasant boy. She is the princess, and soon to be crowned Queen of Treoli." The spokeswoman was a fading beauty, with a nagging hint of matron, probably at least thirty years old. The whole assemblage bowed their heads in respect.

"Princess Anisa? What a lovely name," I said, mostly to myself. Their heads were still bowed, so I joined them gazing at the ground. Another man spoke, and his friend nearby grunted some sort of follow up. Tabuli, noting my confusion, offered an explanation. "These are the two mental insects that chose not to gain the ability of communication."

"What did they say?"

"They said she. . . lovely. . . dead if priest don't come soon," managed the silken lady. She seemed to be trapped in the grip of an endless huff. This adventure was bogging down into a slime of bad attitudes. All I knew was I wanted to be away from these fretting adults, so I could see the princess; tired of discussing herbs and death.

No harm in asking. "Where is the princess?"

Bandi spoke something in what I now recognized as the native language. The two who had admitted ignorance of Aramaic snickered in reply.

"No comments are required from the infantry," corrected Tabuli Manta, turning his searing glance to the giggling trio.

Yet another woman stepped forward, removed her veil, and extended a hand my way, saying, "I am Praella." No bitter tone. Her sudden graciousness surprised me and I stood eyeing the pristine, upturned hand.

This brought more laughter from the enlisted men. "Kiss her hand, peasant," taunted Bandi. I shook myself back into some state of awareness. I had never kissed a lady's hand before. I had kissed my mother and sisters because that was required. This was a strange woman who might laugh if I slobbered. I leaned down very quickly and grazed my lips against her cool, soft hand.

More laughter. I had come, it seemed, to bring pleasure and sport to the Treolian fighting men.

"May I see the princess?" My request prompted a council meeting of the congregated, conducted in their preferred speech. I watched with great interest--very funny, a series of grunts and unidentified words with stern looks and waving arms. I tittered, in spite of myself.

"It is out of the question. She needs her rest," exploded Bandi, returning to my tongue.

"Jesus is young. How old are you, son?" Tabuli asked, turning my way.

"Seventeen."

"Anisa is just one year younger," said Praella.

"Maybe he could transfuse some of his youthful exuberance into her ailing form," Tabuli reasoned.

"Maybe he could brew her a strange-colored drink and make her all better," said Bandi, sarcastically. He translated his comment to the duo standing nearby-- obligatory laughter. Bandi was obviously the leader, the two accomplices maintaining concurring identities of "yea" and "amen".

"I see no harm," Tabuli decided.

"So the absence of harm produces the presence of benefit?" challenged Bandi.

"Please, Bandi," said Praella, "leave the philosophy to Tabuli Manta. Stick to polishing your sword."

I laughed at her comment before I wagered in the potential danger of such a liberty. Bandi stepped toward me, threatening to attack.

Tabuli wedged between us. "Bandi, haven't you ever heard the Greek saying, 'Don't slay the messenger'? Jesus is our guest and I see no reason to forbid him a brief visit to Anisa's tent."

"I will accompany him," Bandi insisted.

"Not necessary," retaliated Praella.

"It is my commission to guard the princess. No one will stop me from my duty," he said, as he grabbed my arm and hauled me across the sand towards the largest of three tents.

"Do not stay long," called the anxious mother. "She grows weaker by the moment."

We arrived at the tent and Bandı pulled back the flap. "Don't dawdle, peasant."

I eased my way past him and into the enclosure. There was a presence in the room--the clinging, stale residue of death. Two women were huddled in the corner, whimpering and heaving huge, pitiful sobs. Mourners. Why do they arrive before the end? It always seems so ridiculous to have them at the bedside of one seriously ill. Wouldn't laughter be a better tonic for any ailment? I decided to leave them to their macabre chore.

My eyes adjusted slowly. Black sheets of cloth were hung to keep the light out, and, I assume, the disease safely within. I caught a glimpse of the form of a young woman, lying very still upon a pile of mats, satin and linen shrouding her visage, giving her appearance a hazy glow, almost like a silhouette. I moved closer, creeping toward the damsel. I gingerly pulled away the layer of cloth preventing me from seeing the lady at rest. I held my breath, fearing if I took another, I might lose·a moment's gaze at the vision before me. Beautiful; no, more. To use that word might cause you to presume she was similar to someone you may have met. Foolish. There was never one to compare with Anisa. I understood what Adam felt when awakened from his deep sleep to first behold his Eve. Anisa had shimmering, dark hair with highlights of gold dancing about the crown. Her lips were full and ruddy with the allurement of virgin promise. I drew closer. A single drop of perspiration careened down her face, winding its way past her slender neck and disappearing in the cradle of her breasts. She was the divine revelation of everything a woman was conceived to be. Nothing else seemed important but being close to her. Mine was not the lusting of a desperate young man, but rather the awe and admiration needfully given to a perfected creation.

I moved and knelt by her side. Though languishing in a fever, she was still stunning. It was beyond comprehension that this lady was dying. I felt like Moses, granted vision of the promised land, only to be forbidden entrance. I just sat and watched.

She did not move. Of course, ever so slightly her chest would rise as she drew her breath. Beyond that, no signs of life emanated from her presence; just the intense radiance of her beauty sculpted into her alabaster skin. I reached out to touch her, but Bandi stepped forward to prevent me, maintaining the scrutiny of a hawk from his vantage point, a mere lunge away.   "No touching," he ordered.

Too late. I ran my fingertips down her arm and tenderly caressed her tiny, soft hand. Bandi pulled me away. As he did, Anisa jostled from side to side, releasing a most audible moan. Her body pulsated, lifted, and then fell back to its former position.

"She moved," said Bandi, relaxing his grip on my shoulder.

"I haven't seen her do that!" I gasped.

"She is alive." It seemed to me his response carried a thud of disappointment instead of a chiming of jubilation.

Anisa's body gyrated, trying to spout the juices of life. Bandi stepped back in shock, horrified; Anisa's face twitched and her eyelids fluttered, as if repelling some displeasure.

"She is moving!" I screamed, scrambling to my feet and running to the opening in the tent. I fumbled with the flap and tripped my way out into the desert heat. "She is moving!"

The entourage was gathered around Hagabus. I could see my father and James coming in the distance.

"She is moving!" I ran full gallop toward the cluster of humanity.

Arriving in their midst, I danced. I think that is what you would call it. I had never danced before; never felt the need. When I touched Anisa it was like liquid fire spilled from my fingertips, more than just flesh meeting flesh; I had reached in and grabbed her soul, snatching her dying frame from the clutch of death. "I tell you, she is moving."

Hagabus marched forward, passing Bandi as he raced his way to our gathering and entered the tent.

Bandi clapped his hands to gain attention. "The Nazarene is crazy. Don't get your hopes up. I was there and I saw. It seems the princess just had some sort of cramp or spasm."

"I do not know why he is lying."

"I don't want you to hurt her mother."

"Why are you saying this, Jesus?" whimpered Praella, as she burst into tears. "I was in there just moments before your arrival. She had the stillness of the dead."

"I felt that, too. Then we touched. Power surged through me and into her body,"

"You touched her?"

"He did," accused Bandi.

Tabuli spoke up, "What is wrong with the lad touching the princess?"

"You know our customs," challenged Bandi.

"The soul cannot leave the body to travel to Keolani as long as one human hand holds it back," Praella inserted, nervously.

"That is merely a legend," objected Tabuli. "Anyway, she is not dying. She lives. Did you hear the boy?"

"I tell you, it was just some sort of spirit seizing her body," Bandi countered.

About that time, Hagabus exited the tent and began to amble across the sand. I ran to meet him, followed by the entire assembly. "Did you see her?"

"That was quite a dance you displayed," he said, frowning.

"Did you like it?"

"I don't quite see place for that in the life of a righteous Jewish man."

"David danced."

"Before the Lord, not the heathen. And you aren't King David."

By this time the entire clan of the bewildered had arrived and anxiously stood awaiting the priestly report.

"Well," he said, uncomfortable with the scrutiny, "I saw her."

"Report to us," demanded Bandi. "This isn't one of your sermons at synagogue. Tell us."

Hagabus grimaced at the insolent young man and continued on at his own pace. "I saw her. Now, Jesus, was she sitting up?"

Pandemonium. A maddened dash was made for the entrance of the tent--jostling and shoving to jam our way through the limited access of the narrow opening, we huddled into the now over-crowded bed chamber. The lady in the veil (whom I later found out was the personal maid for Anisa) fainted. Praella fell by her daughter's bed and Tabuli Manta chanted a prayer. Bandi and his two fellow combatants exchanged glances and finally opted to glower at me in an intense unison.

I heard Papa calling my name. He had just arrived and was outside the tent. Hagabus, having been the last to enter the tent, scratched his head. The two ladies in mourning swallowed their grief in huge gulps of disbelief. I stood back in timid, but ecstatic, adoration. This was definitely better than building walls.

"Silence, everyone," bellowed Praella.

We were all staring at the Princess, who was trying to focus on her surroundings. Beads of sweat had burst on her forehead and cheeks, and her face was flushed.

"Thirs . . . ty," she rasped weakly from what sounded like a very sore and dry throat. The request was greeted with cheers from all except the trinity of warriors, who continued to leer in my direction.

"Bring some wine," commanded Praella.

"Might I suggest water, my lady?" encouraged Tabuli Manta.

"Water, yes, water, mother," said Anisa, clearing her throat.

One of the mourners brought some water and Anisa sipped while her eyes scanned the room. "Where is he?"

Meanwhile, Joseph entered the tent along with the fleet-footed runner. The messenger saw Anisa and clapped his hands. "Herbs," he said gleefully.

Joseph glanced over at me, eyes betraying his curiosity. I could tell he wanted to ask what was happening but decided not to interrupt the flow.

"Where is he?" Anisa asked again, trying to stand to her feet.

Praella tenderly restrained her. "Not too fast, my sweet."

"Who is that young man? Is he the one?" she queried, from her seat of comfort on a particularly plump pillow. She was pointing at me, so   everyone turned to observe. Papa, too. I just smiled. Bandi sneered and sighed. I was keeping my attention riveted on him, because he was intent on being my adversary. (It is always good to keep an eye on your enemy while you learn to find a way to love him.)

"He is just a boy. He is a son of a peasant carpenter. I will escort him from the grounds, your highness," Bandi said, marching toward my   position. Joseph stepped forward and bumped into him, demonstrating ire over Bandi threatening his son, and being called a peasant.

"You will do no such thing," the princess retorted.

"But your highness. . . ."

"I am not highness yet. I am just a princess who would like to meet this peasant boy." Her voice and mannerisms were so compelling I didn't mind the terms peasant or boy. If she needed a peasant let me be destitute. If she wanted a boy let me shrivel away a few years. "Doesn't anyone else see my point? The Princess is ill." Bandi pleaded his case to the room.

"Bandi, is there no camel dung to shovel?" asked Anisa coldly.

Praella giggled and Tabuli Manta smiled, bowing his head.

Bandi stood, steaming and stewing in his anger. "The camels are well provided for," he said with a prideful lilt. "I shall leave and sharpen my sword. You never know when there might be an intruder to our camp that I need to slay." He threw me a defiant look and stomped out, followed by the other two, inseparable.

Anisa paused to allow the infantry to retreat and then spoke. "Come here." Joseph cleared his throat; Praella moved aside. I didn't look to anyone else for approval. I didn't care what Joseph or Praella thought. I had made contact with the princess of Treoli.

"Bring me your hands," she whispered.

I obeyed, deciding to bring everything else attached to them. I sat on the edge of her mats as she gently cupped her hands around mine and kissed each one of my fingers. I had apparently died and entered an afterlife filled with perpetual rapture. No Nazarene ever felt like this with heart still beating and mind intact.

"They are so warm." She stroked her cheek against a callused finger. "You have the gift, lovely one. There is healing in your hands." She lifted her head, revealing the soft, moist, darkened pools that were her tender eyes.

"Thank you," I managed.

I looked at Papa, who frowned, then at Hagabus, who was scratching a hole right through his head. None of them understood. Something had happened in the tent. Some unction had passed between this princess from a foreign land and Jesus, the mediocre carpenter from Nazareth. It was not just an infatuation--not the mere presence of a beautiful woman, and a young man's appreciation of that amazing glory. I had exchanged something with this lady on a personal spiritual level, which needed investigation to a fulfilling conclusion.

Praella moved forward, hovering, like a protective lioness, taking my hands from Anisa's grasp. "Come now, my daughter. It is time to rest. Jesus can return again."

Anisa regained her grip. "I will not release until I know when we shall meet again."

"Tomorrow?" posed Praella tentatively.

Joseph was shaking his head. Hagabus mirrored my Papa's reaction.

"I am without choice," I said.

"What do you mean?" Anisa examined.

"Perhaps the young man has other plans, or another to whom he is betrothed," Praella replied, formally.

"Is this true?" inquired Anisa, eyes widening.

"What is true is that I would be a mad man restrained in chains if I would miss the opportunity to spend time with the Princess of Treoli." I did not dare look at anyone but Anisa.

She beamed a rainbow of satisfaction. "Tomorrow it is, then. I have many questions."

I rose quickly and bounded from the shelter, not wishing to be thwarted from my decision.

Tabuli Manta followed me and caught me by the arm. "Don't listen to the heathen rage. Anisa is a spiritual child. There are those whose love for her is tarnished by their greed. She has sensed an anointing within you. I trust her judgment concerning people. If she is to be queen, discernment will be her only constant friend. You must return. You have done more than touch her body. Her soul has been stirred. She has been refired from the ashes by your passion. You must return tomorrow." He finished and turned to walk away. I had an ally in a camp crawling with critics.

Joseph joined us and lodged his expected objection. "My son is very busy with our family business. I cannot spare him."

The old man whirled around and squared off on Joseph. "If you do not allow this boy to be who he is destined to be, may God strike you dead."

His words were inflammatory, infuriating me. Papa had never hindered my progress; he was my encourager. It was an unfair judgment. I immediately came to his defense. "One with age should speak with greater wisdom or pray for death to silence his foolishness."

Manta eyed me, searching for boyish tantrum in my outburst. At length, a tiny smile jiggled across his lips. He reared back his head and laughed. "Jesus, you have the power of conviction. That will damn your adversaries to a fruitless debate. They better be careful with you. Your enemies will be condemned to ascend barren palms." He bowed and said to Joseph, "Until tomorrow."

The walk back to Nazareth was a quiet one. Little James tried to ask questions, only to be silenced by Joseph. Papa's feelings were hurt, obviously. He was choosing to ignore the situation instead of causing a scene, but tears were struggling for release, restrained only by the fortitude of a man who always chose to take the beating, denying the pain.

"I am sorry, Papa."

"What are you sorry about, son?"

"I am sorry I embarrassed you. Perhaps I overstepped my boundaries."

He interrupted me--not a good sign. "I don't know enough about what happened to be offended. Just forget it. Move on. There will be another day."

"Yes," said Hagabus, "that is wise counsel." He patted my father on the shoulder.

I pressed on. "I am sorry because I would do nothing to frustrate or hurt you, but I am going to see her tomorrow."

A cavernous absence of reply.

Finally Hagabus spoke. "I did not sense you were welcome, Jesus."

"Your mother and I will discuss it," stiffened Joseph, maintaining his composure for young James and the village rabbi.

"Please do discuss it, Papa, but understand. Something happened back there and everyone was in a great hurry for it to end. Maybe they want to cover it up or dismiss it. I have to know why the young Princess is still alive. I want to know who she is to my life, and if I can be something to hers. Papa, you of all people must understand the tug on the heart and aching dread of not knowing. You and Mama fought against all the barricades of acceptability to stay together, to keep us together. If I walk away from this, I will never know what it meant. Don't you understand? I decided two things when I was twelve years old in the temple in Jerusalem. I determined to come back to Nazareth and never give you or Mama reason to fret over my obedience again. I also swore I would not tolerate ignorance to live in me when truth was within my grasp. Don't make me choose between those two convictions. Papa, I need to know. I need to return!"

"You need," charged Joseph with heat, then stopped, just short of revealing the cusp of his anger. "You need. . . to be a man."

"I would agree."

"If I could evoke one trickle of emotion from you about carpentry, you would never want to put down the tools." He placed a firm hand on my shoulder. Hagabus and James looked on, careful not to disturb the sanctity of the moment.

"I have great emotion about carpentry. It is just best kept to myself."

He looked at me, pretending not to understand. "The girl is a princess, and not your kind."

"She is a Gentile dog," inserted Hagabus matter-of-factly.

I waited for Joseph to correct the bigotry. He seemed uncomfortable with Hagabus' phrasing, but chose, for some inexplicable reason, to remain silent.

"Bigotry is so unattractive from the mouth of a man who tries to respect all people." I spoke to the general ignorance of my surroundings. I was disappointed in Papa-- his mute profile to Hagabus' verbal atrocity was an insult to everything I had drawn from the carpenter.

"As I said," he continued, "I would like to talk to your mother on this matter in the privacy of our home."

"The two of you should speak."

"You do not need our approval; you are a man. But perhaps you would welcome our blessing."

I embraced the man, not willing to ruin my relationship with him over some princess at an oasis.

We walked on into the tranquility of the fading day. I felt a burning and itching in my hands--small, white welts appearing on my palms and fingers. I decided to show Hagabus, who would probably welcome the chance to give a diagnosis, and it might get all our minds off tomorrow's visit. "Father Hagabus, look!"

The priest drew near and examined the small white lesions. "Hmm," he said. "Looks like leprosy." Little James gasped, jumping back. Hagabus laughed. "No, no, it's not leprous, but it appears your skin was not pleased with something you touched."

Was he trying to discourage my interest in Anisa? She was the only person I had specifically touched. At least, I thought so.

"Perhaps God is telling you to avoid the heathen," said Papa tartly.

"Seriously, Jesus," Hagabus mellowed, "it is some sort of rash. You have taken in something most disagreeable to you." The priest smiled, cradling my shoulder. "I wouldn't worry about it--gone by morning."

"Could it be a poison?"

"I suppose."

"Then there could be something on the Princess' skin."

"From where?" demanded Joseph.

"Maybe it's monster spit," presented little James with his child-like obsession with the kingdom of the weird. Hagabus shook his head, bypassing the observation. "I cannot tell what it is for sure. It's probably just that you are allergic to work."

This brought a chuckle from Papa, still churning over our disagreement, putting him in better spirits for our arrival home.

Dinner minus conversation. I wondered how much Mary knew about the day's events, troubled about the intensity of my stand with Papa. Who knows, maybe he was right. Certainly not about Anisa being a heathen. Perhaps it was all just a fluke--the Princess, the healing, the heat in my hands. I was prepared to put the whole incident behind me.

Joseph spoke first. "Your mother and I have talked. You have our blessing."

I was dumbfounded. "Why? Where? When?"

Mary laughed and the younger children giggled. "Look at his face!" said Elizabeth, snickering.

"His eyes are going to jump out," little Jacob chuckled.

Joseph continued his explanation concerning the plans--a visit to express our family's best wishes for a speedy recovery.

The evening passed quickly. I retired to my mat to toss and turn, as a sky full of questions swept across my mind, forbidding permission to sleep. There was a burning in my soul, not so different from the stinging soreness festering my hands. Finally, slumber won its nagging desire.

Morning came, confirming Hagabus' prediction. The itching was gone. All that remained were a few tiny white sores in the middle of my palms. What had brought on the temporary irritation? It seemed so strange. Of course, in my life strange was becoming the common place. Yesterday I was a young carpenter, toiling in the heat, at a dead-end career. Today I was off to an oasis to visit a princess--definitely too much to assimilate at the second hour of the day. Jesus of Nazareth was granted audience with royalty, young and female. The bumbling carpenter would soon be with the most lovely lady this side of Damascus.

I fumbled through some household chores, trying to keep my mind from floating away to dreamy destinations, confirming I still had the blessing from Mama and Papa.

After all, it was another day and they were parents. The miracle was intact.

Mary had baked some cakes for the Princess which I was to present upon my arrival. I felt really stupid carrying the small basket, but thought it best not to raise too much of a stir about it.

"Go ahead and go a little early," Joseph advised. "Tools in your hands today would be a dangerous adventure." He smiled and I hugged him. Mary chased me out the door, waving her arms and pointing at the basket I had almost forgotten. A few more seconds and I would have been free of the humiliation. Mothers are always prepared to foil a child's greatest plan of escape. Joseph flashed a bigger smile my way. I think he understood. Sometimes fathers understand even when they can not agree.

Mary shuffled to my side, exhibiting a moody pout, demonstrating her displeasure over her firstborn being smitten by the charms of another woman. "Be careful, Jesus," she warned from brooding eyes. "She is a girl of the world. You are a village boy. Don't get your hopes up too much." She kissed me.

What a vote of confidence; the worst thing she could have said. I was already nervous, my morale having waned somewhere between the sleeping mat and the door. Further evaluation was fruitless. I really needed to have my hopes high. Expectation was never intended to hang low. Hope must be jettisoned to a soaring position by the soul yearning for greater promise.

I arrived at the oasis about the fifth hour of the day. The camp seemed deserted. Truthfully, I expected more activity--perhaps even a lingering jubilation from yesterday's events. Instead I entered what appeared to be a marketplace for the sale of used tents. "Is anyone here?"

One of the tents opened and out crept Tabuli Manta, offering a polite salutation.

"What's going on?" I asked. "I know no one died."

"Anisa is waiting for you. She has prepared some food and will meet you at a grassy area just over that rise. What is in there?" He pointed at the basket.

"My mother made me bring some cakes."

Tabuli smirked. "I think that is every boy's nightmare. I used to hurry to leave my house in the morning so my mother wouldn't give me some mortifying thing to wear or carry with me to the trainers."

I nodded agreement.

"Do you think Anisa might notice if I took one of those cakes?" he inquired coyly.

"I think Mary made enough to sustain the caravan for a week."

Tabuli took a cake and scooted away, pretty quick for an old man.

I made my way up the rise.

There she was. If possible, more beautiful today. Of course, I think most people improve in appearance when they aren't dying. She was sitting on the greenery, carefully placing eateries and dainties on the linen cloth.

"You are early," she said, without looking up from her duties.

"Is that good or bad?" I eased down on the cloth next to her, sitting as close as my throbbing heart would allow. Getting closer would take time and an oxcart of nerve.

"It's good you are here, if you have brought a stout appetite. What is in the basket?"

"My mother sent them," I said, reaching my arm out in full extension to hand the cakes to my hostess.

Anisa laughed at my awkward pose. "What's in there? The way you hold them away from your body it must be asps from Egypt."

"Cakes," I blushed.

She took them from my tentative grasp and decided, "We shall add them to our feast." Her hand brushed against mine and expectation squeezed me. Did she know I was terrified? Did she feel the same way? She appeared quite calm, even though I think she had arranged the dates into little piles about seven times.

"What is it like being a carpenter?" She inched closer.

"You would have to ask my Papa."

"You don't do the work?"

"Yes, I do the work, just that no one would call me a carpenter when I am finished."

"You are being modest," she said, poking me in the ribs.

"No, modest would be to say I never killed anyone with my tools. Honest is to admit I am really quite bad."

She laughed at my observation. It felt good to be laughed at by a beautiful woman. Well, at least in this situation. "That is exactly the way I feel about being a queen."

"But you have to be a queen. I don't have to be a carpenter." I paused, stunned by my own revelation. I had considered those words many times, but had never said them aloud. "I don't have to be a carpenter," I repeated with some emphasis.

"And I don't have to be a queen," she stated, defiantly.

"Yes, you do!"

"If you don't have to be a carpenter, I don't have to be a queen." Her lower lip protruded, permitting a brief glimpse of the little girl cavorting in the flesh of this woman.

"So if you don't want to be queen, what are you doing out here in the wilderness?" I asked, reaching for a piece of rich, dark brown bread.

"It is the laws of my land. A princess must journey the earth for three years before she can ascend to the throne."

"Why?"

"To learn of other people. To grow in her tolerance. To be challenged in the everyday inconveniences of the pilgrim."

"What then?"

"Good question. If I return . . . "

"What do you mean, if?"

"It's three years. Lots of things can happen. That is the true nature of the law. It is a belief that a princess who would be an evil queen will be struck dead by the fates during the journey. If you are able to survive such an undertaking, then the gods have willed you worthy of ruling and reigning." She chewed on a large fig as she explained her mission, her lashes curling so high they almost grazed her forehead; her eyes danced with the energy of a mischievous toddler at play.

"There is no evil in you."

"Are you so sure, peasant boy?" she teased, sitting up on her haunches with her hands on her hips. "I might have you beheaded just to see if there is a brain rattling within." She flipped her hand in the air, mimicking a royal tantrum.

"Then you could keep my head so I could gaze at you forever."

"I could use a man who will not blink in the face of adversity."

"You could use a man who can bake bread. This is terrible." I cast the remains of the piece to the side.

"Well, Lord Particular, I will try one of your mother's cakes to see how they fare." She grabbed one and stuffed the whole thing in her mouth. I burst out laughing, watching her maneuver the mound to make room for chewing. She giggled, and as she did, little pieces of cake spewed in all directions.

"Well, queen. How are they?"   She struggled to swallow so she could answer.

"Well? Answer me!" I commanded.

"Bery goot," she managed past the morsel. A big swallow. "But probably better consumed in smaller quantities."

We laughed again.   Then we talked.   On and on into the day we shared dreams, unearthed our fears, and opened up our hearts to each other unabandoned. Neither of us considered the passage of time.

"I have enemies," she said, changing the subject.

"Who?"

"Who is simple. Why, I even understand. What their next move is . . . that is what frightens me."

I reached up and touched her face, garnering courage from resources unknown to me, instinctively needing to connect with her--yearning to comfort the turmoil in her soul.

"I have something to tell you," I said as she softly kissed the back of my hand.

She sat quietly, giving me time to form my thoughts.

"Look at my hands."   They were red again and the welts had grown twice their early morning size.

"What is it?"

"Do you remember when I touched you?"

"No, not exactly. I do remember feeling a pulling inside, and this warmth tugging me back."

"Tell me more."

"Well, it was like I was catapulted to my bed from somewhere." She paused and crinkled her brow. "I could feel the texture of the mat. Then I was aware of the clothes clinging to my skin." Her face relaxed and she produced the sweetest grin.   "It was like awakening from a very deep, intoxicating sleep, but very fast in a slow kind of way."

"You felt all of this yesterday?"

"Yes. Awareness seemed to avoid me.   Finally I felt my hand touching yours, heat and chill all at the same moment."

"It was much the same for me--I don't mean the awakening part--but the chilling heat was like no other sensation."

"You called me back from death.   Your spirit forbade me to die." She touched my cheek. Every hair in my sparsely-grown beard vibrated in exhilaration. She was so close, I felt her breath warm my lips, the sweet aroma of an innocent girl mingled with the gentle, earthy mustiness of a woman aroused.

"There is a custom in my country," she said, maintaining her closeness.

I didn't care what the practice was. Short of consuming a whole yak raw, I was in for the adventure.

"In my land you express your love by caressing the place on your companion that has greatly moved you." Her words were beautiful but unclear. I gave a tiny squint. "There is no need to explain. Let me show you." She cupped my face in her hands. "Jesus," she stated. "You have touched my mind with yours. I caress that wonderful part of you." She leaned forward and tenderly placed her lips on my head. I fought to maintain consciousness.

She pulled down the top of my robe, exposing my chest. "Jesus, you have opened your heart to me. I caress that part of you." She leaned down and delicately brushed her lips against my chest.

"Anisa, I too have been blessed to enter your mind of great wisdom." I leaned forward and kissed her forehead. Problem. She had shared her heart with me, but honestly, somewhat inaccessible for my caress.

She sensed my dilemma, smiled, and said, "My heart beats here, too." She pointed to a lovely spot on her slender neck. I leaned over and kissed her.

While I was still puckered, she pulled away and stood to her feet, gathering up the supplies and cloth. I was practically flung to the side in her whirlwind of activity. She collected the belongings and ran down the hill towards the caravan. I was confused, overwhelmed, mostly concerned if I had foul breath.

She called back to me over her shoulder, "I will see you tomorrow." She wiggled her backside and then skipped away to the cavalcade below.

"Wait! I didn't tell you about my hands."

It was no use. She had blown away as quickly as a swirling desert storm. Thus ended my first encounter with the ravishing princess.

I came again the next day and the day following, each time brought greater depth to our feelings and more intimate warmth to our romance of conversation. On my third visit, I worked up the courage to ask her about Bandi. "Why do you need a guard?"

"Any specific guard troubling you?"

"I am not troubled. I am interested. In Bandi, for instance."

"Who told you he was my guard? He has been commissioned to travel on this holy journey to satisfy my every need as a blossoming young woman." She tossed her head, causing her dark curls to swirl in all directions. She waited for my male ego to bruise up, and then burst into a wonderful, clean laugh of splashing joy. "Look at you," she said. "An eagle could nest on your lower lip."

"My lip is fine, thank you," I said, trying to restore my masculine integrity.

"I was kidding."

"Of course. I just didn't want to come off callused. I know you needed to sense my disapproval." She laughed harder at my explanation than at her original ploy. "Truthfully, who is Bandi?"

She paused for a moment with eyes dancing, trying to decide whether to continue her game. She determined it best to honor the sincerity of my concern. "He is the son of General Rasuti. The general is my rival to the throne."

"You are being guarded by the son of your chief enemy?"

"Actually, it is the safest selection. They would not try to kill me on this journey; they would be the primary suspects. It is in their best interest to insure my safe return to Treoli."

"Could they still achieve their goals without casting suspicion on themselves?"

Anisa looked at me thoughtfully. She had apparently considered the same thing herself. "That is why I asked Tabuli Manta and my mother to join me."

I could see her logic. It hardly seemed plausible that an assassination plot could be hatched under the noses of these loving guardians. I questioned whether to bring up some of my suspicions to Anisa. For as badly as my hands had itched and burned on that first day, now they were worse. Each day when I returned from the caravan, my hands and forearms swelled with a crimson rash which sprouted fresh welts, stinging. At night, Mary bathed them in water with aloes and cooled them with a soothing salve formulated by Father Hagabus. Every morning I was a little better, so I would once again go to the oasis. At night, I would return in my inflamed condition to repeat the process.

It appeared to me Anisa was growing weaker each day. The original sparkle had been replaced by a false bravado. Something was wrong. An agonizing foreknowledge haunted my mind; I had nightmares of her death.

I needed to talk to her. She had helped me define my life. I had felt like a piece of discarded clay from the potter's wheel, cast to earth to dry up as useless shavings, having never found my value within the mold. With Anisa's help, I was discovering the meaning of the messages from my heart.

I felt a gnawing responsibility to share my apprehensions. If they were unfounded, then let them be ignored. But at least I needed to tell her. "Can you see my hands?" I held them up for her inspection.

"What about them?"

"It's not just my hands that are bothering me. You are growing weaker."

"Mother says I am trying too much, too fast. She tells me the baths will help."

"The baths?"

"Yes, because my skin is so sensitive, they have concocted a blending of herbs to strengthen my body to make me more tolerant to the desert heat."

"What is in the bath?"

"I don't know. My mother and my maid take care of it. Jesus, what are you getting at?"

"I don't want to scare you."

"You are scaring me."

"I am just worried."

"About what?"

"About your safety. Why am I so swollen?"

"You want to blame your stupid rash on me?"

"Not you."

"Then who? My mother? My maid?" She stopped and took a deep breath. "Listen, I love you, Jesus, but these people are my family. You can't expect me to suspect them of treachery."

"Just stop the baths for a day or two. If I am wrong I will never mention it again."

"It may be permissible to discontinue bathing in Nazareth but we Treolians hold great stock in its benefits," she said, trying to regain some humor.

"Then bathe. Just don't use the herbs."

"My skin will burn."

"Are you sure?"

"Are you sure you are sane? I will not sit here and be accused of inflicting you with some sort of dreaded disease." She leaped to her feet.

As she did, she grabbed her head, losing balance, and tumbled onto the sand.

"Anisa!"

"I'm alright," she said, groggily trying to regain her feet.

"No you aren't. See, you can barely stand."

"I can stand just fine," she said, rising, wobbling a little to the right but maintaining her balance.

"Please, just consider my words."

"I will consider . . . Jesus," she gasped as she collapsed into my arms. I lifted her and hurried down to the oasis.

Tabuli Manta met me and said, "What happened?"

"The princess has fainted."

Bandi ran up. "I knew this would happen," he blurted, trying to take her from my arms.

"Leave her alone." I tightened my grip and twirled around to avoid his advance.

Praella rushed up and felt Anisa's face and head. "Do the two of you intend to tear her apart?"

"She fainted in the desert," I explained, anxiously.

"Bandi, you are dismissed," Praella ordered.

"What about him?" Bandi stood his ground, pointing at me.

"Jesus, I will take care of my daughter," said Praella decisively.

"She is being poisoned."

"This is not your affair. You will leave or I will have Bandi escort you home." Bandi moved forward to perform the mission.

Tabuli Manta interjected, "No need for violence. Jesus has the best interest of the princess at heart," he said, attempting to cool the eager rage of the warrior.

I pushed past the trio and quickly carried Anisa into her tent and laid her on her mats. Praella followed. "Thank you for your help," she said dismissively, ministering to her little lady.

"I believe she is being poisoned. I need to let somebody else know."

"What? Who would do such a thing?"

"I think it is the baths."

"I mix the waters for her baths."

"How about the maid?"

"I told you I do it!" She stood and charged towards me.

"Maybe I am wrong." I said, striking a defensive stance.

"Jesus, I think it would be good for you to stay away for a couple of days."

"Why? I want to minister to her. You don't understand. We have become very close."

"Closer than her mother?"

"That is not what I mean. Please, let me touch her," I pleaded as I moved past Praella and fell by Anisa's bedside.

"Bandi!" Praella beckoned.

I didn't care anymore. I wasn't going to let some hot-headed infantryman keep me away from Anisa.

Tabuli Manta entered the tent, glanced at Praella, and came and knelt by my side. "Is this what Anisa would want, Jesus? You and her mother at odds?"

"They are killing her," I pleaded.

"But I am not. Trust me. I have listened, and am well aware of your charges." Tabuli was worthy of my trust.

"Where is Bandi?" raved Praella.

"He is tending the camels, an aspiration much more fitting than pummeling some love-sick boy."

"I want this peasant rabble out of here. He accused me of trying to murder my own daughter."

"I didn't say that . . ." I began to defend myself, but Tabuli lifted a hand to acquire my silence.

"Please give us a couple of days, Jesus, to nurse our princess to health. We are a people of resource. As we have trusted you with our national treasure, now you must give us the same honor in caring for our soon-to-be queen."

I paused, considered, agreed and left the tent, making the lonely walk into Nazareth; not where I wanted to be. My feet were heading home. My soul was with a fragile beauty in a black shrouded tent.

Two days passed. Sun up, sun down; repeated again. Food was offered. I politely refused several times, lost in thought, captivated with memories of delightful times with Anisa and terrorized by images of her cold body lying in repose.

On the morning of the third day I received a message. It was an update from Tabuli Manta. He sent the runner. The communique stated Anisa was still weak, but able to eat a little, say her evening prayers, and remain faithful to her bathing schedule. I was greatly relieved to hear of her improvement, but enraged when I read about those cursed baths. What were the herbs blended in those waters for her so-called safety? I just couldn't help believing there was something sinister in the whole arrangement; convinced Anisa's weakening condition was directly linked to those daily immersions. I could be wrong, but I didn't think so. I tried to dismiss my fomenting notions--fruitless.

I decided to talk to a neutral party, someone with more emotional leverage. I ran my list of options. Mary was out of the question. She would be looking out for my best, and end up advising the most secure option. I already knew Hagabus' feelings on the matter. He considered Anisa to be the heathen princess. Hagabus was religious. Religion and objectivity rarely mingle, let alone unite.

Of my primary choices, remaining was Papa. Normally he would have been my first choice, but he had made his feelings clear about my relationship with Anisa. Still, there was the essence of the man. I believed Papa would give me a fair hearing in the matter. So I asked to see him. We met after evening meal on the third night.

"Well, I know you are troubled," he said as we walked into the cooling evening.

"She is ill."

"Jesus, who is this young woman to you?"

"It wouldn't matter if she were a stranger. I believe her life is in jeopardy."

"But she isn't a stranger."

"Is there something you are trying to ask?"

"I would rather you would tell me what is in your heart."

"I have spent several days with the most intelligent woman alive."

"And what does she feel?"

"Did you know of a certainty what Mama felt?"

"I wondered, continually. I fretted when she walked down the street and smiled at a stranger, especially if he was taller and stronger than me." He paused to rest for a moment.

"I don't feel that way. I really want her to be happy."

"Can you make her happy?"

"I never thought about that, either. I can make her laugh."

"That is more valuable than a thousand kisses."

"Anisa doesn't need me to be happy. I think that is what I love about her."

"So you love her?"

"I love so much about her. I think I could love her and never regret my decision to do so."

"That is not the same thing."

"I like being part of what makes her happy. I like she doesn't need me, but instead wants me involved in her life."

"You have lost me, son."

"The girls in Nazareth need the companionship of a mate to make them feel whole. Anisa is already whole. She is complete without the addition of anyone."

"Even you?"

"Of course, even me. She is sufficient. Except, I feel she needs me to save her from this danger."

"I thought the message said she was improving?"

"Look at my hands, Papa."

"They are better."

"What if they are better because I am away from the evil?"

"Son, you have lost me again."

"What if I am healing because I am away from the thing that infected me? Don't you understand? She is there getting sicker."

He nodded his head. Was it agreement? I wasn't sure. He remained silent.

"What would you do if it was Mary?"

He looked at me, fully aware I expected nothing less than an honest answer. "I would go to hell to save your mother even if I didn't have a plan on how to get back." He peered at me, possibly regretting his wording, a truthful reply, but perhaps not the kind of fire you should build under a young man already half-crazed by his own jumbled passions.

I thanked him for his time, excused myself, and walked away. My heart was in control. Each step I took was one closer to the oasis. I had to see Anisa. I had to know.

Nearing the encampment, I saw a couple of torches burning and a small fire flickering in the midst, but no movement. I laid on the desert sand, creeping closer, probing for some sign of life. The hour wasn't late, but the camp appeared deserted. Anisa was the life of this traveling band of nomads. When she was not around they vegetated in varying degrees of boredom.

I crept to the rear of her tent, lifted the side and slithered into the enclosure. One candle. I could barely distinguish her frail, motionless form.

"Is someone there?" she whispered, feebly. Alive. Should I answer or escape into the night? "If you are waiting for me to get up and greet you, it could be awhile." She coughed.

I laughed, revealing my presence.

"Jesus?"

"How did you know?"

"Who else would try to sneak in to see me when I am at my worst?"

"Now, Jartanza, tell me what you were trying to convey," said Herod magnanimously, restoring the rebuked fellow to a position of prominence.

"If you will, my Lord," said Jartanza.

"I will," said Herod with a wave of his hand.

"He wills," giggled Herodias, clapping her hands.

Herod looked down at his subordinate mate. The two seemed strangely self-assured and confident of one another's choices, like an old couple who had just acquired an excellent price on a young, humpless camel.

Jartanza proceeded, ruefully. "It would seem to me that Joanna and this Chusa must be brought into your watchful custody, lest they escape and warn this Jesus you have discovered his true identity."

Herod sat and considered the words, pleased this small, wise man was fearfully offering counsel for the King's review. Herodias stood back, trembling, not wishing to tip the balance of power.

"I feel Chusa and his Joanna should be brought at once for questioning," Herod decreed.

"If this is your will, my Lord," said Jartanza, careful to subdue his gloat.

"He wills," said Herodias, as she scurried to leave the throne room. "Hurry, and enact the ingenious plan before fate robs us of the victory!"

"I must renew my objections," gambled Blastus.

"You always object to everything." Herodias stopped and interjected in disgust.

"That's why he is my trouble shooter," said Herod, smiling in a fatherly way at the astonished chamberlain.

"What about Jesus?" examined Jartanza, returning to his overbearing manner.

"I will have the religious leaders find him and tell him Herod wants to meet with him. What Galilean would pass up an opportunity to have audience with Herod?" .

Blastus scratched his head. If Jesus was indeed John the Baptist back again, he would definitely have the sense to avoid Herod's concept of hospitality. If he was not John, then the man had greater power than all the lineage of this insipid monarch.

After all, this man won the love of Joanna.

****

A night when the evening fire was greatly needed to take the damp chill away from the flesh and bones of weary vagabonds. All travelers had fallen into an exhausted sleep like dead men struck down in the full fury of motion. I,

Blastus stared at the mutually depraved and menacing trio. By title and authority, they were deemed the reasonable of their fellows. Today they seemed more like ghastly, macabre children, bewitched by a ghostly nightmare. Jartanza elaborated as the superstitious superiors relished each fiendish detail like sucklings drawn to promising paps.

Blastus was silent--the hapless victim overtaken by the maddened assailant.

"Then John lives on in the person of this Jesus," Herod posed as if just discovering the essence of the truth.

"They have the entrails," Jartanza stated simply.

"Then this John the Second must be found," sneered Herodias, fist in the air.

"And then what?" challenged Blastus, carefully.

"We question him. We determine his motives. We take it all under advisement. Finally, we do what is best for the nation," replied Herod, fingering his huge gold ring, straightening his crown, and imitating attributes of leadership.

"We detain him," said Jartanza briefly.

"You mean you kill him," Blastus stated, directly..

"What cannot be detained cannot be destroyed," replied Herodias.

"First we must attend to this Joanna," said Jartanza.

"What do you mean, 'we'?" Herod objected.

"Yes, what are you going to do with Joanna?" demanded Blastus.

"Not just her but also that husband," continued Jartanza.

"Chusa, the court counter," chimed in Herodias with a sinister laugh.

"Do we detain them also, my Queen?" Blastus was no longer frightened to show his displeasure.

"We shall do nothing unless I, Herod Antipas, will it," snapped the plump puppet from his throne.

"Of an eternal certainty, my King." Jartanza produced a bow and a shiver; subservience to placate the man.

"It was not certain or the King would have not rebuffed with his royal displeasure," inserted Herodias in rehearsed, respectful tones.

Herod smiled, having regained the groveling of his queen. Jartanza stepped back assuming the role of the vanquished foe. Blastus observed the posturing, stilled his tongue, lest he become the fourth soul 'detained'.

"No!" protested Anisa as she attempted to wiggle free, held down to the bed by the maid.

"He had his hands all over her," said Bandi, forcing his sandal against my throat.

"Anisa denies it," Tabuli replied, calmly.

"Anisa is afraid of the peasant," growled Bandi.

"He looks fairly harmless now." Tabuli looked down at my blood-soaked robe and broken face.

"The snake is not harmless until the head is severed," said Bandi, putting the cold, sharp blade under my chin.

"You will not touch him until we can hold council on the matter."

"When?" squealed the enraged swordsman. The blade sliced my chin and a fresh stream of blood trickled down my neck.

"If you harm him I will have your father executed for your treachery. Don't forget, in our land the father can be punished, side by side, for the crimes of the son."

"What crime? There is only honor in killing a rapist."

"If he is, as you say, a rapist, I personally will sever his parts and deliver him to the colony of the eunuches." Tabuli stepped forward, holding his hand out to retrieve the sword. Bandi looked at me and then at the aged disciplinarian; much like breaking up a spat between boyhood rivals, only deadly.

He gave the old man the sword. "I will feed you piece by piece to the vultures." He spit on me and charged out, followed closely and speedily by the maid.

Tabuli looked down at me and shook his head. "Were we to expect a visit?"

Tabuli's face blurred and I passed out--the last thing I remember until I awoke the next morning in his tent. My body felt like one gigantic boil yearning to be mercifully lanced. I was surprised to see Rabbi Hagabus on one side and Papa on the other. Perhaps totally humiliated would be better presented.

"Well, it seems he will live," said Hagabus, a little disappointed.

"How are you? You had us all frantic," said Papa, distressfully compassionate.

"How do I look?"

"You don't want to know," Hagabus jabbed, tersely.

"We don't believe anything is broken," said Tabuli Manta, coming into my field of vision.

"That's too bad. It might better explain why I feel like I'm lying in pieces."

"Bandi is clamoring for the council," Tabuli stated, peering over Joseph's shoulder.

"Council?" I inquired.

"Last night," explained Papa, "Tabuli was able to rescue you from Bandi's grasp. To do so, he had to promise a hearing on the charges."

"And the charges are?"

"Rape," answered Hagabus. "Jesus, I thought you were different than the other boys. I believed you had a head for knowledge and a soul for spiritual things."

"I do, Father Hagabus." His accusing words stung nearly as much as my nose.

"You can't possibly believe the charges, Hagabus?" Papa protested.

"Well . . ."

Tabuli Manta interrupted him. "Of course we don't believe them. But it doesn't eliminate the seriousness of the accusation. The difficulty is, Jesus' main witness in his defense is Anisa. As of this morning, she has lapsed into a deep sleep."

"What?" I tried to gain my feet, and fell helplessly on the sand.

"Easy, Jesus," said Papa, picking me up and placing me on the mats.

"Does anyone else in the camp know Anisa is not awake?"

"No, just me," replied Tabuli. "I found her unresponsive when I arrived to join her in morning prayers."

"I need to talk to Papa and Tabuli," I directed to Hagabus.

"Why am I being left out?" queried the priest, displaying bruised feelings.

"Maybe he is affording you time to become confident of his innocence," said Tabuli, a glint in his eye.

"I didn't say he was guilty. I was just disappointed in him."

"I don't believe I like your attitude," said Joseph, with some fire.

I had never seen the two men argue, and I wasn't about to be the cause of it now. "No," I inserted. "It is nothing personal. I have a plan and the fewer people involved, the greater chance for its success."

"Maybe you could restrain Bandi for awhile," Tabuli suggested.

"Does he know much law and prophets?" Hagabus twinkled.

"I would say you are in a virgin arena there."

"I will tell him a story. David and Goliath. Yes, that will do. The children say when I tell that one you can hear the rock hit the giant's head." He waddled out of the tent, engrossed in his part of the plan.

"I guess he will get over not being included," chuckled Papa.

"I still contend Anisa's illness is caused by those baths," I explained as soon as I was sure Hagabus was off and away.

"Well, there is no more danger there," reported Tabuli. "She was due for one this morning, but considering. . ."

"When?"

"In just a few moments. But considering her condition. . ."

"Don't tell anyone her condition."

"Jesus, they will know just as soon as she fails to arrive for her bath," said Joseph.

"Not if she doesn't fail to show."

"I am confused," said Tabuli. "I can not permit the princess to be disturbed."

"I will be the Princess."

"Perhaps it was a blow to the head?" Joseph questioned as he gazed into my eyes.

"No, I will dress like the princess and go to the baths. If what I suspect is right, the waters will irritate my skin and we will have uncovered the plot."

"The plot?" queried Tabuli.

"Well, that part is a little involved."

"How do you plan to get to the waters without being recognized?" Joseph examined.

"Anisa has that large black robe. . ."

"Yes, she wears it for prayers and bathings," Tabuli confirmed.

"It has a hood?"

"Indeed."

"Here is the plan. I will put on the prayer robe and pull the hood tightly around my face. Tabuli will accompany me to the waters and stand guard while I see how the bathing affects me."

"What am I supposed to do?" asked Joseph in a husky whisper, trying to appear the great conspirator.

"Talk to Jesus," I said simply.

"But you are going to be in the waters."

"No, that is Anisa. You stay here and pretend you are carrying on a conversation with me. If anyone comes to the tent to listen, they will think I am still in here."

"I can't do that," said Joseph, timidly.

"Sure you can," encouraged Tabuli, putting his arm around the tentative plotter.

"Jesus, you can't even stand up," reasoned Joseph.

"I can for Anisa." Determined, I eased to my feet, every part of my body joining into a harmony of ache.

Tabuli brought the robe.

I put it on and drew the hood around my face. "How do I look?"

"Ridiculous," dead-panned Joseph.

"Will I pass?"

"Not very well," said Tabuli. "But the baths are not far. If we hurry, and the gods are kind enough to blind everyone, it might work."

"That's the spirit," I whispered.

"Are we ready?" Tabuli gulped.

"Yes. Papa, start talking."

"Now?"

"Yes."

"About what?"

"Tell the pillow how mad you are at me for coming here."

"Can I strike it?" he asked with a small grin.

"Whatever works. Let's go. I think Hagabus is running out of story," Tabuli said, looking out the tent flap.

"Start, Papa."

"Alright. Only for you, Jesus," he said, clearing his throat. "Now Jesus, your mother and I are very disappointed . . ."

"Louder," I insisted.

". . . in you. You should know better. Now you have gotten yourself all tied up in difficulty with these people from another land . . ." His volume increased as each phrase poured from his aggravated heart.

Tabuli and I stepped out of the tent and commenced our trek to the bath.

"Princess Anisa?" A female voice from our side—the maid.

"We are on our way to the baths. We have finished morning prayers and now must scurry along to the waters," Tabuli chattered, a bit too talkative.

"Let me help," offered the maid.

"Not today. The princess wants to rehearse her oaths and principles she will need to know for her coronation."

The maid said something in her native tongue.

Tabuli responded, trying to translate for me as he went. "No," he mouthed. "I will not attend to her in the waters. I will be outside the hanging cloth giving her instruction."

The maid said more foreign words.

"I am speaking Aramaic, because the council about the young Jewish boy will have to be conducted in their language. Even I need the practice."

I peeked through a small opening in the hood and saw the crinkled, bewildered face of the attendant.

"I need help with it too," she said in a passable translation of my language. "It is a talk for goats," she included as we walked away.

I opened the hood and saw we were only a few feet away. The plan was going to work. I only hoped it would be in time to save Anisa.

"Halt!" Bandi. I had grown accustomed to his grunt. We tried to continue but he ran and caught up, standing in front of us, refusing passage. "What is going on?"

"Bath time," said Tabuli cheerily.

"I thought the princess was sleeping," Bandi disputed.

"She was, but now she is awake."

"I checked on her just a few moments before I was accosted by this inane priest," said Bandi, motioning to Hagabus, who had just made his arrival.

"He walked away during the decapitation of Goliath. No one has ever done that," fretted the out-of-breath priest.

Bandi squinted, looking inside the hood. "The princess seems taller."

"She is a growing woman," replied Tabuli lightly.

"In one night? She is as tall as my nose. She didn't even reach my shoulder."

"I saw, too," squawked the maid, joining our discussion.

"It is reported the Great King Rahdandi, as a boy of fifteen years, grew a cubit overnight," Tabuli.proffered.

"Come now," scoffed Bandi.

"And that his horse," continued Tabuli, gaining momentum, "grew a second head in the same evening."

"Yes." Bandi waxed noble. "I have heard the legend of the famous four-nostriled steed of King Rahdandi."

"Then you see, spurts of growth run in the family," Tabuli concluded.

"Where is Jesus?" interjected the unconvinced warrior.

"Being rebuked by his father," said Tabuli.

Fortunately for our cause, Joseph had caught fire with his part; his angry, threatening voice rattling the entire campsite. "You have disgraced our family and made a mockery of the seed of David!"

"Perhaps he will kill the boy so we don't have to go through the formalities of a boring hearing," mused Bandi.

"Perhaps," agreed Tabuli.

My skin itched like it was set ablaze--the hood suffocating me. I couldn't breathe and my flesh was pulsating in pain. I couldn't stand it any longer. I threw the robe off and scratched myself in every direction. "The poison is in the robe!" I shrieked, bobbing around in my loincloth.

Bandi stared at me and said, "Princess?"

Before he could recover from his surprise I pushed him the remaining few feet; he tripped, knocking down the curtain, and fell in the bath waters, letting out a wail, just like a wounded animal imprisoned in the hunter's trap. "Get me out of here! It's poison!" he squalled.

I hadn't even thought of that possibility. They had put the poison in the robe *and* the water. Poor Anisa. They were going to make sure she absorbed the potion of death.

The two other soldiers, Yea and Amen, arrived, and Tabuli ordered Bandi arrested. I don't know if the other infantrymen were involved, but they were more than happy to distance themselves from the waterlogged conspirator.

"It wasn't just me," Bandi protested. "Her, too." He pointed at the maid.

She leaped at her accuser, beating him on his chest.

I slipped away to be with Anisa. All of this discovery was meaningless if the gorgeous lady was a casualty of the process.

I entered her tent, once again sensing the stale habitation of death.. I called her name and touched her forehead. She lay still, a graying of the flesh and a chill to her skin. My effort uncovered the deadly plot, yet its ugly conclusion was still being enacted in the waning life of the innocent maiden. I needed help. There was no sense in having an eternal relationship with the Father if I had no ability to ease the immediate need.

It was time to talk my heart to Him.

"I don't know what to do. I know what you have done. Something passed from me and touched this lady. I felt the presence of warmth and love. You placed your compassion and concern for her into my hands. You raised her up when all hope was gone. Can you do it again? I know you can. I believe this is what you desire. It seems so senseless for her to die. Yet I do not possess the knowledge or insight to be sure. That is why I have always trusted you. You have given me time. You have let me share my life with this beautiful woman. If we are to be separated, let it be with both of us alive to cherish the memory of love. If you see fit, take from me that which will restore her to wholeness. I have shared feelings with her. I have given my life to you. Please, Father, touch her so she may rise from this bed to live a life of freedom and joy because she knows how much you care. I lay my hands on her. I do not demand you repeat yourself. I do not dictate to you what would be the wise choice. I shall touch her to be her healer. For Father, I can never be her tombsman."

I closed my eyes and placed my hands on her brow. Nothing--my heart sank, frustrated with the turn of events. Then faith rescued my sinking vessel. A new wave of belief crashed on the shore of my spirit. I just decided to believe the Father would be inhabiting whatever decision that occurred. My belief grew, faith matured, and I was willing to wait for any result conceived in the gentleness of God.

I didn't need to wait long.

"Jesus, is it time for my bath?" The sweet voice of the blessed miracle dame. I cried. It was all so phenomenal. The Father was greater than any plot, more expansive than any device of my imagination. Anisa was alive and I knew I could never love her as much as the One who overshadowed her mortal frame, giving her fresh being. The tragedy had played its final performance.

The days passed. She recovered beautifully. The revelation of the plot was devastating to her sensibility, not so much the discovery of the involvement of the maid and general's son, but when Bandi disclosed Praella was privy to the details, refusing to participate, but silent so she might gain a part of the throne when the caravan returned with Anisa's corpse.

It fell the young princess' lot to pronounce sentence on Bandi and the maid, ordering them chained together and sent out in the desert--three day's journey. They were given food and drink to last until they arrived at civilization, if greed did not overtake them.

Then there was the betrayal of a mother. Anisa pardoned Praella, deciding it was better to have the connection with an unwilling mother than the head of an executed conspirator; quite a lady. She would be a glorious queen.

"I thought, when I was so ill," she said tenderly, tears in her eyes, "God was killing me to spare my people from an evil ruler. You have taught me that He loves me."

"I know that to be so."

"I wanted you for my lover, but your God has made you to be my Savior and dearest friend."

"I know that, too." I bowed my head. She would finish her trip alone.

"Anisa," I pledged, "because I have met you I will treat every woman with the dignity and honor you have embodied in my sight." I kissed her hand, so much more I wanted. Part of me yearned to leap upon the nearest camel and join this princess to rule in that far-away land. I loved her for so many reasons. Chief among them was she never pushed for me to come with her. I am so glad she didn't. I do not know what path my heart would have chosen.

I let her go.

She let me stay.

The visit ended.

I watched as the caravan gradually dissolved into the horizon. I had never felt so alone, the beginning of my sense of alienation from people, once my own.

I never saw her again.

Months passed, trudging their tedious path into the years. I would visit the oasis, sometimes, just sitting and remembering a conversation. Other times, recalling a fragrance. I recovered from the pestering vacancy. Life provided a diversion, never a replacement, but always the promise of purpose. I treasured the vision of her face.

Four years. A caravan visited our little province. The travelers told us of the great deeds and wisdom of a young woman who sat on the throne of Treoli.

"I know that woman," I uttered slowly to myself.

The memory returned. It didn't hurt anymore; just clean.

She is the woman I loved enough to save and grant release.

She is Anisa, Queen of Treoli.

Brothers, Sisters, and Other Strange Things

Mary gave birth to eight children--six boys and two girls. We all had the same mother, but there any reasonable similarity ceased, as if each child had been plucked from other planets and placed by a cosmic joke into the same family. Siblings and peaceful habitation rarely co-exist, each child oblivious to any other living organism in the household. I know this sounds like the jealous musings of the firstborn, but believe me, I am trying to be as objective as possible.

Now for their names, in order of appearance: James, Simon, Ruth, Jacob and Elizabeth, each tarted with a personality quirk making daily interaction frustrating and futile.

James was quiet and sullen, always tinkering with something around the house, especially when his attention was needed elsewhere. He had decided to be the 'son that Papa could always be proud of'. He never showed much emotion, unless it was an occasional fit of pious laughter at my half-hearted attempts at carpentry. How wretched to be so inept at your trade you are relegated apprentice to your little brother.

Every time I did something wrong, James performed his *Ritual of Correction:* first, letting the tool slip out of his hand and fall to the ground, a look of exasperation as if suddenly affronted with the most astonishing atrocity ever viewed by mortal man, then a sigh--deep, long and exaggerated. Ambling to my side, he gingerly removed the project from my inefficient grasp and muttered his beratement. "No, Jesus, we can't do it that way." (He always used the editorial "we", referring to anyone with an intelligence level exceeding a tree root.) He'd explain, in the most vivid agonizing detail possible, the proper way to perform the task.

Joseph would happen along, and James glanced up from his laborious instruction and piped, "Well, hell-o, Papa. I just had to stop and explain something to Jesus."

I, on the other hand, mustered an anemic smile, trying desperately to hold back the flow of drool at the corners of my sappy-expressioned mouth. Humiliation surprisingly incomplete, next came the straw that flattened the camel's hump. James patted my shoulder and said, "Don't worry, big brother. You'll get it."

Joseph boomed, "Of course he will!   He's the carpenter's son, isn't he?"

The ensuing chuckles afforded me time to reflect on the most torturous execution for my brother.

Simon, on the other hand, was just the opposite. He scorned carpentry--carefree, loud and egotistical, loved to argue and always primed a fight with an hour of complaining.   He tried everyone's patience with comments like:

"Nazareth is a dump."
"My whole family is retarded."
"I must be adopted." or
"I'm really the son of a Roman senator."

His favorite barb was, "Why don't you get married? You're the oldest son. We're all waiting for you to go first."

What, and chance procreating another human pest like him?

Ruth was perfect.   Her physical features were flawless--eyes, hair, teeth.   She was the personification of the "darling daughter"--a girl. I am a great admirer of the female of the species, but Ruth was the kind of girl who insisted on being girlish.   Dirt was too dirty.   Boys were nasty. Sleeping mats were lumpy. Oh, Papa, don t hug me until you wash off all that stuff.   Mama defended Ruth s fetish for cleanliness.   Girls are different from boys. They need to be caressed by things fresh and dainty, so as to prepare them for the gentleness necessary to make them good mommies.   (Motherly logic pearls, ad nauseam.)

Jacob, also called Jude, was typical.   He didn t have any obvious handicaps or pending demonic infestations.   He seemed normal.   In our household of the massively bewildered, he was nearly invisible.   This sequestering prompted a loneliness and melancholy in his spirit. I always tried to include him, but as he got older, he reclused.

Elizabeth was my favorite.   We were sure God originally planned for her to be a boy but changed a couple parts at the last minute.   Elizabeth was reckless and abandoned, climbing every tree in Nazareth, always carving her initials on the side to stake her claim.   She couldn t stand Ruth, and Ruth treated Elizabeth like a mutant plant. The boys considered her to be part of the fraternity, until she began to beat us at some of our own games.   She loved carpentry as long as she could do it fast.   Elizabeth had no patience for work resembling toil.

I loved this family.   Honest insight need not be perceived as scathing criticism, especially amongst kin.

Being the eldest, I often felt a lack of acceptance; many demands for setting an example with little reward for being first out.

I was nearly twenty-two years old when the seventh child was born into the Nazarene brood. He was the child of Mary and Joseph s timely desire instead of the fruit of passion, or, in my case, a parental caretaking mission at the bequest of angelic whim. We were all loved and welcomed, but number seven was the answer to their heart's dream.. Prosperity had nestled into the carpenter s business, and it was a prudently remarkable time to have the child who could glean the benefits of years of family discovery per endless squabble.

Joseph often lamented, The trouble with being parents--just when you finally get the idea and are moved by the magnitude of the importance, you are replaced by raw recruits.

They wanted a boy. He was.

They wanted him perfect and plenty chubby. Request granted.

He was the cooing, kicking, screaming answer to a quietly uttered prayer. They blended their names to give him a special one.

They called him Jomar.

Jomar was just about the cutest baby there ever was. The whole family took him on as a project. Mary practically had to make appointments to see him. Ruth washed him, changed him, and smelled him up with her perfumes. Then Elizabeth would take him out and roll him around in the dirt until the fragrance was a memory. Even subdued Jude joined in the revelry grinning irresponsibly.

As soon as Jomar's little legs could carry him, he would toddle with the girls to our work-site to call the men to meals. Joseph dropped any task in progress, grabbed the little bundle, and threw him in the air. As he gently caught his prized offspring, he would roar with laughter as Jomar released a childish giggle.

Jomar was truly irresistible. He had a name for each of us:

Mary was Ma ,
Joseph was Pa .
I was Jeeee .

Elizabeth was tree . (I assume because she always took him to play in them).

For Ruth, he just sniffed.
James and Jacob were both Jah ,
And Simon was dubbed him .

Joseph, through tenacious effort and quality workmanship, built a loyal clientele in Nazareth. With his profits he purchased land and invested his money, and was always generous with the less fortunate, continuing to multiply his business daily. By the time Jomar was four, Joseph only accepted jobs near home, so close little Jomar was permitted to come fetch the menfolk for mealtimes.

One day we were building a wall at the synagogue. Papa had decided to donate our services to Hagabus. We dug a ditch to make the mortar for the blocks, an effective and well-proven method. You could fill the ditch with water and mix enough mortar for the whole job.

The day was hot and humid. Joseph had asked all the boys to help, both for Hagabus' sake, and to ensure the mortar would not set up before the wall was finished. We had worked hard all morning. It was early afternoon. We kept waiting for Jomar to arrive and relieve us of our arduous task by announcing the sweet possibility of food and celebration, for it was his fifth birthday and each of us knew the festivities would keep us busy long into the night.

Joseph surmised Mary was probably subjecting the lad to unending fittings of some new robe. More time passed. At length Joseph called me. Jesus, would you go and rescue Jomar from the clutches of the adoring women and tell them I m hungry and ready to celebrate?

I was home in a mere three leaps and four turns.

Where are the rest of them? Mary asked, surprised to see me alone.

They ll be along shortly, I replied, adding teasingly, Papa sent me to save Jomar from feminine domination.

Mary whirled around. Jomar? I sent him out to you fifteen minutes ago.

My mind raced, fearing the worse, then reconsidered. Jomar must have lost his way somewhere in town. Mary must have been thinking the same thing, because she said calmly, Let s go find him. She tied a scarf around her head and inquired thoughtfully, You didn t see him as you came?

No, but I wasn t really looking.

Of course not. Well, let s go look.

Do you want me to get Joseph?

No, no need to bother Papa. We ll find him."

We walked, inspecting the streets and alleys, maintaining a composed posture. One couple had seen the boy, and said he was heading toward the synagogue. We searched, growing concerned, not so much for his welfare--

Nazareth was a safe village--more worried about how frightened he must feel to be lost.

We rounded a corner and there, at the end of the street, was little Jomar. We ran joyfully, but when we got there, found it was Nathan, son of the winesman. We continued the search. Mary thought we had better inform the others.

Upon arriving, we calmly explained the circumstances to Joseph. He frowned his displeasure with Mary, but wasn t greatly concerned.

All the family scattered out for a community-wide search. We sought the aid of Hagabus and several neighbors. It soon became a village endeavor; each soul dropping life in progress to find the vanished lad.

Up and down the streets. No Jomar.

Finally Joseph concluded it would be better to call his name and let him find us. We went through the streets, summoning. I shouted until my voice was raw and raspy. Still we couldn't find him. Mary feared he had been kidnapped.

Why would anybody kidnap Jomar?" asked Joseph, aggravated.

Ransom, Mary answered shortly.

From a poor carpenter? Joseph hooted.

You re not so poor anymore.

I am not so rich that I can afford to pay ransoms. Everyone knows that.

The subject was closed, but you could tell Mama was not convinced. Kidnapping did seem like the only logical explanation for Jomar s disappearance.

The hour was growing late when Joseph decided to break work for the day. There was no sense in continuing; the mortar was beginning to harden and everyone was exhausted from the searching. The wall could wait. We could make more mortar.

I was cleaning off a broad-knife when I glanced into the trench. In the background I heard Joseph explaining to Mary that Jomar had probably fallen asleep somewhere. Peering, I noticed a lump--an impression in the top crust-- about two cubits long. Someone had dropped something. I also became aware of a presence behind me. Joseph. He, too, was looking into the trough.

Then, as if struck by a bolt of lightening, a horrible realization hit us both. No, whispered Joseph. No, no, no!

He jumped into the pit and I eased down beside him. The mortar was heavy and clung to our robes. Joseph was thrashing, panting. I waded clumsily through the sludge, scooping the top layer off with my hands.

Suddenly my foot grazed against a solid object. Papa, I wailed. Here. I pointed straight down.

Joseph jiggled through the gray slime and stuck his arm into the mortar. I couldn t breathe, my eyes affixed on him. By this time all the others had gathered around the pit. I looked up at Mama. She looked back at me questioningly, then comprehension flooded her being and she fell back.

Papa was praying and pleading oaths to the darkening sky. Father Abraham, Father Abraham, please stop this. Joseph stopped digging. My God, My God, no, he shrieked, straining to pull something out of the thickening mud. Help me.

I reached into the mess and gripped the carpenter s discovery. We both pulled, finally wrenching free a large lump from the mortar. We lifted it up onto the side and tried to climb out of the closing tomb of hardening clay. Hands reached down to help pull us out of the clinging slime. As we heaved, I heard a resounding crack. Joseph s face twisted, but he said nothing. The ditch was only four or five feet deep, but it took all our effort to get free.

Meanwhile a crowd of frantic people surrounded the motionless form. Flailing arms, screeching suggestions, and high-pitched weeping contributed to a meaningless montage of emotion.

Joseph crawled over, wiping away the mortar, praying fervently. Dear God, please, a sheep, a goat. My God, please!

Mary kneeled across from her husband, scooping away the sludge. Finally a bit of hair. It s an animal, breathed Mary.

Joseph grimly continued. I started at the other end of the mound. Family and friends stood still, silenced by the gloom in progress.

James leaned down and swiped at the drying mass. What are you doing? It s just a lamb. Tears streamed down his face.

I felt a texture beneath the thick coating--flesh. I uncovered something and sat back to see. Pink--a toe--a small pink toe.

Mary looked back at me, her eyes fastened on the small toe poking through the crusty gray casing. No. No, no! Each wailing denial gained volume and frustration.

Joseph shouted, I will not quit, not until I know! He redoubled his efforts. The whole family was weeping.

Mary crept to my side and reached out to touch the soft skin of the toe, her face wet. Joseph cleared away the mortar from the face of a young boy.
He was five years old with brown eyes.
There was a small smile on his lips.
It was Jomar.
Our little one was gone.
Frozen.   Chilled by a blustering crosswind of reality. The scene is forever etched in my mind like an icy, panoramic mural of human devastation, drenched in a veil of suffocating pain.

No one moved, as if the slightest twitch of a muscle would serve as confirmation and permission for the treachery before their eyes. Tearfully and gently, Joseph began a holy vigil of rubbing and stroking, pulling away the cracking clay that encased the body of his son.

Rocking in grief, Mary caressed the tiny toe as she stared into the beleaguered face of her life-long mate and companion.

An amassing of townspeople huddled on the edge of the scene, a retracted cloister, in deference to our dignity and grief; sobbing and blinking away tears, faces exuding compassion, but relief that the inevitability of death had passed over their house--a chilling reminder of mortality. In the shroud of silence my own vexation overwhelmed me with a thunderous rage--mercifully diluted, quelled, and finally quenched by the turpitude of helplessness.

Ruth broke the silence. Do something. Jomar lay still, the only one submissive to the twilight events.

Joseph cursed and wept, his tears softening tiny pieces of clay near the nose and eyes of his departed boy. Look, he whispered, catching Mary by the robe. He moved. I saw him breathe.
What do you mean?
I did, I saw him move. He s alive!
I looked at Jomar--no movement.
Joseph continued to insist Jomar was alive.
Finally Hagabus stepped in. My brother, you are seeing what you want to see. Your mind fills in his breath. He spoke tenderly as he embraced his wounded friend, his gentleness causing my eyes to erupt in tears. Finally, the unthinkable had been spoken and I was granted allowance to grieve. Other men moved to assist the priest as Joseph continued to object.

Mary slumped brokenly, her tears flowing freely with the liberality associated with one who had escaped the foolishness of denial. I could tell she had already accepted

Jomar s death, and her thoughts had turned to the tedium of the days and weeks to come.

Jacob and Elizabeth fled the scene to find solace in solitude. James, Simon, and Ruth looked to me for purpose and meaning. I stood up and gathered my brothers and sister into a circle of grief. For the first time in my life I understood the importance of being the oldest. They needed me, and my God, if they knew how. much I wanted to be of worth at that moment.

Hagabus and the other men tried to help Joseph to his feet, but he slumped back to the ground, releasing a gasp of pain. I remembered the sound in the pit and ran over quickly. Stop, he hurt his leg!

They stepped back and let me through to Papa. You heard it, he said through gritted teeth.

"Papa, it s broken. I placed my hands on his bent left leg. As I touched him I sensed the same connection I had with Anisa; a complete oneness with my father. Warmth passed between us--an assuring anointing of soothing, human compassion. Help him to his feet, I commanded.

They did as I said, and Papa stood and was able to walk back to our home, trailed by a resigned and resolute wife, bewildered children, and a staggering stream of mourners.

Hagabus and some of the neighbors took Jomar s body to prepare for burial.

Back at our house, the birthday preparations lay waiting, serving as a taunting reminder of the absent guest of honor. Mary busied herself setting aside food that would not be consumed. Then, picking up her sewing basket, she sat down on a small pile of mats to finish the hem of a birthday robe--a final gift from a loving family to its youngest member.

The next day we took Jomar, in his new robe, to the family tomb. He was so tiny; so helpless. Except for some swelling and redness of the skin, he looked like the little boy who had left his house short hours before, to summon loved ones to his birthday celebration. No one was certain what had happened on that trek. Perhaps in his haste he didn t see the pit. Hagabus thought he had stopped to examine the trench and fell into the mortar and couldn t resurface to cry for help. We would never know for sure.

The funeral was brief, and the youngest member of the Joseph of Nazareth family was forever sealed into a tomb, until the day of reckoning, which would reunite us all in joyous fellowship and merciful understanding.

****

The weeks passed in sluggish determination, attempting to create distance between the insane tragedy and any life we might discover beyond. The temple wall was finished and dedicated to Jomar--the last job Joseph personally supervised, James taking over. He offered the business to me first. I surprised myself with an audacious and resounding, No Papa. It s not for me. I had known for some time my constructions would not be with wood or stone. I had been afraid to verbalize it to myself, much less Mama or Papa. When I refused, Joseph just nodded--not approval--but Jomar s death had made everything clear. I believe Joseph always suspected my reluctance to inherit the business. Before the tragedy, he was hoping family pride might coerce me into the work force. Now those aspirations seemed empty, vain and futile.

Joseph embraced me and said, You are my son of mystery. I didn t understand your birth, why should I fret because your ways are so strange to me? My dear son, whatever it is you are looking for, find it. When you do, guard your treasure diligently, so your heart won t be broken. I continued to help at the shop as always. Joseph rarely came to a jobsite, complaining the heat would swell his leg.

As the months wore on, a limp festered the tall, proud walk of the carpenter. Flecks of gray peppered his thinning hair and splotchy beard.

I examined his leg one day. Papa, I said, your leg is perfectly straight. Does it hurt you?

He smiled and patted my arm. "It s only being sympathetic to what the bones have told it. And the bones respond to orders from my mind. And my thoughts have surrendered to the insistent demands of my heart.

And what does your heart say, Papa?

He studied his feet, then looked up with a glint of mist in his eyes. "It says, he said, lightly thumping his chest, that I am old and have kept Jomar lonely for too long.

I tried to argue, but he hobbled away. He visited Hagabus frequently, and spent a lot of time with Mama, never missing the opportunity to hold her hand and kiss her cheek. My Papa became the loving grandfather we never had. Harsh words in the household disappeared in deference to Papa s sweet melancholy.

Fourteen months after Jomar s death, Joseph called a family meeting. He stood up. "I am not a giver of speeches or a great orator. The homes and buildings I have constructed will turn to dust and blow away within the passing of time. You, my children, are all I have to tell the world I was glad to have been here and it was worth the time. Just remember, when you are old, tell people you had a Papa and he taught you to laugh. And because he failed, you learned to cry. Tell them he never cursed the God who blew breath in his mouth even when that same God thought it best to draw it back out. Tell them I went out as uncertain as I came, yet strangely satisfied over the whole damn thing anyway. He peered at our bewildered faces and laughed. Aah, good parenting, he boasted. Always keep your children confused so they re afraid not to obey you. Now, let s eat.

We ate and went to bed. I tossed and turned and finally gave up. I crawled out and went into Papa s room. He was sitting up on his mat. I kissed his head and he turned to look into my eyes. I will never forget it.

His face was bedecked with a smile, eyes dripping with tears. Son, you ll explain all this to me someday, won t you?

My throat thickened, but I forced a chuckle. Just as soon as I find out, Papa. I went back to my space and slept a glorious night. I was awakened by the faint sound of sobbing--Mary. Sometime during the night, in his sleep, Joseph had resigned his commission as husband, father, businessman, benefactor, and most recently, philosophical seeker.

He was gone.

The day after the Sabbath, we laid him in the tomb next to Jomar. At long last, the Nazarene who had talked to angels, lived in exile, been slashed by Zealots, and fathered seven children, was granted a reprieve to lie in peace at the side of his favorite son.

I had lost one of my FATHERS.

SITTING 21
From Humble Beginnings

Clinging to the familiar, while suspicious of imminent change, I embraced a lifestyle of convenience, anticipating a mission of permanence and purpose. I had accepted the role of carpenter's son because it afforded me time and space to gather my wits, but after nearly three decades of living, my ambitions remained ill-defined, my future uncertain. Cognizant the tools of another man's trade could never be my passion, each night lying on my bed, I resolved to claim my independence from a treadmill of futility and set out to discover my illusive destiny, so distant from this merchant village. Then morning dawned, and I found myself in a busy household trying to be the role model Joseph deemed proper. Tools were taken from the shelves, food prepared and eaten, hugs and kisses exchanged, and I was swept away into occupational oblivion. Each new job, with its grit and mortar, cemented my commitment to honor my father by embracing his trade. It was totally my fault. Joseph knew my disdain for the trade. There were times, early in my twenties, when he thought I would pursue other avenues. I, and I alone, kept the deception alive.

I vented my frustrations to Master Hagabus, who added his own religious confusion. "Jesus, you must realize God can find you in a carpenter's shop, as He found Moses tending the flocks in Midian. He can certainly contact you in Nazareth. If He has work for you He will find you, but until then, enjoy the friends and family here in town. You could do worse than to follow in the steps of an honorable man like Joseph of the tribe of Judah. We all love you. You are like our son, too. And see, does God not use you as you read for me in the temple? You could do worse."

I heard this speech enough times to have it deeply ingrained in my memory. In many ways he was right. Nazareth had embraced me as a son. The greetings from the townsmen were always warm, with smiles of approval, and nods of respect. Everyone was proud of me; by day I pursued my father's trade, and by night I assisted at the synagogue with Hagabus--a full life.

One evening I alluded to my dilemma. My brother James blurted, "What do you want? You have good work and your God. You have the best of both worlds. You don't work hard enough to get old and you're not in the temple enough to go crazy." James posed a good question. What did I want? Was it simply wanton or a soul-itching quest for place? When I was a child they always asked, "what do you want to be when you grow up?" Not "What do you want to *do* " but "what do you want to *be*?" Intriguing. Frankly, men will forget our deeds, but the person we are will be recorded for all time.

At Joseph's funeral, after all the accolades for his workmanship and efficiency had been bestowed, Hagabus summed up the life. "Before God and his brothers he was a good and just man." My eyes burned with tears--a dynamic epitaph, one I desired. Did I choose the honorable way or resign myself to the path, non-resistant?

The weeks following Joseph's death brought all of my questions crashing in on me with renewed fury. My excuse for mediocrity was gone; my scapegoat of loyalty, entombed. Shattered was the flimsy facade of interest in an undesired trade. Pleasing Joseph had been my only reason for constructing walls and stirring mortar. The other sons didn't need my awkward attempts at carpentry to make the shop work. Joseph had trained them so well the business continued to prosper. I had no reason to stay in Nazareth. Mary no longer needed my emotional support. Joseph's final contribution to the family was planting the seed of another child in her womb. Mary gave birth to one last potential carpenter, and named him Joseph.

I was loved, but basically useless to the flow of this Jewish family. Joseph had been my link. He was gone and I felt orphaned from the culture of the town.

In the midst of my turmoil and troublings, Mary tried to become mother to me. "Well, son, I know at times we have found it difficult to talk."

"No, not difficult..."

"A bit perilous. You always seemed more tuned to your father."

"Well, I worked with him. . ."

"So you did. That brings up my point. Please don't feel I'm interfering. God knows I despise a nosy woman."

"I don't feel you're interfering."

"Let me finish. Then you can better decide. Almost twenty-nine years you have been my son, perhaps half your life. I want it to be yours, not a shadow of your Papa's and mine. A man needs a family."

"I have a family."

"Of his own, borne out of his drive."

"And what if his drive is to delve into adventures other than those of making a lineage?"

"There is talk, my son."

"And listeners, too, I gather."

"There will always be those who listen when others talk. They consider it polite." A small smile revealed the few crinkles around her eyes, the only hint of age.

"Have you been listening, Mary?"

"Jesus, you are my son of destiny. Do you know what that means?"

"Sounds formidable."

"Every mother wishes to have one son to bury her, one son to care for her so she won't have to be buried too soon, and one son to stay at home with her to make sure she is buried right."

"A trifle bleak, don't you think, Mary?"

"I have had too many sons. All the positions are filled. It would be nice to have a son who would make a mother proud she had listened to an angel." Her eyes sparkled with a girlish quality which made me chuckle through my annoyance. Mama had often told me of the circumstances surrounding my conception and birth, but they seemed more like bedtime stories than reality.

"Mary, there are no angels here, just you and me, trying to determine the source of some devilish rumors."

"People expect a young man to marry. When he doesn't, they wait. Time passes--they look for reasons."

"And these self-appointed searchers, what reasons have they come up with?"

"I don't know. I am not privy to their thoughts."

"So I am mistaken to assume you share their concern?"

"I am always concerned about my children. . ."

"Some more than others."

"What is in your heart, Jesus? What prompts a young man to spend more time in the temple than at home?"

"So that's it. If I spent more time at home the tongues of the idle witches of Nazareth wouldn't wag?"

"Are you calling your mother a witch?"

"Only if she has a wagging tongue."

Mary paused, wisely using the lapse to damper the heat of a fiery retort. At length she spoke. "What do you intend to do with your life?"

Finally, a question I could legitimately avoid. I leaned forward and took her hand. "What's wrong, Mother, with desiring more than what you have; wanting your life to mean something?"

"It does mean something."

"To you, perhaps. To the Nazarenes, James and Jude and Ruth and the others, maybe. But for me, there has got to be more. I don't want to sit around and think about my value like some philosopher, while my life ebbs away. I don't want to live, work, marry, procreate and die all in the same place. I want my talent to become my motivation, not merely my frustration."

"And carpentry is such a bad destiny?"

"For another man, a dream of dreams. For me it is a way of achieving tranquility without ever finding real peace."

Mary looked at me a long time. Characteristically, she uttered the   status quo,   while pondering truths more universal.

The conversation was over.

When I left three days later, her good-bye kiss meshed the sadness of a mother with the pride of a parent seeing her child finally excel. It was a long time coming, but Jesus was no longer just of Nazareth.

SITTING 22
The Inn Crowd

Growing up, I was bombarded by warnings about the abnormalities and atrocities of nearby cultures, every adult Nazarene attempting to frighten his children into remaining at home by telling horror stories of life outside the gates of our allegedly blissful village.

There were two favorite targets. The first was a land called Samaria. Recollections of people who had purportedly traveled to Samaritan villages were told and retold, with new lurid details mounting with each airing. I, for instance, was informed the Samaritans never bathe, and of the gruesome particulars of their supposed ritual of sacrificing children. (It seemed they only killed the more handsome offspring. Naturally, everyone felt they were in grave danger.) I don't know where the enmity began between the Samaritan and the Jew; religious intolerance a big cause. Probably generations before, two rabbis had disagreed over a text, time swelling the wound of misunderstanding. The belief, in my day, was a Samaritan man's fondest wish was to have his way with a Jewish maiden. Most of us didn't believe all the wild tales from the town fathers, but no one ventured there, either.

The other place of scorn was a fishing village called Capernaum. The warnings of my youth:

"It is a wild sort of men that walk the streets."

"Too much inbreeding with Gentiles; they're all infidels or sluggards."

"It's a place where the sun will not shine its light on their wickedness--all day long they sit in the darkness and revel in wanton lust and drink." (Eloquent bigotry still reeks)

When I left Nazareth, I am quite sure Mary assumed I would head to Jerusalem. I kept my traveling plans a mystery. She probably felt secure knowing in the City of David I would learn to be "priestly." But I wasn't sure I wanted to be a priest. Does the fact a man loves God mean he has to tie himself to an alter where the only living he does is wedged between animal sacrifices and baking shewbread? I was in pursuit of my Father's wishes, but I desired an adventurous path.

So I went to. . . Capernaum, the friendlier of the two hells available. If I was going to learn of the Father, I had to cease being afraid of His creation. Nestled by the Sea of Galilee, this city was dependent on Gentile commerce for its livelihood. Capernaum had a literal wave of humanity crashing against its shores. There were living souls within, and I wanted to meet some of them.

Despite my statements, the false bravado did nothing to relieve the anxiety eating away at the pit of my stomach as I took my shaky stand. I was a confused mass of apprehension, obviously still a slave of the Nazareth myth. I wouldn't have been surprised to find some beastly beings burrowing beneath Capernaum's wretched terrain.

I arrived late and decided to find lodging for the night. I had two choices--there was a synagogue in the town with an aged priest. I could stay there and find food, shelter and conversation about the law of Moses. The other option would be the local inn. There would be food, shelter and the unknown. I chose the inn, to get my first dunking into Capernaum culture.

I found it easily. The door was heavy and emitted a screeching creak. The interior, dimly lit. I squinted to survey the lay of the room, a few small tables with chairs and mats lying around. I sniffed a mixture of sweat, bread and wine.

I didn't see anyone around, so I called, "Is anyone here?"

"Be a minute," came the reply from behind a narrow door.

"No hurry," I responded, when suddenly this large, tall man, with dark rings around his reddened eyes, was looming over me, wiping his hands on a towel the size of a young man's cloak. His thick, black hair had pure white clumps at the temples.

"What'll it be?" he asked. His manner was brusque, he spoke in a monotone, and it certainly seemed I had located the source of the odorous sweat.

"I need a room for the night," I answered, struggling to sound composed.

"No problem, we always have rooms. No one sleeps here unless they drink too much. What will it be for you?"

"What do you have?" I really wasn't interested in drinking but felt it might be a good way to start a conversation.

"I recommend two, four, and five. Three is too sour and one is better for cleaning a donkey."

I scrunched my face in bewilderment. "I don't understand."

"You know, a donkey. One of those animals with the long ears."

"Yes, I know what a donkey is. I was asking about the numbers two and four. What do you mean?"

"Oh, that. Just something the fishers came up with. You see, the damn Romans and Greeks ship this poison to us with all sorts of fancy names, like of their gods and all. Well, the men didn't feel right about asking for a Venus or Mount Olympus--made them feel silly. So they drank the stuff and found out how long it took them to get drunk and then named it that."

"I think I see."

"Yeah, like this three," he said, pulling a flask from below the counter. "It takes an average boat rocker about three hours to get drunk on this stuff."

"And getting drunk is the object?"

"Hell, what else," he said, peering at me as if viewing an oddity.

I made myself the outsider, so I countered with an order. "Tell you what. Give me some bread and a glass of number five to wash it down." I pulled out my bag of coins and looked up to meet his narrowed eyes.

"You staying long, Nazarene?"

I was sure I hadn't mentioned my city of origin. "What makes you think I'm a Nazarene?"

"Well," he said, glowering, "You haven't done a damn thing since you've been here but squint, sniff and demand. I knew you were some sort of Jewish Princess and Nazareth was the first burg that came to mind."

I was devastated. All my visions of universality were dashed in a brief conversation with an innkeeper. Before I could recover he continued, "You better get that little Jewish alter-boy attitude the hell out of here before the real men come in or they'll turn your little ass into bait for tomorrow's catch." He ambled his way out of the room.

He wasn't mean. He was right. My upbringing was not yet outgoing. Class was in session and I had failed the first test. It was pointless to apologize. I needed to either get over to the safety of the synagogue, or find a way to communicate with the men who would soon fill this room.

I chewed my bread thoughtfully. The wine, though sour, cooled my throat as I struggled to fight back cherub tears. I was a man but my prejudice had made me look small and insignificant. It was important to me to do well in the marketplace. I felt this was somehow a part of my mission. I wanted to minister to humanity with the reality of their Father, bungling my first attempts to live out that dream.

The door suddenly burst open and in walked five men--loud and bawdy but lumbering with fatigue. They headed toward the innkeeper, who greeted them with an enthusiasm notably absent in our encounter. I chose a profile in silence, listening.

The innkeeper embraced the biggest man and inquired, "Jona, how goes the catch?"

"I'm too old to be chasing little things in the water," the burly, heavily-bearded man said, cheerfully.

"And too damn ugly to catch anything on land," said one of the older men in the group, gray, resembling a large bear ready to pounce on the nearest hunk of meat. The group of men produced a chorus of laughter, hooting their agreement.

"Zebedee, even though you are a cagey old bastard, I'm going to buy you a drink," said Jona, eyes twinkling.

No one had even noticed I was there. I was glad. Soon all of the men were gathered around a table, eating and drinking and telling tales of the day's adventures on the sea. I continued nursing my wine, surmising the other three men with Zebedee and Jona were hired servants. Their clothes and carefully-timed laughter displayed a servile position, although any mastering Jona and Zebedee may have had was soon lost as the liquor had its effect.

An hour disappeared as one story after another was passed around the table. I listened quietly from my retreated, observing position. As the drink gained authority, the five slipped into individual stupors of behavior. Jona, louder and incoherent. One of the servants fell asleep and another stared into the candle. The third seemed to be imitating first Zebedee, then Jona, in an attempt to be in the flow. As the night pressed on, Zebedee became more and more melancholy.

The innkeeper watched from the counter, as if accustomed to each step of the process. He gave his first warning. "Boys, I think you have drunk me dry--time to slow up," he said, smiling sheepishly, placing an arm around the flamboyant Jona.

Jona pulled away as if overcome by the innkeeper's odor. "My good fellow, I am of the sea. I ain't gonna drown in this stuff. If the worst comes, I'll just swim." The unsteady fisher stood to his feet, making swimming motions. One of the servants poured wine over his head. They were all laughing except Zebedee, who was looking on in total disdain.

The innkeeper studied Zebedee.

Jona slapped his comrade's back. "Don't you like my fish?" he slurred.

"I see no humor in a servant showing disrespect to his master." Zebedee's voice was cold with no evidence of impairment. I had watched him drink enough to ignite three men, yet he seemed unaffected. Well, there was the unsettling sullenness.

The innkeeper, nervous, stepped in, attempting to pacify Zebedee. "The boy didn't mean nuthin'. He's as drunk as Herod's advisors."

This brought a smile to Zebedee's face.

Jona wasn't content to leave it alone. "Old man, you need to stay out of my business. If I want this son-of-a-bitch to pour wine on my head it's none of your affair."

Zebedee puffed his chest and extended his arms, displaying fists the size of a goat's head. "Jona, you have never had one cubit's sense of decency and order in your whole miserable life."

The two men stood like jackals, squaring off for the kill. The innkeeper tried to quiet the men, obviously accustomed to the routine.

"Decency," said Jona. "That word falls off your lips like dung from the mouth of a queen. At least I'm not whorin' through Galilee."

Zebedee exploded; no other word could describe the sight. He put his hands around Jona's throat and squeezed.

Jona continued to talk as if air was unnecessary for speech. "At least my sin is wine on my face instead of a bastard boy by a Gentile she-dog."

The aged bear tightened his grip, eyes burning with fury.

The innkeeper, wringing his hands, turned to me and said, "Don't worry. They do this every night--your room will be fine."

"What are they doing?"

"Getting sober. A good argument does it every time."

"I thought they came to get drunk?"

"Yeah, they come to get drunk but they know they have to be passably sober when they go home to their old ladies."

All a charade, a business decision made by rational men to maintain a sense of decorum with their families.

Meanwhile, talk had stopped and they stood glaring at each other.

At that moment the door opened and two more customers walked in, younger than Jona and Zebedee, and so ·heavily robed I could only guess where *they* ended and the cloth began.

"Good evening, brethren," spoke one of the men, the taller. "I see the old men are at it again." He shook his head, mockingly.

The innkeeper spoke to Jona. "Look," he said, gesturing, "Simon has come and brought a friend."

So the taller one was Simon, I noted, frantically trying to keep up with all the names.

Then the shorter newcomer pulled off his hood to reveal a head of amazing red hair, luxuriously thick and long, illuminating the room.

Zebedee was distracted, breaking the intensity of his transfixed stare. The unhooded customer glanced about the shabby surroundings with the visible shudder of disgust usually characteristic of royalty.

Jona turned to look at Simon. "Simon," he spat, "is a bastard."

With this, the quintet broke into relieved laughter.

Simon ran to embrace Jona in mock affection, saying, "And you are my father." This brought an even greater roar from the onlookers; I even smiled, though I was careful to maintain my anonymity. The red-head had already seated himself at another table with his back to the whole unfolding, gazing at the wall as if totally indifferent to the dealings of a provincial tavern.

Jona took a seat, too, as if to acknowledge his defeat to Simon's wit.

"Where are your boys tonight, Jona?" said Simon, shrewdly.

"Where they always are--drunk by the sea."

"They aren't worthy to drink with their father?"

"It's not good for sons to see their father drunk," Jona said. "My papa never let me see him drink."

"There wouldn't be any other reason, now, would there, Zebedee?" Simon probed.

Zebedee growled. "My sons sleep with the servants to watch the boats."

I was surprised by how intimidated the old fishermen seemed to be by Simon.

He continued, apparently trying to pick a fight. "They wouldn't be shirking their duty to God and their country, would they, Zebedee?"

Jona stood to his feet abruptly, knocking over a couple of mugs in the process. "Duty," he spewed scornfully.

Zebedee put a hand on Jona's arm. "Let it alone, man."

Jona shook off the hand. "Duty," he repeated. "To what? Your Zealot cause?"

The red-haired man lifted his head to look at Jona, then turned back to his drink.

"Zealots?" said Simon innocently. "Did I mention Zealots?"

"Oh, I forgot," said Jona bitterly. "You can't admit that in public lest some Roman come and cut out your tongue."

"There are some of us with knives who would choose to draw first blood," Simon said arrogantly.

"Oh, yes, brave Zealots who plunge their weapons into the wombs of our Jewish virgins, all for the cause of freedom," Zebedee said, joining the fray.

"Someday, old man, someone will have enough of your sourness and will release the poison from your heart." Simon pulled a sword from its hiding place beneath his robe.

"And if they do, it won't be some cowardly Zealot who hides by day, to rob and pillage at night in the name of country," retorted Zebedee hotly. "Tell me, Simon, do your warriors know the difference between innocent Jewish merchants and Roman dogs who oppress the poor? It seems to me that your swords cut the circumcised as frequently as the uncircumcised."

I glanced at Simon's companion to see if he would respond, but he remained silent. Simon seemed at a loss for words. He strode around the room, swinging his sword. I was afraid his eye would land on me, and it soon did.

He stopped, looked me up and down, and spoke. "You, my brother, are a patriot?"

"I believe in freedom for all people," I said evenly, choosing my words carefully. The fishermen all turned to look at me as if suddenly realizing a rat had crawled from a nearby hole.

"What do you think of this traitor's words?" Simon continued, pointing his sword at Zebedee's chest.

"I think," I said slowly, "we all fight tyranny in our own way."

"And what the hell does that mean?" He shifted his sword point at me.

It would be a mistake to back down. "It means some of us fight with violence because frustration rules our soul. But there are others who fight with honor because we are not quite so convinced the Almighty has orphaned us into the care of madmen."

The red-head turned and smiled. Simon lowered his sword in amazement. "Are you a priest or a politician? And keep in mind, I enjoy killing either one."

"I am neither--a searcher."

"No doubt searching for the courage to do what a man should do in these cursed times!" He took a step closer to me. "What's your name?" The sword was placed against my chest. I looked down and saw dried blood crusted on its blade.

"My name is Jesus."

"Jesus! What kind of stupid Galilean peasant would name her son 'salvation'?"

"One who knew what the people really needed."

A grunt of approval came from Jona. Simon dropped his blade and chuckled. "Jesus of Galilee, you are a fool, but even a fool gets thirsty. Innkeeper, what number is my friend drinking?"

"I don't remember," said the innkeeper, shrugging.

"Really, I'm not thirsty," I insisted, cautiously.

"A good Jew doesn't drink when he's thirsty. He drinks to have fellowship! Bring him some number six on me!" He sat down beside me at the table. "As a token of our friendship and an apology for poking a hole in your robe."

The innkeeper brought me the drink. I knew it was pointless to refuse. So I drank.

As I sipped the contents, Simon leaned forward and said, "When I put the blade to your heart, what went through your mind? Some men shiver, some squirm, some wet themselves, and some fill their loincloth with dung. Tell me, Jesus, did you stain your loincloth?"

I searched his eyes for some glimmer of light. "Actually, Simon, I was wondering."

"Wondering what?"

I stood up and looked down at him. "Wondering when you'd lose your nerve." I downed my drink and said, "If you will excuse me, I need some air."

As I walked out the door I heard the red-headed stranger applauding. Outside, I gulped the fresh air, heart pounding, skin crawling. My head was aching and I felt weak. The journey had apparently taken its toll on me. I walked a few more feet, trying to regain my strength, but my legs were leaden. Then I couldn't get a good breath. Beads of sweat burst on my brow. I couldn't remember ever having gotten ill so quickly. I was close to the city gates when my legs gave way. "Help me," I called weakly. "Someone help me." Two cloaked strangers appeared on my right. "Will you help me?" I muttered.

I heard voices and pried my eyes open long enough to see a thick clump of red hair fall across my face--the last thing I remembered.

The two strangers carried me off into the night, to my next classroom for the study of life.

The Camp of Deliverance

"Who are you? Let go of me!" The voice had a high-pitched, childish petulance.

My brain was struggling to overcome my drowsy resistance.

"I said let go of me!" The voice, louder, more insistent.

Was I dreaming?

Once again the words came. "I said for you to let go of me!"

No, this was not a dream. I was definitely being instructed to let go of someone.

"Wake up! Are you actually asleep? Can't you hear me?"

Again. I could hear but my body was totally unresponsive. I was being rocked back and forth, pushed. I focused on trying to open my eyes, managing to pry them apart for a brief moment, then an excruciating pain in my head forced them closed again.

"You're faking! No one can be that dead," squealed the voice. "I can hear you breathing."

I determined the voice was a man's, directly behind me, and annoying to the extreme due to its nagging, matronly whine. I tried to speak, but nothing came out but unintelligible babble--the pain across my eyes and temples making it difficult to think.

"What did you say?" he whimpered, responding to my moans.

My brain felt like wet, soggy sand which someone had cast against a stone. "I'm not holding you," I mumbled, resembling more of a gasp.

"Yes, you are!"

"I am not," I slurred.

"You are too!"

"Am not. . ."

I became aware of my hands, sore, constricted, and separated from the rest of my body. My arms were pulled behind me. One eye opened, then another--blinked--but couldn't see very well.

"If you don't let go I'll scream!"

I recoiled at the thought, my head pounding. "No, no, please don't scream. I think we must be tied together."

"Then untie us."

A logical request, which I attempted to accomplish, since I, too, wanted to be released. I tugged. Nothing. I pulled again--pain, and the bindings grew tighter.

"Stop it, that hurts!"

Apparently our commotion was drawing unfavorable attention, because a voice possessing the volume of a foursome of fellows bellowed, "Would someone shut that woman up?"

"I am not a woman!" retorted my comrade, using inflections which contradicted his point.

"Please be quiet," I cautioned. Flashes. I remembered the Inn. Capernaum. Fishermen. Before I could proceed any further someone was bending over me; long black hair fell into my field of vision, brushed against my face and tickled my nose. I sneezed.

"God bless you, Nazarene," she said softly.

My eyes were still adjusting, shapes coming in and out of focus, giving the appearance of trees ambling in the foreground.

She straightened up. "Exodusat, this Nazarene is trying to peep down my robe to view my womanly virtues."

"No, I'm not," I protested.

"What are you saying, Nazarene? That you're not trying to look? Or perhaps you're not man enough to enjoy the view?"

This voice came from behind me, not the strong earth-shaking voice which had echoed before, but definitely male. His words were designed to trick me, so I tried to reply quickly. "I'm saying whatever is there I can't see because everything looks like a walking tree."

"What are you, some kind of poet?" replied the softer-speaking male.

The rhyme was unintentional, but it was too much effort to explain. "Some kind, I guess."

"Do another one." The request came from the booming voice which had insulted my co-prisoner.

My mind went blank; no way my aching head was going to be able to duplicate the verse.

The delay angered the speaker. "Poem from you or I'll kill you."

I seized on the blatant ruse of flattery. "See, you did one yourself."

"I did?" he remarked, delighted.

"He's looking again, Exodusat!" the woman teased.

"I'm not! I can't! Perhaps I would under different circumstances, but then again, no," I clarified--a roar of laughter.

"Would someone please let me go?" My partner in captivity spoke up again.

"Shut up," exploded the bellower.

I closed my eyes and tried to recall how I got there. I had been sitting at the Inn. The fishermen came in . . .

"Can you see better now?" The loud-mouthed poet was bending over me.

I could see a little clearer, and my sense of smell was perfect, detecting the fumes of cheap wine and rotted meat on the breath of the immense intruder. Hiding my discomfort, I replied, "Much better, I think."

"Don't look down Sariola's robe again." He grabbed me by my robe and pulled me closer to the open garbage-dump of his mouth.

"Really, I didn't."

"Leave him alone, Beskel. What red-blooded man wouldn't want to eye the milk and honey of Sariola's promising rolling hills?" The second man walked into my limited range of vision, smaller than Beskel, but of course, Beskel was a giant whose gargantuan head and mountainous shoulders courteously blocked the beams of the sun. The other man, by contrast, seemed slight, almost fragile; one more suited to the priesthood than caretaker to foul-breathed mammoths. "I am Exodusat," he said.

"Would you let me go?" my companion asked wearily, his voice cracking.

"No," replied Exodusat flatly, and continued. "Now, on to questions that must be on your mind." He was looking at me.

Yes, questions, so many they were spilling out of my head. "Where am I?"

"This is my camp. I am Exodusat, the Liberator of the chosen people from the domination of Rome."

The statement sounded rehearsed, but actually lacked any egotistical flair; pronounced as a foregone conclusion.

"Exodusat?" I asked cautiously.

"It is an unusually wonderful name," said Beskel, sounding out each syllable as if he, too, had attended rehearsals.

Exodusat stepped in to cover the awkward moment. "Moses led the chosen people from the Pharaoh's bondage. My exodus for His people will be from the Roman devil. The word 'Exodus' means the departure, and I added the 'sat' to place it in the Latin tense of 'you', referring to the Romans. In other words, 'You must let my people go'."

Trifling, but nonetheless passionate, and judging from the discomfort in my head, and blood trickling down my hands--dangerous.

"We have purchased you . . ." he continued.

"Wait!"

" . . .to fight for the cause. Our friend Simon and the brother from Kerioth have brought you here along with him," he concluded, motioning to my fellow-captive, who, by this time, had been reduced to intermittent whimpers.

"You are Zealots," I said, half-questioning. I flashed back to my last encounter with Zealots, with Joseph in the desert as the thieves gashed his face.

"No," corrected Exodusat. "It is more the Zealots are a part of us. They are the fist of God. We also possess His heart."

I heard a murmur of approval from the background. "Then use your heart and free us."

"You have been chosen like Moses of old. This deliverance will take many saviors to achieve. Many rods must strike a blow for freedom. Many climbs to scale the mountains to stand before God, then we will cross the wilderness of Roman oppression into the promised land."

More approval, everything manipulated to eliminate the possibility of disagreement.

"But I am not Moses, nor am I a zealot," I protested vehemently. "I am not going to be bought or sold. You cannot implant your mission on my life. I won't share your cause. I am a carpenter's son looking for my own station, my own reason. I will not share your vision."

"Then you will die the pagan Nazarene we found in a tavern."

I was yanked to my feet, my legs pulsating with pain, and felt a cold sword against my neck. I prepared for the worst, one swift blow from a premature and rather inglorious end. But instead, the sword was lowered and the cords to my partner were severed. As soon as we were freed, he ran off in terror.

"Get him," said Exodusat quietly. Two men leaped like wild beasts in search of prey to chase down the hapless escapee. I was standing, staring into the eyes of the philosophic renegade.

"A man should not die bound," he said. His voice was hollow, as if he had donned a cloak of treachery to produce his desired effect.

"I don't intend to die," I said flatly. Again, I looked directly into his eyes. I don't know what I hoped for or why I wasn't afraid; perhaps angels granted me courage.

"Then I won't kill you." What was this; all just a game to this small man? "But you will learn to fight, Nazarene. And you will learn to channel your hate through your sword as it thrusts into the heart of a Roman pig."

"The fact you are wasting your time causes me to pity you. The fact you waste mine only makes me more determined to see you fail."

Sudden courage. I have often found in the hour of need, the strength rallies; a mighty infilling of energy--a treasure discovered only moments before destitution robs the soul of all hope.

He walked around me once, twice. I fully expected him to have me run through with a sword. But he merely said, "We shall see. It is of no concern now. There are procedures which must be faithfully followed. We will prepare you for your next course of study."

The two men who had chased the frightened whiner reappeared, dragging him into the center of the camp, casting him, shivering, at Exodusat's feet. There were no words, just the sobs of the broken man.

"Now, now, it can't be all that bad." Exodusat assumed the profile of a concerned father. "You must keep strong. Think with a heart of anticipation. You can be the first to show this cowardly Nazarene how a man adjusts to new circumstances." All part of the sport of breaking the man. With a nod, two of the camp dwellers grabbed the terrified weeper and carried him across the compound.

"Come on, Nazarene. You must view your fate," sneered Exodusat as he followed, pushing me ahead, with Beskel the giant skipping before us.

"He so enjoys the feet of clay," said Sariola from behind me.

"Feet of clay?" I inquired.

Exodusat replied, "Yes. You see, most men try to influence the lives of lesser men beginning with their minds-- changing the thinking. But reasoning ability is the final development in a man. I have found it more productive to start at the other end; to wit, the feet. Feet that are broken of running allow us the needed time to reach a man's head."

Taking a quick step forward, Exodusat grabbed my arm and began to propel me in the direction of the procession. I mulled over his words, alarmed.

Lesser men.

Changing thinking.

Broken feet. I saw smoke rising in the near distance, and heard a piercing yelp, not sure if it was man or beast. The screams grew louder. They belonged to my fellow-prisoner.

"Don't start without us," Exodusat shouted as he quickened his step, dragging me along. "Come on, Nazarene. We wouldn't want to be late to the classroom. Learning always begins with a fiery challenge." A quick, chilled laugh. He pushed me through a crowd of men and threw me to the ground next to my sobbing companion. "Make way! The Caesar of Nazareth has come to view the games," said Exodusat, sarcastically.

I looked up to see a path of hot, glowing coals about the length of three men and the breadth of two. I could feel the heat of the embers on my face.

"Stand him up," shouted the excited Beskel. Some men moved forward and lifted my cohort to his feet. He screeched in terror. I looked for Exodusat, but he had melted into the howling horde. Beskel seemed to be in charge of this event. One of the men laid a sword to the prisoner's throat. "What is your name?" boomed Beskel.

There was no reply; too devastated to speak. Another man slapped him across the face.

"Benjamin," he said brokenly. "My name is Benjamin."

"Benjamin, you will walk the feet of clay." When Beskel spoke these words, there arose a cheer of such magnitude it startled me. I looked for a way of escape, but dismissed the possibility; my legs not strong enough. I would be quickly overtaken by the crowd of men. I watched as they shoved Benjamin toward the coals. The meaning of the phrase "feet of clay" was painfully clear. We would have to walk on the searing coals or die.

"Do you understand now, Nazarene?" The voice was menacing. Exodusat had silently slithered next to me. "The fires burn away any notion the feet might have of flight."

"Feet don't plot an escape. Burn them, and the mind still runs free."

Exodusat laughed. "Sear one sole and you greatly discourage the other soul."

A powerful argument.

The captors pushed Benjamin to the front of the steaming pathway. Little spits of fire spurted from the coals. Benjamin glanced wildly between the sword and the fire; a hellish choice--death or agony.

"What is the purpose of this?" I pleaded furiously with Exodusat. "He won't try to escape. I promise! I won't let him!"

"And who will make sure you stay?" Beskel, overhearing my words, turned his yellow-toothed grin my way.

"Then take me through and spare him." The words were out of my mouth. I couldn't take them back. Not that I regretted speaking them, but I was astonished at the swiftness of my choice.

"Then who would keep young Benjamin from running?" Exodusat slipped his arm around my shoulder. "No, it is best you both discover the discipline of the feet of clay." His voice was soothing, as if settling a dispute between two rowdy boys. From his perspective, twisted as it was, both suffer, both stay, both men share a common terror.

They thrust Benjamin roughly onto the coals. He nearly fell but recovered his balance. I could hear the hiss against his flesh. It took a moment for the pain to register. He wailed, frozen to the heat.

"Move!" I screamed loudly, but laughter drowned out my warning. A small reef of fire curled around his foot. "Benjamin, move!"

He began to hop up and down, moaning. The sadistic bystanders shouted and applauded. Then, unexplainably, he stopped and just stood there. "Oh please, God," he entreated.

"God is not in the fire," Beskel taunted in delight.

"Run," I yelled through a lull in the noise.

Benjamin turned and gazed at me. I had never seen that look before, nor have I since. It still haunts my memory--an expression of total despair; the vanquished victim crawling into the teeth of death. He collapsed on the hot coals, his face buried deeply in the inferno, motionless. The crowd was stunned into silence. Was he going to get up? Fire licked his whole body.

"Get him out of there," I screeched.

More delay--endless.

Beskel looked at Exodusat, who didn't move, feeling the luxury of time to make a proportionate decision that might rally the boys to greater admiration.

Then . . . my feet began to run, responding to the anguish in my heart without consulting my good sense. I was dashing across the coals, lifting my legs to my chest to avoid the torment below. I was halfway to Benjamin before the searing agony registered. I looked down and saw flames shooting through my toes. I started to slow, overcome by an all-encompassing fear. I understood why Benjamin had stalled, the misery and anxiety so great you stop dead, trying to alleviate it.

Benjamin's whole body was engulfed in flames. I leaped the remaining distance and landed face-down on top of him. The fire blew past his chest and burned my face. My feet were flailing in the air to escape the heat. I was using Benjamin's body to avoid being burned. I grabbed his blazing robe, and in a fit of desperation, tried to rock us from side to side so we could roll off the coals, his body leaden.

"He's dead," I heard.

I rocked again. We moved.

More strength, please God.

Again.

The fire ignited my robe. One final roll, his body dislodged, and we landed together onto the sand, ablaze. I flopped and beat myself on the chest to put out the fire. I was suddenly surrounded by faces. A cloth was slung over my head with rapid blows coming from heavy hands. I fought, then realized they were trying to extinguish the fire.

"Is he alive?" I said hoarsely through my smoldering veil.

"He's gone."

I threw the cloth off my body. I had to see Benjamin. I couldn't stop now. I struggled to my knees and crawled to his charred remains. There was no sign of life. The crowd stepped back in horror. I looked into the blackened face of a boy-man. I laid my hands on his smoking chest. "Father," was all I could say. I lifted my eyes to the morning sky. "Father!" I squalled, enraged.

Then I heard, no, more like I felt, a winnow of air come from the human devastation beneath my hands. "Benjamin?" I whispered. I looked down into the widened eyes of a frightened child. They softened and welled with tears.

He gasped again, sucking air. "You came," he wheezed. He grabbed the edge of my robe as the words fell from his purple lips. Then he relaxed his grip, slowly releasing the life from his lungs.

Dead.

Jesus wept.

It was all too much; all too foolish.

All too unnecessary.

What followed were eerie sensations, frightful dreams slowly moving through a blurred vision of tenuous consciousness.

According to what I was later told, Beskel carried me to the oasis. Exodusat refused to let him place me in the stream, fearing the water supply could be tainted. The women filled wineskins and stood in line, passing them along, pouring the water all over me.

The more serious burns were on my hands, chest and face. I was told Beskel suggested they amputate my hands, to speed healing. Fortunately, Exodusat dismissed the idea, saying 'he would need both fists to fight Rome'.

My first real memory was awakening to Sariola rubbing some foul-smelling ointment on my hands. She was absorbed in her duty. "How long?" I croaked.

"You scared me," she gasped.

I looked down at my swollen, blistered hands and smiled, "If these don't scare you I don't know why my question should. Didn't you expect me to wake up?"

"I hadn't thought about it."

"How long has it been?"

"Four days."

"Four days?"

"You were hurt very badly."

I looked at my hands again. Then glanced down at my chest--red and raw, peeled back and wrinkled like the dried sun-baked skin of an aged patriarch. "Is my face hideous?"

"No worse than when I first saw you," she replied with a girlish grin.

"Thank you for kind words for a dying man."

"You're not dying. You almost did two nights ago." She was serious and I didn't want to know the graphic details of my near-demise.

"That feels so good," I said as she smoothed some of the soothing stink onto my grotesque hands.

Sariola seemed unconcerned with the ugliness of the wounds. My mind flashed back to the scene of Mary caring for Joseph on the way to Egypt. I remembered how terrified I was to look at the gash on his face. Now here was this stranger tending to the festers on my skin. Comforting, humiliating and aggravating because she was the woman of my captor.

"Feeling better, Nazarene?" Exodusat.

"My name is not 'Nazarene'. Only the ignorant address a man by his race or nationality."

He drew in a deep breath as if sucking in patience. "I see. Well, what is your name?"

"Jesus."

"A common name for a most common man."

The word 'ignorant' must have really irked him. I didn't see any future in exchanging verbal barbs, so I smiled and retorted, "I thought it was the common man you were concerned about, Exodusat."

"He is not a common man," said Sariola defensively. "Didn't you see him cross those coals to save the boy?"

I could tell by Exodusat's face she had spoken out of turn. But he chose to ignore her, probably later to procure her womanly favors. He spoke, appearing to choose his words carefully. "Bravery is saving a life. Stupidity is almost losing your own. The grave has no voice or spark of will."

"And a coward performs to an empty arena."

"True, but enough of words and sayings. Sariola, when will he be ready to fight?"

"Wait," I interrupted.   "What did you do with Benjamin?"

"He died for the God of Israel."

"He burned to death at your hand."

"Your perspective. But as in the case of Joseph, son of Jacob, what was meant for evil, God has brought to good."

"What do you mean?"

"His death brought good to our people." He gazed into the distance with a theatrical reflection associated with a thespian or a madman; he nurtured both.

"Again, what do you mean?   Can't you speak plainly?"

"Very well. As you wish. We took a Roman sword and thrust it into Benjamin's heart. Then we carried him into the village to be found by the townspeople, maybe even his kinsmen. When they see the Roman sword, it will further fan the flames of hatred the people possess for the dogs of Rome. So you see, Benjamin has done great service for the cause."

"The cause," I sneered.

"Yes, Jesus. The cause. There are greater goods than fish and wine and laying with a woman. There is the quest for freedom, a freedom that, in my lifetime, may just be an idea.   But for my children it will blossom, with the sprinkling of blood, into a new nation."

More rehearsed speeches enshrined by grandiose notions. I was in the clutches of a walking nightmare; a martyr looking for a sufficiently painful way to die. I was not going to discuss the horror of Benjamin's death with this patriotic statue. I was silent, giving Exodusat, no doubt, the illusion he had won the debate. It was pointless. I would mourn Benjamin in my own way. My hands would heal and I would sprout new skin. There would be another day.

Exodusat simulated a bow and left.

"I must go," said Sariola, gathering her things in haste.

"Did I cause you trouble?" I asked, realizing her words in my defense might cost her dearly at the hands of her brutish mate.

"No," she said defensively. "I just have a lot to do. There's going to be a big meeting of all the freedom fighters here in the camp."

"When?"

She drew back, not wanting to reveal too much information. Then she looked down at me and chuckled. "Not much harm you can do, right?"

I nodded, sadly.

"Tomorrow," she whispered.

"And Jesus," she drew close to my face, "please cooperate." Her breath was warm and unexpectedly sweet to the smell.

"Cooperate?"

"There will be powerful men, and Exodusat must appear to be strong and in control in front of them. There are too many leaders in our movement. Room will be made. Men will die trying to gain control over the domain of other men." Sariola was wiser than she appeared, or was permitted to be. Women are forced to live out the heartache of the unfortunate choice they make in procuring a lover. The legacy of inanity unleashed by one man's lunacy is bequeathed to his loyal woman. I did not intend to cooperate with Exodusat's deadly delusion. Here was my lady of mercy and I could promise nothing.

"I'll try," I said meekly, feeling a pang of guilt.

She smiled cheerfully, and tenderly placed her hand on my face. "Jesus, that was the bravest thing I have ever seen, what you did for Benjamin."

"What else could I do?"

"Watch. Like the rest of us."

"No, I couldn't watch--too horrible. I think I did something because I was too afraid to just watch."

"You are not common, Jesus." She kissed my cheek and scurried away.

What was Exodusat's plan?

Why was my cooperation needed?

My hands throbbed. If I could bear it for a few moments, my mind would help me to adjust, but it hurt so badly.

Had I caused Sariola harm? How could she withstand the uncertainty of this situation? She was a very attractive woman. She couldn't be very old, yet every wrinkle on her face marked an untold horror. How many Benjamins had Sariola witnessed?

I heard the din of the camp fade as I was lulled into sleep. I had nearly forgotten about my hands. I would think about Sariola and Exodusat later. If later left time for thought.

I was greeted by the golden hues of morning light, apparently having slept the night away. I ached all over and my hands were stiff, like they would crack if I tried to move them, burning with pain.

I wiggled up on my elbows so I could look around the camp. It was barely dawn but already the place was buzzing with activity. I judged the grounds to be a couple of furlongs, maybe about sixty or seventy men, thirty women, and several boat-loads of wailing children. Everything seemed to be fastidiously organized, no doubt the hand of Exodusat. The tents were clean, but stained and threadbare. A few camels, a small herd of sheep, and a half-dozen or more milking goats; the appearance of a camp of nomads. Weapons were nowhere to be seen, possibly hidden to avoid scrutiny from passing Roman patrols. How would they find the place? Even by wilderness definitions, this camp was obscure; danger was present but the real world, far away.

I was hungry but I didn't want to eat; curious, but unable to explore; and worried, but too overwhelmed to plan an escape. So I sat for a long time just watching, hoping something would happen to either change my plight or force me to action. I didn't have to wait long.

"How many swords have you?" I was being addressed by a young man, maybe sixteen, dressed in a robe with some heavy pieces of sheepskin tied on, simulating armor. He had a scarf tied around his forehead and a Roman sword at his side so long, as he walked, the tip kept scraping the ground. He knelt at my side and the handle of the sword popped up and jammed me in the nose. I lurched back in pain, laughing at the comedy of errors perched beside me.

"How many swords have you?" he asked again, impatiently.

"You mean, besides the one you nearly rammed up my nose?"

He blushed. "No," he said intently. "You don't understand. *How many swords have you?* is the password for the meeting"

It all flooded back to me--yesterday's events with Sariola and the meeting which she had so indiscreetly disclosed to me. Was this boy an example of the Zealot army out to destroy Rome?

"What's your name?" I asked, struggling to my haunches.

"How many swords have you?" he replied, persistently. I nearly giggled, then thought better of it. A sword, even in a boy's hands, could still cut.

"I have no sword," I answered.

"No," he said, slapping his leg in disgust. "You're supposed to say, *Enough and plenty'.*"

"Enough and plenty," I said obligingly. "But what does that mean?"

"It means you know the password and I don't have to kill you."

"Then by all means, 'enough and plenty'!"I laughed, unable to stop myself this time.

He scowled to enhance his military image. "I am here to get you ready."

"Ready for what?"

"The meeting, Nazarene. What else?"

"What meeting might that be, Zealotine?" I responded, squelching a smirk.

"The leaders are coming. The great men who will destroy Rome." I looked about the camp at the ragtag group of farmers and fishermen scuttling about. Didn't they realize their swords would have no effect against the brute of Rome? Sadly, this boy personified the myth: they were singular in purpose, desperate by nature and destined to premature deaths.

"Why am I needed for this meeting?" I demanded.

"I cannot say. But I am here to clean you, help you dress, take off your ankle chains, and escort you to the tent of General Exodusat."

I wanted to object, but remembered my promise to Sariola that I would try to cooperate.

"Lead on," I said. The boy took off the chains, warning me "not to try anything or he would run me through like a dog". It was all too crazy, but I continued my submission.

He pulled out a camel's hair brush.

"What's that for?" I asked.

"The general said to scrub you with this to get off all the blackened skin on your hands and chest."

"Oh, he did," I said, recoiling and backing away.

"Don't be such a coward, Nazarene," the boy scoffed. "We're zealots. A zealot would not fear the brush."

"I am Galilean, and we have always had a most religious aversion to the brush."

I attempted to stand. My legs cramped and my feet scrunched inward to avoid the onslaught of pain. I teetered and my ankles cracked, refusing to accept the burden of my weight. The boy waved, and two burly zealots appeared to restrain me. Hardly necessary. Two of the camp women came with water.

The boy smiled and said, "This won't hurt."

Of course, it hurt like hell. He scrubbed and I screamed. He scraped and I quoted every oath and prayer I could remember. A third man came with another brush and began to work on my chest. A woman was shedding the skin on my other hand. I closed my eyes, hoping if I didn't watch it wouldn't hurt so much. They were moving very quickly, which increased the agony. The old skin stunk and bled, leaving behind pink, puffy flesh, hypersensitive to the air.

I opened my eyes, a portion of my hand untouched. "Why didn't you do that part?"

"Orders," he replied curtly.

"You mean I will have to do this again?" .

"Several times," deadpanned one of the maidens.

My skin was stinging, speckled with surface blood. I was in no condition to argue, sitting very still to keep from vomiting.

The scene was interrupted by the arrival of horses, usually meaning Romans, but these were the mounts of the Zealot command. The leaders were arriving. A cheer went up from the scrubbers. The horses were all black except for one, which was a mingled gray and white, ridden by what appeared to be a bearded human head atop a massive heap of animal skins.

"Son of the Father," groaned one of my scrubbing maidens. "I'm going to be his woman."

The mammoth man dismounted from the dappled horse. All attention was focused on him, even though five or six riders had trotted their way into the camp.

The young lady ran to him.   "Barabbas, Barabbas, remember me?" He whirled and caught her in mid-air as she lunged for him. He squeezed her and she squealed.

Exodusat bounced from his tent. "Welcome, my brother," he called, extending his hand.

Barabbas grabbed and embraced him. Exodusat all but disappeared in the newcomer's bulk. The others dismounted, grimly, six in all, sullen from the perceived snub.

Exodusat escaped from Barabbas and hurried over to the group. "Simon," he said, taking the hand of a portly, dark man. He extended his other arm. "Kerioth, welcome."

A tall, golden-haired man declined the offered greeting, heading toward the water.

One of the men had dismounted more slowly, evidently inexperienced with horses. "Phillip of the Essenes, welcome to the Camp of Deliverance."

So my prison had a name. I had not heard it before. "Oh, my Father, *deliver me* from this evil."

The spectacle had a surreal quality--renegades resembling royalty; mythical kings ruling mythical kingdoms.

Exodusat turned away, frowning, peering into the distance as if expecting someone else.

In a few minutes another arrived, dressed in full Roman apparel, red cloak blowing in the wind. My eyes darted to Exodusat and the men to see if some action would be taken against this Roman. He was greeted with the same warmth and respect. "Marius, my brother, come and join us," said Exodusat, as Barabbas buried the Roman in a hug.

Still Exodusat probed the horizon.

"What are you looking for, Master Exodusat?" said Phillip.

"I thought perhaps the one from the Jordan would join us."

"He was told, rabbi," replied Phillip.

"What did he say?" Exodusat was intensely interested.

"He snorted," answered Kerioth, who had just come back from watering his horse.

"Why do we need him? We have you as our rabbi." Barabbas engulfed Exodusat in another massive hug. The group grunted their assent.

"He is important, though," Exodusat objected, gazing afar.

"What is important is to feed this terror of the Roman Army some food and drink!" shouted the rounded Simon. "And soon, we will also need women."

Exodusat shook off his thoughtful mood and slapped him on the back.
"We shall have all that, Simon," he said with the confidence of a well-prepared host. Men entwined, laughing, snorting, and joking, lumbered to an awaiting campfire.

No one noticed me, though I was no more than three lengths away. I was busy trying to keep my robe from sticking to the fresh blood. I was free, but unable to run. I looked at the horses, slathered with sweat, and I didn't know how to ride one, anyway.

Sariola left the uproar of the festivities and was walking very slowly toward me; something was wrong-- brooding, pouting, contemplative features.

"Good morning," I said cautiously. She glanced down at me. A tear welled in her eye, and some unfathomable expression of sadness drew down the corners of her mouth.

"I have been sent," she said heavily, "to prepare you to meet the Zealot leaders."

"Meet them?"

"Yes. Well, actually, to speak to them."

"Speak? Why would I need to speak?"

"Exodusat has told them you were captured. I mean, Exodusat has told them about your capture by the Romans."

"Capture? I wasn't captured by the Romans."

Sariola fell to the ground beside me. "Yes, you remember, Jesus. The Romans burned your hands."

"Exodusat did this," I said harshly, holding up one bloodied stub.

"You mustn't say that" She reached out to caress my face." It is important he look good in front of these giants. He is small but wise. Wisdom is power, don't you think?"

I pulled away. "Wisdom should be truthful, don't you think? That would be smart, now, wouldn't it?"

"Then be smart, Jesus. Your truth is not worth dying for."

"My truth? How about THE truth? You know I cannot tell this lie. What about Benjamin? Don't tell me you've forgotten about him?"

"I have forgotten nothing." She turned her back to me.

"Sariola, I won't lie."

She sensed the finality and remained silent.   Then she turned, softening her approach.   "Exodusat said if you cooperated I could be your gift."

"What do you mean?"

"I have had six children for the rabbi, but he said I could have the seventh child of promise with you."

"You're just as insane as he is."

"Don't tell me you haven't thought of us together," she said, drawing her lips close to mine.

"You're the wife of another man! I'mthe prisoner of the same man.   And thanks to him, I'm burned all over my body!   Another man is dead.   Do you really think I'm dreaming of romance? Can you mingle your kisses so easily with the stench of death?"

She tossed her head, her eyes flashing fire, and jumped to her feet. "Then die, Nazarene.   You will appear before the Zealots.   What you say is your concern.   But you will be there. I would not recommend disappointing the little general.   If you cannot be won over with my love, then be convinced to save your own life. These men are not carpenters and fishermen.   They are vicious.   Choose your words carefully." She turned and departed quickly for the camp.

I considered my plight.   While thus occupied, I was entreated by a giddy sense of well-being.   Peace nestled sweetly into my soul. I share this because of its bizarre timing.   I had been burned, threatened and imprisoned, but I was granted a visitation of reassurance.

My situation was not improving.   "It's time to shear you, lost sheep."   Another new arrival, a slender man--wiry and supple, with an appearance of sinewy power.   In his hand was a knife, a wineskin thrown over his shoulder.

"So, you're going to kill me because I won't cooperate?"

"Kill you? No, I'm here to shave you!   I don't know if killing you will be necessary."

Humor was absent--a serious man, with a knife.   I decided to give him my undivided attention. "Here," he said, "wet your beard with this water. It will come off easier."

"Why are you going to shave my beard?"

"Exodusat."

"I would like to keep my beard."

"If you are to be a Roman prisoner, then you must be shorn."

I understood. The beard was the pride of every Jewish man. When the Romans captured a Hebrew zealot, they always shaved his body hair to make him a laughingstock among his people.

"You're lucky it's just your beard. It can get tricky shaving down there at your seed mountain."

I didn't respond. I didn't want to think about it. It seemed ludicrous to take a stand over the beard, it would grow out again. I splashed the water over my face and beard. It felt so good I did it again, then a third time, rapidly.

"Hold it," said my shearer. "This is a desert. Don't waste that."

"Feels good."

"Hmm," he grunted, heading toward my beard with the knife.

"Take it easy. I was burned."

"I heard. Pretty brave....or stupid."

The blade dug into my skin. He pulled, then yanked. The knife was so dull it wouldn't cut the hair--a tool for pulling.

"Wait a second," I groaned. "Can we sharpen that thing? I mean, just enough to call it a knife?" Bitterly amused. Everything in the camp was an exercise in futility.

"It's dull for a purpose."

"What?" I required, inching away.

He followed me. "If it was sharp, I might cut myself."

"Or maybe the beard."

He ignored me and continued to tear my beard from my face. After about ten ripping minutes he stepped back, frowning critically. "I can't get it all," he lamented

"Maybe if you used a knife," I suggested, rubbing my smarting chin.

"No time for that. I guess this will have to do."

"What does it look like?"

He didn't answer.

"What does it look like?" I repeated, indignantly.

"Hell."

What could I expect? He departed, and I laid back to rest--slumber. I dreamed, passing images: Mary, Joseph, James and Elizabeth. How pleasant to be an inept carpenter!

I opened my eyes, Sariola shaking me. "It is time. They are ready for you. Please do not disappoint them." A sword against my cheek, four zealots pulling me to my feet. "Be wise," called Sariola as they dragged me along. "Wise as a serpent."

Night had fallen. I could see an enormous fire crackling sparks into the sky. The shadowy figures of a herd of men outlined against the yellow flames. I could hear the groans and giggles of men and women at play. Trial beside a fire preferable to in one.

The quartet dropped me unceremoniously into the circle of self-appointed heroes. Exodusat disengaged himself from the group and stood over me. "This is Jesus of Nazareth. He was captured by the Romans, burned, tortured and, as you can see, shorn."

"Looks like the Romans are as bad at shearing as everything else," cackled a voice from the assembled.

This brought a laugh which Exodusat interrupted. "After they interrogated him, they threw him into the wilderness to die. One of our patrols found him and brought him here."

Before I could speak, declaring him a liar, Barabbas entered the circle, his huge form casting elongated shadows. "I am Barabbas, Son of the Father. I am most interested in torture. Tell me, Nazarene, what did fire feel like? I have never been burned. I have been stabbed many times, but never burned. What was it like?" His eyes bored into mine. He evidently was serious, but I had no intention of answering his inane question.

"As you can see," said Exodusat, gesturing expansively, "we have done our best to treat him."

"Did they shave his manly parts?" queried the one called Kerioth.

"I don't think we need to know that," barked Phillip, disgusted.

"Oh, that's right, Essenes don't like manly things!" roared Simon with a laugh. Half joined, the remnant fidgeted, nervously.

"Perhaps you have some other questions," Exodusat posed. "I must warn you the Nazarene has been through a terrible ordeal and his memory may be marred. Questions?"

"What do they know of us?" said Barabbas, leaning over me. I didn't respond and was jabbed in the ribs with a stick by one of my guards.

"I don't know the Romans," I said, my voice so weak I wasn't sure it was mine.

"Tell us about your captor. Was he a commander?" asked Phillip.

"He thinks he is a leader," I said, leering at Exodusat. "Yes, he believes his minute presence carries the power to change men's circumstances."

Exodusat smiled, coldly.

"Why did they burn you?" examined Marius in his Roman garb.

"Because he could," I said, continuing to look fixedly at Exodusat. "To establish an appearance of strength and to disguise his true impotence."

"I have never heard of Romans using fire," challenged Kerioth.

"Nor have I," agreed Marius.

"What are you saying, my brothers?" Exodusat defended.

"Nothing, Rabbi," Phillip reassured.

"I'm saying, why are we looking at this burnt, ugly Jew when there are ripe women here for the picking?" Simon groped for the nearest handful of femininity.

"I just thought the leaders would be interested in our discovery," said Exodusat, exhibiting a comical pout.

"We are," some chorused.

Kerioth didn't join the unison, standing to leave. "Yes, thank you, Exodusat, for displaying this pitiful scapegoat." He disappeared into the darkness.

I struggled to my feet. "Yes, I am a scapegoat!" I squealed because it hurt so badly to stand. "It was your rabbi who performed this atrocity on me!"

"Quiet, Nazarene!" ordered Exodusat.

"He has enslaved me in this camp, and has beaten, burned, and tortured me. If freedom is purchased with the blood of those who most need liberation, then the price is too high!"

"What is he saying, Exodusat?" Barabbas demanded.

"He is delirious from the trial."

"Is he the traitor you have feared is in your camp?" inquired Simon, looking up from the woman in his lap.

"What traitor?" Marius asked with renewed interest.

"Peace, peace," said Exodusat, holding up both hands. "I do not know if there is a traitor. It just seems some of our plans have been foiled because the Romans had advance knowledge of our movements."

"Sounds like a traitor to me!" exploded Barabbas.

"Could be a coincidence," suggested Phillip.

"Behold your coincidence!" An object was hurled through the air landing not more than three feet from me. I looked down, then drew back in horror. It was a human head.

"It's Beskel!" gasped Exodusat.

"Not in entirety!" Kerioth emerged from the darkness with a ferocious laugh.

"What have you done, Kerioth?" cried Exodusat, clasping his robe in fear.

"I took care of your problem, rabbi. I know you have no stomach for violence." Kerioth winked at me. I looked from him to the bulging eyes of the beheaded giant. He continued, "Like David of old, I have cut off the head of your goliath. I followed him to the Roman camp. I saw him talk to them. He was so stupid he never knew I was there."

"I don't know what to say," said a bewildered Exodusat.

"How about 'thank you, Kerioth'?" chided Barabbas.

"Yes, of course, thank you, Kerioth," murmured Exodusat. "Forgive me. It's just that. . .well. . . just yesterday, Beskel and I were talking about the traitor. He thought it was . . .you, Kerioth. He thought you were the traitor."

"Covering his tracks," piped Simon.

Exodusat peered at Kerioth, who returned the inspection with a huge smile. Something was amiss.

"Well, it is certainly good that you didn't believe him, rabbi," Kerioth replied evenly.

"Yes, if I had killed you, then who would I have thanked?"

"And I would have missed the pleasure of meeting this poor Nazarene you rescued from the jaws of Roman tyranny."

The camp hushed, everyone looking at Kerioth and Exodusat, who eyed one another, probing for weakness.

Exodusat turned away. "Take the Nazarene to my private selected quarters."

I was drug backwards out of the camp, the scene retreating from my eyes like a painting preserved for all time. I soon found out about Exodusat's private quarters. About a stone's throw away from the campsite, a pit the length and breadth of two men. I was thrown in, the top covered with branches and leaves tied together to form a frame. All light was shut out by the foliage. So this was Exodusat's private quarters. Repeat guests must be a major concern.

****

Days passed. The black and dreary gloom of my earthen prison-grave was occasionally interspersed with a gleam of light forcing its way through the thick brush barricade overhead. My only human contact was a most welcome daily visit from Sariola, bringing food and water and insisting I use the foul-smelling ointment on my wounds. I learned the meeting of the leaders had broken up shortly after I was hauled away. Even for men accustomed to violence, the shock of Beskel's head had dampered the festivities, retiring to their tents, flasks undrunk and maidens unmolested. At dawn they had made their way out of the camp without explanation.

There would be no alliance.

They would each tread the path of the freedom fighter alone.

Sariola had no idea what Exodusat had planned for me. She had asked once or twice, but he just shook his head and walked away. I continued to eat, trying to exercise my sore limbs, faithfully applying Sariola's treatment to my burns. Despite my surroundings, I felt better.

I entertained myself with memories, thinking about Nazareth, remembering specific details about my village and home.

How high were the walls?

How many etchings on the west wall?

How many lengths was the temple?

Boredom would drive me mad, so I focused my waning attention on detail. I planned.

Where would I go from here?

Which direction was north?

A week passed, maybe more. I tried to count the days, but was never positive I hadn't missed one trickle of light meekly ushering in a new morning. It rained and drops fell through the leafy ceiling--divine, wet and cool.

Then they stopped, the provisions, that is. The angelic visits from Sariola ceased. One day, two. No visit, no food, no water. I longed for the smelly ointment. Where was she? My throat ached for water and my body cramped for food. More days passed; my mouth a crusted sore.

I could no longer move. I constantly listened for footsteps. Each crackling twig startled me to rigid attention. I tried screaming but ended up hacking out a hoarse cough.

Just when I was entering delirium, she reappeared. Food was being lowered, and I pounced on it.

"Take it easy," whispered Sariola.

"Where. . ..been?"

"It's been five days. You'll be alright. He's coming in a couple of days to see you."

She left. Who was coming to see me? Exodusat? Who cared. I tried to pace my food and water but was famished. Everything I ate the first night I vomited right back up--my stomach in rebellion to my fasting technique.
Sariola brought food the next day and the next--strength returning.

On the fourth night I received a visitor. As promised, late as usual, slithering in the darkness--Exodusat. He laid down on the branches above me, prostrate like a child after a hard day's play. I could hear his breathing. Can breathing reveal the anguish of a demolished soul? I don't know, but above me was a defeated man, laboring to retrieve the necessary air to sustain his life.

He spoke slowly. "Nazarene, I ordered Sariola to stop feeding you. It was I who withheld the food."

I listened.

"I had to tie her up to keep her from sneaking off to see you. She loves you."

"She pities me. That's the trouble with women. They confuse the two." What civility did I owe this man? Undoubtedly, my nemesis.

He drew a deep breath and said, "Beware Iscariot, that is what I was warned."

"Iscariot?"

"Yes, Kerioth is Iscariot, the assassin. Beskel is dead. The alliance, a cruel joke. I should have listened to him."

"Him?"

"Beskel. He told me Iscariot was the traitor. I didn't believe him."

"And you were right to ignore Beskel. I don't care for Kerioth but you can't doubt his loyalty to the cause."

"Oh, yes, he's loyal; loyal to any bidder that satisfies his inexhaustible greed."

I waited.

"Do you know why I tried to starve you?"

"No."

"I wanted you weakened. I couldn't leave you here to rot, but I wanted you to know I have power over you. I wanted you thinking of me each time your hunger brought pangs and your throat swelled from thirst. Do you find that perverse, Nazarene?"

"Not really--in character."

"No, you're wrong. I am not an unjust man. I'm a rabbi, after all. A man desiring the mind of God. No, I would not harm anyone."

"Unless they stood in the way of the grand plan for the redemption of the Hebrews, right?"

"They shall be freed. God will kill me if I don't kill his enemies. You must understand that. Did Joshua weep for Jericho? I can't lose sight of the prize, or Beskel died in vain."

"I thought he was murdered by an assassin, not fighting for freedom.".

"The son of perdition killed my friend. He must die. Why do you defend him? Don't you know he's the one who brought you to the Camp of Deliverance?"

My mind flashed back to the night I was conscripted. "My abductor had red hair. I remember it falling in my face."

Exodusat laughed. "Today it's red, tomorrow it's golden. He changes his colors like the sunset before a storm."

Was he lying to me to gain an ally?

"Beware Iscariot, Nazarene." He pushed himself up to leave.

"Where are you going? When do I get out of here?"

"When do any of us?"

"Stop the drama! I need answers!"

None provided.

I screamed--no reply. I collapsed into the sand, weeping madly, until utter exhaustion permitted the blessing of sleep.

Another day.

No food, no drink.

I was convinced the twisted rabbi meant me no good. I plotted, but ended up laughing at my own desperate escape plans.

Then one night I heard the sound of horses. Then shouting, frantic, angry voices, metal clanking, and the horrible shrill pleas of dying children--the sheer, insane, riotous squeals of human slaughter. I heard harsh voices speaking in a language I did not know. Fire crackling, smoke, screaming men and women; all gradually dissipated and was replaced by the breeze blowing an infrequent, elongated moan through the macabre stillness. Then suddenly the snorting of horses and the mumblings of men. The voices grew louder, more distinct, coming my way.

I prepared to die.

"Lift," said a voice in my own language.

"What are we doing, Judas?"

"Don't use my name."

I couldn't place the voice, but I definitely had heard it before. The frame of branches above me lifted, permitting a flickering of light to dance down the sides of my sandy tomb. I looked up trying to make out images.

"Here's a rope, Nazarene. Wait until you hear nothing; then take your freedom."

I knew him--the shadowy form of Kerioth and a man who appeared to be a Roman soldier. The hair was dark. Another transformation?

They slipped away before I could respond. I stayed where I was, shaking, for a good while. I didn't hear any human voice, though I could still detect the burning odor of fires.

When all was still, I gripped the hanging rope. I climbed. Dear God, how it hurt. I clawed my way to the top and wrestled my weary frame over the edge. I lay there, panting. I realized I should rest somewhere else. I slowly pulled myself to my feet. The camp no longer existed; just a heap of rubble and glowing embers.

I walked.

All along the way there were bodies. A few of them were armor-clad Romans. But mostly they were the limp remains of zealot men, women and children, dressed in the homespun rags of defeated dreamers. As I crossed the camp I was overcome by grief. Children were dead in the arms of mothers who clenched the robes of renegade husbands.

And then, I came upon the body of my captor--the little rabbi with a spear standing erect in his chest. Sariola lay next to him. I stooped down and looked into his features. I don't know what I expected, but there was no expression on his face at all. No rage or nobility.

He was asleep.

"Sleep on, Rabbi," I whispered.

I cried. Why should I mourn my tormentor?

The answer came quickly.

I was alive. It is the duty of the living to mourn all tragic and useless loss.

I lifted my eyes and stood up--time to move on. The wilderness awaited me; a wilderness where I could search for a better way to be a rabbi to this people.

SITTING 24

Well, Lions and Other Bugs

I picked my way through the darkness. I could see a gray haze which promised new dawn. I ached from nose to toe, and my head throbbed with each step. I wasn't going to last long.

Lingering images of the burnt out camp and dead bodies with eyes bulging towards the heavens--Zealots destined to behold only their Maker--bewitched me.

What had happened back there?

Why wasn't I dead?

I stumbled and nearly fell. I chuckled at myself. Maybe I was being optimistic. I was in no condition to survive this wilderness. There would be a deadly heat in just a few hours. I had no food, and worse, no water. I tripped again, and this time, collapsed in a heap.

I hadn't made much progress. What if the Romans returned? They might regret their generosity in sparing my life.

I forced myself to stand. Immediately I swooned, blacking out for a moment. I sat up, my chest heaving. I decided to rest. I had to stay in control of all my faculties, at least those that remained intact. I wondered why I had been saved.

Kerioth.

Why had he come to my rescue?

It was Kerioth, wasn't it? But I thought I remembered the other man calling him something else.

Judas, that was it. And Exodusat called him Iscariot.

A man of many names; diverse appearances. The questions whirled, but I didn't know the answers.

It was time to move. I stood, slowly. My knees locked. I shuffled my feet forward, but my legs buckled.

The morning light was creeping its way through the darkness. I could see an area just ahead which was shadowed against the horizon. Could it be a grove of trees? In this wilderness? It was too much to hope for but I decided to try to get there anyway. I stood again, but could not walk. I eased back to the ground; I would have to crawl. I lay on my stomach and pulled with my arms and feet. Shooting pains reminded me of my unhealed chest burns. I flopped over on my side. It still hurt, but I could make some progress. It would probably take me hours to pull myself to what was most likely a mirage.

I wanted to feel grateful for life, but what was the point in being saved from fire, only to be thrust into another impossible situation?

I paused to slap myself. Of a truth, I really did. It was a soft slap on a tender cheek. Here I was, alive, and still complaining. Didn't I realize I had made it out of there? I mulled over the events at the Camp of Deliverance. What an absurd name. Deliverance from what? Exodusat had only managed to deliver his people into the jaws of death.

But Kerioth. . . why was he there?

The more I thought the slower I crept. Still I had to think to keep my mind off the pain. I would have to quicken the pace. If daylight exposed me to a passing Roman patrol, I would be squashed like a bug. I tried to coordinate my musings into a cadence with my sideways progress.

Why was Kerioth with a Roman soldier?

Why would a Roman soldier help me escape?

And. . . why didn't the Roman kill Kerioth?

I'm sure I must be a most pitiful sight. Probably make a leper look fresh and healthy.

I remembered Exodusat's warning: beware Kerioth. I'm sure Beskel would agree, if his voicebox were still connected to his befuddled, barbarous brain. Was Kerioth the traitor? Was Exodusat right about him, this human changeling?

I began to grab handfuls of sand and lurch myself forward. It was all such a charade. Men motivating to manipulate other men while wiggling to gain position. Exodusat masquerading as the controller until a fiercer master eliminated him.

That must be it; Kerioth had brought the Romans. Then it was true. Maybe he was Iscariot--an assassin. A man generals deem indispensable until he changes allegiance and betrays them.

I seemed to be getting closer to my destination. It was most assuredly a small clump of trees. To me, it was a little heaven. I looked behind me and suddenly realized that it was not morning at all. The sky was lit, not from sunlight, but the flames from the destruction. It was an inferno of human debris. If the remnants of the camp had not reignited, I would not have been able to see the grove of trees. The destruction of one man's sinister dream was the light for my path to salvation--a grim thought.

I wondered if I was becoming delirious. Perhaps misplaced metaphor is the precursor to mental incompetence. Maybe I needed to put an end to all these swirling questions.

The conclusions were actually very simple.

Kerioth had betrayed Exodusat--an arrogant, cruel, zealot rabbi. My release was his devious way of disgracing the little tyrant; liberating his prized prisoner hammered the last nail in the cross of Iscariot's former ally.

****

I was almost there. The grove of trees, miraculously, appeared to surround a grassy area. A few more pulls and thrusts and I arrived at the sanctuary. I lay face-down in the cool, moist grass, then struggled to a sitting position and leaned against one of the trees.

I remembered nothing else.

When I awoke it was morning. I had survived. I waited for the predictable onslaught of pain. It didn't come. I didn't hurt. I know that sounds like a simple statement, but I was pain-free. I mean, there were some twinges. Nevertheless, the pain which had been my constant companion since my arrival at the Camp of Deliverance was simply. . . gone. It was wonderful! I laughed out loud. I could stand up. I could walk! At first I was suspicious of my new-found healing, then I realized analyzing a miracle serves no function except to delay the enjoyment.

I walked around the grove. Although I had some stiffness, it was as if I had been granted the grace of movement.

My next sensation was the growling revelation of a powerful hunger. Even stronger was the thirst that left my throat parched and sore. If I could find something to drink, I might have the strength to search for food. I looked above me at the leaves on the trees. I reasoned that if the sun had not absorbed all of the dew, there might be some moisture. Even a little water would be a blessing to my crusted lips. I picked a leaf and sucked it. Then I chewed on it. At that point I didn't care if it was poisonous or not. At least I

182 *I'M...the legend of the son of man*

would die with some wet in my mouth. I picked more leaves. I chewed, licked, sucked and squeezed. Every drop of fluid was captured. The fluid gradually permeated the dry sandy layers of my tongue. Even that little dribble was enough to give me some energy. My mind cleared, and I began to scout the terrain. walked around one large tree and there it was. I was so startled that I drew back.

There, before my skeptical eyes was a well. I felt so very foolish. I had been sucking leaves when, eight lengths away, was a well. Then, with a sensation of pure joy, I ran for the holy sight .

Water!

My days in the Camp of Deliverance had rendered me somewhat cynical. It occurred to me that the well might be dry. But when I peered over the side I could feel the coolness of the water. There was a rope hanging from the side. I pulled it up, but nothing was tied to it. I had a rope but no bucket. I took off my robe, tied the rope around it, and lowered it into the well. The water was quite far down. I drew up the robe, but as it came to the top, the water spilled out. I couldn't bring myself to suck from my robe. Leaves were my limit; I had my standards. I crossed my arms in frustration. There had to be a solution.

Finally I had a moment of inspiration. I checked the rope carefully. It was strong, with no fraying. So if you can't take the water to Jesus, take Jesus to the water. I held onto the rope and pulled myself over the edge. Holding on tightly, I began to walk myself down the inside wall . It was quite deep--somewhere between twelve to fifteen cubits. It became much cooler the further down I went. I began to slip as my hold on the rope weakened. Then I began to slide in earnest, so fast I lost my grip altogether and fell into the water. It was fantastic! I submerged deeply and pulled myself to the surface, drinking as I went. I was like a boy again in Nazareth. I dunked, resurfaced, drank, dunked and drank. I filled my stomach until it became difficult to stay afloat.

I began to cramp. Was I going to drown in my own solution?

I grabbed the rope and lifted myself slightly, which relieved the cramping. If I could hold on I would be alright.

But how was I going to climb out? Not that it mattered at the moment. I lay back and floated. The well was barely wide enough for me to stretch out all the way; I shifted from side to side. Fatigue began to take over. I found myself trying to fall asleep. Not a wise move; a little nap in this place would produce a most permanent sleep. I dipped my face in the water to stay awake.

It was time to get out of the well. I tested the width of the enclosure, stretching my legs to see if they could brace me to climb up and out. But the well was too wide for them to reach. I pulled on the rope again. Could I climb with just the rope?

While I was deliberating my plight I heard a rustling from the opening above. "How's the water?"   A man's voice--one I had never heard, I was sure.

I froze. I was trapped. Did he see me, or could he just hear me splashing? I tried to be motionless.

"I know you're down there. That is, unless you're a monstrous eel." The voice was friendly, but the reference to an eel made me pause. I hadn't even considered the possibility of another occupant in the water. "What is your intention?" the amiable voice continued. "It seems that your answer has created new questions. Perhaps your desire to survive has limited your chances for escape."

Why did he use the term 'escape'? Perhaps it was a Roman soldier toying with me. But why? He could just let me die.

I decided to speak. "I seem to be a bit water-logged," I said sheepishly.

"Yes, I would think so, unless you've sprouted fins," he said with a chuckle.

"That hardly seems likely." I couldn't think of anything clever to say.

"So, perhaps you will trust me to help pull you out."

I couldn't decide if there was a degree of sarcasm in his voice or not. "I can't see you," I called. "I mean, I just hear you."

"Do you think it would be to your advantage to see me? What if I am weak and small? You might not have the will to try to climb if you felt that I could not sustain your weight on my end."

He was certainly provocative. He proceeded with his logic. "And if I looked big and strong, you might

depend on me to pull you out without your own hard work.
I might fail you."

He was unmistakably intense.

"I don't know the answer," I said dully.

"True. And what you don't know might hurt you.
But you have to get out of there. You can't do it yourself,
and you don't know me. I will pull if you will climb."

I was cornered with my back literally against the
wall. Around me was the illusion of safety, but it would
eventually mean death. Above me was the friendly voice of
the unknown. But it, too, could be death. I fretted, trying
to think. The man above remained mute.

"Are you still there?" I called.

Silence.

"I need to hear that you're there," I squealed,
frustration taking over.

Still there was silence. I finally realized that the only way to
find out was to try to climb. I pulled on the rope. There was
a sharp tug from above.

There was somebody up there. I pulled myself up and began
to climb. I could feel a gentle pull from the surface. I
yanked. At the same time I was being aided. It wasn't easy,
but it wasn't impossible either. Every time I stopped, he
stopped. But I made progress. I understood that there would
be no shortcut. I wouldn't get out of the well as easily as I
had gotten in. Every good idea has to be reinforced with
hard work. Now I was getting philosophical again!

Stop thinking, keep climbing. It was really an
intriguing experience. I could always feel the support from
the companion up above. Inch by inch, I was almost there.

"Looks like I'm going to make it," I declared
elatedly.

"Either that or you're going to take your worst fall
yet," came the wise but creepy reply.

He was right, though. One false move now and I
wouldn't survive. I tightened my grip. He did, too. I pulled
with new vigor; he answered in kind. As I reached the top, I
was so involved with grasping the side of the well, and
getting turned around and out, that I didn't immediately
look for my rescuer. I fell to the ground in relief.

As I did, I gasped, "Thank you, thank you. You
saved my life."

There was no reply. I struggled to my knees, looking up. I couldn't see anyone.

I stood up, beckoning, "Where are you? I want to thank you!"

There was no answer. I walked around looking for him, and took some steps into the noonday sun of the desert. No one in sight. I stepped back into the grove and discovered a small fire blazing near a tree. I called louder. Only the fire crackled in response. I stepped closer to the warming flame. Though the day was hot, I was cold from my stay in the water. The fire felt good.

But where was my helper?

There was no doubt about it. I was quite alone. Of course, that was impossible. Just as impossible as trees in the desert, and a well sprouting from nowhere.

****

I had just drawn myself from a very deep well, not discounting the help of my invisible benefactor. I felt a confident strength nourishing my every weary fiber. In fact, I felt better than I had in weeks. I had no desire to loiter by the fire--ready to go.

But where?

My original plan had been to view life in other towns. But maybe my approach had been wrong, too complex. Perhaps I should start with simpler forms of life. Non-human forms.

Before me was a great wilderness. I could begin there.

Due to my misadventure, it was already late afternoon. The fire was crackling its invitation to stay and refresh myself. I decided not to travel on today. I felt like Adam in the garden. I was solitary but not alone. My thoughts turned back to my friend at the well.

Who was he?

Was he a survivor from the camp?

I scanned the horizon. The camp was still in sight across the flat terrain. Surely no one had survived that smoldering mass of annihilation. Could it be that my stranger was someone who had hidden away from the Roman troops?

My thoughts quickly turned from my rescuer to an emptiness in the pit of my stomach. I was famished. And, unlike Adam, I didn't have countless groves from which to glean. Some of the trees in my oasis were fruit bearers, but it wasn't the season. It made me angry. I felt foolish for wanting a tree to bear fruit outside the natural order, but the feeling persisted. Why couldn't some tree just rebelliously bear fruit when it wanted to? No, not my trees. I ended up with my own little forest of mature, proper, fastidious season counters.

I peered at the horizon again. Was I stalling? Surely I wasn't expecting some miraculous provision to sprout from the desert sands? Not that I would reject it if it appeared. I couldn't stop myself from gazing in the direction of the camp. Was there food there? If there was, could I go back into that crematorium to get some?

Some time passed.

I tried to get my mind off the hunger, but it was hopeless. After an hour of sitting and thinking, I realized I needed to go back to the camp and see if I could scrounge up something to eat. The sun was beginning to set. I would need to hurry.

With my new strength, I covered the distance quickly. Carefully stepping over the carnage, I tried not to look into the faces of the dead. The bodies had bloated from the sun. Flies had gathered forming an ignoble funeral procession of buzzing, hungry mourners.

Most of the camp had burned to the ground. I walked a little further, lifting debris and poking through the ashes.

I could find no food.

I came upon the carcass of a horse with the rider still attached.. The horse meat could be salvaged. I leaned down to inspect the animal, but drew back, grimacing. Here was the noble steed of a Roman warrior, reduced to a hunk of dinner for a starving Nazarene. I was repulsed. I was also starving.

I found a discarded sword, and cut into the side of the horse. As I was trying to figure out how to dislodge the meat to roast on my fire, I heard a swish of movement from behind me. Quickly I ran and hid behind the charred remains of a lone-standing tent. Was someone alive after all? I heard it again. Darkness was beginning to fall, and the sound seemed louder. It was coming from my rear, to the right. Then I heard a clatter, this time directly in front of me. The two sounds were closing in on me. Did I have the strength to elude two enemies? Struggling to see something over my barricade, I suddenly viewed the form of the intruder coming from my rear.

It was a lion.

My flesh crawled with fear. Had he seen me? But there was no sign of interest. He was delicately stealing his way past the human remnants, and was drawing a bead on my horse. I had almost forgotten about the other sound. That is, until *the other* lion appeared. He, too, crept stealthily toward the horse. The two lions initially seemed unaware of each other. And most blessedly of all, they were oblivious of me. They sniffed about on different ends of the huge carcass, circling the prize. I watched, fascinated in spite of my trepidation.

What would they do? Would they dine together, sharing the spoils? More importantly would there be leftovers for an undernourished Nazarene?

They began to circle more quickly. A deep, guttural growl rumbled from the throat of each predator. They circled faster. I realized there would be no breaking of bread here. The lions had no intention of sharing with each other. They were going to fight over the meat.

I was trapped. I knew that if I ran away I might incur the full fury of two wild beasts who would probably prefer my fresh meat to the horse. I sucked in breath, frightened to move.

The circling continued. Faster and faster they went. One nipped at the tail of his opponent, and the other would swat a clawed paw to the snout. Then, as if on cue, they vaulted skyward, colliding in mid-air. The night reverberated with the screams of the huge cats as they scratched and tore at each other. Once again, the camp was arena to a life and death struggle--two desperate beasts lashing out for the meat of sustenance. The lions sprang, then fell, and leapt again. A cloud of dust rose from the battle. All the rage of nature was being acted out before me. I crouched and observed in total awe. One lion would gain an advantage, only to be struck by an unexpected blow, and reel back in agony. At length, the intensity waned as each warrior recoiled from deep wounds. Would there be a winner? Would the victor have the endurance to claim the prize?

Eventually, they attempted to battle from their wounded positions. Neither would give ground. They gnawed and snipped, but there was no clear victor. The beleaguered duo wrestled in the anguish of fatigue and pain. Finally, one of the pair just collapsed. He twitched once, then twice, and lay still. The other beast gazed for a moment at his fallen comrade. What was he thinking? Was it compassion? "I'm sorry, old friend. Nothing personal, you understand."

I wondered why the surviving cat hadn't claimed his reward. Where was his voracious appetite? Horse meat was just a few feet away. Then I understood; he couldn't move. The battle had taken its toll. He slumped, then strained to get up, only to fall again. He was gasping for air. He had vanquished his foe, only to gain a few moments to await his own demise.

Here I was again, watching something die. Did this stunning creature have regrets? Did he think that it might have been better to share? Was he capable of remorse for the destruction of two lives--his enemy, his own?

He slipped, then resisted. It crossed my mind that I might help him, but I felt no compulsion. This was a ritual beyond my domain.

He fell for the final time. There were no twitches or twinges. The defeat was complete.

I took the sword which was still in my hand. I eased my way over to the battlefield. It was mind-boggling. The scene was so like the night before. Before me were two crafty members of the same kingdom, who could find no room for each other. They decided to battle to the death. It was so much like Exodusat and the Romans. A battle of wills always produces a meaningless extinction of all foolish participants.

The difference was that I was going to take the two fallen warriors of this night's conflict back to my campsite and devour them. This was fresh meat. It would be delicious. I poked the lions with my sword. They were dead. I grabbed them both by the tails and began to drag them across the sand. They were much too heavy. Deciding that I was suffering from massive greed, I picked up the least battered lion, slung him over my back, and headed towards my gleaming fire.

As I gluttoned on roasted lion that night, I was sobered by the sense of purposelessness. Not that it hindered my appetite. But as I chewed, I considered that it is sometimes better to let the lions of life destroy one another, and to meekly wait to inherit the remains. I was not bruised, or bloodied.

I was full.

I had picked the bones of the greedy to satisfy my hunger.

We inherit nothing until something dies. The lions could have cooperated with each other and had me as fresh meat. Instead, they chose to flex their wills instead of their intelligence. The result was a futile battle, gaining nothing. They gorged on greed.

I received the lion's share.

****

The next day I headed into the wilderness with no point of reference, because I never knew the location of the Camp of Deliverance. My last stop had been Capernaum before my abduction and exile into this unknown stretch of repetitive rock and sand formation.

I decided to go in the opposite direction from the camp, walking until my legs demanded rest. I drank some water and scrounged around for food, astonished at what was acceptably edible. An unknown berry, some greenery near a ravine, and a fat green lizard, all became palatable to me.

Alone. I had been alone before, but had always known there was humanity nearby. Now, truly alone and uncomfortable with the solitude. It seemed a bustling environment was needful to create the background for my sense of purpose. I became bored with my surroundings; watching a bird soar and descend to land gracefully, and imagining it was as disgusted with the environment as me; totally unimpressed. The bird soon launched skyward, an enviable capacity for changing point of view. I lamented that earth-bound bipeds such as myself had no creative design to ascertain such a panoramic vision.

A snake slithered his way across the molten sand. Side to side he glided, with the progress of an old man climbing a hill. Did the serpent wish he were me? Did he desire to be upright and tall? I watched in amazement as the snake struck down a bird, tarrying on the ground for too long. It didn't seem right--the slimy swallowing up the glory of heaven.

Days went by with no real change, filled with nothing but survival. My first nights in the wilderness were fretful and sleepless. I was terrified of the teeming forces of nature around me. Perhaps one of the cousins of my lion might return to revenge his relation.

After a few days I found it easier to sleep. My dreams were absent the horror I had just escaped. They were full of Nazareth--faces of home mingled with a foreboding sense of dread and failure. I awoke in frustration and fatigue.

Let me tell you, though, I was blessed by an abundance of water. I never once had to resort to sucking on leaves. I traveled on. An occasional scorpion darted across my path. At first I flinched and shuddered, but then realized that the creatures were much too busy with their own affairs to be concerned with me. The scorpion was more intent on dodging my huge feet than biting them. I was learning.

Most of my discoveries were disheartening, such as overassessing my personal toughness. I was grateful for the solitary field of activity, not desiring an audience for all of my nervous twitches and wild-eyed looks when something rustled in the night. I was disappointed, believing myself to be more secure. Each day there were new revelations that contradicted my self-image. Was I pathetic or funny? I concluded God was right when he said it wasn't good for a man to be alone. At least, not for too long.

Being a man. What was it anyway? I had never been with a woman. Most men my age were married with a brood of little ones. Why not me? I was attracted to women. Yet thoughts of marriage always stirred up confusing contradictions about my real needs. I grappled with appetites and desires; part of me wanted the glories of love, caresses, and fulfillment. I remember as a boy, listening to Mama and Papa in their room. They thought I was asleep, but I could hear the pants and pleasures of tender love. It made me giggle, but also tingle with anticipation. Someday I would be a man. I would hold my own virgin.

As I fantacized, my heart cried, UNFAIR, stagnating in self-pity. Didn't I deserve the pleasures due a man? I contemplated satisfying myself, one way or another.

Raging need wrestled with my spirit's cry, in an agitated, tumultuous attempt to achieve balance.

My heart released a coliseum of feelings and insecurities. Sometimes my self-revelations were dazzling and brought joy; other times grueling and draining, producing tortuous vulnerability. I was becoming exhausted from the unmerciful exertion of deliberation.

A time of discovery; a time for being alone with myself.

****

Fidgeting in an oppressive gloom of monotony, I walked further and further into the depths of the unknown. I succumbed to an itch to move as I tackled the adventure of survival, surrounded by a revolving cycle of life and death. Fits of sleep, moments of discovery, and lapses into self indulgent grumbling speckled my seemingly never ending days.

Even eating became predictable. Although I had no control over what food would surface, I attempted to recreate a common meal. Lizard was terrible, but preferable to the unknown flavor of snake. (I relinquished kosher traditions with my first juicy insect) I had an occasional treat of figs, and devoured them with a bizarre sense of unworthiness.

One day I happened upon a vine of wild grapes. They were so delicious that I almost decided to make a homestead near this miraculous vineyard. I stayed for two days, but finally moved on, realizing there was really no future in grapes.

Having little else to do but muse, I considered nature, and she peered back, suspiciously. I felt that every creature, tree, and rock was fully aware that I was an alien. I wanted to explain my presence, to share with them that I had not chosen to invade their territory. Mine was a journey of necessity lacking any design.

One night, particularly overtaken with a self-imposed boredom, I consumed my dinner and attempted the lost art of falling asleep. I noticed a small bug crawling along. I decided to study his progress. He scurried past me, gathered a tiny provision, and pushed it towards his rock home to squeeze it to safety. As I watched, he repeated this process over and over again. Ten, then twenty times. I scooted over to discover the source of his labor. I found a tiny morsel of dried bread, which my insect friend was transferring one crumb at a time. I lay on my belly, getting my nose as close to the ground as I could. He scampered, so I decided to follow him, my face brushing the ground. I tried to duplicate his spindly crouch. I was amazed at how different everything appeared at earth level. For one thing, his rock sanctuary loomed large in the distance, and must have seemed a vast expanse to my minute friend. Not to mention how much work it was to maintain the crumbs during the journey! I continued to creep and follow the multi-legged wonder. How intelligent of the Father to give him so many benders. Did he rest some of them on the trip over so they would be fresh on the return excursion?

I was so close to the ground that I inhaled a nose full of sand. I sneezed, spraying in all directions. The bug was completely overturned by the blast, and rolled a few feet across the path. He turned himself upright, and gave me a look of utter disbelief.

Quietly I said, "Excuse me."

The bug paused in bewilderment, which seemed reasonable to me. First of all, he had no idea why this huge flesh-mound was crawling along behind him. Secondly, he had almost been blown away by my poorly-timed sneeze. At length, he continued on with his work, as if resigning himself to the fact that he was unable to change his circumstances. He would simply have to continue his business under the scrutiny of this massive crawling imitator.

It upset me that my sneeze had caused such a furor, so I decided to help my little friend. I carefully picked up the small morsel and gently moved it closer to the opening of his rock home. The determined worker was under his rock at the time and didn't see my gracious maneuver. He popped out a moment later and started out on his usual routine. He passed right by the morsel I had situated and returned to the original spot. When he got there, he looked around. It was gone. He scuttled right, then left. He whirled in a complete circle. I could sense the desperation flooding his black, hairy soul. "Where is my morsel?" I could almost hear him screaming. He was frantic. I had totally demolished his life. From his perspective, I had moved his manna miles away. I thought I was helping him, but all I succeeded in doing was confusing the ingenious instinct of a highly efficient organism.

"Over here," I said sheepishly, trying to make amends. Of course, he didn't know the language. I decided to take the food back to its original spot. The bug scurried in terror from the monster hand to the safety of the rock. I waited for him to come back out.

Much time passed. I inched my way over to the rock. "It's okay. I moved it back," I pleaded softly. "I'm sorry I interfered. I won't do it again."

"That's okay. I'm a rock. I'm used to people chipping away at me."

I lunged backwards, heart pounding, and landed on my rear.

A bellowing laugh ensued. "You know," said the voice, "talking to rocks is one of the danger signs of wilderness fever."

Walking up to me was a man--a fellow member of the human species. I hadn't seen one in a long time.

"I wasn't talking to the rock," I said defensively, pulling myself upright.

He was a small, roundish man, with a light, fuzzy beard and friendly brown eyes. "Then to yourself?" he responded lightly. "He who talks to himself must always question the answers." He chuckled.

"No, I was talking to a bug." It popped out before I considered the stupidity, and I groaned inwardly.

The newcomer didn't pass up the opportunity. "Oh," he said, nodding with widened eyes. "That's a different story. Conversations with insects? Much more acceptable! Probably not wilderness fever at all! Forgive me for thinking that you might be losing focus. Were you able to get through to the little crawler?" He definitely had the upper hand in the exchange. Not to mention the fact that he was standing up and I was splatted on the ground like a bowl of discarded stew. .

He continued, "May I help you up?" He reached out his hand invitingly.

"No, I'm fine. I just feel. . .stupid."

"Well, I can't argue with that," he said in his friendly way. His voice was so musical that I was disarmed. I laughed. He joined in, and I led him towards my fire.

"Please allow me to introduce myself," I said, then felt foolish for my formality. I smiled ruefully. "I'm Jesus."

"My name's Mekel, Jesus." He stretched out his hand again. I shook it. It was small and moist but had a firm grip.

"What are you doing out here, that is, besides harassing defenseless bugs?" He smiled again. There was an endearing quality to his humor; it was without cynicism.

"It's. . . a long story. I know people always say that, but in this case it really is true," I said awkwardly.

"Well, I figured something must have happened. You weren't born talking to rocks, were you?" He feigned a serious look.

"No, this is my first contact with that world," I said playfully, enjoying myself. It was so good to talk to another human, especially one with a sense of good cheer.

"Come, tell me. The fire is warm and I love a good tale." He leaned back as he spoke, setting a relaxed mood. I looked him over. Old, but not grizzled; with none of the obvious crippling of aging. His white beard was wispy. His playfulness gave him a youthful quality which I suspected would be with him always. But mostly, he was human.

I began to tell him my story. On and on I talked. I was starved for personal contact. Even in the Camp of Deliverance my human interaction had been constrained, to say the least. I told him about Benjamin and the irrational rabbi, Exodusat, of my burns, the zealot meeting, and Kerioth. I shared about the massacre at the camp and the healing at the oasis. While relating the events of my rescue at the well, I stopped abruptly.

"Was it you?" I searched his twinkling eyes.

"Was what me?" he asked as he leaned forward.

"At the well, somebody pulled me out."

"Oh, not true, Jesus. No one pulled you out. You were assisted as you helped yourself. It is the way of the Creator." He stated this so matter-of-factly that I was astonished. I was swept with the realization: Here was my salvation. How else could he know about the well?

"Messengers of mercy need not remain once the soul has been set free," he stated. He had anticipated my question. I was about to ask him why he had left.

"Thank you," was all I could get out.

"You did it, my boy. I just steadied the rope." He bowed his head humbly.

"I couldn't have made it."

"Are you sure? That's the problem with humans. They refuse challenges because fear is greater than the potential of the victory celebration."

He was quite sure of himself.

"Why do you refer to humans as they? Don't you share in our plight?" I asked in amusement.

He continued, "There are humans who are born and there are those blessed who put on human flesh in obedience, that they might work some higher purpose." He stopped. He assumed he had made himself clear. I waited for him to continue but he didn't.

Finally I said, "Your wisdom escapes me."

"Now Jesus, I think you play ignorant," he retorted. "You could not have survived this long without possessing some eternal, privileged information." He eyed me.

"The only information I wish I was privy to is knowing what to do next." I was in the mood to change the subject back to reality. I continued to tell Mekel of my dreams and memories of Nazareth. For some reason, my heart opened to this stranger. I told him of one intimidating dream that particularly haunted me.

In the vision I see my mother, Mary, walking towards me. She is naked from the waist up. She is pregnant and almost due. I don't know how I know this, but I sense that her time is at hand. Her breasts are enlarged with milk. She laughs with glee, then almost simultaneously begins to weep like the mourners at a funeral. In my dream I am confused by the mixture and the intensity of her emotions. While I stare in confusion, Joseph enters the scene and points at me. His eyes are filled with anger. He doesn't speak but I know I have displeased him. I try to talk but no words come forth. Suddenly, blood begins to flow from Joseph's beard and trickle down on to Mary's protruding belly. As the blood flows, the stomach shrinks and Mary begins to fade. There is terror in her eyes. As she disappears, Joseph slumps to the ground, his eyes blazing with consuming anger. I hear a scream, and then I awaken.

I related the dream to Mekel, being shaken anew by its macabre content. After I finished I looked at him, waiting. I was hoping that Mekel, like Daniel of old, would be able to interpret its meaning.

"Who can tell?" he said, gesturing upwards with his hands.

I was surprised, and a little perturbed. I knew he didn't owe me any answers, but I thought he might at least consider it. Had I bored him? Or perhaps, offended him with the perversity of the images?

But then he leaned over and patted my shoulder. "What I mean, dear son," he said warmly, "is that answers don't lie here among the rocks. You must return to Nazareth to unmask the interpretation of your heart's plea. Stay there until you receive the peace that makes this passage liveable."

"Nazareth?" I cried. "Nazareth is why I came out here in the first place. There are no answers in Nazareth. . . just caverns of questions."

I spoke with bitter certainty.

"Then why do your dreams transport you to her gates?" he asked gently.

It was a good question. Could it be that there was unfinished business in my hometown? Could there be a family need that I was unaware of?

"Find your mother, Jesus," Mekel said tenderly. "She is waiting for you." He stood to leave.

I was rattled by his words. Could he be right? Had he been granted insight into places in my soul that I had still not touched?

He walked from the fire into the surrounding darkness.

"Where are you going?" I asked as he began to blend into the velvet shadows.

"Your answers are in Nazareth," his voice sounded distant. Once again he was leaving me. I felt bereft. Was Mekel right? Did I need to return? I pondered his words as I prepared for sleep, suddenly so tired I could scarcely keep my eyes open.

My last waking thought was, "Can any good thing come out of Nazareth?"

SITTING 25

A Reminder to Welcome

Ruth was the one who found me.

They say she ran away screaming in terror--thought I was a leper.

I was unconscious, babbling incoherently from a burning fever, my flesh mottled and dead skin hung from my body like a tent flap blowing in the breeze.

She ran to get Mary.

My own mother didn't recognize me.

Several of the men from town carried me to the carpenter's house. I was laid outside in a makeshift barricade, protected from the sun. When I was placed in the shaded pavilion, Mary took a long look, then drew back in horror. Could this battered man be her oldest son?

I awoke to discover myself in Nazareth; once again an outsider, unaware how I got there. The last thing I recalled was my conversation with Mekel, who had advised me to return to Nazareth. I spent a day or so thinking about the things he said, then headed out, confused which way to go. After one day's journey I happened upon a caravan of merchants who graciously provided me with food and shelter. When I told them my destination, they invited me to join them--Nazareth was on their way. Then things got hazy. I remember becoming very ill and stumbling into a tent. The next thing I knew I was struggling to regain my faculties back in Nazareth, trying to surface from a pool of murky water, my body listless and my reasoning eluding me like a moth fluttering in a springtime meadow. Gradually I made out a face, the dimmed countenance of a bleary eyed Mary peering down at me with a mother's deepest concern. My last memories were of men, camels and caravans. Now the face of my mother. I couldn't move, so had no way of letting her know I was alive. Of course, maybe this pallid portrait was the lingering apparition of a dying man.

A large, plump face lunged before my half-open eyes, the appearance so abrupt it jolted me into a nerve-tingling alertness.

"He's alive," said the giant mouth.

Mary rallied to attention as if awakened from a deep and dreamy sleep. "Jesus," she squealed into my face.

"Yes," I replied weakly.

"Are you sure it's Jesus?" said the face, which I finally identified as my little sister, Elizabeth.

"Yes, it's your big brother and he's home. He'll be alright." Mary dabbed at the corners of her eyes with the homespun robe hanging from her body.

"He's ugly," said Elizabeth, curling her lip and wrinkling her nose.

"Go get Mama some water for Jesus. Hurry!"

Elizabeth backed away as if mesmerized by the decadence before her eyes.

"Where am. . .?" I couldn't finish.

"You're home, Jesus," Mary said softly. "We found you outside the gates. You were very sick, but now you're going to be fine. Just fine."

Elizabeth was back with the water and frightened stare.

"That. . .bad?" I said, trying to make it sound like a question.

Elizabeth looked at Mary. "Is he talking to me?"

"I think so."

"Yeah, it's bad," Elizabeth said. "You look like a butchered sheep."

"You rest now, son," said Mary firmly. "I'll be back with food. Are you hungry?" As she asked this, she reached down and stroked my hair. For a moment I felt like a boy again, receiving Mama's full attention. I pulled away, the man in me suspicious of the gentle intention.

Mary paused, lips pursed. I thought she was going to say something, but evidently thought better of it. She arose and departed.

I was alone. Apparently I had fallen into the throes of an unrelenting fever and the caravan had delivered me to Nazareth. How long had I been sick? How serious was it? Did I really look like a bloody lamb? I was back in Nazareth in the position I least needed to be, helpless. I had come back from my time of discovery like a wounded animal. My life was out of control. I was just tired of feeling incompetent.

While contemplating, *he* came through the door. I had only been gone a few months, but he had aged several years; Master Hagabus, his face a mixture of concern, fright and delight. Perhaps concern for my health, certainly fright over my looks, and assuredly delight to have his fellow-student of priestly elocution back again. I felt the same--good to see the sage of the synagogue.

"Master Hagabus," I said.

"Oh, good, you can talk. Mary was concerned you had lost your tongue. I told her that was impossible. I'm quite sure you will continue to ask questions long after death."

I chuckled. I would survive. No rabbi would have the poor taste to make jokes about death with a dying man.

"I see. . ." I said, pausing for breath, "that you have gotten no younger."

"And I can see you have gotten no prettier!"

"Eliz. . .says. . .I look like. . . butchered sheep."

He smiled, sensing my effort and fatigue. "You rest now." He stood up to leave then paused. "Butchered sheep usually have a better coat of wool." He departed, chuckling.

I considered his comment. The fires had burned my hair and my beard had been shorn. I was a hairless, wounded sheep--certainly not the image I would have selected for my return home.

I rested, dozed and dreamed, opening my eyes only to have slumber lure me back. My body took over. I wanted to think, it wanted to heal. I vaguely remember drinking water and eating some crumbs, but mainly I collapsed into the arms of fatigue. At times I sensed a presence at my side, but when I awakened no one was there.

Time passed; I was aware of no passage, experiencing the bliss of oblivion; my will succumbing to the regimen of restoration.

One day I looked up to see my bed surrounded by the full contingency of Joseph offspring, all wearing stiff, unnatural smiles; evidently Mary had warned them not to be visibly shocked by my appearance. They were all there, except Simon.

"Where's Simon?" I inquired, counting heads.

"James is here, Jesus. He's been so worried about you, right, James?" Mary pushed James forward. He was uncomfortable, having the social graces of the Nazarene carpenter he was.

"It's good to see you, Jesus. I mean, it's not good to see you like this. This is bad--you look like hell. I don't mean in a disrespectful way. You look better when you don't look like this. You know what I mean?"

I did know what he meant. "It's good to see you, little brother."

Each of my brothers and sisters made a speech, obviously orchestrated by Mary, who was, as usual, trying to restore balance and purpose in the wake of tragedy. Everybody was mortified, but that was irrelevant. We were family. We were together and no matter how wretched we might feel, we were going to make the best of it.

"It's time for you to stand," announced Mary ceremoniously.

Stand? The thought hadn't even crossed my mind. "Perhaps tomorrow, Mother."

Too late. James grabbed one arm, and Jude the other. Mary was pulling on the front of my robe.

"Another family project, Mary?" I squeaked as I felt the blood rush, throbbing painfully, into my unwieldy legs.

"No time like the present," grunted the determined matron.

Spoken like a person devoid of agony. I achieved vertical balance. They were so pleased they let go, applauding. I plopped down. They all rushed to catch me, missed, and I landed rear-end-first, on the floor.

"Well, that's enough exercise for today," said Mary, justifying her mission.

"Can't he walk?" asked Ruth, looking at the others with a puzzled expression.

"He never walked real good in the first place," said James. I waited for a chuckle, but it didn't come. He was serious.

"Of course he can walk," replied Mary. "We've just got to give his legs more notice the next time."

Next time? I knew Mary. We were going to do it again, and soon. She wanted "us" to walk. It wasn't just me that needed to walk; it was both of us. She wanted no crippled children. Not that she wouldn't love us if that was our fate. But, bless God, if she had anything to do about it, WE were going to walk again.

The family went out in single file, the ordeal over. The welcome-home party (*even though he's ugly and don't act like you noticed*) was completed. What could follow this? With Mary in charge, it could only be outrageous.

After three days, I began to make my own way around my little enclosure. Mary had argued for a more ambitious recovery program, but I was able to compromise with her. It did feel good to be up and around. I wanted to be well, even though I was growing impatient with the whole recuperative process.

On the fourth day, I decided to join James at one of the job sites, anxious to break a sweat and feel my muscles ache from labor instead of injury. James was edgy. Every conversation begun died within one or two exchanges.

At dinner he didn't say a word. Was he thinking about work? Or perhaps he was worrying over Simon, who had been fighting off a fever. Mary was so busy with Simon she had little time for anything else, which was a relief for me, because I didn't have to dodge her doctoring.

After we ate I caught up with James, who had quickly left the house to take a walk. When I approached him, he tensed, looking around the deserted street, avoiding my eyes.

"Hey, little brother," I began, feeling my way.

He didn't respond.

I continued, "Is there something wrong? Is it the work? You know I'm not very good at the trade, but I sure do enjoy the labor and fellowship. And the sun feels wonderful. . ." James had turned and was striding away. I ran after him and grabbed his arm "What's going on?"

"Why did you come back?"

"It is my home."

"It was never your home. You were always a stranger here." He bent down, picked up a rock and threw it aimlessly to the ground.

"Am I a stranger to you?" I needed to know what my relationship was with this man. For he was, indeed, a man, becoming one without my help or notice.

"It's not personal, Jesus. Life is not the way you believe. You think it's made up of ideas and feelings. Life is work and success and grabbing a few minutes of pleasure here and there. You want to be at peace. Well, it doesn't come with an afternoon of prayer and thought. It comes at the end of a day of hard work and lasts just a few moments before sheer exhaustion forces you to drop."

"Listen, James, I have learned many things since we last butted heads. I'm not some temple dreamer. I have tasted my own blood and languished in pain   I've scrounged through the ditches and ravines just to find something to eat. I have grown. I'd like to start again."

"It's not that easy."

"It can be. Unless there is more wedged between us."

"Chiolita. . ." he said, then cut short. The pause grew longer, and made me wonder if he had finished.

I jumped in. "What about Chiolita?"

"She thinks you have leprosy and the whole family has been infected. She is spreading it all around the town that Simon has fallen to the disease."

"That's ridiculous."

"It doesn't matter if it's ridiculous. It just matters that it's being said and heard. People don't even need to believe it, but they'll decide to be careful. I've had three jobs cancel, and I'm having a hard time getting workers, especially with you coming to the sites."

"I'm sorry. I. . . didn't know."

"You never know, Jesus. You always want to believe there's an answer. Sometimes there isn't, big brother."

"How can you live like that?"

"How can you live like you do? Chiolita is a witch. There's nothing good in the woman, but she lives here. We all have to walk around her like a pile of fresh dung in a stable. It's always there, and the smart ones learn not to step in it."

"Maybe I could talk to her."

"Maybe you can't! The woman respects nothing and nobody. She makes the witch of Endor look like Samuel's loving mother."

I chuckled at his reference.   James was not an insensitive drone. He possessed the wit of a poet. "What do you want me to do?"

"You're asking me?" He was legitimately surprised. I realized my openness was new to him. I had always considered myself a good listener, but now I saw myself through the eyes of a younger brother who had spent his whole life trying to find independence.

"Yes. I need to know what you want me to do."

"Talk to Hagabus. The town has planned a meeting to discuss the situation. Hagabus will certainly be the man in charge."

"Hagabus knows I don't have leprosy."

"What Hagabus knows, and what Hagabus can convince a mob of, are two different things."

He was right. I might not continue to live in Nazareth, but these people would. Hagabus would have to exceed common sense, and calm their fears by getting them to laugh at their own accusations. "You're right. I'll talk to Hagabus tomorrow."

"Tonight. You can't go to him in daylight. No one will come to Sabbath."

"Alright, then, tonight it is! Now, may I walk you back home?"

"Wait," said James, pulling a small bag from his loin cloth. "I have a gift for you." He reached into the pouch and pulled out a little rattle. He shook it, creating a tiny clinking sound.

"What is it?" I asked, holding it at arm's length.

"It's your leper's rattle. I got it so you can shake it and warn all the women and children you're near." He burst out laughing, turned and ran down the path. I caught up and tackled him. We wrestled and rolled in the sand like two giddy boys released early from synagogue.

"Leper, leper, leper," he giggled and choked.

"I can still whip you." I rolled him over and punched him playfully in the stomach. It felt good to romp. He grabbed me by the neck, flipping me over, trying to pin me.

"Oh, you think so, do you?   We'll just see about that!"

I struggled fiercely, impressed by his strength. We rolled again, and suddenly we were staring at a pair of sandals, which encased two stubby feet joined to a pair of swollen ankles. Looking quickly up the body we met the frowning eyes of Chiolita, the town matriarch.

James quickly rose to his feet, throwing me to the side. I remained on the ground staring up at her.

"Good evening, Mother Chiolita," said James respectfully.

"James." She spoke to him but never took her eyes off me. She pulled her veil carefully over her mouth. "So, Jesus, you are back in Nazareth," she said slowly.

"Yes, Mother Chiolita," I answered, following James's lead in manners.

"Is it true Simon is ill?"

"He does better, Mother," James quickly interjected.

"Jesus, you have been ill, too."

"More exhausted than sick," I said directly, quickly hiding my leper's rattle from her intense review.

"As a matter of fact," added James, "Jesus was on his way to see Father Hagabus about offering a special sacrifice on Sabbath in gratitude for his healing."

"So you are healed, Jesus. Maybe your sacrifice should be one of supplication for God to spare your brother's life. Good evening." With this frigid remark she disappeared into the night. We watched silently.

"I know, I know. Go see Hagabus," I said.

"Tonight," was all James replied.

We walked to the house without speaking, unwilling to rouse any other creepers in the night.

****

A golden glow eeked through the cracks and crevices of the tiny stone room housing the aging rabbi. It was adjacent to the synagogue, and so tiny four men could not stand in it without touching the walls.

I made my way up the path and stood before the small, arched opening which served as a door, with a homespun robe hanging across it, aspiring to privacy.

I was calling for my friend, when it occurred to me it was late and Hagabus might consider my visit an intrusion. I decided the importance of the conversation outweighed propriety. I called again.

"Yes, who is it?" came a crackly, sleepy voice.

"It's Jesus, Master. I'm sorry to awaken you."

The curtain was drawn aside, and an unkempt Hagabus appeared. "I wasn't asleep, Jesus. Rabbis must always be alert. Watch and pray. Remember, I taught you that as a boy. Because everything always happens in the hour you least expect it. Do you remember?" He was energized with the verbosity peculiar to people who insist they were not asleep.

"I remember, Master," I smiled. I glanced about the room. Despite the diminished domain of the domicile, the furnishings failed to fulfil function. Hagabus was not a man enamored by the prospects of elegance. Simplicity reigned supreme in his space.

"What can I do for you, Jesus?" Hagabus asked, smoothing his hair with his hands.

"I just saw Chiolita."

"Oh, I see," Hagabus said slowly. I realized he would not divulge anything I didn't already know.

"We had a talk."

"You listened and she talked, am I right?"

"It seemed the best profile for me."

Hagabus grinned gayly. "I, too, have found that to be the case. A man can stand and argue with the rain, but he'll find he gets wet anyway."

I understood. Hagabus was more comfortable with parables than candor. "Standing in the rain does give the illusion of the sky falling. Is the sky falling on me, Master? Should I be wary of the thundershower from this old cloud?"

Hagabus scratched his beard. "I am weary of verbal paths leading into darkened caves. Let us speak frankly. But keep these words in this holy of holies. Am I clear?"

"Clear."

"Mother Chiolita has many concerns."

"You mean she makes many her concern?"

"Isn't that what I said? Well, anyway, that's what I meant. She is a widow and she's lonely. That's why God had the notion to keep women busy taking care of the inefficiency of men so they wouldn't trouble themselves into a storm of gossip about things that aren't their affair."

"You mean, things like. . . fatal diseases? Do I look like a leper, Master?"

"No, you look like--what was it Elizabeth said--a prickled goat."

"Butchered sheep."

"So it was," he conceded, easing himself onto a rickety wooden chair.

"I do feel much better now."

"And you look a bit better. What was the source of your infliction, anyway?"

I wanted to tell him about my capture and imprisonment at the Camp of Deliverance; perhaps he would empathize if he knew the details of my fiery trial. I decided against it, not wanting to divert from the subject "There are many surprises beyond Nazareth's gates. Let's just say I stumbled on some of the more alarming possibilities."

He nodded as if resigning himself to my ambiguity.

I added, "You do know Chiolita has told the town that I have leprosy and that Simon contracted the disease from me?"

Hagabus placed his hands on his knees, leaned forward and studied me, deliberating, like a physician pursuing a diagnosis. "Do you know how long you were in the grip of fever?"

I didn't. I had been so busy trying to regain my strength it hadn't occurred to me to ask.

"It was three weeks ago today they found you outside the gates."

"Three weeks?!"

"A frightful thing. You cried out in the night. First people were concerned, then terrified. Disease is a specter looming large in the soul of the Nazarenes, Jesus. We didn't understand why you didn't get better."

"You say 'we'. Were you a party to this leprosy hysteria?"

"No, because when I came to sit with you I studied your features. I determined you had wounds, not lesions. Burns, I presume."

I was impressed by his astute observation and unaware of his personal care and ministry. This touched me, and made my next question more difficult. "If you knew it wasn't leprosy, why didn't you stop the vicious rumor?"

"What could I do? Would they believe me?"

I was irritated at his cavalier attitude. "Well, in the absence of an angel, the report of a passionate fool might at least garner an ear."

"But the foolhardy run the risk of death upon arrival of the angel. What if I was wrong, and you were leprous? I would have endangered the whole town. And a point, my boy. Why did Simon fall ill?"

A good question, but not one, in my opinion, which should have silenced this most respected rabbi. I was trying to understand, but was beginning a slow burn. "You played it safe. Was it to maintain your place, or keep the coffers full with Chiolita's gold?" I was goading him. Hagabus rarely revealed his heart unless he lost his well-constructed control.

"What are you accusing me of?" he retorted angrily, rising to his feet with a youthful spurt of energy.

"Playing it safe. My mother is a widow, too. Or does she lack the finance and power to gain the protection of the local holy man?"

"I have always. . ."

"Is the memory of the generosity of my father so faint in your mind that this bitter old woman can drive you into a profile of silence?"

He glared at me, not the animosity of a wounded man, but rather the shamefacedness of an appeaser who had sought peace at all costs. He was trying to maintain an order in his little Galilean province, but complacency minus conflict leaves an unfulfilling compromise. "Have you talked to your mother?"

"We've talked."

"About Ratheal?"

"The herdsman?" What did Rathael, the plump animal keeper, have to do with anything?

"He wanted to marry your mother. She refused."

"Why?"

"You, and a house full of other reasons. She said she couldn't think of her own life until her two oldest sons were happily betrothed."

I sighed. Would the marital issue ever cease to haunt me? I looked up at Hagabus. "What does any of this have to do with Chiolita?"

"Three days ago, Mary arranged two marriages--you and James. Ratheal offered his daughter to you and Chiolita offered her granddaughter for James."

Why hadn't James told me about this? Or better yet, Mary? How could she make plans for my life?

Hagabus, sensing my outrage, said soothingly, "It was beautiful, Jesus. Chiolita was quieted and Mary was overjoyed."

"And when was I to be informed?"

"When you were better. Now, I guess. I don't know what they planned."

"So if I am willing to marry a girl I don't know, then Chiolita will stop saying I'm a leper? In other words, I am clean enough to gain the favor of a lady, but perverse enough to be perceived by the whole town as defiled!"

"I guess. I remember the love you had for that heathen girl."

"You mean Anisa? She wasn't a heathen. Not every girl who is not Jewish is a heathen."

"You loved her. You are capable of loving a woman."

"I didn't know we were discussing my prowess. Anisa has nothing to do with this. Ours was a romance of conversation. We never had the reason or the season to develop it to anything more."

"But she has everything to do with it. Do you remember when she was ill and you touched her and life came back into her body? You said it was a heat or warmth. Do you recall? Of course you do. How could you forget?"

I was shocked Hagabus still retained the memory. What did that anointed moment have to do with devilish gossip and forced nuptials? "Hagabus, you have lost me, old man. What are you talking about?"

"You have a gift, Jesus," said Hagabus, his eyes shining. "It is from God. Use it, on Simon. Heal the need in your own house. Share your miracle."

"So you believe God has granted me a gift, and he would have me produce a family and use my hands to warm my children's bread?"

"Heal your brother!"

"You think the power is mine?"

"Try it! It would go a long way toward answering people's questions about your soul and heart."

"Let me understand this, rabbi. I should use the power of God to prove my own worth to the surrounding skeptics?"

"So," Hagabus said triumphantly, "you admit to the power of God in your life!"

"I receive the intervention of my Father into every crevice of my imagination."

"Father? You speak of Joseph and I speak of the Almighty."

"Your Almighty is my Father. He always has been."

I was stunned by my own words, and even more surprised I uttered them to Hagabus. He was theologically devastated by his former prize student. "He is father to no man. He begat us in spirit. No man possesses His Seed and the God of Sinai impregnated no human female to give birth to a son. I would request you cease this blasphemy in my home, so near the Sacred House." All warmth had departed from his demeanor. He was back to posturing about His deity, the *idea* of God--a pious, purposeless, pursuit.

"I must talk to Mary."

"I would suggest you speak with Mary and use the respect of a circumcised son," he replied, obviously indignant I would refer to God as "Father".

I stood and thanked him for his time, a chasm between us. Things would never be the same; never again interacting as student and teacher.

I stooped through the archway and headed through the starlit night for my home. Was it a good time to talk to Mary, or was it too late? Was there ever a good time to change your life?

****

Nazareth. A peaceful hush lay over the village like a blanket of warmth and tranquility tenderly placed upon a mother's favorite son. Each step contained a memory; each little stone disclosed a sacred impression from my childhood. I knelt at the wall where little Jomar met his tragic end. I stroked the rugged stone cemented in place by the skillful hand of Joseph, the carpenter. How much of the town had that man built? The rocks cried out the praise of the industrious worker. He was gone, but the memorials of hearth and home still exhaled the essence of his excellence. I saw places where we used to play as children, the faces of those who still lived, and others who had passed through to unveil the Great Mystery. I was transported on the wings of a soaring nostalgia, as I pined with the melancholy of my boyhood passions.

I crouched in the street to survey my habitation, remembering the Egyptian boy who was transplanted so precariously into the vineyard of his heritage. This had become my home, by the sheer magnitude of unrelenting time, I had grown here in wisdom and sprouted in stature. I believe I had found favor with my fellow man.

I recalled those nights, returning from my studies with Hagabus, when I would hear the inner voice of my heavenly Father sanction, *"This is my son. I am well pleased."*

Here I had emerged from a boy to a man. I looked up; the stars seemed to move from behind their cover of clouds, as if they were granting illumination to my late-evening meditations.   Perhaps I was trying to delay the meeting with Mary, the carpenter's wife. Certainly, to these Nazarenes, that is what I would always be, Joseph's boy. No matter what discoveries of the spirit filled my time on earth, to the residents of this Galilean town, I would always remain, "Jesus, the carpenter's son."

"Is there more for Jesus of Nazareth?" I asked a distant star.

It twinkled at me.

Stalling.

I was trying to convince myself it was too late for further conversation with Mary. I walked on toward my home, or whatever it was.

As I rounded the corner I saw a faint flicker of light in the window. Someone was awake. I ambled towards the door, and thought about just going to my sick-tent, to bed. But curiosity overtook me and I stepped through the opening.

Mary, sitting cross-legged, staring off in no particular direction.. The candlelight was merciful to the aging process which had etched its work across the young girl's face, sculpting the image of a Jewish matron. Tonight, in this light, she was my mother again. Youth graced her features. She looked beautiful. I could no longer be angry with her. She was waiting; the role of an ingenious woman who had learned the power of well-timed submission, not lacking spunk, but lending grace to the sanctity of the moment.

"I spoke to Hagabus," I said from my position at the door.

"You once called him master."

"I still love him, but I have only one Master."

"And that master is the God of Moses?"

"I call him Father. I mentioned that to Hagabus. He was rather. . .upset at my familiarity."

She surprised me with a sympathetic glance. "Perhaps God would welcome a bit of intimacy."

"Perhaps we all could." I crossed the room and lowered myself to sit next to her. "Why, woman, have you tried to control my future?"

"Woman?"

"Let's not argue titles. First master and now woman. You're my mother, but if we are to remain friends until the end of our times, we must reckon with one another as man and a woman. I can no longer swear a false allegiance to mere words. I need a relationship with you and this whole house that grants space for me to mature into whatever my Father wants me to be."

"Marriage is a good thing, Jesus. I loved your father for many years. It wasn't always great. As you age you tire of the hunt for perfection. You accept the good that falls your way. The wisdom bestowed by age tells you to snatch the blessing quickly, and make it your own. Rathael is not my love. That was Joseph; the young, stammering boy that whisked me away into adventurous times. But this herdsman is a good man, solid, not given to wine, and willing to accept my children as his own."

"I'm happy for you and Rathael, Mother. I know love is a good thing. I'm not some dried-up old prophet who disdains the beauty of romance and the joining of a man and woman. Mama, it's like when you cook a stew for the family. You keep adding things and stirring   ingredients until you arrive at just the right taste. Then you stop fussing with the broth, sit back and let the brew of nourishment blend together to create the ideal mix for the dining pleasure of those you love.   That's the way it is in my life. I have all the ingredients I need. It's not the other things aren't good. They're probably wonderful. My Father has placed a fullness in me that now must simmer in turmoil, so I can pour myself out to others as meat and drink. I have to do something besides duplicate what I am. I have the heart to create and I must see the work completed, so I can determine if it is any good."

Her eyes were moist. "So, it's your mother you hate," she deadpanned, the corners of her mouth turning up.

"Are we back to being female and not human again?"

"Are you saying women are not human?" she responded playfully.

"No, I'm saying I'm leaving tomorrow at first dawn."

"But you can't. It's fine you don't want a wife, but you have to be here for James' marriage."

"I'll come back for it. When is it?"

She jumped to her feet. "You need to be there. I can't trust your roamings will return you to our gates. Look at you this time. You have to stay. It's only twenty Sabbaths and a day away."

"Twenty Sabbaths, might as well be a lifetime. Just give me the time and place and I promise to be there."

She turned her back to me, planted her foot and whirled around for confrontation. "What will I tell the family?"

"Tell them I went away to find an appropriate gift. Now, where will the wedding be?"

"Someday, Jesus, I will take all the things I know about you, that I have pondered in my heart for so long, and maybe, just maybe, I will be able to form them into one brief, reasonable thought." She had her finger in my face and her eyes blasted fire.

"And then again, maybe not," I smiled, and she laughed out loud. "Now, where's the wedding?"

"As I said, twenty Sabbaths and one day. In Cana."

"I'll be there!"

"No you won't," she said with mock sarcasm. "You'll be off slaying some dragon in the name of the Most High."

"No, I'll be in Cana, and you shouldn't think of yourself as a dragon. A bit cranky maybe, but not fire-breathing."

I tickled her to hear her laugh again. "Mary, before I leave, I would like to see Simon. . .alone."

The transition was abrupt, but I was afraid I would forget. She nodded and kissed me lightly on the cheek. "The real kiss is waiting for you in Cana. Be well, my son." She waddled out of the room.

I eased my way into the dark corner of the side room. .As I drew near the mat, I felt the heat from Simon's body. I didn't know what to do. I didn't want to awaken him. I knelt down by his bedside. It was past time for prayer. I needed to make real contact.

"Father, good evening. Things have been busy tonight. I might have offended some good people. That was never my intention, or my heart. Maybe Hagabus is right--I mean about Simon, here. You love him. I mean, I think you more than just tolerate us. I think you want to be with us. I think you're fascinated by our actions, and you won't be satisfied until we know you want to link with our dreams and to teach us how to live fully. Would you, Father, touch my brother with the fullness of your love for him?"

The warmth in my hands. Was it the fever or unexplained glory that sometimes just happens? I placed them on Simon's head and then lightly upon his chest.

I stood to my feet, my work complete. Any more involvement on my part would be futile. I turned to leave, and saw a slight movement in the dark. "Is someone there?" I whispered.

Silence. I went to my enclosure and laid on my mat. I was asleep immediately. I awoke still tired, but as I had promised, at dawn I was on my way. I walked from Nazareth, not knowing when I would ever return. Would I ever come back? Dear God, please, not on another stretcher.

I had heard my cousin John was in Bethabarra, near the Jordan River. Time for another family reunion.

SITTING 26

Smotherings

I heard the door creak and a slender shaft of light coursed through the encompassing bleakness. My thoughts were transported back to the stables in Bethlehem.

"Master Jonas, sir?" Relah. "Is that right? I forgot your name."

I could see the hem of her garment as she descended the stairs.

"My name is Jesus, Relah."

"That's right. Jonas was the guy in the whale. You're the Nazarene."

She turned and whispered. It appeared she was helping someone down the stairs. "I've got somebody who knew my grandfather. I thought maybe he could. . ." She paused at the bottom step, squinting into the darkness. "Where are you?"

"I can't see a thing, " said her companion, whining.

"Just stand still a minute. Your eyes will adjust pretty soon," I reassured. It was a man, though the tone was deceptive.

"What's he doing down here anyway?" he whimpered breathlessly, exerted from his decline.

"I told you, Matthan. He was born here," said Relah impatiently.

"Recently?"

Inwardly I groaned. "No, sir, I'm a grown man now. I'm over here."

The old man shuffled. "Of all the crazy, fool things."

"I would offer you a chair but there is none."

Just then the stair door slammed shut, and a draft of wind extinguished my candle. Darkness.

"What in the hell's going on, Relah?" squalled the aged gent.

"It's just my brother. He likes to shut doors."

"That's about the only thing he can do," he muttered.

.   Relah fumbled around until she found my candle, and relit it.

I reached out and put my hand under the old man's arm to steady him, and settled him next to me on the ledge.

"Matthan? I like that name. My grandfather's name." He was bony and frail beneath the over-sized robe, and stiffened at my touch.

"I brought Matthan because he was a friend of my grandfather's, wait I said that.   Anyway, he was around during tax time." I nodded my head. "Well, you might say thank you. I didn't need to bring him. It's not easy to unearth these old people."

"You watch your tongue, missy.   I'm not buried yet."

"I thought you might be able to ask him some questions about your birth," Relah concluded, ignoring the rebuke.

"I'm sorry if I didn't seem. . . well, please forgive me. I was lost in thought."

"Well, you seem reasonable enough," said Matthan. "When Relah said there was a man in the stable, I thought we had a crazy on the loose."

"I have been accused of worse." He peered into my face, squinting, as if attempting to excavate a reminder of who I might be.

"Do you need another candle?" asked Relah, turning to leave.

"Do you have to go?"

"I have to go feed Gretoon. I let him feed himself once and I still can't get the stain off the wall," she laughed. I joined in, but Matthan just grunted, the kind of sound old ones make when they know they should laugh but years of false maturity have suffocated the inner giggle.

"We'll be fine, Relah. Just come and get me in an hour. I don't want to fall and break my neck on those crumbling steps," Matthan huffed with a widow's complaint.

Relah was gone and we were strangers in a candlelit stable--looked to be a long, slow hour. Matthan hadn't taken his eyes off me.

"Gretoon?" I asked him.

"What was that?" He cupped his hand around his ear.

"Gretoon," I repeated with greater vigor.

"What about Gretoon?"

"I never knew his name."

"Well, now you do. It's Gretoon."

"Thank you. I do."

Going nowhere.

"Crazy, you know," he said. I wasn't sure who he was referring to. "Crazy," he repeated. "Gretoon. Like a loon."

"Hmmm. That rhymes."

"Are you crazy too?" He came closer. We were nearly nose to nose. I could smell his sour breath.

"No, I'm not crazy."

"Well, what do you want to talk about?"

"I don't know. I appreciate your coming."

"Well, you should appreciate it. It's hard enough for me to walk, much less go prancing and darting around town."

"So you were here during the tax."

"Who could ever forget a tax? But who can remember one over another? All Roman thievery blends together after awhile."

"My mother and father came here for the taxing. They were House of David. I guess I decided to be born while they were here."

He sat and stared at me, anticipating more information. "And. . .well, I wanted to come see the place. Back then there weren't any rooms available in the whole town. The innkeeper let them stay here."

"Berkiel. That was his name. He was a businessman." He let out a short, hacking cough. "He knew how to turn a good profit; just how much water to add to the wine before risking being run through by a Roman sword. So, he gave you the stable?"

"Well, actually, my father. I wasn't here yet. I came later."

"It's a wonder Berkiel didn't charge extra for another person," Matthan snickered.

"Did you ever hear about a child being born here? And after that, we lived here. In Bethlehem. My father apprenticed with the carpenter for a time. He would have been very young."

"No, I left for a time, right after the taxation. I was a merchant. I often traveled to the East to purchase cloths and spices. I brought 'em back and sold them to the damn Romans--at a healthy profit."

"Well, thank you for your coming." I was done.

"I returned right after the slaughter of the children."

My heart stopped. My skin went numb, the words hung in the air. "The slaughter?"

"Yes. They tried to cover it up, but it was Herod. He sent assassins to Bethlehem. There was something about the children having a disease. He killed them all."

"All? How many?"

"I don't know. From age two or three and below. I don't remember, maybe a dozen or more."

"Why?"

"Only the young still ask why. Kings don't need a reason. That's why they're kings, so they needn't be questioned. I always heard it was a wager he lost. The bastard was always making crazy promises and having to back them up."

"Did you question it at the time?"

"Why run into the wind? I've found it's best to turn my back on what I can't control. But you know, that's what happened to Relah's brother."

"Gretoon? What happened to Gretoon?"

The old man stood up. "He's a lot older than Relah. I guess about thirty or thirty-two. I'm not really sure. Anyway, what was I saying?" He inched his way towards the stairs.

"We were talking about Gretoon, Herod and the children. What happened to Gretoon?"

"Oh yes," he said, waving his hand. "Gretoon was just a baby. Really, just born a few Sabbaths earlier. His mother--Relah's mother--heard the screams of the children when the soldiers were rounding them up. I guess some sort of mother's instinct took over, because when she saw them coming to her house she tried to hide him. He was crying and she couldn't get him to stop. She gave him the breast, tried everything, but he couldn't be quieted, so she finally put him under her robe and shoved his whimpering mouth between her thighs, deep into the warmth of her womb. She squeezed her legs tightly together until all the cries were silenced. The soldiers came and searched the house, and she clung to Gretoon the whole time. When they left she pulled him from between her legs. Thought she had killed him. Just about went mad. He finally started breathing and was asleep for five days. He woke up drooling and babbling. We thought he was going to be alright, but he never stopped. She saved his life, but the demons had come to punish his soul. He would have been better off dead." Matthan shook his head and started to climb the steps.

Gretoon. I realized when he said "Grt-oot", he was trying to say his name. There was a mind buried under all that confusion. He was robbed of his life, but mine was saved. He was another victim of Herod's paranoia and vengeance on the wise ones from the East.

Matthan paused on the third step.

"Here," I said, coming to his side and offering my arm. "Let me help."

Matthan waved me away. "Nah. I can use the challenge. Don't say anything to Relah. Her mother died when she was three. I'm the only one left that knows about it. Relah's mother thought she wouldn't be able to serve the garrison if she knew about Gretoon. Relah thinks Gretoon was her mother's punishment for adultery. Best left that way."

He turned, disengaged, slowly ascending the stairs, creaking and wheezing as he went.

Behind every miracle is a horror making divine intervention a necessity. I felt indebted to Gretoon, Jeremiah, and all those little chubby faces who never got to live. My heart ached. Still, Gretoon wasn't dead. There was a human being in the shell.

Maybe there was more to my Bethlehem visit than memories. Maybe Relah needed to know the truth. Maybe Matthan needed to see some of God's compassion. Maybe the brutality of Herod needed to be exposed.

He was dead, his arrogant butchery lived on.

Maybe it was time to discover greater possibilities of what may be.

A lot of maybes.

Still . . . *maybe.*

SITTING 27

The Repentant Leap

somewhere in the rugged terrain of Galilee, near Samaria:

I really think my face is looking better. Ruth might not even shrink back in terror. I don't know if time heals all wounds, but these are improving. My skin is still discolored with different shades and textures, but the raw patches are healing over, and the beard is slowly returning to its former freelance station. I think I could pass, in a large crowd, for average. After being considered a grotesque contagion, to go unnoticed is a delight.

I have decided to take my time making the trip to Bethabarra. One reason is I need the opportunity to sort through my feelings about the latest Nazareth encounter. The second is I am lost, not knowing where Bethabarra is on the Jordan River. I am certainly not heading for some sort of palatial kingly retreat. I don't know much about my cousin John, but from the bits and pieces I have gathered, he doesn't seem the sort to lounge in luxury.

I have passed some travelers along the way and am following their non-specific directions to find the man they now call "the Baptist". Some of them were pilgrims returning from the Jordan experience. They described an energetic, if not frantic, man preaching to the assembled multitudes a voluminous, rugged doctrine of repentance. He seems to have little regard for finery, nor is he impressed by a person's status.

I smile just thinking of it. The Jews can use a prophet who smells of sweat instead of reeking of the sweetness of aloes.

I am anxious to meet this relative.

I've been considering what profile I should take. I don't want to dash to his side and claim him as family. I barely knew him as a boy and never as a man. But I also don't want to be timid, standing in the shadows. I have a feeling John would welcome a straightforward approach. So what will I do? Why am I here on this quest? It just seems logical. I mean, if you wished to purchase a camel you wouldn't frequent the goat herd, and if you want to find the truth, it seems prudent to go where God seems to be spending His time, which at this juncture, points to a watering-hole where a bearded fanatic is dunking people in filthy fluid.

Most interesting. What will I find?

Does God actually inhabit a place where men may uncover the hidden meaning of all things?

Probably not, but it beats staying in Nazareth shaking a leper's rattle.

So clearing my mind to set a purpose for my journey: *I'm going to the Jordan River to escape the insanity of home life and to hear my cousin preach, hoping I will find a clue as to what my Father wants me to do. A trifle bizarre and self-indulgent, don't you think? It is where I begin.*

I've decided once I reach Bethabarra to camp outside the area and sneak in and out to observe. I have always found open-minded inspection the best way to reveal the reality of any situation. Perhaps I will build a fire and offer a spot of rest and nourishment to passing patrons, a wonderful way to find out what is going on and meet some fascinating people. I can hardly wait!

****

Actually, it became a simple matter to find Bethabarra. As I neared the Jordan River, a small stream of flowing humanity converged to form a wave of jubilant celebrants heading for a river of decision.

I also watched those returning from the Jordan, searching their faces for the light of God. Some would smile, some shout, and some would stare blankly into the distance, displaying disappointment over what the Baptist and his watery solution were able to accomplish in their lives.

The people going my direction grew in numbers as the roads from Galilee, Judea and Samaria came together. All types of humankind: merchants and workmen, tax collectors and soldiers, the learned and ignorant, sharing a single purpose. Prejudice was abandoned for a season of reverence for the greater aspiration.

I marvelled--marching, sweating, smiling and laughing with the medley of comrades. I had never seen anything like this before. Maybe this was the real miracle; not some magic river which would wash away our sins, just a common thread weaving human hearts into a glorious tapestry.

Men who never dreamed of personal contact with one another were now racing towards a mutual goal. God most certainly was on the trail leading to Jordan.

As we neared our destination, you could hear shouts and squeals coming from ahead, not screams of pain, but exultant cheers by fulfilled praisers. I lagged to the rear, searching for a campsite near the road where I could peruse the flood of fellows bound for the depths.

I found a promising spot and cleared a small camp, hoping it would be inviting for visitors. I started a fire and went down to the river, away from the activity, caught some fish, and brought them back to broil over the blaze. The smell of cooking food can snag a man who, in his excitement, has forgotten all about eating.

It didn't take long. Soon half-a-dozen, maybe more, were lounging at my roadside inn. Some boys went back to the river to catch more fish. The entourage grew. Truly, a transcendent moment; one of those special interchanges that make you proud to be a son of man. Everyone shared what they'd brought: some had dates, bread, wine--all blended to create an abundant meal, partaken in an atmosphere of gleeful commonality, the way God intended food to be eaten.

Our numbers grew until we had to clear more space. An energetic, young, dark-skinned man took charge of the fishing detail. His name was Andrew, from Galilee. He, too, had come searching for soul-stirring direction, and kept us in fish as the gathering expanded.

I listened to stories: one woman was recently widowed, a soldier tired of war, a Sadducee disillusioned with religion, a carpenter from Samaria who had thrown down his tools (I could really sympathize with that!)

None of us had seen the Baptist, but we were part of a crusade which drew out the best in us. We were all searching, so it was alright to be lost.

Someone started a song and we all joined in. Young ones played and babies cried; mothers scurrying around trying to appease childish needs, and little boys chasing and tackling one another. There were older people; aged souls in prayer with glistening tears glossy on their cheeks; a carnival of emotion spiraling around a backdrop of human expectation.

As the food supply depleted, more mysteriously

arrived. It was no longer my campsite; no one even remembered how it began. I laughed out loud, but the sound was swallowed by the sheer volume of giddy gratitude. It felt wonderful to lose control--the end result a holy cause. How much God must be revelling in this treasure of people excellence! We were needy but not greedy, uncertain but not befuddled, and sinners but not condemned. I chomped on some fish, and smeared the meat on my face in abandonment. Children came around, and I entertained them with silly stories, imitating animals and giving them rides on my back, finally tumbling to the ground in exhaustion.

Night fell; people finding their place to sleep beneath the stars. God
gave his blessing and dwelt among us.

****

I slept without the uneasiness one might experience in the proximity of strangers, surrounded by little ones who had nodded off during story time, and warmed by a fire which was tended by an unspecified procession of observant caretakers maintaining the integrity of the blaze.

A sweet sleep. I dreamed of hope--no specific images. It was more a presence. Yes, a presence of hopefulness permeated my heart and allowed me to relinquish all the cares of my day. I was where I needed to be.

The heat of the morning sun had already caused beads of perspiration to burst on my forehead. I didn't want to move, gently lulled back to sleep. Then I smelled food, my eyes blinked, and my ears tuned from inner voices to outer chatter.

Apparently I dozed in the interim, because my young sleeping companions were gone. I felt so lazy. Was it the sunshine, peaceful surroundings, or an annoying character flaw present since my youth? I heard two men conversing. At first my hazy thinking prohibited understanding. I peeked in the direction of the droning voices.

What was this?

I trembled and chose to lay very still, not breathing.

Where was I?

Had I been thrust backwards in time?

Wasn't this Bethabarra?

What were these two doing here? Was I at the Camp of Deliverance? I wanted to jump up and run, but my better sense compelled me to remain still.

Sitting in the camp next to me were two of the men who had been by Exodusat's fire--the meeting of the zealot leaders. The heavy-set one was Phillip, yes, that was it. I could never forget the other one. Still dressed in the war garb of a Roman centurion, Marius. What were they doing here? Even worse, what was I doing here with them?

I feigned sleep.   My tension had escaped their notice. They continued to talk. I decided to listen and learn as much as I could before--well, honestly, I don't know what I was going to do.

Phillip spoke first. "I have joined him."

"I never thought you would leave the Essenes," said Marius with a chuckle.

"Does one leave the Essenes? They make sure to imprint your soul for all eternity." Marius laughed.   Phillip continued, "It's just that John, I mean the Baptist, has his hand on God's heart. When I hear him preach. . ."

"Preach? You mean scream. I have to concentrate until my head hurts to make out a single word.   Just an unruly upheaval."

"Exactly, my brother. A lake in a desert. Our people have been so vacant of emotion it's like being splashed with cold water. At first you're shocked; it even makes you angry. Then you realize you're more alive than you ever thought you could be."

"Your words resound with poetry. It is the mission of a man to disdain soft words. I hear John's cry, but he still tells us to remain in servitude to the chains of bondage."

"I don't think I agree."

"Then what is 'be content with your wages'? 'Do violence to no man'? That's what he told the soldiers yesterday. What does he expect us to do? Are we to drown all the Romans in his baptismal river?"

"Show me the fruit of violence," Phillip protested. "Where does it get us? So many dead. Don't you see we'll be drained of blood long before the Romans? We must find a new battle plan."

"There is nothing new here, Phillip. The Baptist told the Pharisees he was not the Deliverer of the people. He is waiting for another. He stands and dunks the deluded masses in the muddy Jordan under the guise of remitting their sins. I say, sinless or cursed, they are still damned in

Roman bondage. I fear for him."

Phillip was awaiting further revelation, as was I. None came. Finally he inquired, "Do you believe the Baptist is in danger?"

"I know he's a dead man," Marius snorted. "The Zealots have decided he's worthless to the cause of liberation. They have hired an assassin to drown him in his own river."

"Why did you tell me this?" he gasped in despair.

"I want you to warn him. Tell him to change his message. Tell him to run, or hide, whatever needs to be done. I think John is a good man; he's misguided by his obsession with God, but he's not worthy of death. Some of us feel the Baptist's execution might backfire. We might get a whole wilderness full of mimics who continue this insipid message of repentance. Why should we, the oppressed, repent? Why doesn't he preach his burning message to the Roman devils? But believe me, Phillip, they are going to kill him." Marius stood. "You have the information. Do with it what you want. I don't know when it will be, but it will be public and it will be ruthless. The Zealots won't tolerate the Baptist's weakness. Hear me, man, the Baptist is dead." Marius ran from the camp. Phillip stood, called after him, then trotted away in pursuit.

My eyes popped open and I sat up. John was in danger, and if I didn't hurry I might not see him alive.

****

New information, new revelation. New responsibility!

Such is life.

My mission was two-fold: one, to be a student of the spiritual phenomenon going on; and two, reconnoiter and try to identify the would-be assassins. After all, John was family. (Of course, it is always prudent to hinder assassination attempts.)

Nevertheless, too much to think about before I'd had anything to eat. I tromped down to the Jordan and knelt to wash my dirtier, more exposed, areas, the endeavor, fruitless. It became clear to me why they called this body of water the Jordan Sludge. My cleansing experience ended up being an action of replacing old dirt with new.

A lovely lady gave me a generous portion of bread which she had warmed on the coals of her fire. Delicious, from my lips to my deepest growling innards. I felt nourished and ready to make my way into the mainstream, as it were.

I didn't want to be seen--keep my distance so I could be the discreet observer. I desired to capture the whole Bethabarra adventure in its natural flow.

I inched my way down the bank, walked around a bend, and came upon an inlet surrounded by water--people everywhere. Merchants had even set up booths and were hawking their wares. There was a mingling of the colorful robes of the affluent with the customary tan and browns of the poor. Everyone seemed to be in a rush. I stood still, people whizzing by me.

As I looked around, I noticed the traditional cliques were still operating. The Pharisees, in full gala wardrobe, remained distant from the tumult, sitting and scowling suspiciously, casting an air of superiority; the whole endeavor outside their jurisdiction.

The Essenes clumped in a conclave of rigorous scrutiny.

The soldiers were munching, slurping, and laughing harmoniously.Mothers swatting children, children scampering, pouncing upon anything that moved.

Heard above the chaos was a booming voice--John's. His bellow exuded an earnest desperation squeezed from a soul enraged.

"Repent, for the Kingdom of God is at hand!" he howled.

The crowd cheered, though others listened quietly, as a smattering whispered opinions to preoccupied neighbors. I pushed forward to get a better look at the prophet, who was also kin.

I climbed a small knoll and crawled on my belly to get above the crowd. Pulling back some greenery, I could see perfectly down below.

John, the Baptist.

He was a huge mound of hair sprouting tiny patches of darkened skin. Bushy locks and billowing whiskers merged with the camel-hide garment to form a tangled web of manly overgrowth. There was one round balding spot on the top of his head that shone forth like a halo from the shaggy mass of curly brush. His skin was baked, burned, and ravined, giving him the appearance of a much older man.

His baptizing technique was truly eccentric: he grabbed the person by the robe, pulled him upward into a leap and plunged them both into the river in a frenzied, rapturous joy, emerging with the penitent from the murky depths, leaping again into the air, slinging water in all directions.

The convert shrieked in delight, and John shouted, "Repent! The kingdom of God is at hand!"

I laughed and ended in a hoot--so unorthodox, so fervent, so fragrant with a divine sense of humor.

One by one, each person came into John's arms to be plummeted beneath the muddy Jordan in a bath of radiant glee.

I was transfixed. Then I remembered the Baptist was in danger. He seemed immortal in this setting. I scanned the crowd. Somewhere in the mob was an assassin determined to pin John down for one final plunge in death. Where could he be?

Before I could even figure out how I would recognize such a person, I gazed in horror at the next candidate in line for baptism. Could it be? Maybe it was a coincidence. Would they carry out their sinister will this soon? Marius had only spoken of the plan this morning. Yet, there in line, waiting his turn to be immersed, was Kerioth. He had his head, red again, reverently bowed. He glanced up, squinting into the sun. Iscariot, the zealot assassin. Why else would he be there? They had sent the slime of their corps to do the deed. How vulgar to feign a repentant heart to enact this hellish execution.

I had to warn John, but I was too far away to race to his rescue. I yelled. The crowd drowned out my screaming with their chants and singing. All I could do was watch the travesty unfold.

Time stood still. Kerioth was in the Baptist's arms. I screamed again, but to no avail. I watched as the Baptist leaped into the air, taking Kerioth and himself deep into the tide. The splash sent a spout of water propelling skyward. The crowd cheered. No heads emerged from the water. Kerioth was making good on the plan, drowning my cousin, and no one realized it.

At the top of my lungs, I cried out, "Stop him!"

Just then the water separated and the two entangled men leaped toward the heavens. The masses wailed in ecstasy. Kerioth danced in a circle, raising his hands to the bright morning sky. John clapped and pounded on the back of the freshly redeemed soul.

He didn't kill John! Could it be Kerioth was here just to be baptized? Had I been so mistaken about this man?

I felt a sudden shame at my lack of charity. How could I be so judgmental? Didn't every men deserve to be cleansed of the inner filth clogging the passage to newness of life?

I came down from my perch to join the praising throng.

God had called a prodigal home. I, more than most, knew Kerioth's deeds. This was a great victory for the forces of light. Kerioth came to the shore, as man after man pummelled him in joy. Already the next soul had dived in the depths with the hairy baptizer, but the crowd of men was still congratulating the former betrayer. I wondered if I should say something to him. I edged forward, craning my neck, I couldn't find him. He had disappeared. Then, for a quick flash, I saw the blazing hair, and something else. He was with someone I recognized. Then they were gone, swallowed up in the crowd.

"Very exciting, don't you think?" said a voice to my rear. I started, turned around, half expecting to see Kerioth. "But a bit overwhelming, too." It wasn't Kerioth, but a kindly man, a bit past fifty years of age, I estimated.

I smiled. "Yes, very exciting."

"Are you here to be baptized?"

I was stymied. I hadn't really decided whether to join my cousin in the repentant leap. "I. . .don't know. . .I mean, I think so."

"Well, no hurry. Lots of water and plenty of God's grace to go around. My name is Alphaeus. I'm John's assistant."

"Assistant?" I asked, surprised. The spontaneity of the surroundings didn't promote images of organization and titles in this anthill of activity.

"Well, not in the sense of organizing. We don't do a lot of that. I assist him in one specific way."

"And how do you assist John?"

"Well," he said, putting an arm around my shoulder, "I baptize the women."

It hadn't crossed my mind that only men were being

baptized at this site.   The women were few, and onlookers only. "Where?"

"Just upstream. Women from everywhere. All classes, colors, and dispositions, I might add," he said with an impish giggle.

"Why doesn't. . . ?"

"I know what you're going to ask. Why doesn't John baptize the women? Now this is private, right?" He lowered his voice to a clandestine whisper.

"Of course."

"Well, John told me if he ever got his hands on an excited, wet woman, he didn't think he could let go, if you know what I mean." He continued, "I mean, he may be a prophet from the heart up, but he's a man from the loin cloth down. That Nazarite vow can drive you nuts if you're not careful." Alphaeus's honesty was refreshing. Cousin John avoided baptizing women for fear of getting immersed in a scandal. "What are you doing tonight?"

"Nothing, nothing at all."

"You must come by the fireside. We have people from everywhere gather, eat, laugh and share until we all fall asleep."

I realized my campsite idea was not new.   People will always find a place to warm body and heart. "I'll be there," I assured him, patting his arm.

"Sometimes John joins us."

He scurried away to dunk more contrite ladies.

I thought about Alphaeus' invitation. A darkened sky lit by a blazing fire, with stories so plentiful they nuzzle the mind with a lamb's caress. And, the chance to see John away from the water.

I would certainly be there.   Alphaeus, I wouldn't miss it.

****

I was so excited about the coming evening the morning dribbled away, relenting to what ended up being an endless afternoon. I was a trifle over-anxious. Of course, with anxiety comes the temptation for boredom and the inevitable sour stomach.

I was determined to entertain myself. I resorted to eating to relieve the sour stomach. I liked eating; I always have. My favorite part of being a carpenter was completing the day's work and being able to eat. I have often dropped a rock on my toe because I was deeply engrossed in a daydream about some desired delicacy. I always looked forward to supper. "Come and dine." Such a sweet phrase. And because we were hard-working providers, we could eat large manly-fellow portions without shame or guilt. I have tasted foods I didn't like, but have always devoured them anyway. As a result, I became quite adept at putting on weight. I was often grateful my robe provided such generous latitude for my expanding form. As long as I didn't gain enough for it to show in my face, no one could ever tell.

I think one of the reasons I enjoyed food so much was the potential for fellowship, adding the final garnish to a delectable meal. Two brothers, having a heated disagreement, could always, with the arrival of warm bread, a flask of wine and a fine roasted lamb, relish mediation.

However, it is difficult to fill a whole day with eating. I know this from personal experience.

My starvation ordeal at the Camp of Deliverance had taken a toll on my body, and my appetite seemed to be making up for the lost time. Inspecting my protruding middle, I would soon need to seek a good spiritual reason for a long fast.

At any rate, I did a lot of eating.

Evening made her belated appearance, time for the sunset meal (not that I needed any more food). I ate with the children. First, because they were more fun. Secondly, maybe their fussiness over food would encourage me to consume less. The mamas watched me carefully as I sat with their sons and daughters, perplexed, perturbed, but also delighted to have an adult male helper. I guess most men feel a sense of responsibility toward children, but to me they are kindred spirits, always passionate about their play and annoyed when the atmosphere becomes too dull.

This particular night, though, things did get out of hand. One of the boys decided he was the "baptizer" and poured water on everybody's head. I tried to be adult, but when he doused me, I instinctively crumbled some bread and threw it at him. Needless to say, this inspired all the children to toss figs and bread; I, their favorite target. Two irate mothers arrived and quickly restored order, glancing their disapproval my direction. I ducked shamefacedly. I was guilty, and not just by association. I was covered with food and had some water in my hand I was just about to fling on a nearby little person; humiliating, in a fun sort of way. I excused myself from the skirmish and went to clean off before too many adults saw me.

Twilight gently extinguished the light of day, allowing the fires to express new brilliance. Soon it would be time for the meeting; an aggregation of the freed.

I decided on invisibility--to sit and glean the harvest of human testimony without needing to react or approve.

Alphaeus mentioned no specific time. There was no summons given. But as if an inaudible clarion had chimed a decree, people rose and spirited their beings to the wilderness shrine for the redeemed.

I followed, mingling with an expectant, chosen few yearning to be with one another. Then, I sat still, absorbing a buzz of conversation magnificently laced with mirth, swirling its infectious thrills deep into my heart.

One of the brothers stood to speak. "I came here to die, or maybe it was to confirm I was already dead, just flesh and bones looking for a place to find a grave for my weary self. My spirit was crushed. My family was all killed by leprosy, but God would not grant me the disease to end my meaningless journey. I was hungry to hunger no more. Does anyone know what I mean?"

The gathered congregation released an affirming groan of understanding.

The man continued, "I heard of the Jordan. Now understand, I didn't come here to gain life. Life was gone for me. I came to confirm my own death. I wanted God to let me die. I went into the water. . ."

When he said this, there were some chuckles interspersed with shouts.

He paused and then said, "I couldn't even feel the wet. My heart was numb. My body destroyed. The Baptist grabbed me and lifted me in the air. I was prepared to die, to let the Jordan waters fill me and kill me. I went under the water, and when I did. . ." He stopped, choking back tears.

Gentle breathings of love and encouragement emanated from the encircled friends. One stood and embraced him.

The speaker pulled away. "Let me finish. I want to tell you. When I was under the water, I heard a voice inside me. . .inside my head. . .my heart. I am not sure. It said, *'Live or die, but decide to do one well. I will be with you whichever path you choose.'* My heart erupted. I leaped from the water a new man. I chose to live and will spend the rest of my life doing it well."

With this, he plopped back down and the crowd cheered--a wonderful story. How awesome to hear the voice and truly inspiring to be alive!

A young lady jumped to her feet. "I can't sit still any longer. I was a prostitute." Her candor evoked a gasp from the surrounding mass, but she didn't pause to react. "I came to the Jordan to make money. I figured, where there's men, there's need. I thought they would soon tire of God and dunkings in the water, and would yearn to be embedded in the arms of a woman. A lot of money to be made. John could save their souls and I could profit from the rest. I came to bed with every man in Bethabarra until I either died or walked away a very rich woman."

A hush fell over the crowd. No one moved, shock written on each face; a stillness settled on the assembled.

The woman took in their reaction impassively. "I thought the best way to solicit business was to pass myself off as a repentant. If I could get the women to trust me, I could seduce the men. I went into the water with Brother Alphaeus. He just stared at me. I said, 'Come on, old man, take me down.' He gazed into my eyes, gave me the shakes."

Someone from the crowd hollered, "He does that to everyone!"

The whole gathering burst into laughter--a much-needed relief of the tension.

She smiled and continued, "I said, 'What are you staring at, preacher?' Now get this, he said, 'An ass.'

More laughter.

"I said, 'I'm not an ass, I'm a woman.' So he says, 'Not quite so. You're an ass impersonating a woman, and God is here to arrest you for your crime.' Well, I was ready to climb out of the river and run for my life. But before I could go, he says, 'You can repent, you know. Why don't you try laying down once in the arms of God and get a lasting satisfaction for your soul?' He had me. He knew I was here to whore. I just stared at the brown water. Before I could speak again, Brother Alphaeus grabbed me and took me under. I want to tell you, I have been grabbed by men before and taken down. But this time, God took me down and held me there until my pride was drowned and my heart surrendered. I came out a. . ." she shivered as tears began to stream down her face.

"Bless her, Lord," intoned a sweet female voice. The tender utterance broke all remaining composure of the witness; she fell to her knees and wept. Alphaeus came forward, knelt, and embraced her.

He looked up at the people and finished the story. "She came out a new being. Would some of you wives come and love this woman, because she is your sister, and because she will no longer be on the prowl to take your husbands?" A flurry of movement as matrons and maidens sprang to embrace their new sister. The men stood back, in awe of the miracle before their eyes. I lifted my head to the sky and sobbed in joyous gratitude that God would salvage this damsel in redress. We all were witnesses to a sanctioned miracle, retold again and again in Eternity.

The sharing could have gone on for another hour, but a man strode to the center dressed in the colors and garb of a zealot, with skins, wearing a sword at his side. His husky, basal voice demanded attention. "Wake up, sons of Abraham! You're celebrating the story of a whore while Rome makes prostitutes of us, for her own pleasure."

Alphaeus stood and spoke. "It is a time for celebration, brother. Grasp the moment, if not the concept."

"You grasp onto this, old man," said the warrior, drawing his sword.

A voice from the midst of the crowd. "What is your intention, brave freedom fighter? Do you plan to kill off your countrymen as a practice session for your final slaughter of the Roman hordes?"

Everyone looked around to see who had spoken. Even the pompous warrior seemed confused. A man stood up, clothed only in a loincloth and body hair--John. He had been there all along, blending into the assembly. "It's me, my brother. What's troubling you? Aren't you moved by these testimonies to God's grace and power?"

Excited conversation swept the group as they became aware of John's presence at the gathering.

The Zealot snorted. "Roman blood excites me, Baptist. I want these people to be free once and for all. You can give them release, maybe a temporary taste of salvation. But my sword can break the real chains that bind them!"

"And the death of Romans," John said evenly, circling carefully amongst the seated people, "will that cause this prostitute to stop spreading her legs for every buyer?"

"No, but maybe she could earn a decent living if she were free from Roman taxes and tyranny!"

"So, you are saying all sin is caused by the deprivation of basic privileges. You would have us believe we would never foul our consciences if we just had enough denarri; that this brother's dried-out soul would be refreshed, if only the Romans were overthrown. Am I correct in my interpretation?"

One, clothed in the customary drapings of the Essenes, leaped up.

"John," he said in a placating manner, "we realize that men need God to enrich their beings, but shouldn't we have the right to pursue God in liberty?"

"No," answered John abruptly.

"What do you mean, 'no'?" shouted the Zealot, brandishing his sword and taking a stride toward John.

"Freedom is not a given," answered John. He spread his arms again, including the whole crowd in his gesture, endued with the grace of a Greek orator. "Life is what we have. God is the one who can explain that life. Freedom is an honor, to be sure, but life can be lived in dignity and power, even if one is shackled in chains."

The crowd listened quietly, awestruck by the eloquence of the utterance; dwarfed by the significance of his speech.

"Alright, John," said the Essene in his reasonable way. "We know you have a desire to change the inner man, but can't you see the need to address the outer circumstances?"

"This is what will change the outer kingdom, Baptizer!" the zealot roared, wielding his weapon in the air.

"The sword does make holes in men, but never truly makes them holy," John said with a smile.

The crowd roared its approval.

"All we would ask, brother," the Essene said, moving closer, "is that you be intolerant of sin in everyone, including Herod and his adulterous wife, Herodias!"

Mutterings and murmers--the Essene struck a chord. They all hated Herod for his excesses as well as his betrayals. He continued, "Preach as fiercely against palace sin as you do pauper sin."

John looked at the faces around him. "When Herod comes to the Jordan, I'll preach the message of repentance to him as well." He departed. I also chose that time to leave. As I made my way into the darkness, I mulled over the evening's events. My breath had been taken away by John's powerful speaking; such a simple, yet profound way of putting things. I was so engrossed in my thoughts I bumped into someone making his way to the fire.

"Excuse me," I said, embarrassed.

"Quite alright. It's dark." Mekel, my wilderness confidant. At least, I believed so.

"Mekel!?" He was walking toward the gathering. "Mekel!" He didn't answer. Perhaps I had been mistaken, or he didn't recognize me. I found a place to sleep. The ferocity of the rally increased until it sounded more like the clamor of a riot. Soon it ended and I watched and listened as the people came back to find sleeping space, most reserved, stomping to their resting places.

Something had happened. I didn't know what it was, but the freshness was gone.

****

I dreamed

I was lying flat on my back, immersed in a shallow pool of water. I could see the sky; the shimmering water made it look like crystal. Suddenly there were angry men before my eyes, shouting and cursing. Mary was there, weeping and looking down at me through the watery window. Soldiers passed by, busying themselves at an unseen task. Was I going to drown? Was I holding my breath? No, I was breathing, or perhaps felt no need for air. Maybe it wasn't water at all, but instead some sort of transparent veil.

I saw Mekel. He leaned over me and smiled, and spoke in a harsh, raspy voice. "You should have listened." Then he covered my face with a black shroud.

I jolted awake, my heart pounding--morning.

Before I could contemplate the meaning of my dream, I noticed people were rushing around, frantically gathering their belongings. What was going on ? I asked a passer-by, but he shook me off. A little boy ran up to me with a wooden toy sword, the same one that had begun the food fiasco the night before.

He had tied an old piece of robe around his neck, simulating a cape. "Caesar is dead," he proclaimed, flailing his pretend saber. "We have killed Caesar."

I stood up and grabbed the arm of another stranger, his eye wide and fearful. He didn't want to stop to talk. He pulled from my grasp and galloped off.

Another man, running by, turned his head and panted, "You'd better hurry. The legions will be here soon."

"Legions?"

"Yes. Do you think they're going to overlook one of their own being killed?"

"Who was killed?"

"Where have you been, man? One of the Roman soldiers is dead in the Jordan. They'll surely take revenge." Shaking his head, he scampered away.

A dead Roman soldier. I headed for the river, only a short distance, and probed the water. Downstream was a gathering of men, peering down, as if inspecting the earth. I trotted cautiously to the group, keeping a careful eye out for possible danger. In the middle of the circle, lying in a clump, was a Roman soldier, or at least, a man wearing the garments of one. I knew this legionnaire. It was Marius, his body blue, almost gray. He was very dead.

"What happened?" I queried.

"Isn't it obvious?" snapped one of the men. "He's dead."

"Murdered," said a second.

"By the Essenes," declared a third, who sounded very much like the argumentative zealot from the night before.

"You don't know that," piped another man.

I looked up from Marius' remains to see Alphaeus.

"Who else slits throats like that?" replied the zealot decisively. "Like an animal for sacrifice--ear to ear."

There was a span of silence, as each man assessed the validity of the zealot's accusation.

"I know this fellow," I said. "He's not a Roman. He's a Zealot spy." I spoke without thinking, surrounded by men who were either members or sympathizers. Three of them moved toward me, threateningly.

"Wait," said Alphaeus, stepping in between. "How do you know this?"

"I met him. Name is Marius."

"That's a Roman name!" hooted the Zealot.

"I know. He used that name and the clothes to move in and out of the Roman garrison to gain information for the rebel cause."

"You're a lying Galilean bastard." The zealot thrust his face into mine.

"Why would he lie?" said another of the men.

"Yes, zealot. Why would he lie? What is his gain?" said Alphaeus reasonably.

"To keep us here until his Roman friends can come and kill us all," said the brutish warrior. A couple of men snickered at the ludicrous image of me being allied with any Roman friends.

"Laugh if you want, but I'm clearing out of here before the local centurion shows up." The zealot lumbered away. There was a pause and the other three followed, surmising, I would assume, that even though the zealot was overwrought, he still might be right.

I was left standing with Brother Alphaeus.

"Well, good morning, friend," he said with a smile.

"Good morning," I replied, smirking over the absurdity of the greeting.

"Now to start the day," said Alphaeus. "First, get cleaned up, then, morning meal. Then dispose of the dead Roman's body. Such an exciting life, this work of God."

I laughed out loud. Alphaeus was truly a delightful man.

"What I didn't tell you, Alphaeus," I said, "is Marius was here to warn John."

"Warn John?"

"There was, or is, a plot to assassinate the Baptist."

"Oh, is that all?"

"Yes, and I know it was serious." I was shocked, and a little disappointed at his lackadaisical reaction to my report.

"My dear friend, what is your name?"

"Jesus, of Nazareth."

"Well, Jesus of Nazraeth, if everyone who wanted John dead would line up, we could stack them from here to Jerusalem."

"So you feel there's no danger?"

"I didn't say that," said Alphaeus, reaching down

Would He be man-like, or endowed with advantage?

God the cheater.

"Cheater, Cheater, Cheater! Cheaters never prosper."

Nail the imposter to a cross!

WAIT!

What if he didn't cheat? Is there a Jesus? Was he a man? *If he became the kind of man described in the Synoptic accounts, and he had to learn all those lessons to get there, then like any other flesh unit he had to experience certain discoveries to become the person he was proclaimed to be.*

A carpenter who tells no parables of carpentry. *Did he like it?*

A single man surrounded by women. *Monkified or tantalized?*

An intense man with great emotion. *Mellow or passionate?*

A cleanser of temples. *Dutiful or angry?*

A family man. *Reluctant or motivated?*

I wrote this book because I thought it might be nice to speculate on how Jesus might tell his own story based upon the events surrounding his life and who he turned out to be. Maybe you can write a better one. I shall be your first sale.

Just remember:

It is not a new Bible. *The old one is fine.*

It is not a prophecy. *I am no prophet.*

It is not religious. *I am a bawdy man, I be.*

Suspend disbelief and let the tale weave some wonder. You will receive what you carry out with a child's heart.

My protagonist phrased it this way: *Your faith will make you whole.*

Well said!

Enjoy--Behold the man!

Author's Comments

Shhh, Ahh-mane, shuffle-shuffle, rustle-rustle, ooohhmmm, swat-shhh, hal-lay-lou-yeah, mumble-mumble, cough-cough, wahh-waah, look-look, giggle-giggle, glare-glare, clap-clap, whisper-whisper, give us this, we thank you that, shh-shh, benedic-devo-sanctifica-invita-emo-TION, sneeze-sneeze, gesundheit, tick-tick, tock-tock, snore-snore, sigh-sigh, shh-shh, in closing, creak-creak, waddle-waddle, shake-shake, vroom-vroom, yawn-yawn, go-go, bye-bye, home-home, cluck-cluck, snooze-snooze, rrrring-rrring, **Monday.**

The sounds of religion; listening for more, hearing the hum of silence disguised as reverence.

A man lived, if he did.
He worked in a shop, if there was.
A man of destiny, if such exists.
Gave his life, if there was life to give.
He loved people, if they knew him.
Had the touch of healing, if an anointing flowed.
Raised the dead, if rumors can be believed.
He was tempted, if he got around.
Like us, if he was part of the gang.
Talk of God, if one can be found.
Women around, and never kissed?
Books written, no suspense.
Story told, empty pews.
Son of man, son of god.
Human life, or just a fraud?

The reason we can't hear from the horse's mouth is because the beast can't talk. We could follow it around and observe its ways. We could watch how it drinks and runs and learn of its drive and passion. After such a lesson we might not call the beast a 'beast' and it an 'it'. Who knows?

If god became a dog, would he bark and growl at strangers, poop on the carpet, and beg crumbs from the table?

God, as a worm--just good bait, or burrowing in the ground making a muddy nest?

How about God "donning the down"--a duck? Would he quack or possess the ability to appear Mandarin, but have the unfair insight to stay south all year 'round to avoid the foolish flight back and forth?

If God were a man . . . aah, now there's the test.

taxation of Jerusalem for Caesar Augustus. I was a little intimidated by her family tree, but the simplicity of her manner created a wonderful equality.

She had been injured at fourteen, while riding a horse. The animal had taken a fall and rolled over on her. Countless physicians later, she remained bed-ridden.

"I came to the Jordan to heal the crippling in my soul, not my body," she explained.

"So, have you been baptized?"

"No," she answered with some hesitancy. "I haven't. . .found the right time."

"Hmmm, you're scared."

"I am not."

"Then let's go." I stood and began to pick her up.

"Wait! I can't swim!"

"Oh really? That must be because your legs don't work."

"If we applied that logic, then you shouldn't be able to think," she replied.

"Keep in mind, I'm carrying you over water, and having no brain could damage my ability to hold on." I pretended to lose my grip.

She screeched in delight and gasped, "Ok, ok! Let's pray you have some mental capacity left!"

By this time we reached Alphaeus, watching our approach with his bemused expression. "What have we here? My fame is spread so much that they're carrying them in from everywhere. What is your name, my lady?"

"Joanna, dear brother," she said, with a fresh joy almost able to cleanse the muddy tide.

"And are you here on your own free will, or has Jesus become over-zealous?"

"Actually," Joanna replied with a side-ways look my direction, "I was just sitting on the bank minding my own business, when this tattered gentlemen told me he knew a great place to catch fish."

I groaned, and Alphaeus laughed in delight. "Well, since you're here," continued Alphaeus, with a grandfatherly tenderness, "would you like to have God fill your heart with his forgiving grace?"

The words were so warm and gentle tears sprang into my eyes.

"Oh, yes, sir, I would," Joanna gushed.

Alphaeus took her from my arms and walked a few feet deeper into the inlet. "Don't be afraid," he comforted. He gently took her under in his arms and just as gracefully surfaced.

Joanna was radiant.

"Here, Jesus," Alphaeus called to me. "You have done well. You have become a fisher of women."

I waded through the river, carrying Joanna back to her couch. I noticed a man standing with the servants, short, lean, pale, with a closely cropped beard.

Joanna clapped her hands. "Oh, Jesus, that's my husband, Chusa. I want you to meet him."

Chusa appeared distracted and skeptical. Evidently her spirited love of life was not shared by her mate. Joanna made the introductions. I was going to shake his hand, but his quick nod determined the extent of our contact.

"I see you were baptized," he spoke, feigning interest..

"It was glorious, dear," bubbled Joanna.

"Thank you for helping her, Jesus. I'm sure the servants could have done it."

"It was my joy, sir. She is a wonderful woman." I placed her on her cushions.

Chusa decided to make conversation. "What did you make of the death of the soldier?" he asked. Before I could say anything, he went on. "I just came from downstream, where the Baptist is. No one there. The shores are empty, but he's down there, preaching. No one for miles, but he's roaring anyway." He looked at me, mystified. "It's ridiculous."

I excused myself, and walked until I found a private stretch on the riverbank.

John was preaching to the wilderness.

Father, why was I here? I had absorbed this adventure at arm's length. I had wanted to observe, without being associated with the unconventional nature of the movement. I had enjoyed without joining. And now, my cousin alone, I was here with the women.

I was a coward. What, after all, was I going to take from the Jordan?

Time to decide.

The day was fading as I headed down river. Chusa was correct. There were only three old men, praying. John was in the water, pelting the vacant shore with his diatribe on repentance.

I came down into the water, within five lengths, but he didn't see me. Then, as if alerted by an angel, he turned to me. His eyes searched my features, like he was trying to remember. Then, he gazed above my head and a beam of ecstasy spread across his bearded countenance, tears ran down his cheeks. "Finally," he moaned, opening his arms to the sky. "Finally."

"I have come to be baptized." He didn't hear me. The sun was beginning to set and I shivered, feeling the loss of its warmth.

. John was muttering softly; I had to strain to hear. "He told me the one nestled by the dove would be His son. I have baptized thousands, looking for the sign.. And then. . .now. . .today. . . you." He looked directly at me for the first time, his dark, piercing eyes gleaming. "I saw the dove, and I heard his voice. He said, 'This is my beloved son, in whom I am well pleased'."

As John spoke, a shower of warm rain fell from the sky. I did not question. It was from the Father, for John, not me. It was his epiphany--a fulfilled odyssey.

"Baptize me, John."

"No. You baptize me! I need the cleansing. I'm tired. I need to be baptized by you."

I frowned. After all I had seen at the Jordan, I knew I had to be baptized by John. "Just do it, brother. It's the right time, and it's the right thing."

He gingerly waded my direction.

"And I want the full treatment. The whole leap. Don't you hold back."

He grabbed me by both arms and we leaped into the air. I felt his strength. I was a part of it, but I wasn't controlling it. I remember opening my eyes under the water and seeing the puffed cheeks and effervescent smile of my cousin, John the Baptist. We surfaced giggling.

John embraced me. I didn't feel any need for words. My heart was crying to move on, time to discover something beyond Bethabarra.

I took one last look at him. Little did I know I would never see him again. John was waist deep in the brown water, preaching, oblivious to me.

A voice crying in the wilderness, unconcerned if acclaimed, or even heard.

The wilderness.

I felt driven to go to the wilderness; my own wilderness--a spirited choice.

SITTING 28

Dinner-less Conversation

The primal misconception: at some point during a fast the hunger stops gnawing at your entrails and appetite decreases until the participant is free of discomfort. Wrong!

Fasting--suicide simulation for the more perversely religious.

My particular re-enactment had lagged on for forty days. I had lost considerable weight, felt weak, but still alive. But, and this is a most important but, I was famished. I could have eaten my robe. I did, in fact, chew on it a time or two to relieve the aching emptiness in my stomach.

I didn't start out to fast long, but had a voracious curiosity to learn more about myself; to examine my appetites and drives.

It is fruitless to undertake personal mission without first garnering inner revelation about self:

Anticipating a blessed event--*like a young woman who clings to her mother right before birthing her first child.*

Sensing a closeness--*hearing John's words echo in my heart; "This is my beloved son in whom I am well pleased."*

Considering sonship--*always called a son--Joseph, Hagabus, Xantrippe, proclaimed me the same.*

I have always known only one as my Father. My heirship is neither stimulus nor an ethereal belief in a Universal Creator.

I know God, just like I know anyone. He has entered my life.

Known to me as I am known to Him. Perhaps unique, but mortal.

Therefore attainable.

A worthy mission; to share with others His fatherhood, for creation craves intimacy with God.

John said the heavens pronounced me beloved. What if I see weakness in my cloak of humanity forbidding such a generous term? Can I still believe in confidence this Father of mine is well-pleased with me? I am not always well-pleased with myself. Yet, I have been granted favor. Many a child has destroyed body and soul in the quest for such approval.

God's son. I've always wondered.

On one hand, I have believed myself to be a son of man, birthed through the water, blood and pain of a woman's travail. . . yet more. At age five I knew in a youngster's way I was cuddled in heavenly arms. When I was twelve, and went to the Temple, and knew in a young man's way I was about my true Father's business. Each year brought a fresh, invigorating revelation.

What shall it be? Am I to become some watchful priest studying the Law of Moses until my aged, decrepit, bent form frightens the children as I hobble down the street?

Father, I don't want to be a holy man. I don't want the juices of my youth to dry up in the prison of a useless frame.

I contend it's preferable to be drained of all energy in the pursuit of a worthy whim, than to become a dusty wilderness in the acquisition of a safe, complacent peace. I don't want to be God's son if God is like the fables of Sinai; reeking of the mustiness of preserved scrolls. What joy is there in being the offspring of a rock formation? I don't want to be begotten of One who only maintains a cosmic order with no creative power to change the circumstances in the life of a hopeful searcher.

The frigid soul of religion makes me shudder in this desert heat. Father, why would you make such a dynamic world and then whittle out one small slice of holiness?

God's son.

You did not make me an angel, barren of human discovery. I am tempted as every man and only time will determine my mettle. I shall revel as a son of man. Give me the power through your Spirit to keep you well-pleased.

"Am I beloved?" I spoke aloud. "Am I your beloved Son? Does that offend you, Father? Am I too audacious?"

"God's Son? Can there be documentation for such a claim?"

Assuming I was in solitude, I had developed some oddities, like talking to myself. I was not alone. I recognized the voice. It was Mekel.

"Do you know me this time, Mekel?"

"More importantly, do you know yourself? Why would God starve his own Son? You look terrible. What kind of messenger does an emaciated son make for His Father?" He slowly emerged from the shadows.

"I needed to fast."

"I suspect you have wandered too far from reality, my friend. If you are as you say, God's Son."

"How do you know that?"

"Why, I heard you say it. Just a minute ago." He stood directly over me and continued, "Jesus, if you want a mission, I'll give you a worthy one. Think of the starving world.. What do men need? Is it bread, or. . . " He bent down and picked up a rock, thrusting it into my face, ". . . another stone?"

"What is your point?"

"Think of it! If every stone were bread, men would never feel hunger again! What do they   require, rocks or enrichment? Be the Son of God! Set the example!   Why should stones be stones when God is able? And, of course, the man with this bread will rule the planet. You are hungry. Correct the oversight of the original creation. Please your Father. You can bring balance to his order while providing the blessing of nourishment to a starving world. He is waiting for his son to lead the way. Baker, feed thyself. Can you see the logic? Don't come to a disheartened mankind claiming to be God's son with your weakened, starving body. Come strong, or don't come at all. Make use of the useless. What a message! If stones can be made into bread, then lunatics can be rendered sane! Lepers can be healed, and the blind can see! If you are God's son, as you say, change these stones to bread!"

A variation on the old drivel: *Since I have need, life should adjust to me.* "Mekel, let the stones be stones. We already have wheat. Why not just grow more? Leave the stones alone. Anyway, you can feed the body but the soul still needs every word that comes from God."

Mekel feigned a puckered pout. "I just thought you might be hungry."

"I am hungry, just not foolish enough to try to turn rock into ration."

"You will let me help?" He squatted down to get closer to me.

"I have no idea what I'm doing, Mekel, so it seems fruitless to solicit assistance."

"That's when you need the most insight, when you are just starting out. I know Jerusalem. I know the scribes and Pharisees, and the Essenes too. They're all educated men. Unfortunately, they are jaded by their own abundant learning. I know what they want. I know what would enliven their bored, religious tedium."

"Is that why you were by the fire at the Jordan?"

"The fire? Oh, you mean John, the Hairy's little escapade. Yes, in a way. I was helping them to ask the right questions. You cannot acquire meaningful answers without first formulating an articulate inquiry." His smirk exuded neither warmth nor joy.

"Evidently you did a good job of it. At least, judging by the results."

"What do you mean?"

"The people I saw coming back from the meeting had neither answers nor well-thought-out questions. They were just confused and upset."

"Confusion is the father of disruption, which is the fire burning away the chaff of fruitless labor!"

"Once again, Mekel, you sound enlightened without shedding the slightest glimmer of light."

"Might I continue?"

I chuckled. He didn't desire my blessing.

"Men demand to see the power and the glory before you can establish a new kingdom. It's all visual! How do we begin our day? We open our eyes. Nothing is begun until the eyes are enticed with a vision of earthly wonder. Listen, I know this special place at the temple, it's spectacular. It's the apex, the pinnacle of The House, visible to all. All of Jerusalem could behold a person who stood on that precipice, and God wouldn't allow his son to be hurt. Am I right?"

"Are you right about what? You have said many things. Which one do you want me to evaluate?"

"That God wouldn't hurt his son."

"If pain brings salvation, then the final result is righteous."

"You don't know God if you think he would cause you pain. If you leaped from that pinnacle, he would send angels to catch you. If you don't know that you don't know the Scriptures. This is a promise from the holy scrolls."

"Then what?"

"Then what? What do you think would happen if all Jerusalem saw you borne by a legion of angels?"

"Oh, surely I wouldn't need a legion. Two or three at the most."

"God never sends a few to do anything. It's big all the way. A legion would draw a crowd and then you could lead the people into the ways of truth. They would see the power and the glory and be open to you starting the kingdom! Don't you see? Trust me. I know religious people. You have to set them on their ear. This is fool-proof."

"Mekel, it would take a fool to try to prove anything by diving off the temple. Why would I want to test God? He's always been with me in everything. You, of all people, should know that. He even used you to pull me out of the well after the Camp of Deliverance."

Mekel was silent.

I probed further. "Remember the well, Mekel?"

"I remember the well."

"It was you who pulled me out, wasn't it?"

"I said it was."

"You're an angel, am I right?"

"Yes, and I said, you did it by yourself."

"I had help. The help was you. Do I have this straight?"

"You know the rules."

"What rules, Mekel?"

"Don't play stupid. I hate it when your people get condescending! I am allowed to deceive you as long as you play along, using your own ego and stupidity. I can't lie to a question asked from an honest heart. Of course, I'm not telling you anything you don't already know."

As a matter of fact, he had told much I didn't know. "So it wasn't you?"

"I was there . . . watching."

"But not helping?"

"Stop the act. Why would I help? If I could have destroyed you in the well we wouldn't have to be going through this shit."

His voice had changed, in tone and texture, no longer the erudite scholar, but rather a befouled renegade. I wasn't safe at home in Nazareth anymore.

A nagging uncertainty often accompanies an unsettling circum-stance, the nerve-bending, gut-wrenching realization of discovering half a worm in your half-eaten loaf of bread; the abdominal cramp twinging the nausea, bursting beads of sweat on the frantic brow--the chilling realization of being alone, and surrounded by a foreboding wilderness of unidentified creaks and swishes: exactly what I felt in the presence of the sinister Mekel.

He continued the conversation I wished to end. "My father was a Gnoshi tribesman--a nomad--the medicine man, the necromancer."

"Your father? I thought you were an angel?"

"Jesus, you suffer from the decadence of stale thinking. Why can't I be both?"

"I wasn't aware the angels procreated."

"No sex in heaven? Then why bother to leave our mortality? Do you think God can come up with something better than the pleasure of sexual delight?"

I didn't respond.

"My mother," he said, returning to his original thought, "was a Chaldean princess, adept in the Mithric art of human soul removal and transplantation of spiritual wills."

"And what does this mean to me?" I let my head fall back, closing my eyes. I slowly re-opened them.

Mekel was glaring at me, his eyes red with bloody fire. "Incarnate! You know that word, don't you, Nazarene?"

"Are we playing word games? Yes, I know it."

"To become flesh. That's what you are, right? Or at least, what you might become."

"Mekel, you strike me as a man with a tale to tell who only asks for opinions out of forced humility."

He pouted, then rose to his feet proudly. "Incarnate. That's what we both are."

"Please sit down. You're making me dizzy. I can do without your theatrics."

"Your hunger has weakened you to the point of breakdown."

"Perhaps so. But I see how silly it is to stand when you don't need to make such an effort. I'm never going to do it again if sitting is an option."

"Slothfulness! Such a distasteful trait in the son of God."

"If you just want to insult me, Mekel, I can give you better ammunition than that."

"Then you admit you're incarnate?"

"I am in the flesh. That's why I'm so hungry."

"And you are totally ignorant of me?"

"And many other things, obviously."

"How senile of Him to make the same mistake twice."

"I'm tired of this. Who is 'he' and what mistake do you feel was made?"

"You really have no knowledge of me? I, too, am incarnate, but my father has done a much better job preparing me. I have studied you, Nazarene, the way a bored child gazes at his hand on a hot summer day. You have been in my thoughts from morning till night. You have invaded my dreams. You have been the focus of my whole life."

"Are you trying to flatter me?"

Mekel's face twisted. "I wish to see you destroyed in the most humiliating and public way possible!"

"These words are not going to increase the possibility for ongoing relationship," I responded, trying to lighten the wearisome exchange. He had the vocabulary of a priest and the disposition of an ass with a boil on its backside.

"He made the same mistake with the garden couple," Mekel said incredulously, as if thinking out loud.

"You mean Adam and Eve?"

"Of course. He didn't warn them about me, either. As if I were not a threat. He always underestimates me! And now, a second time, he leaves his incarnated word oblivious, bathed in an arrogant state of unawareness. It's outrageous!"

"If you're talking about my Father, information is given as the need arises."

"You're wrong, Nazarene."

"My name is Jesus."

"That remains to be seen."

"You're like one of your own riddles, Mekel. Always twisted, leading nowhere."

"Oh, I shall not disappoint you, Incarnate."

"Then play out your rampage to some sort of conclusion, preferably in the realm of sanity."

"You don't want sanity! You want submission; an insipid surrender to the higher will. In so doing, the human intellect forfeits the opportunity to drink from the cup of knowledge."

"I see no cup," I said, raising myself to my knees, mustering a burst of energy. "Nor do I need to drink poison in order to justify some juvenile sense of discovery."

He appeared astonished at my display of renewal. I had been granted an endowment of strength. He scooted himself closer, putting his protruding nose in my face. "You remember that garden couple, Jesus? They were so enthralled with the surrounding foliage, with discovering each other-- sexually, you know--and with having chit-chats with Him, they were deadened to the greater glories! Now the woman. She knew! She was already discovering God intended her to be subordinate. She wasn't hungry. But I, I made her eat!"

"You do overestimate yourself. I was hungry, and you couldn't even whet my appetite."

"Are you being smug?" Mekel pretended to be shocked.

"I'm just observing."

"Women. They're always the cursed. So strong-minded, but weak-willed. They have such promise, but never the function to control their destinies. They always depend on others to fill them with food for their souls."

"So that's why you choose them to torture. You use the damned and cursed fellows at your resource to take their trust and desecrate their beings in rituals of evil pleasure." Women were always the victims, along with children, of every atrocity perpetrated since the beginning of time.

"I thought you were going to be a worthy adversary, Incarnate. We're back to the same old brick and mortar, spouting this nonsense of evil being embodied in the person of my father. And I guess you contend all good is encased in the essence of your begetter."

I didn't answer. Mekel was an educated beast, the worst kind.

He ranted, anew. "Man is the source of his own evil. He doesn't need any help to degrade everything decent. I am not evil--I'm knowledge. I am the schoolmaster to the student of inquiry. I am the hunger for the sweet nectar of learning. You might say I produce the unanswered questions, which cause men to eat the fruit of knowledge."

He paused and I jumped into the space. "You just don't get it, Mekel. Yours is a knowledge revealing facts without releasing the purpose behind the truth. To see the grass and fathom the breadth of its blade is not the same as languishing in a pasture and feeling the cool dew upon your skin on a springtime morn."

"Oh, I see, it's experience you crave--a carpenter chained to a bench by family loyalty and fear of the unknown. You have the audacity to speak to me of personal revelation?"

"You, Mekel, are the one who encouraged me to return to that village."

"I merely echoed the foolishness of your heart. You are bound by that shrinking world, and always will be. You may not turn stones to bread but it's not out of some sense of overcoming temptation. It's because you have the stench of complacency!" He stood to his feet again and thrust a finger in my face, nearly poking my eye. "If you're the second Adam, he's failed again. He's made someone who can curtail his appetites, but lacks the fortitude to birth a creative effort!"

Blood rushed to my head, a vicious reply forming on my lips. I paused, searching for words to strike him down. The delay was good; I began to see Mekel's ploy. He was desperately prodding, attempting to expose the fear of my own heart, that I would waste my vision through timidity. Points were due the master deceiver for cleverness. But praise was due to my Father for granting me wisdom in my hour of need.

I drew a breath of deep consideration before I spoke. "As always we must play it out one day at a time. Tomorrow offers no provision, unless you arrive early to run the race."

"We aren't much different. Another place, brothers."

"Now you're resorting to insult."

"Don't trivialize genius. Your father created knowledge, but mine reveled in it. Isn't that praise? Your father made man, and mine exposed the flaws. Isn't that loyalty? Your father created the need for God and mine created   religions. Why isn't that seen as an act of faithfulness?" He stopped, heaving an exasperated sigh. "We have an opportunity here, my brother, both incarnate sons. Why can't we, the next generation, resolve this feud? Our fathers were bound by their allegiance and trapped by stubborn wills. But you and I, we can stop the pain; soothe the turmoil in men's souls--the battle between personal identity and alignment with the will of God."

"You really believe you are Satan's incarnation?"

"When your creator put the star in the sky and those stooges from the East spoke to Herod, it became necessary to have another incarnation. My father felt the need for equality. I was born two years to the night after you were regurgitated in that filthy stable."

I was stunned. Mekel had made contradictory statements about his origins. This one contained some truth. How, otherwise, would he have known about the circumstances of my birth? "You seem so much older than me."

"You mistake maturity for age. Who do you think Jerusalem is going to listen to, a scholarly man with a priestly bearing, or a splotchy, two-toned, back-woods Galilean?"

He had a talent for accentuating my negatives. "I guess we'll just have to pray people listen to their hearts."

"As I said, there's no need. I'm willing to worship you. See?" He knelt at my feet. "I believe in you. Didn't I call you God's son?"

"Not really. You challenged my authority to presume such a relationship."

"Isn't it worship you want? Isn't that the whole thing? My father was cast down because he yearned for appreciation. Your father wanted it all. Believe me, they both would be glad if we resolved this thing here and now. Yours wants all the glory and mine is sick of having all evil blamed on him. I'll agree to worship you, and I'll lay all the kingdoms of the world at your feet, if you'll . . ." A clumsy pause.

"What, Mekel? You're not at a loss for words are you?"

I stood up, which demonstrated, to me at least, I was being empowered from on high. I burst forth with renewed confidence. "Speak up, man! What do I have to do to bring about this unity?"

He shivered, reaching his trembling hand toward me, fingertips quivering. "There must be a joining. I believe in you. You just have to believe in me. All we ask is you kneel and acknowledge the beauty of Lucifer--the Angel of Illumination, and the need for him to be returned to his rightful position in heaven. Kneel before me and send a message to every heart that there is forgiveness at your father's throne. This will make you, Jesus, the salvation of all creature's souls. All kingdoms shall be yours forever. Just kneel, and admit the punishment administered was too harsh, delivered by an over-wrought God against a trusted angel, who only made the mistake of believing in his own worth."

Remarkable. He was weeping, frothing at the mouth- -a veritable madman.

I had a flitting moment's pity, quickly replaced by righteous indignation over the atrocities this alleged incarnate and father had placed on the hearts and lives of all mankind. "Get out of here, you freak and pernicious bastard. I'm not going to worship you. I'm going to worship God, and him alone, until he shows me how to be Jesus to all people."

Mekel leaped to his feet, howling. "Once again cast to earth! It's not over, you Nazarene! I'm not defeated! I've just sampled the same treatment at the hands of the son my father suffered from your Tyrant!"

"Get out!" I shrieked

"I'm going! But only for a season . . . you'll see me again."

I closed my eyes until I knew he was gone. I stumbled back to my resting rock, lowering myself to a seated position, and leaned my head back, closing my eyes. My heart was racing. My eyes fluttered open and widened. There were three men standing over me in white robes.

"Not again. Are you angels, too? "

"That sounds fine," replied one with a chuckle.

"Am I dead?"

"No, I don't think so. Are you hungry?"

"I just had another so-called angel ask me the same thing."

"Yes, but did he bring bread?" He proffered a fragrant, golden circle of loaf.

"He might have gotten a little further if he had," I said, taking the bread in my hands. I inhaled the warm, rich aroma, and looked up at the three visitors. I didn't question my good fortune.

The angels came and ministered to me.

SITTING 29

And So It Begins

Twenty Sabbaths and a day, though it seemed longer.

She was lovely.

She was radiant with a glow of expectation.

Her eyes darted back and forth between the floor and my throat, as she aspired to look me in the eye, timidity inhibiting such a bold maneuver.

She was the young lady to be my betrothed. Mary had convinced her to come along to Cana; my latest journeys might have rallied some reason into my shortsighted bachelorhood--Mary thinking.

She stood patiently, waiting for my greeting. What should I say to a perfectly wonderful woman who was more than willing to be my life partner, and I am about to make groom-less? Your worst enemy wouldn't place you in the middle of such a mess. It takes family to mastermind the more embarrassing scenarios in our lives.

I certainly didn't need the pressure. My thoughts should be on my brother James. After all, it is his wedding that brought me to Cana of Galilee. He already felt I had stolen focus from his life. I didn't need to be the center of attention on the day he took a wife and started his new family.

Meanwhile, back to the damsel in waiting.

She smiled at me.

I smiled back. "Hello, I'm Jesus," I said with all the grace of a wind storm on the Sea of Galilee.

"I know," she said in a whispery breathiness, capable of weakening the knees of any rational man.

"I'm sorry about the wedding. My mother should not have interfered."

"So, you don't want me?"

What was the appropriate response to that question?

"I'm sorry. You are beautiful, but I have made other plans."

I frowned at myself. Other plans? What did that mean? What a horrible job my mouth did trying to translate my heart.

"There is another woman?"

"No, actually, these are my companions," I said, pointing to the five men who had decided to come with me to the feast. They were comrades I had picked up along the way. There was Philip and Andrew, who had been with the Baptizer. Then there was Nathaniel, Philip's friend. A guy named Thomas had appeared, and attached himself to our troop. Also Andrew's brother, Simon, had relented to join us, definitely there for the free eats.

"So you like men better than women?"

I peered at the conglomeration of aromatic male specimens, and realized how odd our entourage must appear. I obviously had confused the girl. "No, women are wonderful. It's just that . . ."

"Were you always so skinny?" she interrupted, playfully poking at my ribs.

I had lost weight in the wilderness. When Mary saw me she didn't know whether to hug me or stuff me with bread. I had tried to pick up some of my lost girth the last week or so, but ended up getting sick trying to break the fast too quickly. "I was on a fast," I explained.

"Oh, did somebody die?"

"No, just an average fast, I guess."

"So, you will not share my bed."

You had to admire her directness, charming in its alarming way. "You are better off. I am a weird sleeper. I get up a lot in the night. I think I even snore."

"There are things to do in a bed that might keep you there all night," she said with a mischievous grin.

"So I hear," I gulped, mouth devoid of fluid.

"It's never too late," she said, inching her way to my side.

"You will make some man a beautiful bride."

"Some man who is not Jesus, right?" She planted her foot and jerked her hip.

"Excuse me, miss, this man is going to be Israel's next great prophet," inserted Philip from over my shoulder.

Interruption helpful, content lousy.

"Prophet?" she screeched.

"Is this going to be religious, Andrew?" asked Simon from across the room. "You told me it was food and wine, as much as I could handle."

"Alright, Simon. So now you know. Jesus is the lamb of God, too. Now are you happy? You know everything," said Andrew, huffing from the other side.

"Lamb of God?" gasped the perplexed maiden.

"I doubt if we can advertise him as a lamb and get any men to listen to him," said Thomas matter-of-factly, from yet another corner of the abode.

.   "I think you are all nuts," said the logical and lovely lady, pulling away.

"No, no," I said. "You just caught us in a bit of disarray." I reached for her hand. She pivoted and scurried away.

"Wait," I called after her.

"Don't worry, old man," said Simon, slapping my back. "There's lots of food and drink to take your mind off lost love."

"She's not my love."

"If you are the lamb, then she would be your ewe," observed Nathaniel thoughtfully.

"No, he would be his own you," chimed in Thomas, attempting to sort out the meaning.

"No, dear brother, not 'you' like you the person. It's 'ewe' as in female sheep," explained Andrew meticulously.

"I don't like sheep," blurted Simon.

"If you get them in the right sauce you might change your mind," jabbed Philip.

They all burst out laughing, causing the whole house and outside pavilion to fall silent and turn in unison to stare our direction.

"What's wrong? They never heard laughter?" roared Simon, glaring at the quieted gathering.

"Make an announcement," said Thomas, turning to me.

"Yeah, tell them you are a prophet," said Nathaniel, nudging me forward.

We had achieved the focus of the entire assemblage.

.

"This is Jesus of Nazareth," announced Andrew, lifting a cup of wine. "Listen to him talk. He really knows his stuff. Go ahead, Master."

I was trapped; the guests awaited my wisdom. I quickly took the cup from Andrew and lifted it above my head, proclaiming, "To the bridegroom!"

A brief pause, followed by a resounding cheer.

"Beautiful words," slurred Simon, patting my shoulder.

"Please excuse me," I said, thrusting the cup into his hand and hurrying away.

"Can we eat now?" shouted Simon to my retreating back.

I didn't exactly know where I was going, so many disasters to address.   Enroute my arm was grabbed and I was tugged to the side.

It was Mary. "Can I speak with you?"

"I should see . . ."

"She will be fine. I need to see you."

"Of course, Mary." She motioned towards a private place to the side.

When we were alone she continued,   "I saw what you did with Simon."

"Oh, he is just a fisherman. He will learn."

"No, Simon your brother."

My mind went blank. She apparently recognized the dull expression, so she clarified. "You know you healed him. He arose the next morning whole and has been fine ever since."

My mind flashed back to that last night in Nazareth by the bedside of Simon while I talked to my Father. I remembered hearing a noise. It had been Mary, she had heard it all.

"I'm glad," I said.

"Me too. It is a great gift. Not one that should be hidden. Do you remember when you were a boy and you would have a present for Papa and me, and would hide it under that basket in the room?"

"I remember. You knew? Did you peek?"

"No, but it was a most ingenious hiding place. It could not be seen. But this gift you have needs to be brought out from under the basket and shown to all." She pointed an aging finger at my nose.

"When the gift is completed and it is time to display its wonder, I will know," I said, squeezing the finger and giving it a soft kiss.

"James needs your help."

"What does James need?"

"Not just James. Everybody here. It is time for you to give your gift to the bridegroom. They have run out of wine. The local winesman has depleted his supply. He failed to tell us he was running low. Do something. Now is the hour."

"Woman, what is this to you? Would my Father have me known as the provider of food and drink for parties? This is not the time and place. I have come to honor my brother in his day, not to trivialize God's presence in my life." I was not trying to be abusive or bruise her feelings.

Her wince transposed into a patient smile; she had counted the cost and was prepared for rejection. She toddled off, stopping briefly to speak to a servant.

I was left alone in my quandary. She loved to do that; disrupt my life by presenting contrary views, then bustle away, leaving me with the perplexity. I looked around at the festivity: my new colleagues feasting in their own realm of gluttony--my brother James sitting next to his wife, grinning from ear to ear. He was quite a man. There was Simon, my healed little brother. Ruth and Elizabeth scurrying, giggling at the attempted jokes by would-be suitors. The moment was rich with emotion; the kind of transforming mere happenings into lasting memories. I had learned so much since I last saw this family. My battles with my own appetites in the desert had served to enliven my senses instead of turning me cold and dead to life. It was time to decide what kind of man Jesus of Nazareth would be. I certainly did not want to become some agitated scribe, disdainful of the happiness of others. I wanted to bless James. This was my heart. The gift just needed to have purpose, and not be the whim of an over-promoting mother.

If God wanted wine, then God must provide the creative energy to spill the blessing. So, Father, do you want me to bring wine to this celebration? Should an outpouring of wine be the first evidence you are with me and want to bless your people? Am I to be a son who brings festivity to the mix of humanity? What am I saying? You love to see your children happy, enriched and expansive. You stand at the edge of the marriage bed and applaud the ecstasy. Heaven paints the portrait of pleasure and hell distorts the image.

I took a deep breath and spoke aloud. "Yes, we will add our blessing to this remarkable moment."

Nearby were some huge pots which earlier had been filled with water for cleaning the feet and legs of arriving guests. Now these same containers sat empty, to the side. Each pot was large enough, if filled, to provide wine for all the celebrants. I had an idea, an ingenious notion.

I beckoned one of the servants, an older man with a boyish glint in his eye forewarning of mischief.

"The lady told me you might summon me," he said with a grin.

"The lady?"

"She is your mother, is that correct?"

"Mary? Yes, she is my mother."

"She told me to do whatever you say. I am prepared for anything," he said as he simulated a soldier's rigid attention.

"And what if I choose to do nothing?"

"Then I will be most disappointed. I was looking forward to someone livening up this droll gathering."

"So you feel the need to be busy?"

"Oh, no, sir. Busy is what I avoid. I often appear to be, so I don't have to do."

"I stand corrected. Perhaps it would be better stated, do you want to put some spice in this wedding pot?"

"Oh, yes. There are so few joys for the slave. Chief among them is disrupting the complacency of your master."

"Take those waterpots over there."

"All six?"

"Yes, why not? All six."

"You know they are purification vessels."

"You mean it is where the people wash their feet so they don't stink."

"Quite so, and much more accurate, my Lord," he replied, relieved of his ceremonious attitude.

"Go fill them with water."

"Easy enough."

"Then draw a cup and take it to your headmaster."

His brow twitched and his countenance grew somber, squinting at the pot, then back at me. "I know my master is well drunken, but not so rattled as to mistake water for wine."

"I thought you were to do as I said?" I picked at him with a teasing tone.

"Not if doing what you say will cost my head."

"Then we must pray this water will possess a blessed fermentation to become wine before it reaches the governor's lips."

He looked deeply into my eyes, trying to ascertain the depth of my motive and the breadth of my sanity. "Shall I say it is from you as a gift to his highness?" he said with a bow and a twinkle.

"Playing it safe, my friend?"

"Giving honor where it is due."

"And responsibility where it should fall, right? No," I continued, putting my arm around the old provider, "let the miracle speak for itself. Just present the drink and allow the master to provide the insight."

"Very well. I shall not tell him the source of the offering or inform him from which vessel it came." Another bow and he was off on his business.

"What's going on?" enquired Andrew, passing by just then.

"Just contributing my bit to the celebration."

True to his word the servant told no one of the source of the newly-found wine. True to His word God squeezed a blessing that astounded and delighted the bleary-eyed governor of the feast.

My brother James found me alone in a room.

"All is well, little brother?" I probed.

"The governor says it is the best wine he has ever tasted," said James with glee.

"It is a gift to the bridegroom and his exhorters from my Father."

"There is so much! There is enough for four villages. Mama said it was you."

"Interesting. Actually, it was a group effort. There was a child-like servant draped in old man's skin, some willing wet, Mary's persistence, my remembrance and love for a departed carpenter, and the Father's desire to amen the joyous revelry of your wedding." I embraced my brother and friend.

"I didn't think you would come."

"Well, I did have a devil of a time getting here," I inserted with a laugh, "but I needed a place to break my fast, and where better than at a feast?"

Precious, nervous, heartfelt, clumsy, pure, sweet stalling. Our souls drank deeply of the pensive tenderness.

No more words.

Two short embraces, one prolonged look into each other's eyes, a mutual sense of knowing, and James was gone to his bride. I stood alone in the room, hearing an occasional shriek of delight as one of the invited guests became aware there was wine for all the hosts of Galilee in the confines of one sun-baked home.

I lifted my eyes to the ceiling. "Father, you did good today." Tears came to my eyes. I heard my heart whisper a gentle reassurance to my bewildered mind. "And so did you, my son." I was satisfied. I needed nothing else. I had encouragement to sustain me until my next defeat.

A gushing Mary entered my place of solitude, agog with "Mama-ly" gratitude, repressed only by the need for propriety. "Thank you, it means so much."

"My Father's wish."

"I know you did not do it for me."

I took her hand. "Miracles are just like the breath in your body. They are granted to maintain the beauty of life. Remove them and the flesh decays. Release them at the right instant and we are overwhelmed with newness."

"Now I have a present for you." I never knew what to expect from Mary's presents. "They came from the East, to Bethlehem," she began.

I nodded, waiting for her to establish some meaning to the statement.

"They brought frankincense. The gift was stolen by the zealot in the desert. They brought myrrh, most of which I used at the oasis for your Papa's wound. And they brought this." She held aloft an ornate wooden box with images and symbols carved on the side, trimmed in glistening gold.

"What is it?" I asked, for the container didn't seem to fit into the humble surroundings nor in the hands of the simple woman displaying it.

"It is gold from the star-gazers of the East. They brought it for you. I have saved it. I'm sorry we had to use some of the contents to take care of you and the family a few times."

I stared, agape.

"It's for you," she insisted. "I was saving it for your wedding day. But since that's not going to happen--at least not now--I thought you might fund your journeys with it." While she talked I was lost in a memory over thirty years old, when wise travelers came to a tiny village and brought presents to a child born beneath a star. This, truly, was a blessing which had waited many years to find destination.

"Thank you, Mama," I said softly.

Mary, seeing I was overcome by the gesture, left the room and me to my thoughts.

I considered Santere and his seekers, and was infinitely grateful there were those who existed in this world able to perceive heavenly purposes. "Thank you, dear souls from the East," I spoke aloud through my tears. "Thank you for not being blind to a star's beauty, nor deaf to its silent call."

I considered Santere and his seekers, and was infinitely grateful there were those who existed in this world able to perceive heavenly purposes. "Thank you, dear souls from the East," I spoke aloud through my tears. "Thank you for not being blind to a star's beauty, nor deaf to its silent call."

****

Departing the next morning, we discovered the servants had not managed to keep secret the source of the wine. I couldn't blame them. Everyone likes to embellish their portion of a winning effort.

When we stepped into the morning air, we were surrounded by gawking expectant fellows, each carrying a flask of water, hoping I would recreate the wine bestowal for their own consumption. Where was yesterday's overflow, I wondered?

Mary and the rest of my family traveled with us. My new found friends and I decided to make Capernaum our next stop, the home of Andrew and his always-ravenous brother, Simon. Both of them were anxious to get home to their father, Jona, and the sweet smell of the catch. The other three gentlemen just followed along. I suspected they were hoping I would change guppies into whales at the Sea of Galilee.

We all stayed at Andrew and Simon's home for a few days. I was very pleased to meet their father, Jona, and his sea-faring buddy, Zebedee. They were the same belligerent couple I had encountered before my abduction. I was a little surprised they didn't recognize me, but remembered they were rather involved in drink.

I had a wonderful three days enjoying my family. I spent most of my time toting baby Joseph. His resemblance to Papa was comical. He even had his smile; a half-moon of lip which threatened to turn downward with any provocation.

. After a few days it was time to leave. I wanted to go to Jerusalem for Passover. I needed to be there. Also Simon and Andrew's house was overrun by curiosity seekers, most carrying some sort of container of water in great expectation of a holy sign of some fine wine. In addition, members of the wedding party had brought some of the Cana fruit of the vine to Capernaum, and were selling it, claiming it had supernatural healing properties; even reports of miraculous transformations taking place.

"Drink the Cana heavenly flow and you will be made whole," they would advertise to the awe-struck Capernaum folk.

Nathaniel confronted one of the sellers and attempted to expose the charlatan. "This wine is from foot-washing water," he presented, hoping to startle the crowds. Unfortunately, he was followed back to our camp, so we were surrounded by even more water-toters.

I compared this scene with John's ministry at Bethabarra. He, encompassed by the repentant, and I, pursued by winebibbers.

We left the next morning before daylight. The family returned to Nazareth and I journeyed to the headquarters of Judaism.

****

Something was wrong with me. All the way to Jerusalem, I battled depression. I was bound for the City of David and Passover, with its yearly promise of atonement and forgiveness. Still, my heart was full of anguish and doubt. I tried to lighten my mood by talking and laughing with my companions, but as soon as I was alone the sense of dread returned. I even cursed a fig tree along the way because it didn't have fruit. Of course it wasn't the right season, but that didn't stop my little temper flare.

I stayed in prayer all night to purge my soul of the gloom--no avail.

Arriving in Jerusalem, I was shocked. This was not a House of God; a marketplace for the greedy. The temple was riddled with corruption and the ceremonies stank of religious bondage. Nowhere could I find the 'fatherhood' amongst the abstract worship to the "most high". The practice of animal sacrifice was bigoted, favoring those of certain nationalities and skin color.

This was not my Father's house. I scoured the proceedings for a portion of purpose in the midst of the pernicious pandering. The temple rulers were nothing but merchants, bartering and haggling, marketing a nationalistic god-head.

It made me sick. I stood watching the chicanery until I couldn't tolerate it any more. I rushed into the courtyard, running from wall to wall, turning over tables and scattering the money on the ground. Grabbing a rope from a nearby donkey, I whipped the oppressors.

I was furious. "Get this all out of here!" I shouted hoarsely. "You're selling God to the highest bidder. This should be a house of prayer! You have made it a sanctuary for robbers!"

I was a man possessed. Yet, in a sense, my actions seemed apart from my own bidding, as if I stood back and watched myself explode with emotion. I certainly hadn't planned the outburst. I was unacquainted with this temple purger, in awe of this Jesus. I watched in fascination at the ferocity of this newly emerging being. This was not the man who had deliberated and delayed turning water to wine. I beheld a manic zeal quite unknown to me. If I were wrecking havoc on the temple as a mortal act of self-righteousness, it was sacrilege. Still, if I believed I was acting as the arm of God, the implications were mind boggling to say the least.

I (or he), finally finished the cleansing ritual. The last dove fluttered away, and the moneychangers, smarting from smacks, scurried to safety.

People were petrified, standing as fleshy statues, staring at my panting presence.

A timid voice floated from the back. "Tell us by what authority you do this."

A deeper voice, more boldly, chimed in, "Give us a sign."

"I'll give you a sign," I said, angry they couldn't see what was so obvious to my eyes. "This temple will be destroyed, but in three days I will raise it up."

A grandiose declaration initially received in silence.

Then someone giggled. Soon the whole courtyard was swept by a wave of laughter--the perfect time for me to slip away and get this raving Jesus out of there so I could figure out why he was beginning to act without my permission.

. The five of us were camping on the outskirts of Jerusalem. Simon was not with us. He had stayed in Capernaum to pursue his trade.

Tension. When Philip and I reached for a loaf of bread at the same time, he jerked his hand back in fright. I shook my head, smiling. There was no way I could explain the scene at the temple. What was the motive?

"Well, another exciting day." Andrew was the one who broke the silence.

"What did you think?" I asked the small gathering of men.

Nobody responded, all hoping I would shed some light on the day's activity.

"Well, let me tell you my feelings," I finally said slowly.

"Please do," Andrew said gratefully.

Nathaniel nodded vigorously.

"I think. . ."

They leaned forward, hanging on my every word,

"I think . . ."

They were eagerly awaiting my insight.

"I think we should avoid the temple for awhile." I jabbed a piece of bread into my mouth and grinned at them. They all gazed, bewildered.

"Now, Master," said Thomas. "Can you tear the temple down and build it back in three days? I really doubt that."

Andrew punched Thomas in the arm. "If Jesus said he can do it, he can do it."

"Why would anyone want to destroy the temple?" queried Nathaniel.

"I guess to build it back in three days," responded Philip, logically.

Again they waited for me to offer an explanation about my statement. I didn't know what the phrase meant. Words come from different territories in a man. Sometimes they come from the heart, full of heat and fire. Sometimes from the mind, tapping   all available wisdom.   But sometimes they come from the spirit--uncharted, secretive, ethereal regions.

"What did you mean, Master?" Nathaniel possessed an inquisitive nature, free of cynical guile.

I looked at him. We were interrupted by rustling footsteps.

"They're coming to get us!" cried Andrew. "I should have stayed with the nets!"

"Don't be frightened," said a gentle voice, "just an old Pharisee on the prowl."

Standing in the firelight was Nicodemus, the brother of Hagabus. I rose to greet him, then dismissed my companions. Nicodemus didn't recognize me, our earlier meeting many scars ago.

"If you need help, scream," whispered Thomas as he prepared to leave.

"Scream?"

"You know, in a manly way."

Nicodemus was a man who pondered, which is a few unspoken questions away from a searcher. He gathered information. never positive   he was receiving, or had arbitrarily rejected the ideas. He quietly absorbed.

He liked to talk about God.

I talked about the Father.

He wanted to exchange compliments.

I revealed human need.

He wanted decisive ideas.

I spoke in parables.

His main purpose, I think, was to incorporate me into the existing fold; an independent representative of the temple law keepers.

I chose to remain autonomous.

An intense conversation, leaving both of us unchanged.

I wanted to ask about Madez, but decided it was not the time for personal chatter, which is one of the reasons the discourse was a failure. Nothing personal, nothing lasting.

Nicodemus left, still in need of rebirth. I went to sleep, wondering what was happening with Hagabus and my little family in Nazareth.

I'd had enough of Jerusalem. I wanted to go back to the warmth of tender friends.

Thus ended my first adult excursion to the City of David. I would come again.

The next time I would be better prepared.

And so, of course, would the

SITTING 30
Profiting With No Honor

Could there be anything as soul-settling as experiencing a night of blissful sleep in the bed of your youth, nestled securely within the walls of your family home?

Two nights in the Joseph-the-Carpenter house rejuvenated my heart. I was completely exhausted from my harried lifestyle, a busied course, often tempting me to become the predictable frantic soul.

Jerusalem and the temple scene, a constant influx of new traveling companions, the discourse with Nicodemus-- all just an appetizer for the full banquet of activity which lay ahead.

Leaving Jerusalem, I stopped at the Jordan and decided to indulge in a season of baptisms. In addition to the spiritual significance and symbolism, the water was invigorating during the summer heat. I let the other men do the dunking, while I cooled in the stream, enjoying the spectacle and delights of the baptized, in no hurry. It just seemed right to continue my work near John's creek for the repentant, adopting my cousin's catch-phrase: "Repent, for the Kingdom of Heaven is at hand."

The people flocked to the river. I taught, and seized the opportunity to touch their lives with healing. I could have stayed forever. But the pompous gained notice of our efforts, so alas, it was time to leave the Jordan. Two prophets on the same river hatched a fretful predicament for the religious hierarchy out there peddling the status quo. I surrendered the flow to my cousin.

I needed to go through Samaria. As I stated earlier, in my upbringing, Samaritans were considered to be worse dogs than Gentiles. So it was time to challenge another piece of my inherited bigotry.

My fellow travelers, about twenty-five in all, were perturbed with my touring plans, not wishing to revise or even question their views on this hated race. I remained true to my itinerary.

Samaria was magnificent, thanks to the efforts of a feisty woman I met at a well in Sychar; kind of lady people relished criticizing until she came into the room, then, intimidated by her persona, they hushed their gossip, and bowed for her to speak. She was the catalyst for God's miracle. Still, the transition from hatred and prejudice to human communion is always most delicate, fostering the true meaning of the phrase 'awkward exchange'.

As my entourage discovered Samaritans really didn't belch demons, a giddiness permeated the scene. We were all grossly embarrassed over years of anger. Comical how Samaritan and Jew became overly-talkative, to the point of silliness, trying to compensate for years of stern, unyielding silence.

Samaria was beautiful--an interval, in the space of a movement, never to be taken for granted or foolishly imitated.

While in Samaria, I received news of John's imprisonment The Baptist had caved into pressure from the Essenes to sermonize against the atrocities of Herod, alias the fox.   When Herod entered into a relationship with Herodias, one rumored to be adulterous, John fired off verbal barbs within the earshot of palace loyalists; ill-advised.   I wish I could have counseled and warned him. Politics by its crude nature will embrace the acceptable organized religion, while hastening to dispose of pesky, non-conformist prophets. I prayed for him.

It was then I decided to return to Nazareth, homesick for family, wanting to talk with Hagabus, share my life and fresh mission with the village of my youth, and rest, becoming invisible for a day or two.

Relaxation. It reminded me of the message of a Levite, extolling the virtue of 'tireless effort'. I chuckled when I heard his words. Everybody knows there is no such thing as a tireless effort. Everything worthwhile brings the ache of fatigue no matter how divine the calling or miraculous the conclusion. True success is discovering the path that still fulfills even when exhaustion has depleted our desire.

I needed replenished having endured such emptiness during days when I touched the bodies of human sufferers until my hands seeped blood from my raw, irritated skin. I wanted to give up and be normal but purpose raced forward to reinforce passion; determination energized my fainting spirit of willingness.

Welcome, Jesus, to Nazareth--nothing to accomplish, little to do, and much to be gained enjoying the commonplace.

I slept, dreaming I was flying over my home village. It was evening and there was a slight chill in the air, the kind of cool clearing the mind for an excursion in memories. I soared, looking down on the candle-lit houses-- a city on a hill, unhidden.   Though the village seemed minuscule compared to the vast array of stars above, it still shone forth; a single candle from each house. As I climbed higher the town grew distant and dim. Was I too high to see, or had it lost the glimmer of its glory?

I descended to regain my perspective; recapture the glistening vision.

Voices. Were they coming from people in the village below? The mumblings were not from the dream, but rather my brother and sister, Jude and Ruth, arguing in harsh but muffled tones.

"How long is he going to stay this time?" whispered Ruth.

"I don't know," answered Jude flatly.

"I can't take this anymore. I am getting older and still have no children."

(enter James)

James: That's not Jesus' fault.

Ruth: If he would have been here more often I wouldn't have needed to help Mama so much.

(enter Elizabeth)

Elizabeth:Well, you aren't the only one unmarried.

Ruth: I know. We both have practically raised little Joseph.

Elizabeth:I don't know what we would do without him.

James: Who are we talking about?

Ruth: Little Joseph. Please keep up.

Elizabeth: James, Little Joseph gives Ruth and I a sense of mothering that keeps our sanity in this pressure to perform family duty.

(enter Simon)

Simon: You are being your usual dramatic self.

Well, now all the family was involved in the early morning dis-cussion. Everybody except Mary, Little Joseph and James' wife.

Ruth: What is he doing with his life?

James: He is called of God.

They were trying to maintain a silent discussion, but the volume was increasing, if for no other reason than the mass of numbers.

Simon: Why not be a priest? Hagabus could use the help.

Ruth: Why not anything normal?

Elizabeth: Normal isn't that great.

Jude: I love him. I just wish he wasn't so weird.

Elizabeth: He's not weird.

Simon: Have you heard some of the things he has done?

James: No, what do you know about this?

Simon: I just talked to Hagabus.

Jude: Me, too.

Elizabeth: Are you guys talking about that guy, Veshioli?

I perked my ears--a new name.

Simon: Yes, from Jerusalem. I think he is a Pharisee. Well, anyway, he has been commissioned by the San Hedrin to follow Jesus.

James: What? A spy?

Ruth: No, an information gatherer.

Elizabeth: Sounds like a snake to me.

Jude: Anyway, go on, Simon.

James: I don't know if I want to hear this gossip.

Ruth: He is a religious guy. Why would he lie?

Simon: Anyway, listen if you want, or close your mind. This Veshioli said Jesus vandalized the temple and threatened to tear it down.

Jude: How would he tear it down?

Simon: I don't know. He also said Jesus was in Samaria sacrificing baby goats to pagan gods and dancing with loose women.

Elizabeth: And you believe this?

(enter Mother Mary)

Mary: Yes, Simon, answer the question.

Simon: Good morning, Mama.

Ruth: Why would he lie?

Mary: Why would he tell the truth?

Simon: I am just tired of all the uncertainty.

Elizabeth: We all are.

Jude: I don't like being the brother of the town freak.

James: Jesus is not a freak.

Mary: No, he isn't.

Jude: Of course, a freak in Nazareth is anyone who doesn't do what is expected of him.

I was eavesdropping to hear the heart of my own family. Jude was right. I was guilty of being the freak show in my own town. I couldn't decide whether to remain silent or enter the room and share a thought or two. What would be my motive? If they felt they could open up to me they would have done so. They needed their secret opinions to remain private. After all, candor is a virtue of the Divine, only tolerated by the natural man. This conversation was not meant for my ears, certainly not for my input. The drama continued.

Mary: It is a family thing.

Gone was any attempt to maintain metered tones. Each family member was now in full voice, concluding I was either deaf or my feelings were secondary to their compulsion to express.

James: Mama, what do you mean by a family thing?
Mary: I mean when the time comes we will do all things as a family. We will deal with Jesus as family. If he needs assistance in any way, we will give it. We will certainly encourage him to settle in among us and join our daily efforts. If we discover he needs our help in other ways. . .
Elizabeth: Other ways?
Simon: You mean if he is crazy?
James: Jesus is not crazy. Have you all forgotten the water to wine and those wonderful days in Capernaum with him?
Ruth: No one has forgotten.
Jude: That was then, this is now.
Simon: What does that mean?
Elizabeth: Are you saying you can be a miracle man in Cana and a crazy man in Nazareth?
Mary: Calm down, children. Jesus will hear.
       Too late. I was hearing. I was not angry. I felt like a man gazing at his own reflection in a pool of water, discovering the extent of his ugliness.
Mary: What I mean is, if Jesus is having some difficulty adjusting to Jewish life in a small town, we must bond as a family and protect him from the onslaught of criticism. He has had a most tumultuous life, filled with twisted paths. Perhaps he is confused. I am not sure. But he is still family.
Elizabeth: What if he is not confused? What if he is right and we are wrong? What if his ideas of life are ripe with God, while our ways are rotting, meaningless pursuits?
Ruth: What are you getting at, Elizabeth?
Simon: Are you asking if I could go his way?
James: Wouldn't that be something? If we all ended up following him?
Jude: Do you think we are going to change our minds?
Simon: Maybe, end up writing about him?
       (Simon giggled, stimulating the lot of them)
Mary: Whatever we do later will be affected by what we do now. We must prepare for Sabbath. Let us eat, love each other, and remember to include big brother in everything we do.

The End

The drama was over and it was time to exit before they discovered me. I climbed out of a window and headed to see an old priest who might shed some light on this visit by a Judean Pharisee named Veshioli.

****

I descended the stony path to the small cave-like abode of Nazareth's resident priest. How many times had I made this journey? How many nights as a boy did I meander my way to the door of my scholarly sparring partner? Now, coming as a man to discuss very adult matters.

I paused at the entrance. Hagabus was speaking, giving his austere discourse about Sabbath etiquette. I peeked though a crack in the robe covering the entrance to see a small boy, about ten years old, standing petrified, shaking, listening to a warning, packaged in a rebuke, cushioned with some fatherly compassion.

"God likes his house to be clean, my son," crackled the priest. "Dust is for the grave, not the altar."

"Don't worry, little Samuel," I comforted, entering the room. "Master Hagabus growls like a bear, but has never eaten a child yet."

"Jesus!" He ran into my arms. We embraced and I kissed his forehead. "Jesus is here, Master Hagabus."

"Master Jesus, little Samuel," corrected the priest.

"Right, father," he apologized, and continued excitedly, "May I run and tell the others that Master Jesus will join us for Sabbath?"

"Yes, you may," I provided.

"Jesus will read for us today," added Hagabus.

The boy gave a cheer and ran out the opening, pumping as much speed as his little legs could propel. I clapped my hands and laughed, totally absorbed by his infectious enthusiasm.

"The children love you, Jesus," noted Hagabus, busying himself.

"They are the only piece of the Garden of Eden we retain," I presented.

Hagabus scratched his beard and studied me for a moment. "Ah, because of their innocence," he assented, suddenly discovering my mean-ing.

"That, and how unashamed they are of their own nakedness," I poked at him playfully.

"That's because they have no wrinkle or blemish to hide," he grunted over his shoulder.

I had caught the rabbi in good spirits. "Veshioli." I said nothing more, careful to convey curiosity, free of incrimination. I wanted an honest answer without small-town priestly diplomacy. Hagabus didn't respond so I said it again. "Veshioli."

He stopped organizing and turned toward me, struggling to look into my eyes, speaking slowly, labored, "I do not know the man. He came late last week before Sabbath, with letters of introduction from Malchus, a servant of Caiaphas in Jerusalem." He hesitated, perhaps weighing the wisdom of further disclosure.

"So now I know where he came from. Why is he here?"

"He was here about you. I would assume to inform us . . ."

"Or warn. Isn't that more accurate, Hagabus?"

"I received his words more as opinions than warnings."

"So, what opinions did you hear from this spy?"

"He feels you are dangerous. Taken some of your words and actions out of context and is levying charges against you. I admonish you, Jesus. These men are experts at the turn of a phrase. If they so desired, they could make God seem overwrought and pretentious for thundering out ten whole commandments." Hagabus smiled, hoping I would follow his example and lighten the mood. I returned the grin. It was difficult to imagine this priest was my enemy. Perhaps he was cursed by caution, but a rich heart beat beneath his parochial manner. "There will be a large crowd today," he bubbled, changing the subject. "Samuel will make sure of that."

"What did you believe, my brother?"

Hagabus sighed with a heaviness of soul caused by the burden of too many years of too many petty problems about too many irrelevant issues. "I believe when God touches a tree it should bear its fruit without believing it has become a forest." He rubbed his bald head.

"So, am I the tree with the exaggerated sense of importance?"

"You are a good man who is about to be swallowed up by the mass hysteria of lesser fellows," proclaimed Hagabus as his eyes met mine for the first time, filled with tears. Was it sadness for my plight or the overwhelming drain of fatigue?

"As Jonah spent three days in the belly of a whale, perhaps when I am swallowed, the Father will vomit me onto a new shore."

Hagabus just stared at me. "Sometimes I think I will never grow weary of the parable. I love the glorious hidden meanings in each tale. Then you come back to my door, either mastering or mangling the art of the story well told. Whichever, this last Jonah one totally eluded me."

"What does not elude you, sir, is the fear in your heart, caused by the visit from this Jerusalem dignitary."

"What do you mean?"

"Jerusalem in any of its forms still scares you."

"It is a city. I am not frightened by buildings and streets."

"Jerusalem is where your dream died and was buried by judges who once were your friends."

It was out. He knew I knew his secret.

He paused and peered at me. "Nicodemus?"

"Yes, many years ago when I was twelve. What happened to you was a mistake. Your term of punishment is over. You can live now."

"He is well?"

"He is searching. I talked with him one night."

"What did you tell him?"

"He must be born again."

"More parables. Do they ever translate into real answers?"

"It is not a story. I am speaking of an experience."

"Veshioli is a potent personality, Jesus, possessing the intellect of a caesar and the cunning of a viper."

"My dear Hagabus, they are a brood of vipers."

"It is not the bite that kills, but the poison that remains," he said, pulling himself up and heading for the door. He was finished. I knew his ways. He would talk no more on the matter. "You will read for us today, Brother Jesus?" he said, donning a renewed cheeriness.

"I would be honored." I swallowed a question as I nodded in his direction.

With this he was out the opening and gone. I was left standing in the midst of the meager material possessions of one very damaged but consecrated priest.

Coming out the doorway, I was nearly knocked down by the leap of four flying children--Samuel, along with three wiggly companions.

"I told everybody, Jesus," said Samuel as he hugged my leg.

"Everybody is coming," said one of the little girls. I believe her name was Naomi.

"Everybody but Chiolita," said a third boy, frowning.

"What do you mean?" I asked calmly.

"When we told her you were coming, she grunted and stomped off," said Samuel carefully, so as not to show disrespect.

As Samuel spoke I looked up and saw Chiolita, heading our way, apparently coming to see Hagabus, but when she saw me, turning and beating a hasty retreat.

"Wait, Mother Chiolita," I called. I excused myself from the children and pursued the matriarch. She tried to accelerate but my youthful legs won the race. "Wait, Mother," I said as I caught up and nabbed her arm.

She whirled around and glared at me. "That hurts. You squeezed my arm. Now I will be black and blue for days," she panted, melodramatically.

"I didn't mean to hurt you."

"You never mean to hurt, Jesus barJoseph. Not me or Matthan's daughter or anyone, right?"

"Mother, what have I done to you?"

"I am not your mother. It is what you do to everybody. What your family has done for years. Some people in this town can make one mistake, and they are damned. But you and Mary and Joseph can drift back into this community at will, your sins and stupidities obvious to everyone, and you're embraced and forgiven. I am sick of it, and there will be a payback. You, Jesus, better watch your step. There are people mightier and wiser than you who see your arrogance and are prepared, for the good of the nation, to expose your presumption and reveal your insanity."

"What have I done to you, Chiolita?"

"You are a bastard. I'll bet they never told you that! You don't have a father. No one knows who he is. Mary got pregnant with you before she knew Joseph. You are a bastard, walking around trying to preach God to people who are already better than you. But Jerusalem knows all about it. I told the fine gentleman . . ."

"Veshioli?" I asked, barely able to squeeze the name in.

"It is none of your business," she squealed, foaming at the mouth. "He has been my guest for the week and I have learned all about you, and Jerusalem, and the whores of Samaria, and how you told those hungry people along the Jordan you could turn stones into loaves of bread."

"What? Stones into bread?"

"Don't try to deny it. He was there and had to comfort those starving, confused souls when you ran off with their money." She glared, blinking with a nervous twitch. I would not be able to reason with her. I was stunned by the bite of her words and their venomous content. Merely calling them lies did not seem sufficient defense.

She pushed past my desolation and ranted, "Let go of me, I have a guest to feed."

"Of course, I'm sorry, I mean about holding your arm."

She pulled away and clogged up the rise to her home at the foot of the Nazareth cliff.

I watched her climb, my soul slain by the swift sword of her surreptitious slander. I stood transfixed as people passed by and gave greeting to me on their way to Sabbath service. My ears were deafened to their warm words.

Then a warm embrace of a fellowman. He took my arm and moved me to a safe haven, sat me down, and patted my shoulder. I was alone with Matthan, Mary's suitor.

"Are you all right?" he asked with a warmth causing me to fight back tears.

"No, I don't think so. I don't want to lie to you. No, it is not all right. I don't understand."

"Well, don't you think, Jesus, understanding is the luxury granted to those easiest to deceive?"

"No, Matthan, I think we need it. Without understanding we try to gobble up life, and end up choking on the sheer glut."

"She is a bitter woman, Jesus."

"Did you hear her words?"

"I heard it all."

"What have I done to her?"

"You were at the wrong place at the wrong time, you and your whole family. Listen, come here." He led me to a quieter place.

"About a year before Mary and Joseph were married there was an . . . accident around here."

"Accident?"

"This is not easy. Chiolita was married to a man named Daniel. He was a good man, a hard worker, but had a gentle side that made the other men in the village nervous."

"Gentle?"

"He was softer in his touch, quieter in his way." He looked at me for a glint of recognition. Being satisfied I understood, he continued. "Daniel met a man from a nearby village. At first they did business together, then became friends. As their companionship grew it changed; more the closeness of two in love. I am not very good at this."

"I understand, brother."

"Anyway, the two men met in a cave outside Nazareth. One night some of the young boys from the other village caught the men. I am not certain what happened next. There were and still are so many stories. The companions were found at the bottom of that cliff right up there." He pointed to the summit where rested the small shops and tiny houses that made up what was known as Nazareth. Matthan continued, "They were naked and bloodied. Chiolita believes the young boys stoned them and threw them off the ledge to make it look like an accident."

"Accidentally naked?"

"People tend to believe the first explanation to get the tragedy out of their lives."

"So what has this got to do with me?"

"You see, Chiolita believed, well I guess she still does, your father Joseph and I were with the boys who killed her husband." He stopped. I looked at him. "We weren't," he added in haste. "We tried to tell her we were home, but she never accepted it. So when you were returned here with Mary and Joseph, and everybody accepted the family without question, Chiolita felt cheated and has been trying to gain her vengeance ever since."

Matthan sat quietly staring at his own callused, weather beaten hands, the narrative finished. A wretched story. My heart was torn between fury over Chiolita's accusations and compassion for the torment in her soul.

Matthan rose to leave. "It is time for Synagogue. The people will be expecting you."

"How many heard Chiolita?"

"Many heard, but few listened. We are a decent people, mature enough to know when to don our ears and when to become as deaf as the rocks that clutter our streets."

I nodded, not in agreement, but more to acknowledge the generosity of his spirit. "I will be along, brother."

"You are a good man, Jesus. How proud Joseph would be." He walked away.

It was the second time that day I had been called good. How casually praise is offered to soothe hurt feelings. I did not feel good. I felt used, like the road winding its way to the garbage pit. Gehenna, the waste dumping area for Jerusalem, where everything rotten, misused, and worthless finds a final place for deterioration.

It seems in Nazareth, Gehenna was at the bottom of the cliff where they cast all their rejections.

Was Matthan telling the truth? Was Joseph with the murderers? Did Chiolita know something we didn't, or was she just brutalized by the agony of nightmares about the horrid deed? Chiolita, Hagabus, Veshioli, Matthan, Mary, and Joseph--strangers to me, displaced in my hometown.

Sabbath, a time for healing. I was late to share my life with people who really didn't know me. It was finally time. My hour was come.

****

A chain of events, an explosion of fury, and a mob's thirst for violence left me dangling from the cliff where Daniel and his companion had plummeted to their untimely deaths.

How did it happen?

Reading for Hagabus in a synagogue jammed with people, each one scrutinizing the carpenter's son turned miracle man; a local son--a disconcerting blend of pride and embarrassment.

Hagabus handed me the scroll of the prophet, Isaiah. I read aloud.

"I have been sent to preach the gospel to the poor."

Poverty was not a stranger. It was the worm gnawing at the hope of every Nazarene.

"To heal the brokenhearted."

Victims fail to attend their restoration. Chiolita was not present to have her heart healed.

"To preach deliverance to the captives."

Mankind--captivated by an allegiance to failing tradition.

"Recovering of sight to the blind."

I remember the first blind man I saw granted the miracle of sight. After he screamed in delight for a while, he whispered to me, "What do I look like?" He could see everyone but himself. The common impasse.

"To set at liberty them that are bruised."

The choice to choose a well-chosen path. The freedom to walk away from the tolerated abuse.

And finally. . .

"To preach the acceptable year of the Lord."

Passage completed, congregation silent.

All the poor, brokenhearted, captive, blind, and bruised sat, staring anxiously, desperately needing intervention.

I closed the scroll and looked at them; the room silent with a disquieting apprehension.

I understood. They desired more than the words of a very dead, though well-meaning, Isaiah. They were disappointed and confused. Had I come here to read Scripture and perform sacred rites like some efficient holy man? After all, they already had a priest. Nazareth needed the supernatural. But wait. What piece of their honest humanity had the people brought to exchange for divine intervention? Moses was dead, his laws debated. What remnants of faith still pulsed in their veins?

At length I spoke. "Today this Scripture is fulfilled in your ears and you can become the benefactors of all of its promise if you choose to believe. But you must reject your dull training and the futility of repetitious unbelief."

I sat down. A pause, followed by a buzz of conversation. A whisper of dialogue soon erupted into a swarming agitation from the disturbed hive.

"You are just a carpenter's son," one scoffed.

"Where did you learn anything you can teach us?" sneered another.

I stirred the nest again. "Don't forget. There were many lepers in Israel. God ignored them and healed Naaman the Syrian. There were many widows amongst the chosen people who were hungry during the drought. God sent Elijah to a widow in Sidon. Think about it. It is not a people blessed by genealogy that God visits. He is looking for one person who can be touched by rebirth."

This infuriated the pride and sensibilities of the already resentful gathering. They, like their Jerusalem cronies, mistakenly believed birthright carried clout in heavenly decisions. Years of frustration and disillusionment descended on the hearts of the Nazarenes like a thundering cloud in the desert heat, igniting their parched, dried souls.

I was grabbed and pushed to the ground. (All wars begin with an ill-timed shove.)

Some stepped in to help and were thrust aside by a new wave of the enraged.

We were out the door, propelled on the tide of an angry sea of disconsolate fellows. I had struck the community nerve and now I must suffer the pain. It was no different than the vigilantes who cast two innocent souls from the ledge so many years ago. What did they shout at Daniel and his friend? What did they feel as they watched the two fall to their deaths? Was I to become the latest victim of Nazarene bigotry?

I heard the children scream and saw little Samuel beat the leg of a nearby attacker. I was afraid he was going to be swallowed up in the melee, so I grabbed him and hurled him in the air to an observant mama who scurried him away. Samuel was safe, but I had lost precious time to escape. Muscled up the steep grade to Nazareth's pinnacle, I looked into the faces of my attackers and, strange as it may seem, I recognized no one. They were strangers to me. No words, just the huffing of men on a mission to dispose of the undesirable.

How humiliating to be mastered by this surge of insanity. Had I driven these men to this stupidity? Was this an attack against me or a riotous reaction to unfulfilled lives? It made little difference now. None of them, individually, meant to kill, but as a swarm they would dash me headlong on the rocks below.

It was fruitless to fight the fury. If I objected it would only fuel their intent; struggle, and I would secure their grasp.

We passed Chiolita's house. I caught a glimpse of two forms in the window. Did I see a slight smile on her thin, crusty lips? Was this what she was waiting for? Could this be her rendition of justice? Perhaps in some twisted and perverse way it did seem fair to her; the son of Joseph lying battered on the rocks which were previously stained with the blood of her executed husband. I squinted to make out the second form looming behind Chiolita. I suspected it must be Veshioli. What was he thinking? Perhaps the enraged crowd would simplify his task so he could return back to Jerusalem and indulge himself in less perilous social climbing. Veshioli. Was he behind this? Here was a religionite on a most dastardly mission--such rumors and lies.

A man spit in my face. I fought to gain release, not about to die on this cliff. I leaped to secure footing--no avail. My meager efforts were useless against the singularity of the crowd.

Nearing the top. My heart was pounding. Could sheer lunacy supersede the will of the Father? Gaining speed. It was a steep climb, and fatigue was taking its toll on my assailants. They released me for a moment to regain their grasp and catch their breaths. As they did, a man leaped from the crowd and threw three or four of my attackers to the side.

"Leave my brother alone!" he screamed.

Jude--at least, I thought so. A Jude I had never seen before. His rage exceeded the fury of the whole mob.

His voice echoed with the intensity of a higher will. People were not accustomed to hearing Jude speak, let alone reverberate like the God of Sinai. They stepped back, and when they did I took my opportunity to push through the midst. They fell back in sheepish submission, responding to the authority of Jude's demand. He had broken a heinous spell with his decree.

I weaved through the horde and out the other end without looking back, headed down the hill at a clip just short of a gallop. I heard the clump of running feet behind me. I hadn't considered what I was going to do if my assaulters elected to follow me.

What should I do, Father? I haven't come to fight my way out of tricky situations. Am I going to have to wrestle my way to freedom?

"Jesus, wait." I sighed in relief. My trailer was James. I didn't stop, but instead slowed my pace, allowing my younger sibling to catch up. "Wait, Jesus. Simon has been hurt."

This declaration brought me to a halt. "Hurt? What do you mean?"

"When they drove you from the temple, he tried to stop them. He fell and several of them stepped all over him."

"Is he all right?"

"Mary is with him. I don't know. It's his leg. I think it may be broken."

"This is not what I planned."

"You never get what you plan, Jesus. These people are hard-working folks who don't understand oddities."

"Are you defending their actions?"

"No, I am just understanding."

"Then you go back and understand. Pick up some rocks in your little village, James, and see what crawls out from under the hiding places. Grow up! Real life is happening while you mortar yourself into complacency."

"This is my home," he screamed.

"That's right, it is your home, but it isn't the world. It isn't even a good representation."

"What about Simon?"

I did not know what to say. What was the answer? I knew Simon would be fine. Mary could nurse a demon back to heavenly status. Should I return?

Before I could decide, Elizabeth came running up to me. "Jesus, go on. Get out of here," she ordered breathlessly.

"What about Simon?"

"He will be fine. He has hurt his leg but he will be fine. You must get out of here."

"I can't leave Simon."

"They will kill you,"

"I don't think they will hurt him," James objected.

"You weren't there. They don't see Jesus. They see blood. They feel insulted and angry. These are no longer our friends and neighbors. They are a pack of wild animals."

"I know these men," James said.

"You know nothing, big brother," she proclaimed. "They are not in your control. Don't you understand? They have risen from the synagogue to kill your brother. Use some sense. Jude is up there now trying to break up their craziness."

Jude was still there. Would they turn on him? Revenge loses its trail injuring the innocent. What was I to do? Father, please help me. Don't leave me without your counsel.

"Jesus, don't you feel any responsibility for this?" James demanded.

"Where is Hagabus?"

"You're changing the subject," growled James.

"He is in his home," Elizabeth stated, sadly.

"He is an old man, Jesus. These are his comrades and friends. You must stop asking people to fight your battles. You have put him in a horrible predicament."

"I wasn't trying to put him in any predicament. I just wanted to know he was safe."

Actually, I wasn't sure what I felt about Hagabus. He couldn't have stopped the people from ascending the hill. I don't know what I expected. Whatever it was, it needed to have been done years ago, long before this congregation turned into a murdering rabble. Maybe if Chiolita would have been ministered to instead of tolerated. Maybe if Hagabus, himself, would have exhumed the dead bones of his past and given them a decent burial in God's grace. The tragedies that befall men are often the weight of accumulated indecision breaking the backbone of mercy. What I mean is, Nazareth went berserk today because people had allowed little festerings to find hearth and home in the lives of friends.

I decided it was time for me to go. I had dreamed of being a helper to the city of my childhood, yet I think part of me needed an affirming pat on the head, given in a community unison, to confirm I had finally achieved success.

There would be no approval. My God, what was I saying? There would never be another visit. Nazareth was no longer a refuge for my exhausted, uncertain, childish fear. I was a fox without a hole. It had taken me too many years to discover Nazareth was never my home. It was where I had passed my youth--where I sprouted the hair of a man.

It was time to find my place in life; a station of purpose not redeemed by the sentimentality of locality.

"I must go, James, I have nothing more I can give here. I have nothing more to learn here. Patience is a mothering process, and I must go where she can complete her perfect work in me. "

"That is just a fancy way of saying you are running out on the family again."

"James, calm down," said Elizabeth as she squeezed his arm.

"No, Elizabeth, let him speak."

"I have nothing else to say. You are the one that musters the words which produce this outrageous response in good men."

"Good men?" queried Elizabeth outraged.

"What? Is Jesus the only good man? Can't these men be good? Must we pray all the time or change water into wine to be called good?"

"I don't claim to be good."

"No, that's right. You are the Son of David. God's Anointed One. Or what is the title this week? What claims will your followers make tomorrow? Are you going to destroy Rome?"

"To me and to you, I will always be Jesus. I am a son of man and proud to be."

James was not finished. "In Nazareth you are the madman that the elders had to try to destroy."

"Shut up!" Elizabeth pressed angrily. "You are saying things that will not return to you with any peace. You will despise yourself for this, James. The words are gone and you cannot get them back. Think about this. Jesus is your brother. Don't say anything you can't retrieve."

"I hear his heart," I said to Elizabeth. "A heart does not always speak the truth. It can only share the burden of its abundance. I love you, James." I embraced him before he could resist.

"And I love you, brother. You are family. As family, we will handle this. If the stories of your deeds return to our homes and those actions continue to be peppered with craziness, we will come for you. We will not wait for Veshioli or Jerusalem or some mob to fling you from a cliff. We will honor the name of Joseph of Nazareth by returning his confused eldest to the safety of his home. My brother, I believe you have a passion and desire which is misguided by your own limited understanding. The family will find you. So, live and be well. But know this. We will not allow you to destroy the reputation of our kindred. Do what you will, and we will do what we must."

I understood. If I were in his sandals, I would have delivered the same speech. We stared at each other for a long time, like we did as young boys; stare until one loses the glance and looks away. Neither of us would surrender the blink on this day. It was no longer childish games. To James, it was integrity. To me, eternity. We were so close in spirit, yet worlds apart in the matters of heart. "I have one Father to please, James."

"I know who that should be," he said as he flicked a glance at Elizabeth.

"I am going to come down to Capernaum, literally, my brother. It was my dream to be of ministry to my home. Now I know if you chase a dream too far, you may fall off a cliff. It is time to accept reality and take what has been given me."

James remained frozen.

Elizabeth hugged me.

"We will find you, big brother," he warned.

"I won't be difficult to locate."

"Do great things, Jesus," said Elizabeth, tears on her cheeks.

"Do the right thing," said James firmly as he grasped my hand.

"You two must make up your minds. Which is it? Great things or right things? You know, carpenter, they don't always agree."

I winked as I eased my grip on the callused hand.

Time to leave. I would never see Nazareth again, never darken her borders, run the streets, or climb that hill.

I was reminded of an old proverb a medicine man from a caravan once told me. "There is a place we run and play, but then as men we walk away."

Playtime was over--time to walk.

****

Never wanting to do my work in Capernaum, unable to imagine how it could be of any use to my life, it ended up being exactly what I needed.

Simon and Andrew became my constant comrades, along with two of their friends, James and John. The foursome had been inseparable in youth, competitive in business, and now voracious in their appetites for this new work which we dubbed "The Kingdom", wanting to differentiate our ideas from conventional religious thinking. Little danger of being lumped in with the pious--truly a renegade movement, populated by the most unlikely crew to ever be proclaimed god-worthy.

Both Jona (Simon and Andrew's father) and Zebedee (James and John's papa) were infuriated because I ripped their sons from the moorings of the boat and the family business, counting on their offspring to take over the commerce and provide for them in their old age.   Plans change.

Simon turned his house into a headquarters for the new Kingdom movement. People were in and out night and day. Peter's wife and mother-in-law gyrated between fits of disgust over the people trudging through the house, and a deep sense of awe over what God was doing to touch the lives of those visiting intruders. Honestly, we were all overtaken by a magnificent reverence, sometimes feeling like children playing with fire, deluded, we actually controlled the flame. However, in our saner selves, we knew we were not the masters of this miraculous manifestation.

Cripples, lepers, blind, and maimed entered the door of the fisherman's humble abode, leaving healed, restored, enlightened, and transformed.   I marveled, overwhelmed by a joyous befuddlement; no opportunity for faith to wane, and no logical motivation to take credit for the awesome awakening in this little fishing village. God, dwelling and creative, in the floor plan of one stone hut in one tiny village on one so-called sea, in Galilee.   I sat amazed as people, devastated by the daily affliction of aggravating illness, often for years and years, would hobble, creep, or crawl to attempt one final feasibility for wholeness. Equally astounding were those, so imprisoned by the restraints of traditional values, who would walk away, rejecting the miracles raining from the sky above.

I was teaching in Simon's house one day when there was a clamor on the roof. Suddenly pieces of clay and palm branch fragments began to drizzle, then deluge us, from the ceiling. Light flickered through the rooftop, followed by larger pieces, pelting on the listeners below.

Cheers and stomping feet.

Gradually, through an ever-growing hole in Simon's ceiling, a bed of mats and blankets eased down, suspended by a force unknown. The crowd gasped. In the eerie golden light, it appeared the heavens were presenting a body on a bed for our review

Then came a voice from above. "Sorry about the roof, my Lord. It was too crowded to get through the door and too important to wait." Everyone laughed and cheered.

So the bed was lowered, the man was healed, and Simon leaned over and whispered in my ear. "About the house . . ." he said.

"I know, the roof is a mess.   I'm sorry," I whispered back.

"No, I just wanted to let you know. The house is now yours, such as it is."   He gazed upward at his new window to the sun.

"Really, Simon, you can keep it."

"No, I would rather remember it as my house when you couldn't look up and see the heavens looking down. "

We were partakers in a greater good, no one manipulating the work. God was at His task and had granted us seats in his chariot to tour the wonders of His handiwork.

Life continued, fluctuating impatiently between glory and trial. By day we fished, talked, and worked with our local brothers. As night fell, a row of torches and candles would wind its way to the door of Simon's-- pardon--my house; each a heart to listen, a mind to learn and a body racked with some form of pain. Young men and women came from all over Galilee. I was only thirty-one, but was quickly becoming the old man of the troop; a wonderful outpouring--a revolution, as such a phenomenon should be defined.

Soon our house was filled with the very young and also the very old. The middle flock of souls stood back and watched. We became the gossip of the village. I tried to bridge the gaps, reasoning with the priests, and answering the questions of the Pharisees. I attempted to meet with Jona and Zebedee. But no effort at unity or reconciliation moved anyone. They were swallowed up in the gullet of everyday life, digested by living. The Father showed me I was chasing a faint whistle in the wind; by the time the music was heard the tone faded. God was using this message of Kingdom, with its ragamuffin adherents, to create His own separation. *Verily I say unto you, Without the open disapproval of the bored, the searching soul will never pursue.*

The Father was inviting a new breed of people to his freshly concocted feast. Some were ignored so many more would gain interest. Capernaum was God's experiment and He, alone, controlled its factors.

New faces: Matthew, a tax collector, turned Kingdom. Mary from Magdala, a demon-possessed woman who had been the source of great amusement to the surrounding hillsides, abandoned by her evil forces, brought her freshness and honesty (and also a goodly sum of money) to the cause. The financial aid was a blessing. We were a group of people who could catch enough to eat, fix what was broken, but found it difficult to secure the funds to buy other needed provisions. Simon of the Zealots joined us. He was the Simon I had encountered at the Camp of Deliverance. When he first came to Capernaum, he listened and then disappeared. I would see him again in a day or two and then he mysteriously vanished. Once he was gone for nearly a week. I thought surely he had moved on to other battles. One night as we all sat by the fireside, he walked into the house, sword drawn. If he was going to kill us we were suitably stunned and ready.

He grabbed the sword by the blade and with one swift motion he broke it across his knee. "Your words, master, have broken through the prison of my heart. Now I break the sword that forged the chains of that prison. I do not understand your ways, nor do I know if your words of the Kingdom of God will work, but I do know my ways of death bring no hope of life."

"And what am I to do with a broken sword, Simon?"

"It is not a mere piece of metal. It is the blade of a tale rehearsed and told many times with the same bloody conclusion. I used that sword as a boy when I killed an innocent man in the desert."

"This man, was he alone?"

"My memory is hazy, master. I believe he was with his family. Yes, I believe there was a young boy."

"And you spared the boy?"

"I frightened myself into flight. I remember it, because it was my first kill. I acted as if I was the victor. In my heart I was terrified. I had been taken captive by a devil of treachery."

"And what did you do with the frankincense?"

He jerked his head upright. "How did you know about that?"

"Perhaps this man you assumed slain did not die, but lived to relate the tale," I said as I stood to my feet.

"The frankincense was stolen two weeks later by thieves who murdered my father," he said, once more lowering his head. "I brought this flask of frankincense in honor of the repentance my father would pledge if he had ever heard your words." Simon broke into choking tears.

I sat in silence listening to his sobs. So the cycle was complete. I had the gold and the frankincense brought by the wise few; Mary, the myrrh. I hugged the patriot and welcomed him into the cloister. We fueled the fire and threw the sword into the blaze, and watched as the instrument of death blackened, but did not melt. The fire burned all night, the sword simmering in the heat.

In the morning Simon of the Zealots said sadly, "Look, Master, the sword still lives."

I looked at the charred, broken blade. "Does it?" I asked as I reached into the deadened fire. I grabbed the blade, still warm from the coals, and squeezed it in my hands. It crumbled into clumps of ash. "You don't have to be afraid anymore, my brother." We embraced and walked towards the sea.

The weeks were so filled with activity, often I forgot what day it was. Inspiring work. I longed for contact with the family in Nazareth. Nazareth was nearby, but still inaccessible for a visit--too much flaring pride and smoldering rage. I thought about going by night to visit them and returning before dawn. Still, if someone discovered my presence, I would just complicate their lives.

I traveled to other Galilean towns, searching the crowds for a familiar face. Certainly fabrications about our seaside shenanigans would be trickling back to Nazareth. What must Hagabus think? Chiolita--moved or stoic? Veshioli must be exhausted convoluting and cavorting.

Holy men began to converge on the little sea town. Alphaeus arrived one Sabbath, having just visited John in prison. He helped me identify the newcoming "old spirits".

"That one is from the Council of the Elders," he would say, pointing with a smile. "San Hedrin." His eyes widened in mock astonishment. "The Long Robes must really be concerned, you crazy Nazarene. John never got anyone higher than the temple guard to come and annoy him."

It was good to see Alphaeus. He stayed and fellowshiped for a time, but was uneasy with the miracles.

"I feel ashamed of myself," he stated in his simple manner. "I mean, as a Jew, I should be thrilled God is moving and doing miracles before my eyes, but heavens forgive me, I find myself suspicious--even cynical."

"What do you mean?"

"Oh, we Hebrews are all alike. We have no bread, God gives us bread. Then we complain of no meat, so God gives us quail. The quail is salty, so we complain of thirst. Moses gets frustrated at all the fussing and hits the rock and we look at each other and say, 'What's with him'?"

We both laughed. It was the nature of man to be overly observant of difficulty but leery of solution. Yet I had never found this to be a flaw in Alphaeus. I wanted him to make the transition from John's Jordan to our Galilee Kingdom Movement. He was attending, but distant. Was it loyalty to his dear comrade, John, prohibiting his full measure of involvement? The times were different. This was no longer Bethabarra. We would not be returning to the repentant leap. The Zealots, Romans, and Jewish elite were squeezing the remaining innocence from the hope-starved masses. Was Alphaeus anticipating a pardon from Herod, and a return to the glory days on the Jordan? The season was past. I was concerned about his unguarded idealism. He needed to stand watch on his own heart--his allegiance. Yet, I did not know how to reach him.

One day he came to the house escorting two young men. "Jesus," he said, "you are surrounded by followers. Each of them has a motive for being with you. It is true they love God and see His hand in your life. But they are men, and quite susceptible to their latest whim."

I listened to the tender lecture with great interest. Before me was a man, a well-preserved artifact from a gentler time, teeming with experience and character. He had even navigated the intricacies of the female unknown. His was a treasure chest of knowledge being graciously opened to me.

"What you need," he continued, "are two comrades you can trust to not seek their own. You will need a pair who will follow in faith, react to the need, and stand till the end." He placed an arm around each of the sturdy lads. "These are my sons. This is James. He has neither intuition nor intelligence."

I looked at James for some grimace at Alphaeus' assessment. He stared straight ahead with a slight smile, either unoffended or unaware of the meaning of the words. Whichever, he seemed content.

Alphaeus proceeded. "This is my other son, Jude. He is an inquisitive one, but unable to really grasp the answer to the questions he asks, if you know what I mean."

"In other words, he finds joy in asking, if not understanding," I presented.

"Precisely, rabbi. How insightful," replied the proud father. "He is also as strong as an ox and can kill a camel with one blow."

I decided not to ask where this ability would be of use, or how it had been tested. "I am glad to meet you, gentlemen."

"No, you don't understand, Jesus. I am not introducing them. I am giving them to you." Alphaeus was serious.

"They are a gift?"

"They are your helpers who need no boost of personal reward to maintain the tenacity of their loyalty."

I studied the boys. More smiles. "What do they feel about it, my brother?"

Alphaeus peered at me, a bit perplexed. "You see, Jesus, that is the beauty of James and Jude. They don't need to feel. I have taught them to love and give. I have taught them to find fulfillment in these actions. Children find their value in whatever we tell them has worth. If it is money, they will not be satisfied until they are rich. If it is war, they will not be complete until they have shed blood. If it is giving, they will not find peace until their offering is received and finds appreciation in the life of another. I have taught my sons to hunger and thirst for righteousness."

"Then that is why they are so filled?" I patted two very broad and muscular backs.

"They will serve and find their joy in doing. They do not submit to gain any other recognition or favor. They yield to find their purpose." Alphaeus embraced his sons and kissed them deeply on the mouths. How clever of my Father to send another James and Jude to fill my life in the absence of my brothers.

"You will join us, Alphaeus?" I was hoping he would make the leap of faith.

"No, my Lord. This is a young work needing legs that grow stronger with toil."

"But the little chicks need a rooster to teach them to forage for the grain."

"Actually, Master, the old chicken best serves in the stew," he laughed. "Anyway," he continued, "I must see to the needs of John. It is hard to find his locusts at Herod's palace. John is the one I was called to serve, just as my sons will serve you in your greatest hour of need."

He made his departure. I couldn't help but feel something very special was ending. Would I see him again? What would be the circumstances of our meeting?

His offspring remained; eager, if a trifle delayed in perception.   James and Jude became my dependable protectors on the uncertain road ahead.

Meanwhile, my ministry became plagued with the pesky questions of religionists on a mission to disrupt our movement.   Along with the teaching, fellowship, and miracles, there was also a barrage of legalistic inquiry and concocted arguments over the finer points of Mosaic law and traditional practice.   These "men of letters" were trying to categorize this seashore phenomena into an acceptable, existing explanation.   Many of the common people became bored with the constant pecking of tedious bickerings. The people shrank away from the dark cloud of boring exchange.

One hot Sabbath day it all came to a much-needed confrontation.   People were everywhere, and the house was full.   They had come from nearby villages, which is significant, because of the laws regarding travel on sabbath-- no more than six furlongs. People found exceptions for the rule.   These revisions were attempted, but the religious leaders cited the letter of the law to quell any notion of individual liberty, unless someone wished to journey for a noble cause such as an offering to the synagogue. Grace was proffered for such generous overtures.

Andrew came and whispered in my ear, "We are not alone." It was a code we developed so all would be aware when some of the "men of old" were lurking about. "We are not alone" meant there were spies in the house.   The observers from the religious community had begun to disguise themselves as common laborers to gain our confidence and trap us into stumbling over subtle interpretations of Jewish law. For example, there was one particularly nefarious fellow who pretended he was blind and had come for healing. I was a bit skeptical because he had arrived alone and moved around the enclosure with some ease, as if familiar with the surroundings. I scolded my own cynical nature and asked him if he wanted anything from the Father.

"Yes," he said. "I know it is Sabbath, but I would desire God heal me."

Why does a blind man care what day it is? "We shouldn't do work on the Sabbath. You must come back again," I replied, testing him.

"No, dear rabbi. God loves me enough to heal me on the Sabbath. He has made you above the rule," he said loudly.

"No one is greater than the law. Often the principle is misinterpreted by frustrated men who have a cause to promote, an article to sell, or a personal axe to grind." I reached out and touched him.

His eyes flew wide open. "It is a miracle. I mean I already feel the power."

I took a coin from my girdle and flung it in the air. He dropped his staff and disguise, bent down and caught it right before the money hit the ground.

"It is a miracle, my friends. Or is it?" I asked in a mock whisper. "Is it miraculous to see a Pharisee leap for the sweet possibility of money?"

"No!" they all screamed and laughed.

"The miracle may be the speed in which he devours our funds," one jeered, sustaining the comedy.

The exposed, pompous charlatan turned and huffed, "You saw it. He was going to heal me on the Sabbath!"

"Not even Jesus can heal a fake," said James the son of Alphaeus.

"Very good, James," I said, bowing. The gathering cheered.

The Pharisee turned stomped to the door.

"Wait, my brother," I called. "Might I have the coin which I gave as alms to a poor blind beggar? I feel such conviction I did it on the Sabbath."

He looked around the room and with a grunt, threw the coin back to me.

"Thank you, kind fellow, and please, if you must travel, keep in mind no more than a few furlongs." The room reignited with laughter.

So today, once again, we were not alone. Andrew had spotted a goat in our sheepfold. "Dear Father," I prayed quietly. "Help me to get my mind off foolish games and think about those who have come to gain life."

The heat was growing with the intensity of a furnace as the people crushed in on one another gaining entrance to the tiny house. The air was thick and steamy, reeking with the odor of men's sweat, mingled with the aromatic scents of the foods they had devoured. The door was jammed with people, closing out the light of day. The only illumination was from the hole in the ceiling which this retired carpenter had failed to take time to repair. The golden sunlight danced through the splintered rooftop, giving an iridescent glow to the center of the room. The heat of the noonday sun burned the crown of my head. I sat for a moment, clearing my mind from the torpor of heat

A grunting. A pig. No, a higher tenor. A grunt mingled with a muffled shriek. Others heard, too. Coming from the back. The audience drew silent. Louder, surrounding us. I whipped my head, looking for the source; behind me, now to my right, suddenly above my head and before I could look and investigate, a form dropped through the ceiling and landed in front of me in the middle of the dusty floor--screeching, rolling in the dust, raising a cloud which choked the onlookers and prohibited me from seeing the intruder. The people gasped, retreating. The high-pitched squeal continued. I had better fix the hole in the roof. More squalling. I decided I'd better find out what had befallen us. If this creature kept moving we would all choke to death. I reached into the swirl of dust. When I made contact I realized it was human. There was soft skin and narrow child-like shoulders. When I touched them the writhing stopped but the groaning continued. The dust began to settle, giving way to some field of vision. I turned the small one over and saw for the first time the hideous, twisted features of what appeared to be a young boy, his mouth foaming, depositing frothing spittle all over my robe. He screamed and twisted again. If I allowed him to escape we would never regain control. I grabbed him and pulled him to my chest. He struggled and spit, yapping and yelping incessantly. He stunk, and I noticed pieces of dung were caked in his hair.

"I am sorry, my Lord. He is my son," came a sorrowful voice from the doorway. "I thought I had him tied securely."

"What's wrong with him?"

"He is blind and deaf and cannot speak. The demons have filled the vacancy of his soul."

"Come here, man. We must untie this boy once and for all."

The child was skin and bones, but possessed the strength of two men. How horrid his world must be--no sound, light, or feeling, besides the unexpected touch of another. I struggled with the boy but lost my grip. He jerked free and growled, spitting in every direction. Suddenly Jude, Alphaeus' son, leaped to his feet and tackled the young boy and sat on his chest. "You'd better hurry, Lord. I am losing this battle," he grunted as he was bounced into the air by the gyrations of the tortured lad.

I froze as the whole scene moved in a slow whirl before my eyes. What was this? Could it be another trick by the Jerusalem slime? Was I being tested again? Were they trying to create this spectacle to further discredit the work?

I came to my senses. This was a boy needing help. Not even the finest Greek thespian could manage this performance.

I joined my brother on the ground beside the body of the imprisoned young soul. "You foulest of hell, arrogant of all that is damned, come out of this boy and seize him no more."

The writhing ceased so suddenly that   Jude, who was in mid-air, fell on his buttocks to the side.

No breathing. No life.

"He is dead!" exclaimed a man from the gathered, fearfully.

"No," I said. "He is not dead. He is just emptied, waiting for life." I spoke the words, but did not know my own meaning. Come on, son," I pleaded rubbing his arms and chest.

"He is dead," said the doomsayer again.

"What's with you? Are you some sort of undertaker standing to profit?" A chuckle trickled across the room. As the laughter gained momentum the boy twitched. "Laugh some more," I said in a loud voice. People tried.

"Think of something funny," said John the fisherman.

There was a pause as the pressure drained the room of all levity.

"Think about how you will explain this to your wife," I suggested over my shoulder. A brief burst of laughter and the boy jerked and sat up.

The congregated gave a collective gasp.

He rubbed his eyes, looked into my face and said, "Who are you and why are you sitting on me?"

A screaming, rejoicing, tear-filled cheer rattled the house as the boy shivered in terror. He had never heard the faint blowing of the breeze, and now was surrounded by a noisy arena of well wishers.

"Silence, you rowdy Galileans," I requested charmingly.. "You are frightening enough to each other. Think how you must sound to this boy on his first visit to our earth." I helped the boy to his feet, embracing him. "Welcome home, my son. The days will get better."

I walked him back to his papa. I couldn't find him. I asked if anyone claimed the boy.

"Master, he is over here. He fainted when the boy spoke," called out a concerned soul.

"Well, it is time for another resurrection!" I announced, rubbing my hands together in glee. We helped the man to his feet. "Papa, meet your son." I presented the lad, and the two of them enjoined in the most outstanding reunion I ever experienced in mortal body.

"Papa?" The boy hugged his neck.

The room melted in the warmth of adulation for a Father who had such compassion on one disembodied family.

"You are the son of David!" hollered a man from the rear.

It soon was a cheer, and then became a chant. "Son of David!" regaled the room.

A man in the front stood and shouted, "You are fools! Who else but Satan has rule and reign over devils?"

"God?" rejoined one of Alphaeus' son, Jude.

Everyone laughed, concurred with yeas, and resumed their chant-- "Son of David."

"What you have seen, my brothers, is Satan casting out himself to gain your confidence," the man bellowed again, insistently.

Our guest spy had revealed himself.

The chanters fell silent. It only takes one complaining voice to subdue a legion of praisers.

"If you divide a kingdom, my friend, then where shall you place the throne?" I posed. "By separating the authority you decapitate the head. No unity. No kingdom. No king."

As I spoke, I saw a familiar face. My brother James, with an expression which, if translated into words, could fill volumes on the subject of terror. I glanced around and there was Simon, and in another corner my brother Jude. What a day they selected for a family reunion!

Once again the intrusive religious figure rose to speak, but I interrupted. "A house divided against itself," I said fiercely, looking into James' eyes, "cannot stand." I paused, held the glance for another moment, and then continued, addressing the assembled. "There has to be agreement, binding brethren with a loyalty, which exceeds reason." My eyes darted first to Simon, smiling, and then to Jude, eyes burrowed into the ground.

"You speak parables to try to disguise the devilish nature of your business," the spy charged.

"Neither can Satan divide his efforts by saving this child; even if he felt it might deceive. Each soul is too valuable to his evil cause. And what about you?" I squared off to my challenger. "You might go ask your brother

Veshioli about such matters. He is more qualified on the subject of deceitful darkness than I."

The nay-sayer stomped out of the room as the witnesses of God's goodness applauded and hooted their approval.

A pharisee named Simon came to my side. He had been one of the religious visitors who had brought some curiosity instead of condemnation. "Your mother and brethren are here to see you," he said in hushed tones.

"What is he whispering?" demanded a fellow in the middle of the crowd.

"Tell him," I suggested, looking at Simon.

Simon rolled his eyes and said, "His mother and family are here to see him."

I reasoned James intended to make good on his threat. The stories trailing back to Nazareth were undoubtedly filled with treacherous lies. I loved my family, but it was time to shed childish things.

I jumped into the crowd, grabbed a young man and pulled him to his feet. Then I lifted up an old, grizzled chap with yellow teeth. I squeezed them both in a vigorous hug, peering into their alarmed faces, and then spoke to the assembly. "This is my mother," I said, kissing the young man on the cheek. "And this," I continued, "is my brother." I gave the perplexed aged man a big kiss on the forehead, glaring into the eyes of my younger brother, James. "Anyone who does the will of my Father is my mother, brother and sister."

A nod of approval and small smattering of applause followed.

James rose quickly, and exited the house, followed by Simon and Jude.

I was free of a tormenting responsibility. I was sad, but had made my choice, one in harmony with every fiber of my being.

It would be a Day of Atonement in the future before I would see them again; a Passover when I would need family and they most certainly would want to make their peace with me.

SITTING 31

Life, Adventures, Perversions, Healings, and Death Amongst the Four J's. . . Plus Me

The dreams are back--more vivid. Waking and sleeping have coagulated into a malaise, causing me to rise in the morning exhausted from the interplay and turmoil of the previous night's visions.

Visions. Perhaps I am transported to another place, duly summoned to partake of two worlds. The night realm is tangible, a vista of intrigue, struggling to penetrate my conscious mind.

A precursor to insanity? I have wondered. Certainly those tormented possess a heightened spirituality prior to lunacy. Do we teeter between warring awarenesses, selecting to acknowledge the one and deny the other?

The latest was the most disturbing. Everything seemed so real. I was the dream; it flowed from me, linked to my soul.

I was in the desert: no, I was the desert--I'm not sure. Joseph was there, struck by the zealot's sword. No young boy; a sword wielded by its own design, falling hard and true, gashing the face of a horrified Joseph. The flesh split, spurting thick, red blood. I, myself, entered the wound in my father's face--the warmth of skin and oozing stickiness of blood, hearing his inner scream of pain. Then I was dispelled from the gash, and the self-propelled sword turned and thrust itself into my side. I looked down and saw the blade peel back the skin. The wound was mine. Then I became one with the sword, my eyes entering my own body. I followed on as the sword slashed my heart, splattering blood everywhere until I could see no more because of a veil of crimson, which began to fade, gradually revealing the hazy, golden glow of a spring-time day.

Fresh. The fragrance of blooming flowers and the greenness of growth. There were young men and women walking back and forth in stately splendor, some carrying chubby children, others holding hats, nodding to each other. I looked down at myself, covered in blood, but felt no pain. Passing, the strollers would greet me with a smile, then scurry on about their business. I was ashamed of my bloodied state. I did not belong in this serene scene. The couples, with their children, seemed unaware of my condition, oblivious to my blood-soaked cloak.

Finally a tiny child, barely able to toddle, came to my side, carrying a gorgeous, gleaming garment.   It shimmered and shone, stinging my eyes with its radiance; a brilliance transcendent of mere color. The little one presented me with the robe. I touched it, and fell headlong into the depth of its pristine glory, uniting with the glistening greatness. I giggled like a young boy at play.

I awoke. The transition from ecstasy back to the fireside in Galilee seemed accursed, taking me hours to calm the restlessness in my soul. Disjointed, as if the fragments of my life would never connect to form a whole.

I struggled to sleep, partly due to panic about my night-time spectacles, but mostly because I knew if encompassed by rapture again, I would never wish to return.

One night I was awakened by Levi Matthew. "Rabbi." .

I jerked to an upright position.

"There is a man to see you," he said softly to soothe my frayed nerves. He gave a long sigh, I assumed, for my benefit.   My traveling companions were always concerned I was not getting enough rest.

"Who is it?" I asked, rising to my haunches.

"He says his name is Alphaeus and you would know him."

"He is right."

"That is strange."

"My dear Matthew, what is so strange?"

"Alphaeus is my father's name, too."

"No, Matthew. You are strange," I smiled, rising and passing him enroute to the visitor.

I came up over a small rise.   He was turned sideways. His features were stern as he stared into the crackling fire. He was not alone. Two young men stood at his side, at rigorous attention. There was a third companion. Sitting on a small pile of garments and skins was . . . Joanna, smiling, indiscriminately.

"Joanna?" I said quietly, barely able to believe my eyes.

She tried to stand up, giving a gleeful squeal. Years of crippling limitation disappeared. She believed she was the little girl who could walk again. "Jesus!" she screeched.

Alphaeus ever-so-gradually turned to me.   He was vastly different. Gone was the aging pixy with the cherubic features.   A soured countenance   was mortared onto the features of this old friend.

"Jesus," said Alphaeus in an uncharacteristic, careful, basal tone. "Meet my associates. This is Michael and this is Justin."

I looked into the stony faces of the overly-mature boys and opted to head for Joanna's warmer greeting.

"What are you doing here?" I asked as I bent down to hug her.

"It was time for my evening walk and I got lost."

"Serves you right for hiring a blind guide."

"Can the blind lead the blind? I heard you say that yesterday," said Alphaeus as he stepped my way.

"Yesterday?"

"Yes. We have been listening for three days now."

"Please forgive me, brother. I had no idea. I would have . . ."

"We kept our presence a secret for reasons we will speak of later."

"Well, you call it secret. I will call it a wonderful surprise."

"You speak so wonderfully," Joanna gushed, with the flattery of an over-zealous sister.

"Well, I see the weakness in your legs is now affecting the discretion of your ears."

"And I see the holes in your manners are almost as large as the holes in your robe."

"You always have to get the best point, don't you?"

"It's just you make it so easy to win." She laughed and we hugged again.

"I have brought a new friend who has heard of your work and requested to join our delegation," Alphaeus interrupted

I turned from my hug with Joanna, and released an involuntary gasp. Kerioth--a black-haired version of the Iscariot.

"I am sorry, Rabbi. Did I startle you?" said Kerioth as he reached down his hand to help me up from my hugging position.

I looked at his hand, envisioning all the deeds it had performed. I saw that same hand holding the head of Beskel. "No, I was just preoccupied with Joanna," I said, accepting the gracious boost.

"My name is Judas barSimon."

I looked into his eyes and he into mine. Did he remember me?

"I have enjoyed your teaching. I have many questions." He squinted for a moment as if trying to reconnoiter, and then smiled, broadly.

Alphaeus interrupted. "There will be plenty of time for such things.   You men take Joanna over near the followers fire. I would like to talk to Jesus alone."

"As you wish," relented Judas.

"Just don't drop me into the fire," said Joanna as the two somber young disciples picked her up.

"I am quite sure-handed," said Michael as he lifted with his comrade, Joanna's humor escaping him.

"Would you hurry, Jesus? I think these guys don't fathom my wit," pined Joanna, feigning exasperation.

"I will be along. Just don't run too far."

"You should be glad I'm crippled so you don't have to explain to your male ego why I'm faster."

We sat. Alphaeus stared into the fire. There was no need for me to make small talk. This was his conference.

"I have come from John," he said at length.

"He is well?"

"He is in prison. I did tell you that."

"Yes, I knew."

"He wondered if you had forgotten.   No communication. No visit. The questions do tend to pile up and baffle while one sits in the rotten straw of a cell."

No time for excuses.

He continued, Information is scarce, but what is coming forth to Herod's Palace, or rather, to John's chamber, is sometimes troubling."

I remained silent. He filled the space. "John is a man. A fine man. A godly man, yet a man. A man who tires of chains.   Perhaps dreams of rescue.   Sometimes believes he should still be preaching. He often wonders if he was filling a need to his people others could not satisfy."

"Quite an array."

"Well, 'if' and 'perhaps' become your two closest friends in jail."

"So you are here to solicit my support in the plans for an escape?"

"I did not say John requested or even wanted an escape. The absence of freedom can be a thorny prickle to the captive soul."

Again, I remained mute.

"He has asked me," he resumed, "to lead this small delegation to see you."

"Delegation? Well, John has become more formal since the last time I smelled him, sweating, in his soiled loin cloth."

"He is wondering if you are just a second voice still crying in the wilderness and perhaps there is another to come." He paused, chest heaving, cheeks red, eyes black, darting.

No surprise. When I saw Alphaeus' doleful features I figured there was trouble from John's followers. The Baptist's people had found it difficult to make the transition from John's stern overtures of repentance to the Kingdom Movement--free and far less Jewish. We had dodged many an attack as they joined forces with the pesky Pharisees. Frankly, I found it boring. Any group of people maintaining identity by erecting an unyielding legalism has lost the spontaneity making life expandable. Their demise is accelerated by the inflexibility of their dogmatic character.

He continued on, not needing my input. "We are concerned about the miracles."

"Concerned, why? Because you need one?"

"As you know, John did none. What is the purpose for these carnival tricks?"

"Carnival tricks?"

"I mean, men need God and you are trying to solve all their problems so they don't place their dependence in His Greatness. Secondly, you do not honor the traditions of the fathers. This causes people to speculate what the source and power might be behind these outbursts."

I was incensed.

"Take this thing with the centurion, a Roman, and you said he had greater faith than anyone in Israel."

"He did."

"He is a Gentile, heathen, a soldier."

"I know. Which gives you some idea of the famine of faith in Israel."

He winced. I hungered to see the twinkle in his eye, shining when he was bested. It was gone. All business from the Baptist's agent.

"A widow at Nain," he pressed on. "They say you raised a boy from the dead because his mother was crying. Is this true?"

"The young man really appreciated it."

"You can't interrupt funerals, Jesus. They are sacred services. People are going to meet God. The relatives need time to grieve and release their frustration. You can't break the tradition . . ."

"Wait! Nobody missed the funeral. Everyone was glad they could go home and eat the prepared food with the young man alive. The glory of God was achieved."

"But we cannot dictate God's glory."

"Let me get this straight. You do not doubt the centurion's servant was healed, nor do you question the possibility of a boy being raised from the dead?"

"No, I have seen such outpourings for myself over our three-day visit."

"This is new, Alphaeus. You are not questioning the validity of the miracles, just the propriety and source, am I correct?"

"Precisely," Alphaeus said with a relieved smile, content I finally understood. He continued, "Thirdly, we are concerned with the back-grounds of your adherents."

"Friends."

"Friends, then. It is a smattering of tax collectors, whores, cripples, pagans and common fishermen."

An accurate description. "And you don't like them?"

"I love them as sinners who need to change. But as front people for a movement of God, they are not credible. Take Judas," he prodded on.

"Take Judas where?" I asked with a smile.

"Take him as an example."

I was trying to imagine Kerioth being an example.

Alphaeus instructed. "He has been visiting John--consecrating himself, studying and growing in God."

I listened. Maybe I was being judgmental of this damaged soul. Men change. If not, I was out of business.

"I hope I am not interrupting," said a voice which blended in with the sounds of swishing grass and crackling branches.

'   Alphaeus lurched back, displaying a hideous countenance of fear.

"Relax, brother," I said. "It's Judas."

"I startled you, Rabbi Alphaeus."

"No, my son. Come here. We were just talking about you." Alphaeus patted the space next to him.

"If you both don't mind." Judas bowed his head.

I smiled and nodded my approval. He bolted the few steps to Alphaeus' side and sat down, smiling like a boy ready to receive a tasty, sweet reward. The man was changed. First, he seemed much younger than before. His hair was darker and cut in the front, revealing more of his face and allowing for more expression from the eyes. I deemed such an action positive.

"I know I am being presumptuous but the other fellows had gone to sleep and I really don't know Joanna well," he shared smoothly.

I never knew Joanna to remain a stranger. She would talk anyone to life, pursuing their friendship. I decided to ask her why she hadn't overwhelmed young Judas with the same treatment.

"Glad to have you, my boy," said Alphaeus as he patted Judas' shoulder. The smile was back on the old baptizer's lips; the joyous grin I remembered from Bethabarra. I had to be careful my new feelings were not jealousy over the loss of Alphaeus' affection to this new prodigy.

"Master Jesus, I loved your words this day," Judas presented with a bit of awkward formality.

"Well, I am glad you are here."

"I have some questions, if you don't mind?"

"Oh, I do love questions," said Alphaeus. "Perhaps as I listen to you answer young Judas I can learn more of this Kingdom Movement myself." Alphaeus returned to a youthful demeanor. The whole exchange smacked of theatrics, rehearsed days before, to be performed tonight.

"Of course. I will try to answer."

"What should we do about the Romans?" Judas fired with a newly-revealed intensity.

"Are you having a problem with one?"

"Problem? We are their captors."

"No swords in my camp. No swords around my camp. Tonight I am free, as are you, as long as you dwell with us."

"You are speaking of the proximity of evil."

"No, I am speaking of the reality of the time and how we wish to view it."

"I am an old man," said Alphaeus, beginning a thought.

I interrupted. You didn't used to be. You were as spry as the rodent running on the desert track. What ages us are fears we fail to confront."

"Then you do not fear her, this wolf of Rome?" Judas interrogated.

"So now Rome is a she. And she is a wolf?"

"The wolf eats when not hungry, runs in no particular direction, and hunts for the thrill of the kill," said Judas, hauntingly.

"And what would some student of Moses' Law know of the thrill of the kill?" I posed, staring into his eyes, searching their translucence.

"As Moses found out, there are many roads and much wilderness on the way to the truth of Sinai. Mine was an arduous journey with the benefit of very little manna from heaven," Judas spoke, casting his glance to the ground.

"Well spoken, my son. Certainly, Jesus, you understand the boy's questions?" jabbed Alphaeus, slipping an arm around the shoulder of the one presumed offended.

"I understand questions. I treasure them. I can give answers. But I too, am cynical of carnival tricks," I barked, glaring at Alphaeus.

"Should I be honoring Moses and my people?" Judas requested as he slowly lifted his head, disclosing moist vacant eyes.

"You must take what you can from every experience and find something of God in an otherwise predictable sojourn. Where Moses had insight, listen to Moses. If your people can give you the treasure to make living meaningful, then call them blessed. Embrace them and kiss their necks. But if you merely honor traditions that have proven to be deadly burdens, then you will be like the camels, faithfully lining up to bear loads and falling dead in the heat of the afternoon sun."

"I think I understand."

"I wish I did. I really do tire of all your parables, Jesus, Alphaeus retorted gruffly.

"And I, gentlemen, tire of religious discussions. I live a life free of theological entanglements. If you will excuse me, I have some common Galilean riff-raff to prepare for another day of carnival tricks and poorly-timed miracles."

They both grunted, feigning bewilderment.

I strutted away, knowing exactly where I was heading. It would be dawn soon and my soul felt there was still some spirited magic lurking in the shadows of this evening of surprises.

I found Joanna surrounded by sleepy Baptists. Her eyes were wide with wonder, gazing intently into the surrounding shrubbery, maintaining the alertness of a sentry at watch.

"Jesus," she screeched as I came into view. The two ardent young men rolled over, deep in sleep.

"I can see you are well-protected," I smiled as I looked at the snoring corpses.

"They are young. They eat, sleep, and overreact," she giggled.

"I should have you write my material."

"I should be your seamstress," she said, eyeing my robe again.

"And you think this was purposefully designed by a weaver of cloth?" I spread my arms to display the dilapidation of my frock.

"So, just as I thought, you stole it off the back of a dying ox," she punctuated seriously, which launched us into uncontrollable laughter. "What did Alphaeus want?"

"He had questions."

"Young men travel to ask. Old men travel to tell," she said, placing a finger on my lips.

"Then he had much to tell. My work worries him," I said, kissing her hand.

"What bothers him?"

"Miracles, harlots, timing, traditions, I don't know. All of it. None of it. Or probably mostly what he can't discover for himself. I love that man." She was hanging on my every word. It was no wonder Adam clamored for his Eve. Women allow men to indulge in self-pity without ever bringing up the indiscretion again; at least, good women do and Joanna was a good woman.

I looked at her. She remained silent so she would not interrupt one single syllable of my meandering introspection.

"When I saw you tonight," I said, changing the subject, "you tried to walk."

"What are you talking about?" She tried to hide a grin.

I chased her face and caught her eyes. "No, I saw you. You were trying to rise. Before you thought about being crippled your heart and spirit said 'get up, there's Jesus'. Am I right?"

"Yes, it happens sometimes. I forget I'm a cripple and my heart says leap before my legs remind me I am earthbound."

"How wonderful. After all these years."

"I'm not that old," she said, punching at me.

"No, but your passion says you can walk. I'm here. It's Jesus. Wake up! Excite your spirit and you will walk!" I stood to my feet, still holding her hands.

"Come on, now. Stop it." She was still smiling, but her voice was laced with aggravation. "I am as I am. Why must you change me?"

"It is your heart that wants the change. I did not reject you as you are. But your spirit pleaded to come and run with me." I gently tugged on her arms.

"They hurt, stop it!"

"What hurts?"

"My legs. They're burning!"

"Have they hurt before?" I asked quickly, falling back to my knees.

"No, not since the accident. They are on fire!"

Michael and Justin woke up. "What's going on?" said Michael through a groggy haze.

"Be silent. Alphaeus wants you. It is the hour of sacrifice. There are turtle doves to find and sheep to slaughter. Be off!" They jumped to their feet, scattering into the darkness.

"This is horrible," she panted, as she rocked back and forth on her buttocks.

"They are trying to live. Your legs are being brought back to life. Pain lets us know something living is hurting. Don't be afraid."

"Well, then, these legs just got the full travail of birth!"

"Come. Stand up! Let the little girl win this one. Let your heart set the way." I tried again to lift her to her feet.

"This is not the Jordan River with you carrying me, Jesus."

"I know. But it is real, and it is now."

"It's easy for you to say. You suggest. I agonize. You are whole. I have no footing in this matter."

She stopped in mid-thought. I had pulled her to her feet. She was wobbling, threatening to topple, chuckling within a gasp. "I didn't know I could do this. My legs are killing me."

"No, they are trying to be un-killed--much more difficult."

Amazingly, she found her balance. "There is not one inch of me that does not hurt or throb or want to vomit."

"If you do that vomit thing, be a good Jew and point towards Jerusalem."

She laughed and as she did, I gently pulled her forward. She lurched as her leg convulsed, stiffened, and then nearly collapsed into a new stance about two scoots from its previous resting place.

"That's called a step," I regaled.

"My God, this is insane."

"Walk to me, you beautiful hunk of a woman."

"Yuch, I've never seen your robe while standing! It is ugly up and down!"

"Walk, princess."

Her legs jiggled and she weaved back and forth like a drunken fisherman, almost falling, catching her balance just before crashing to earth. She wiggled forward again. Then there were two little drags and slides of painful progress. She was so close. I wanted to reach out, grab and embrace her, and never let go. But this was not my time; this was Joanna's miracle.

"My God." It was Judas.

"Get back, Kerioth," I ordered.

I immediately realized what I had said, referring to him by that name. There was nothing to do now. More important things were afoot.

He obediently stood at a two-man distance, his mouth agape.

"Come on, Joanna," I encouraged.

"I walk funny."

"Funny is good."

There were two more glorious lunges and she was in my arms.

Laughter, enhanced by tears, relieved by more of the same.

"I have dreamed of this," she whispered into my ear.

"Wake up, my dear. Your faith has made you whole."

****

The camp was startled to station by all the noise of jubilation; Camp Kingdom, waking to begin another boisterous day.

Judas grabbed my arm, pulling me away from Joanna. She whirled, twirled, and folded into an inglorious plop.

He stared in astonishment at the transformation and embarrassment at casting the healed soul to the ground. "I'm sorry, but how did you do that?"

I reached down and helped the young calf to her feet and said, "Do what? Pull on arms, or hug a beautiful woman?"

"No. You healed her. Didn't you know?"

"Seems to me she did all the work and the Father just approved the procedure."

"I didn't do anything," piped Joanna.

"You can walk," reasoned Judas.

"And she hugs quite nicely too," I said as I tickled her ribs.

She squirmed from my grasp. "My legs are still killing me."

"You can walk," repeated Judas, flabbergasted.

"Well, Jesus. I assume you know this woman," came a rich, deep, feminine voice from behind me.

I twisted around, being careful not to drop my fledgling. "Mary, I want you to meet Joanna. Joanna, this is Mary of Magdala."

"How do you rate hugs so early in the morning?" she asked Joanna with a wry smile.

"She can walk," expectorated Judas, hoarsely.

"It's the new rule of the order, Mary. Hugs in the morning for every ex-cripple who can walk to eat," gurgled Joanna.

"Miracles before morning prayer and bread? Really, Lord, how will we stay healthy and spiritual?" deadpanned Mary, as she came and added her warmth to the hug.

I stepped back and said, "Joanna?   This lady, Mary, once had seven demons, before the Lord relieved her of that burden in exchange for the trauma of traveling with sweaty, grumpy men."

"I am pleased to meet you, Mary. What is it like to have seven demons?"

"You know that crampy, bloated feeling you get once a month in your stomach during your womanly time?"

Joanna acknowledged without hesitation.

"Well, demons are like that, only it's in your heart, soul and mind all day and all night."

Joanna recoiled.

"She can walk," Judas croaked, his voice raspy and weak.

"Mary, I would like you to take this lady and traipse her about until her mind gets used to the idea of walking."

"What if she tries to give up? She looks like a little bit of a palace princess to me," posed Mary, in her droll manner.

"Palace princess?" Joanna attempted a hastened hobble in Mary's direction.

"If she tries to quit go ahead and drown her in that ditch water and bury the body where no one will ever find it." I joked without laughing.

"Oh, I see. The usual treatment." Mary flipped her hand in the air, and with that, the two of them were off, Joanna limping, determinedly.

As they left, a trail of early-morning risers arrived at the origin of the din.

Philip was the first. "Didn't that lady arrive here crippled?"

"What are you suggesting, Philip? Do you actually believe in miracles? Remember, last week you told me five thousand people could not be fed by five loaves and two fishes."

"Forgive me, Lord. It was my first time to contemplate such dinner preparations."

"Well, at the very least, there's one cripple who won't have to remain confined to her bed."

"The Romans should reward you for keeping the streets clear and the gates uncluttered," Philip touted.

"She can walk," Judas said in a dampened whisper.

Alphaeus stomped his way to our position. "Did you tell Michael and Justin to prepare a sacrifice?"

"Joanna can walk," inhaled Judas, grabbing Alphaeus by the arm.

"What do you mean?"

"Jesus healed Joanna. She is walking."

"What is the meaning of this?" postured Alphaeus as he turned a defiant glare in my vicinity.

"It seems your mind would be more at ease if she remained crippled," I shrugged, legitimately bewildered.

"I welcome God's intervention. I always am suspicious of man's interference."

"I saw her walk," huffed Judas.

"I did too," Philip inserted, matching Alphaeus' defiance with some of his own.

"It seems a bit twisted to argue the good fortune of another." I appealed to his better nature.

"I am not crazy, Jesus. I have my reasons. I am concerned about false hope. I am fearful of hysterical reaction."

"Reason is the sole bastion for the stubborn unbeliever," I observed pointedly.

"I know what I saw," Judas said, revived.

"You know what you think you saw in an emotional moment. Will it last?" Alphaeus seethed.

"How can anything last unless it is begun?" probed Philip.

The discussion had garnered an audience, listening and trying to determine the topic.

"And nothing begun in deceit will bear heavenly return," jabbed Alphaeus in response to Philip.

"Is it all right with you if Joanna walks, Brother Alphaeus?" I asked quietly.

"Don't challenge my compassion, boy. I have loved that sister ever since I met her at the Jordan."

"The same is true with me, sir. Did you know she wanted to be well?"

"Everyone wants to be well."

The gathering ensemble gave a groan.

"Not so," said one from the crowd.

"Sickness can be like a mantle of protection from the harsh and cruel realities of living," shot a most astute John.

"Very true," agreed Matthew.

"So I am to be mobbed by your deluded mass?" said Alphaeus, exasperated.

"There is no solace for hopelessness. It can't even tolerate being with itself. These people are compelled to believe Joanna is walking as a result of her faith. If they don't believe for her, then maybe their miracle was a lie. Maybe they will lose their second chance, too." I reached out and grabbed the arm of an older chap. "Look at him, Alphaeus. Three days ago he was leprous and dying. Don't you think he wants to partake in Joanna's miracle?"

The aging man smiled at Alphaeus, proudly displaying the fresh pink skin of a newborn child.

"And this former blind man. Do you think he can afford to doubt God's mercy in the life of another? He lives to see a daily confirmation what happened to him was no accident, that he will never have to walk in darkness again."

Alphaeus paused to reflect.

"But what if it begins and ends with no explanation for its origin or promise to return?" It was a new voice, a Pharisee.

"What do you mean, man?" growled Judas.

"What is your name? Identify yourself," commanded Matthew.

"I am Simon, a Pharisee."

A rumble of disapproval.

"Silence, my brothers," I said. "Welcome, Simon. Please speak."

"What if it stops as quickly as it starts?"

"Then we make sure we don't miss a minute of the glory," said Simon the fisherman, just arriving on the scene.

"Well, good morning, Simon, meet Simon," I smirked, nodding a greeting. "How was the fishing?"

"We are having bread this morning, if that answers your question."

"Everything has a time and those endowed with wisdom jump on quickly and desert late," I said to Simon, the non-fisher.

"That is all I'm trying to do," said Alphaeus. "I was with John from the beginning and don't want to leave him now in the wake of some populous movement." He scrutinized the faces of the gathering numbers, looking for understanding, needing affirmation.

"Now concerning this rogue named John." I addressed the assembled. "You certainly didn't go out to see a man dressed in fine cloth, nor one fragrant from exotic oils from the East."

The whole crowd laughed and Alphaeus smiled. I walked amongst them.

"What did you go to see? A prophet? No, more than a prophet. Sweet-smelling dainty men live in palaces and have calluses on their backsides instead of their hands."

A hearty grunt of approval.

"John was not rattled by every wind blowing an opinion. He cried out when no one was there to listen. He preached when no one heard. You wonder how long this will last, like I am sure John does from his cell at Herod's palace. Beware! Pharisees want to know the origin of everything from the yeast in their bread to the miracle of a soul raised from the dead. It is not always so convenient. Life is not so generous to the stringent and demanding. Some mornings we awaken filled with energy. Then there are days when our bodies ache and we feel lazy and heavy laden. Do you control this? Can you make your hair change color? Can you give yourself another breath of time? Yet you fuss about what you can't change. You dream for more, and lose the precious little entrusted to you. My friends, drink the cup filled with the freshness of new wine." I looked down at Alphaeus, who had found a seat in the midst. "John the Baptist is greater than any man born of woman. None greater--truth. But the one we consider the least in our kingdom is greater in God's eyes than the Baptist. May God inhabit our day. John's was then. Ours is now."

A hushed stillness--the morning cool emptied of clatter, providing space for men to absorb. Unfortunately, too brief. The Pharisees commenced to grumble, but Simon, one of their own, cocked his head, pausing for deeper contemplation. Judas looked to Alphaeus, and Alphaeus studied me, then stood and walked away.

James and Jude followed their Papa.

"I must learn more. I must know more," Judas announced, further breaking the thoughtful silence, as I quietly watched an old friend leave.

James and Jude caught up with their father, who had established a healthy clip in exiting.

He stopped and turned, sensing their presence. "I committed your lives to Jesus. I presented you as my sons to labor with this man as I had with John."

Both boys nodded, respectfully.

Alphaeus continued, "Perhaps it was not right of me to commit you in such a bold manner. After all, no one forced me to serve the Baptist. It was my choice. I selected to be part of each eccentric, holy, insane maneuver. It was not right for me to compel you to work with another man without giving you the dignity of deciding for yourselves."

The young men stared, puzzled by his words. "What are you saying, Papa?" asked Jude.

"I am saying you are free. I don't know where Jesus is heading, but you are no longer bound by family responsibility to stay with this movement."

James patted his father's head. "We love you, but we would not stay with Jesus on the strength of your decision."

Jude joined in. "I love you, Papa. You just don't know Jesus."

"You are our father. He is our life." James straightened tall.

"And if he is wrong," demanded Alphaeus, "and just another erratic character on the very uncertain field of our time? What if he leads to nowhere? What if he becomes preoccupied with his own sense of importance? Then what, my sons? What will become of you?

They looked at each other.

"Move towards life," said James.

"That is what you taught us, Papa," reminded Jude.

"John was good, but now his life is gone. He is followed by those who remember instead of those who live," James replied, directly.

"People like me, you mean," Alphaeus sprouted a slight smile.

Jude answered. "Yeah, Papa. You don't mean to be old but you have chosen to think, instead of do from your heart."

"You have both learned to speak freely. This is good as long as you can back it up with experience. I did not select to retire to memories. My body initiated the response," declared Alphaeus emphatically.

"And someday we will get tired, too," James agreed. "But for now we run toward the life--Jesus. He is the man of everything you taught us to think."

Alphaeus surveyed the men standing before him, looking for uncertainty and gauging the depth of their loyalty, a father relinquishing authority to his independent sons. "I will always be your Papa."

"You just can't be our life," said Jude with stinging honesty.

"I will be with John." Alphaeus quickly turned, beating a hasty retreat. His heart was swollen with sorrow and pride.   His head throbbed from the pressure of unreleased tears and the stress of the early morning conflict.

Jude reached out and grabbed his arm, pulling his papa close for an embrace. James joined. "And we will be with Jesus." He kissed the aged baptizer on the lips.

Meanwhile, I had accepted the invitation of Simon the Pharisee to dine at his house, not far. The Pharisees were using his home as a headquarters for viewing our kingdom movement. Simon's house was filled with heat and dust, a staleness hanging in the air. The room was occupied by austere holy men, mumbling, praying, reclining, dining on meticulously prepared food, in exacting proportions, served in overly-cleansed bowls.

Though invited, at no time was I to feel welcomed.

I had only brought a few of my companions along. Judas had pleaded to attend and I saw no need to deflate his enthusiasm.

We all laid down and waited in the steamy closeness, no longer in the fresh air I preferred. This was their arena.

Food was passed without comment, adding to the bleak environment.

Suddenly the door opened, allowing a stream of light to infiltrate the dim situation. The beam was so bright we were all temporarily blinded, not knowing who had entered the room. The door was left open.   Then the strangest thing happened. I felt someone kissing my feet, and the sensation of moisture trickling on my toes.

One of the Pharisees shut the door. "Were you born in a manger?" he shouted at the unseen arriver.

The kisses were followed by the stroking of my hair, disconcerting considering the dinner party was all men. I thought a dog or sheep had entered the room and selected my feet because they had the most recent residue of meat.

There was a gasp. The kissing or licking continued. The moisture fell on my feet like rain. I raised to see what had made its way to my side.

A woman, weeping, kissing my feet and then drying the freshiy fallen tears with her long, chestnut hair.

"Would you like me to get rid of her, rabbi?" Judas offered, leaning across my chest.

"What is your name?" I asked her.

She did not answer, timidly refusing to lift her head to look at me. She pursued her ministry of kisses, tears and strokes.

"My child, what . . ." I did not get to finish.

"Susanna," she answered, head still bowed.

Judas moved to stop her.

"Leave her alone," I whispered.

"The Pharisees are watching."

He was right. Everyone was staring at us. She and I had something in common; both unwelcome strangers.

I reached down and stroked her hair. She wept bitterly, as the hostile men hissed their disapproval.

"Simon," I shouted through the commotion.

Gradually the complaining subsided.

"Yes, rabbi," Simon replied cooly.

"I finally feel welcome in your home and it didn't come from you."

"She is a whore," spewed a voice from the corner.

"You didn't give me water so I could wash myself, nor a kiss of greeting."

Simon remained silent, fully aware of his oversights.

"Now this woman has not ceased to kiss me and has washed my filthy feet with her tears, and, even though her sins are many, they are forgiven because of faith."

More rumbling dissatisfaction.

"Be careful," cautioned Judas.

Rejecting his counsel, I continued. "You have built your faith on the actions of sacrifice. This woman has taken what she has--her tears, kisses, and soft hair and applied them, in hope, to her situation. That is faith. Use what is available. Kisses and tears have garnered forgiveness and salvation. Susanna, go about your way. You are forgiven."

"Rabbi, you have no power . . ." began Simon.

"It is you that have no power, Simon. You have no power to help this desperate woman nor the privilege of having me as your dinner guest anymore." I arose and left the house, trailed by a small delegation of nervous friends and one frantic former prostitute.

When we had distanced ourselves, Judas spoke. "Rabbi, I know you don't do anything without purpose."

"You mean, you hope I don't." I quickened my pace.

"Why do you choose to offend those leaders?"

"What was their purpose in offending Susanna?"

"She is a whore."

I stopped, causing my fellow-escapees to run into me. I smiled at Susanna. She was unscathed by Judas' observation.

I put my arm around Judas and pointed in the distance. "Do you see that small plume of smoke way over there?"

He squinted and said, "Yes, I believe so."

"If you were cold, Judas, would you head toward that smoke, assuming there would be a warm fire waiting?"

"I suppose so."

"Or would you look around and see if you had the kindling to start your own fire right here?"

"This is a trick."

"Staying warm does come up. It is a need. Which would you do?"

"In the distance," he mulled, "is the potential of a fire already started. I may be just a short journey from its warmth."

"Or is it merely the final smoke of a dying ember?"

"True. But here I may struggle to build my fire and fail to ignite the wood."

He was a son of reason. "Also true. It is a risk, but it is your chance, taken by you, using your own resources. Do you understand? You see, Judas, the Pharisees puff great smoke and promise great warmth. You may find it, or journey to their hearth where you remain frigid. But if God can teach you to be content using what is within your grasp, you may never be cold again."

Judas nodded and rubbed his beard, in deep thought.

"Come with us, barSimon, and build your fire." I offered my hand to the young inquisitor.

"Perhaps we both can warm by its blaze," he said, grabbing my hand. He smiled at Susanna.

"What are we waiting for? All this talk of fires has made me cold!" she joked.

We laughed and sauntered off to better places.

****

Joanna was afraid to stop, walking continually day and night for three straight days, driven to march because of the awesome nature of the miracle, but fearful if she rested, her legs would settle back into their leaden, useless position.

Making her journey back to the palace, she had decided to have the consorts carry her to the chambers on the couch--the bed of her former affliction. Even though it appeared to one and all she had adjusted to her handicap well, she hated her cushioned, purple silk divan-prison, never feeling comforted by its comfort.

She was grateful for her miracle but plagued with doubts. Would it last? Would she be crippled again? She was happy Jesus was not around to see her anxiety, even though she missed him very much. Still, she wondered why thoughts of the young Nazarene brought both joy and sadness. Maybe it was his tattered robe. Perhaps, the exhaustion etching its way across his features, or the nagging dread she might lose him.

A stark realization. It was not the loss of her healing she feared. She remembered back to one evening at the palace. Chusa had left for a meeting, dismissing the servants. She was alone and he was late returning. She needed to get to the trough to relieve herself. The time passed as she cried out for the servants. Her stomach muscles cramped. She tried to move but could not get down from her bed. She screamed for help--no response. Such a simple thing, a process normal people repeated several times a day, but she laid in pain, imprisoned on her bed. She restrained, squealing, unwilling to surrender. Overcome with exhaustion, she released--the simple waste of the day. She would never forget her humiliation; Chusa returned and found her soaked and rancorous in her own dung. The sheer damnable loss of control. This was her greatest fear. She never wanted to be that dependent ever again. Love and devotion were commendable, but she would walk proudly to the trough--a declaration of victory.

She wanted to run into Chusa's arms. She loved him very much, though never quite sure of the depth of his passions. He wasn't interested in other women. He was a man with a tepid deportment; pallid skin, emotions buried. Yet, she believed within his subdued demeanor there was an intelligence capable of solving any problem.

Yes, she would run into his arms, shattering his stony heart; a second miracle spawned from the power of the first. Chusa would be overwhelmed with joy, and she would know the fire of his enthusiasm.

They arrived at the palace. It was time. They hauled her to the door. She barely could sit still. The servants opened the door and Joanna leaped to her feet, ran into Chusa's arms, and wrapped her miraculous legs around his lean middle. Pulling back, he tripped over a footstool and fell on his backside, Joanna still attached. She was aghast, wanting to surprise her love, not maim him. She reached over to help him to his feet.

He pulled away, horrified, his narrow eyes widening, threatening to leap from his face."What happened?"

"Jesus healed me, even though he insists it was my faith that did it."

"H-h-how?"

"When I visited him in Galilee. No, that didn't really answer your question, You wanted to know how, not where." She knelt down and encircled his neck with her fragrant feminine arms. "Chusa, I can walk. I can run. I can go to the trough."

"You mustn't," he said mouth agape.

"No, I don't need to go to the trough now."

"No, you don't understand. You can't walk," he insisted as he moved with haste to his feet.

"Yes, I can." She marched, twirling.

Chusa grabbed the swirling Joanna. "You can't walk in Herod's palace. He is a superstitious madman. He will want to know the details of your good fortune. Worse yet, he will want to know who and why."

"I can walk, husband. Rejoice with me. For God's sake, dance with me," she pleaded, trying to catch his hand.

"We can dance quietly in this room, but you must never allow yourself to be seen by the members of the court."

"But the servants . . ."

"We will give them money for their silence." Chusa chewed on his thumb, his selected profile for interludes of tension and devious planning.

"I can't do this. Each step I take is an honor to the God who healed me. I cannot hide this miracle in the back chambers of a king's palace."

"Then prepare to be a widow. When Herod has questions and I cannot satisfy him with answers, he will torture or kill me to prove his royal authority."

"Are you serious, my love? I am never quite sure. Is this what you want?"

"No," he said, clasping her arms. "I would love to dance into the palace court and show off my beautiful miracle lady. But we must be careful, and for the time being, let's not tempt the powers that be."

This was not the homecoming she had anticipated. Then again, Chusa was her husband and usually had greater

wisdom on matters of palace etiquette. She submissively
nodded her head, as a tear squeezed its way from the corner
of her eye, falling upon her breast.

She would obey the wishes of her husband.

She could still walk to the trough. It was in the
house.

****

The watchman was alarmed. By day, Herod's
palace was a bustling arena, but usually darkness brought an
eerie stillness. Tonight a visitor made his way to the walls,
a stranger to the vigilant night guard who took great pride in
recalling the names of the travelers darkening his portal.
The visitor was small in stature with a crown of white hair
and a gray, woolen beard which came to a sharp point near
his stomach. His bearing was regal and manner bold, as he
trudged like an infantryman up the tiny hill leading to the
gate.

"It is late, traveler," declared the watchman with
authority.

"My journey forces me on into the night."

"What do you seek?"

"I seek an audience with the queen, one Herodias."

The guard eyed the stranger. Arriving late was one
thing, but to request an audience with the queen, well, that
was presumption bordering on lunacy.

The stranger continued his discourse. "She will
want to see me. It is in her best interest." He turned his
back as if preparing for a substantial wait.

The guard smiled at the little man, who possessed
audacity, if nothing else. "The queen is at rest."

"So may I have your name so she will know who
to behead on the morrow? She will want to know which
dense gatekeeper offended her honored guest."

The sentry frowned. Beheading was never out of the
question. "Whom should I say is calling?" he asked,
hoping to gain insight from the name.

"Jartanza of Smythania of the Chaldean host," he
stated importantly, without turning around.

"Jartanza?"

"Correct."

"Will she know you?"

"Here. Give her this to jostle her memory." He
handed the watchman a tightly wrapped piece of goat hide.
Staring at the lump, he wondered. What should he do? Just
a guard, questions of policy were beyond his domain. If
Herodias was going to behead someone let it be the intruder
instead of an over-zealous doorman. "I will return."

"Be quick about it. The chill stiffens my bones."

The gate-keeper was fortunate, the queen still awake. Her chamber-maid took the wrapped bundle and closed the door behind her, but not for long. Herodias came storming out, pointing a long, slender finger at the guard, bellowing, "Did you know what you brought to me? What was your ploy?"

Stepping back in panic, feeling the heat of her breath, he prepared to die. "No, my queen. I was unaware. It was a gift from a noble visitor. He seemed to know you, said you would be expecting him."

"Send him to my chambers. The audience is granted, but tell him I am unimpressed with tricksters. Prepare to be of merit."

The soldier tripped out the door and ran back to his post, finding Jartanza at the gate, still facing the darkened wilderness. "She will see you but you need to beware. She is angry at whatever it is you sent her. This had better be good."

Jartanza turned and smiled. "I can see why you are a lowly door watcher. You are frightened of what may happen. I would suggest you look at your meager life and be much more afraid of what is happening."

The diminutive one pushed his way past the affronted guard into the courtyard.

"Wait! You don't know where she is."

"We will find each other."

And so it was. Jartanza was confronted by Herodias scurrying down the palace steps. She halted, glaring, posturing above.

"You are Herodias, Queen of the Jews," he breathed, mustering a charm absent from his gate-side manner.

Herodias gazed down on him. "You are a man who has the head and features of a god and the body of a young stable boy," she said with a curled lip.

"I see you received my gift."

"Yes, a rather unusual present. It is a human ear?"

"Yes--freshly severed."

"I saw the blood was not yet dried."

"A delightful way to gain your recognition."

"To gain my ear you bring one of your own," she sang, descending a step.

"A most clever observation," he complimented, slowing easing up a step, careful not to disrupt the precarious balance of power.

"I see, however, it is not your ear," she said, reaching down short of his face and then pulling back.

"No. I'm sorry. I cannot provide you with a specific name. The donor must remain anonymous. A pilgrim who slept a bit too close to the well-worn path."

She piddled a faint smile; disgust mingled with impishness, betraying a sadistic curiosity.

He seized the moment to close the distance between them. "I am Jartanza of the Chaldeans," he said, bending on one knee.

"Chaldean? Then you are a sorcerer."

"Now, Queen Herodias. Everyone knows there are no sorcerers in Judea or Galilee, among the seed of Abraham."

"Oh, yes. Then shall we call you a wise man?"

"You may call me Jartanza, the servant of the queen."

"Will you join me in my chambers?"

"Though unworthy, I would be honored," he said, rising from his kneeling position.

"The night air has too many ears," she whispered, ascending the stairs.

"Aside from the one you carry," he inserted, trailing behind her, through the door, down the darkened corridor to her chambers.

She pushed the door, entered, tossing the ear on her purple bed. "What is it you want?"

"You offer no drink for a stranger?"

"I didn't know you were staying that long," she said, lying across the regal bed.

"I have no plans to depart," he said, inching to her side.

She lifted a hand to stop him. "What do you do, little man? That is, besides ear removal."

"I have come to solve your problem," he stated quietly, taking a couple of grapes from a nearby bowl.

"I have those poisoned to kill off overbearing guests."

"Then you don't want me to solve your problem?"

"Which problem? The boils on my thighs or the rotten meat shipped from Sidon?"

"I was thinking more of the stinking prophet you have in your dungeon," he proclaimed, popping a half dozen grapes in his mouth.

She sat up on the bed. "John? You know John?"

"I do."

"The one they call the Baptist?"

"Every single hair of him."

"Why do you think he is a problem to me? I am a queen. I am mother to the Jewish people."

"He is a problem to Herod, and Herod is a problem to you," said Jartanza as he sat down on the bed next to her.

"Herod is my husband. He is not my problem," she said, standing and moving across the room.

"Where is the king? Does he frequent your chambers? How long has it been since you have felt him inside you?"

"Perhaps I should cut off your ear, so I can have a matched set." She stumbled towards him, brandishing a small dagger.

Jartanza tried to remain calm, but a fine stream of sweat dribbled down his brow. "Is it always the Jewish way to kill the bearer of truth?"

There was a long, cold space while the two contemplated their options.

"How can you solve my problem?" she asked, throwing the blade on her bed.

Regaining presence of mind, he said, "I am a Chaldean, wait, what did we say--wise man. I am adept at the elimination of difficulty for those souls who believe in the powers dictating destiny."

"Speak plainly."

"John claims your husband is an adulterer and you are the whore of his iniquity."

"Untrue, but go on."

"Herod is so convicted by these accusations he chooses to, let us say, be self-sufficient in his sexual activities, no longer feeling the need to solicit your involvement."

"And how would you know all this?"

"How does the wind know where to blow? It allows itself to be taken by the forces in power. As do I, not trifling in mundane affairs like other men, I allow myself to be caught away by the delicious opportunities to witness the magic in the here and now," he postulated, boldly stroking her cheek.

"Do you believe in soul displacement?"

"Belief is too often just what a man hopes. I do not believe, I perform."

"I have sought pleasure amongst the eunuches. They are a clumsy brood, some too large, most too soft, smelling of aloes."

Jartanza smiled. The plan was unfolding with greater ease than expected, unlocking the heart of a queen. "Your problem is John. I can talk to him."

"Talk? Yes, this is what men do best. Maybe you could negotiate. I want my dignity back."

"And you shall, all the dignity you deserve. But I must see John."

The doors to the queen's chambers opened, and a young girl entered like a whirlwind, leaping on the bed and groping for the queen, needful of a hug. "Mother, he was at my door. I barely got away this time. I know he will find me. I will be alone," she shivered in tears.

"This is my daughter, Salome," Herodias said, embracing the frightened little lady.

"I am Jartanza, my princess," he said, bowing.

Salome ignored the introduction. "What can we do? Mother, he is going to have me." She fell on her mother's breast, sobbing.

"It is Herod. He yearns for my daughter. We have foiled his advances by pleading her unclean, but I think he is wise to our ploys."

Jartanza gently moved toward the mother and child, touching Salome's hair. "Do not fear, my lady. Your beauty will grant you the greatest desire of your heart."

Salome wept without comfort.

"I will see John," Jartanza determined.

"Please stay in my chambers," mouthed Herodias.

"I am not adept at granting favors for womanly pleasure."

"Too bad. Stay anyway."

"Yes. But I will see John."

Herodias nodded, and buried her face in the dark hair of her harassed young maiden.

****

Jartanza made a small pallet for himself in the corner of the matriarch's chambers. The first to awaken, he gingerly eased to his feet, muscles stiff and joints creaking.

Herodias was sprawled naked across her bed, an emptied cup lying on its side just beyond her grasp. He stood, considering the attributes of the Queen of the Jews-- bronzed, wrinkled skin, ribs protruding, with breasts resembling desolate plains of what once might have been tiny, firm hills. Her nose wiggled with displeasure even in the sanctuary of slumber, the girlish frown furrowing additional wrinkles like tiny levies constructed to dam a flood of tears.

Lying next to her, in a tiny human ball, was Salome, partially covered by the Queen's robe. She slept like a child, her feet scrunched underneath her, jutting buttocks pointing skyward.

Jartanza reflected, a wry smile curling across his dry, crusty lips. So this was royalty, he thought. No wonder the quest for wealth. Not only does it afford the luxury of possessions, but also permits the perniciously idiotic sluggard the benefit of survival.

He was careful to be quiet, not desiring an early morning conversation with Herodias. He had permission to see the prisoner. He didn't want her unpredictable memory to delay his mission. He would be to the dungeon to see John before she even discovered his absence.

A last glance at the prostrate monarch. Not so different than some prostitute lying on animal skins in the back stable of a Babylon inn. Yet this particular aging mass of flesh was a queen, endorsed by husband and Caesar.

He muffled a giggle as he inched his way to the large cedar door, bones cracking so loudly he was certain their chorus of complaint would startle the young girl.

Jartanza slowly opened the door and slid through the smallest opening possible, leaving it ajar, anticipating a thunderous thud if closed. Out of the chambers and on to the prison beneath. The palace was damp and chilly. The evening fires had released their warmth hours before. Dank, dark, foreboding, reeking of spoilage was the residence of Herod Antipas. Jartanza felt his way down the darkened corridor by touching the moist, slimy walls, attempting to avoid the sleepy dogs lying in wait for any unsuspecting rat.

Stairs, slippery from the dew--a final obstacle--as he neared the cell and found the guard asleep on the hay, snoring, mouth agape, sucking air like a drowning pig. The cell was open and a drone of hushed conversation came from within. Jartanza stepped across the plump body of the less-than-vigilant keeper. He listened at the entrance, careful not to be seen. Gathering his nerve he took one additional giant step and found himself inside the cramped enclosure, white hair grazing the roof.

He found two men sitting in a corner talking privately

"Aren't they afraid you will escape?" asked Jartanza, interrupting the exchange.

The burly, bearded one glanced up and said, "Escape to where," then turned and resumed his conversation. Glancing about, Jartanza realized he was right. Many walls to climb and guards to avoid.

"I'm Jartanza," he said, offering an outstretched hand.

"Are you prisoner or reasoner?" queried the bearded man, ignoring the hand.

Jartanza assumed he was John. "I don't think I understand."

"Well, there are only two excuses to be in this place," said John. "You are either put here for contrariness or sent here to get me to recant my allegations against Herod."

"I am neither. I, like you, am a holy man." He crouched, feeling for a dry spot to sit.

"Did you hear that, Alphaeus? Our friend here thinks I am a holy man. It doesn't seem right that they can imprison a man and then send strangers to his cell to insult him on top of all the other indignities." Alphaeus smiled. "I am not a holy man," stated John, flatly.

"A man of God and words, then?" suggested Jartanza.

"What is it you want?"

"Well, of your two choices, I guess I am a reasoner."

"It would have been my assumption. You aren't fragrant enough to be a prisoner." John gave an echoing chuckle which in most taverns would qualify as a bawdy laugh.

"What is your business? We were involved in some discussions," interjected Alphaeus.

"Let me not interrupt," said Jartanza, leaning back trying to appear comfortable in the surroundings.

"The matters were private," Alphaeus emphasized.

"Private or secret?"

John shifted to his knees. "We were planning my grand exit from this palatial accommodation. We thought if I grew just a bit more hair and beard and wallowed about in the mold of the hay, they might throw me out of the gates, deeming me the wretched remains of a diseased ox."

This time Alphaeus laughed, choking back the sound, respectful to the guard.

"You would pass better as a beaten ass," said Jartanza, dousing the levity.

"Now that I have been called before." John cast a fiery gaze at the uncomfortable visitor. Rebuffed, Jartanza turned and studied the wall.

"We can continue this later," sighed Alphaeus, rising to his feet.

"You were talking about Jesus," Jartanza gradually pivoted his head to reveal a sinister grin.

John, shaking his head, remanded Alphaeus.

"No, Baptist. Your friend did not tell anyone. What else would a prematurely retired prophet talk about than his latest competition?"

"I have no competition with Jesus."

"I know you have said that, but there are those of us in Israel who would love to hear your message alive and well again, being boomed from the Jordan."

"Why are you here?" demanded John.

"I represent the countless thousands of brothers everywhere who were moved by your call and are left cold by this Nazarene."

John squinted at his intruder, then peered at Alphaeus, who shrugged his shoulders.

"Who do you represent?" asked John cautiously.

"Your message was more powerful in the wilderness. Oh, Jesus is quite a miracle man. But here, among the seed of Abraham and the adherents to Moses, we do not sanction alleged acts of the supernatural conjured before our eyes, having no sense of Godly authenticity."

"That is what I was telling John," bubbled Alphaeus, leaning forward.

John lifted a hand, demanding silence.

"You made two mistakes, Baptist," said Jartanza, testing his liberties.

"I made more than that. They just didn't catch them."

"The first was taking Herod so seriously. Don't you know he is the joke of the empire? Pontius Pilate has court jesters that do nothing but perform spoofs of him."

John allowed the hint of a grin to cross his stern features. "I love Herod. I love him the way you would love your cross-eyed brother whom your father has assigned you the responsibility of teaching how to hunt. You must point him the right way, show him what to do, and just make sure you are standing behind him when he finally lets loose the fury from his bow."

Jartanza released a spontaneous laugh in spite of himself. He plodded on. "Your second mistake was turning your ministry over to Jesus of Nazareth."

"I must decrease. He must increase."

"Decrease perhaps, but disappear?" challenged Alphaeus, wearily.

"Decrease to achieve what?" posed Jartanza. "When have the armies of the Lord ever retreated in the presence of the enemy? Jesus speaks of a kingdom of heaven, and lives as a gentile in the hills of Galilee. He extracts his followers from amongst the self-indulgent, the afflicted, and unmotivated dreamers. It is a not the army of repentant souls you enraged and empowered through God to restore the promises of Israel."

"And what is the source of his power?" inserted an agitated Alphaeus.

"I don't need both of you to hear one truth," said John, raising his hands. "Alphaeus, leave me with this brother. I will see you later." John reached over and gave as much of an embrace as the confines would allow. Alphaeus glanced at John and then over to the visitor. Jartanza mustered a compassionate, warm smile.

"All right. I can see you two have much to talk about," Alphaeus said, struggling to exit the cell.

"Come soon, my friend," said John, absentmindedly.

Jartanza was confident. He had acquired the ear of the Sage of the Jordan--poised to gain his comradery. Now, he was alone with the great prophet of Israel. Mission accomplished.

As Alphaeus was about to leave the cell, John lifted his head. "My dear comrade." Alphaeus stopped, turned and fell to his knees before John, who looked into his eyes, giving a passing glance to Jartanza. "Have you thought what you will do with my body?"

"When, John?"

"When I am dead, of course," he said, irritated. "We have never really determined the destination of my remains."

Alphaeus was visibly shaken.

"Elizabeth and Zachariah are both gone," said John mostly to himself.

Alphaeus nodded and Jartanza twitched impatiently, preparing to speak.

John pressed on. "I think I would like to be near them. I am not even sure if they have a space in their tomb for me."

Jartanza could stand it no longer. "The two of you can discuss such far-reaching plans later. You, I, and John must talk of the ministry to our people."

John ignored him. "If there is no place for me amongst my kin I think I would like to be immersed one last time in the Jordan," said John, glaring at Jartanza.

"Of course," agreed Alphaeus, perplexed but obedient.

"So you want to die?" said Jartanza, with an icy spit.

"You may go, Alphaeus," said John. "Just remember to take my body far from this palace."

"Of course, John," said Alphaeus with a tear in his eye. He backed out of the cell and turned to make his way over the sleeping guard.

"You don't have to die, Baptist," said Jartanza, uneasily.

"Your name again?" examined John, cocking his head and scooting closer to the stranger.

Jartanza was bewitched; the sensation of being in a room with a powerful, imbalanced inmate who had just gained advantage. "Death is not the answer. You are a great prophet."

"And the alternative to death? What might that be, Jartanza?" He was disquieted; John referred to him by name, the first time the Baptist had specifically uttered it. The sound fell cold and deliberate from his lips.

"Herod is weak and easily led in the direction of most flattery. He could be convinced to disregard his differences with you."

"And what of Herodias? She seems to have a deep stake in my demise."

"I have met with Herodias," said Jartanza with the glee of a child possessing a secret.

"And from the smell of your clothes, you have also slept with her."

"Yes, I have been in her chambers but not as a lover. I have interceded for you."

"And she is willing to forget I called her an adulteress?"

"She is willing to do what is best to prosper the palace of Herod and to further procure her comforts."

"How would Herod and his brother's wife prosper from my release?"

"If he was on the throne and you were back restoring the people of Israel to their traditional practices in honoring God, then . . ."

"Let me stop you there." John paused as Jartanza fidgeted. "When I was twelve years old I had a dream. Didn't have that dream again until three nights ago."

"Dreams are important. They signal a beckoning from the forces which determine our purposes."

"I'm glad you feel that way, because in this dream, I am alone. I know it is me even though I do not see myself."

"Did I tell you that I am an interpreter of dreams?" Jartanza inched closer.

"Then perhaps you can discern mine."

"Like Daniel of old, with the Almighty's help, I will try."

"In my dream, there is a man who comes up to me and, as I said, I know it is me even though I cannot see myself. He comes very close, and pulls back his cloak and says, 'Would you like to see'?" John mimicked the raspy, hollow voice of his dream-stranger.

Jartanza leaned forward, scratching his beard.

"I hear myself saying, 'Yes, I would like to see'. 'No, you can't', replies the man. He laughs and then pulls a human head out from beneath his garb. He swings it by the hair, dripping blood."

Jartanza tried to maintain a scholarly calm.

"As I told you, I had this dream as a boy of twelve. You can certainly see why it remained in my memories. After all these years, I had the dream just a couple of nights ago, three to be exact. I said that, didn't I?"

"A most intense and revealing dream," said Jartanza in an overly analytical way.

John ignored his intrusion and continued, "In both dreams, my head was as I am--a man--not a boy. You know something else?" breathed John, leaning toward Jartanza.

"What is it, my friend?"

"The man holding my head?"

"Yes?"

"He looked just like you." John thrust his face into the surprised sorcerer's nose.

Jartanza gulped. "Me? I would do you no harm!"

"No, it is not your fault. The snake was born slithering, striking out. It's me! Oh God, please forgive me for my self-pity in this jail cell."

Jartanza was speechless, wary of his own tongue.

"How stupid I was to doubt Jesus. How weak I must have appeared, for the forces of darkness to think they could scrape the stables of hell and send some ass like you to guide me into dark defeat. Did they really expect me to be party to a plan to destroy what I have lived to usher in?" John was weeping, jowls flushed with anger, volume exploding, rising to his feet, moving threateningly towards the retreating Jartanza.

The guard awakened from all the commotion.

Jartanza, fearing for his life, screamed for help. "Guard! Your prisoner is escaping! He has gone mad!"

The guard entered, yawning. "Are you alright, John?"

"Fine, Samuel."

"I am the one who is in danger, you camel-brained lunatic!"

"Be careful, you will have two of us after you," said John, laughing heartily.

"Should I run him through, Baptist?" questioned Samuel drawing his sword.

"No, we must allow him to return to my lady unharmed, so they can plot their devious scheme and get me out of this whole mess once and for all," said John as Jartanza scurried to hide behind the guard.

Samuel shook him off like a crawling creature discovered in the night covers.

Jartanza ran to the stairs and started to climb.

"By the way," John screamed at the scrambling little man, "repent, you shrunken sack of goat vomit!"

It hadn't gone well. What happened? Jartanza fretted and fumed, stumbling, as he groped his way to the top of the dungeon stairs, too terrified to look back, and much too humiliated to listen to the taunting laughter billowing from the prison beneath. Burning with resentment, he swore John would pay for his eccentric behavior. Such shortsightedness would be rewarded with deadly consequences.

Rants of rage and revenge boiled in his mind as he opened the door and raced into the hall. Turning the corner he ran headlong into Chusa, equally harried, coming from the other direction. Chusa knocked the sorcerer back on his behind and scuttled on without saying a single word.

Jartanza lay bruised; buttocks, feelings, and ego-- seething.

****

Chusa ran through the shadowy halls, aided by candles and the first beams of morning light. Summoned-- not unusual, part of his job. After all, he was in charge of the king's household affairs, and the king would periodically make the household his affair. Fastidious care was taken to anticipate the royal whim, but Herod's appetites were notorious, leaning to the bizarre.

Though being summoned was part of the job, it was still odd for it to come this early in the morning, and a little peculiar for the request to come from Blastus.

Blastus was King Herod's chamberlain, the eyes, ears, mouth, and often, the punishing hand for the erratic monarch. He dutifully enacted Herod's moody edicts. A summons from Blastus usually meant a complaint from the disgruntled king.

So. . . hustling along, scouring his memory to anticipate the nature of the rebuke, preparing a suitable excuse, certainly not wanting to collect his thoughts on the spot, often coming across bumbling and contrived.

He arrived at the door, inhaling with a wheeze and releasing a ragged breath, he tapped lightly. No reply. He wanted to leave, hoping time would blow away the whole affair, whatever it was.

Yet, this was not the chamberlain's methodology. "Deal with *now* this minute so you will be prepared for the next *now* when it comes along," he would storm at the quaking servants.

Chusa knocked again with more vigor. He would be able to tell by Blastus' face the seriousness of the charge.

The door was whisked open and Blastus said, "Come in, Chusa." The chamberlain walked over to a chair, plopped down and spoke without looking up. "Sit down, frosty this morning."

Chusa was puzzled, unable to gauge his mood. "Good morning, Lord Blastus."

"The reason I called you in--we have some discrepancy in the household accounts."

Chusa shuddered in his belly and stood weak-kneed in silence. His mouth dried up, throat swelled, leaving no passage for speech.

Blastus paused for a moment and then glanced up at the statue-still accountant. "Please sit down," he said with a greater degree of authority.

Chusa obeyed, easing his way onto the chair provided.

"Herod was desirous of figs." Blastus studied a parchment.

"We have figs," said Chusa, surprised.

"Not Macedonian figs."

"I see. He does not like our local figs?"

"Not just figs. Let's see--aloes, the Egyptian bathing oils, oleander, the Greek wines, the list is quite lengthy. I spoke to the cook and the household staff who informed me the budgets for these items had been trimmed . . . by you." Blastus lifted his head to achieve full eye contact.

Chusa squirmed in his over-sized chair--trouble The chamberlain's countenance was immutable, a stern man, demonstrating the glare of an unrelenting disciplinarian.

"Finances are meager," said Chusa sheepishly.

"Kings do not care about budgets. Those are concerns for weak-willed servants. Kings want their desires. It is your job to prepare for such requests and set aside money for King Herod's divergent tastes."

"I ran out of money." He immediately realized his lapse; a most unfortunate choice of words. Pleading poverty to a taxing individual invites an audit.

"Then bring me your accounts and we will go over them together."

He did not need assistance in reviewing the palace expenses. Chusa knew the records: money spent, what had been allocated to each department, as well as how much *he* had claimed.

Mind you, he was not a thief; not pilfering in the conventional sense.

He had simply granted himself advances which were, as of yet, unpaid, giving himself financial boosts which he felt would have been rewarded were Herod the type to participate in such acts of generosity.

A record of palace affairs. The tally was clear to Chusa. Each shekel had been fancied and placed with care into scrutinized events and projects. Yet the account of the dealings might be confusing to the financially austere Blastus.

Moments passed. Blastus sat and stared at the deliberating Chusa. The silence was much too long for him to justify, so he decided to pretend he hadn't heard.

"Well?" Blastus said at length.

"I'm sorry, my lord. Did you say something?"

"Yes, I want you to bring your records here to my chamber. And I want them this very day." Blastus stood to his feet.

"Today? Oh, that is not possible."

"I will decide the feasibility of the timetable."

"No, what I mean, Lord Blastus, is I would like some time to gather the material and do justice to the chamberlain's request."

"How long?"

"A week?"

"First thing tomorrow morning."

Chusa swallowed the large lump in his throat. Negotiations were over, this he knew. He stood, tottering, backing towards the door. "Thank you, my Lord, for your consideration. I want you to know there is nothing wrong, just I need my work to be presented excellently. This is why I asked for the time. "

"I am not concerned about the quality. I am most interested in the accuracy."

Chusa muzzled himself, for errant words had already deprived him of his secret world. Discarded, he quietly evaporated from the room, shuffling his way down the hall.

The records were in shambles. He would never be able to formulate an explanation by morning. His only hope was to have as much gold and silver in hand as possible, to alleviate suspicion of embezzlement; much better to be considered an overly-zealous spinster. His case--just saving expense on the palace budget. In the process he had failed to execute some necessary duties. Blastus, seeing the funds in hand, would give a rebuke for poor management, but would withdraw his request for a full accounting.

Chusa felt much better. He had saved a large cache of money for just such an occasion.

Joanna was just awakening, as Chusa bounced into the room, whistling.

"Good morning, my sweet husband."

He headed straight to the closet containing his emergency withholdings. He had wrapped them in a purple silken robe purchased for Joanna from merchants of the East. She had showed no interest in the lavish garment. Joanna's tastes were simple, and due to her crippled condition, she never attended a palace banquet where such elegance might be appropriate. Chusa knew she would never wear it; she never even looked at it, probably forgetting it was there. An excellent hiding place.

He found the robe. What was this? It was loose, not wrapped tightly. He picked it up and shook it. Nothing came out. He scrounged about the closet looking for the provision.

Gone.

Frantic. Calm down, he thought. Don't let Joanna know anything is wrong. She probably just moved it. "My dear Joanna," he said with uncharacteristic kindness.

"Chusa! You are so pale! Are you sick? You must get into the sun and out of this dreary palace." She reached for his forehead.

He pulled away. "No, I just exerted myself a bit in the closet," he said. "Do you remember that purple robe I bought for you?"

"Yes, I tried it on a few days ago."

"Where is it?"

"It's in the closet."

"No, not the robe. I need what was in the robe."

She smiled. "I found all that treasure. I didn't remember we had saved anything. I was sure you had forgotten it too."

"No, I hadn't forgotten."

"Were you saving it for some reason?"

"Joanna, where is the money?"

"I didn't know it was yours. I mean, I didn't think we were saving. We are comfortable."

"Joanna, where is the money?" he panted, grabbing her arms and squeezing.

"Chusa, what's wrong?"

"I just want to know where the money is!"

"I sent it to Jesus, for his ministry."

Chusa sank to his knees like a man stricken with palsy. "You what!"

"I didn't think we needed it right now. I knew Jesus did. It seemed right. It was in my robe and I thought you were saving it for my happiness. I knew nothing would make me happier than to provide for Jesus' ministry."

"You gave him all of it?"

"I didn't want to hold back."

"I am a dead man."

"Chusa, what is wrong?"

"Blastus will . . ." He started to explain and then stopped.

Joanna shook her husband.

He buried his head in her bosom and began to cry like a baby. "It wasn't my money. I took it from the treasury."

"Took it? You mean you stole it?"

"For you, my love. I wanted you to have fine things."

"I didn't need anything! I didn't ask you for anything."

"A man knows what a woman requires and he yearns to give it. Don't you see, Joanna? We both are in danger."

"What can we do?"

"I don't know. Can you get the money back?" He peeked up, earnestly.

"I don't know," she groaned, troubled.

"I don't know what to do," he said, staggering from the room, slamming the door behind him.

Joanna sat quietly, alone. It was the first time in many years he had included her in anything of consequence. Chusa was her husband. He could be right. Maybe it was her fault. Had she been demanding or sent signals of dissatisfaction? She would have to help.

****

Having survived the Baptist's scrutiny, the sword of the guard, and the collision with Chusa, Jartanza gathered his wits and headed back to Herodias, arriving in a huff of aggravation--disheveled, unkempt, and red-faced from all his humiliating exploits.

"What happened to you? Did one of your hexes backfire?" Herodias stood back, bemused.

"I have been to see John."

"You didn't ask permission."

"Yes I did, my Queen. Last evening you gave me your most gracious blessing for my adventure."

"A nod is not a royal bidding."

"Forgive my oversight, my lady. I felt a nod from the Queen of Israel carried more authority than Caesar's Legion." Herodias smiled, remarkably duped by the flattery. "Would the Queen like to know of my discoveries?"

"No! Not if it is going to disrupt the flow of my morning. The early hours are so important to the structure of a balanced day." As she spoke, she posed, staring off in the distance to add credence to her homespun philosophy.

Jartanza smiled, remembering the naked drunken woman he had snickered at hours before.

"Do you mock me with your smirk?" she snarled.

"Not at all. I was simply considering how one so powerful and beautiful also possesses such insight into the human soul."

"I study. I struggle. I experience and . . .   I become," she said, pouring herself a cup of wine.

"I do not wish to disrupt your flow, but something must be done about John the Baptist."

"I do not wish to hear his name or any more of his lies," she said, gesturing with her cup. Droplets of wine pelted the tiny warlock's head.

"As you wish," said Jartanza, drying off on a nearby robe.

"Then he did speak of me?"

"I thought you didn't . . ."

"You thought. You thought. Do people stand around in expectation of your thoughts, little man?" She bent over and stared at him, her right eye refusing to focus.

"No, my Queen. I am at your bidding alone."

"Well, tell me what he said." She climbed up on her bed and sat cross-legged, like a young girl readying for a bedtime tale.

Jartanza unleashed his contrived tirade. "He must be stopped. I do not wish to bore you with the drivel from his uneducated lips. We must devise a plan."

"There is no 'we', sorcerer. There is only me and those I beckon to perform my will."

"How rude of me. You must forgive me, but each moment that. . .that religious tyrant lives in defiance to your rule and authority is an insult to all that is holy." Herodias appeased, Jartanza continued. "Herod will not punish John for his insults. There must be a well-executed plan to rid you of this damnable torment once and for all."

"You do understand," said Herodias, reaching out her hand. Jartanza stretched but she pulled away and said, "The problem is, Herod respects this prophetic vermin. Respects and fears." Climbing down from the bed, she crossed the room and poured another cup of wine.

"Herod has other concerns." He paused. Herodias turned and waved her hand for him to continue. "I have a plan."

"I am amused by plans, especially those promoted by unkempt, impotent underlings." Jartanza remained silent, awaiting the flick of her hand. She delayed, simpering a humorless curl from tight, thin lips, testing his subservience, visibly aroused by the new game. "Go on," she decreed with a fanciful flutter of her fingertips.

"What would happen," Jartanza began, "if Herod were not able to find Salome?" Her smirk exited, ushering in an irritated glare. "I mean," Jartanza hurried, "he feels he will eventually attain the favors of the girl. It seems he is correct, considering she is right down the hall and he is the king." Jartanza risked continuing without the permission wave. "If Salome could be hidden until Herod realized he had. . . lost his. . . ability to dabble with her," Jartanza said cautiously, fearful of making too much innuendo to the mother, "then he would be nearly insane with his own lust."

"And what value is Herod's lust to me?"

"If Salome could reappear at your selected time, my Queen, the grateful King might be vulnerable to her charms and be willing to negotiate the fate of one dungeon locust-eater."

Herodias cocked her head, eyes gaining a brief glint of comprehension. "I would get two things from this. First, my daughter would be safe from the ravages of the pig-man.

And, at the juncture of my choosing, I could release my flower for the bee to buzz and sniff."

"Herod will be ready to burst in his fantasy."

"And I will manipulate his delight to gain my will."

Smiling, both were content each had conceived the plan while the other was captivated by its devilish ingenuity.

****

Standing before me was the graying father of the man I once met many years ago as a boy in Jerusalem.

Aging--some people's countenances reflect perceived horror and ongoing anguish over the whole life process. Others, like Jairus, become a wrinkled visage of their younger selves; features only slightly marred by time and sagging.

He arrived, his little daughter sick, hopeful--greatly concerned for her well-being, yet still feeling energized he had taken steps to resolve her condition; coming to me, a difficult decision for a father to leave his child's bedside during the season of her greatest need, still, believing God, who performed magnificent deeds throughout Galilee, would have a blessing for his little girl.

"Move toward the movement" had become my personal creed. Jairus had the activated faith. I followed him, wondering if he would remember me from the temple so many Passovers before.

Then, messengers arrived from his home.

Bad news.

"Your daughter is dead. Don't trouble the master anymore."

Watching Jairus. My words were useless. This was his decision. His eyes, a harvest of tears from a furrowed brow of increasing doubt.

Did he blame me? For although we set off at a quickened pace, there had been a delay. Surrounded by an immense gathering, someone touched the hem of my robe. (In retrospect, I don't know if I felt the touch, or sensed a connection; the same chilling warmth flowing through me in Anisa's tent.) I turned to discover a crouched mass of weeping middle-aged woman, hunkered down, kneeling at my feet, making her latest attempt to improve her faltering fortune--common sense temporarily relieved from its ardent duty.

The result, she was healed.

I was compelled to stop and celebrate with this daring soul, commensurate with the dynamics of such a ferocious faith.   "Your faith has made you whole!" I squealed in delight.

I always marvel at faith, both great or small. Great faith is such an unexpected pleasure. I am in awe of the faithful one striking such a blow of unearthly intelligence. On the other hand, little faith always makes me equally awe-struck; dumbfounded by the short-sighted one who feels he can dictate life's unpredictable flow without any help from the Father.

The celebration with the woman was a needful act, stealing precious moments of traveling time to reach a very sick little girl. Did Jairus think such a demonstration for an already healed woman was prudent, given the urgent need of his daughter? Undeniably, his child was dead; however, I could not believe because one woman was granted the dignity and space to experience her own miracle, a little girl would be cursed to death.

I looked at my friend. Was there any faith left in him? Was he willing to see the saga through? "Don't be afraid. Just believe," I said, touching his arm. He raised his head; the bewildered countenance of a mourning father.

Starting to speak, stopped. I sensed his dilemma, being torn between *What in the hell is going on here* ? and *What have I got to lose?*

I walked on toward the house, not certain Jairus could manifest belief, but maybe he could follow my faith as I had moved out on his. He decided to risk it; after all, he had to go home anyway. . . for a funeral.

As we neared the house we heard the wailing mourners who had gathered to comfort and, unfortunately, confirm the family's loss. The household was involved in the hustle and bustle of preparations. Except, sitting in the corner with a vacant stare, was a disconsolate woman whom I decided must be Jairus' wife. The passage of just a few fleeting moments had transported her from mother to the shattered caretaker of a lifeless form.

"She is not dead. She is sleeping," I announced to the assemblage.

No response, a sigh, two giggled, and then a small burst of laughter. Mama turned and gazed at me disapprovingly, as Papa Jairus bowed his head; reverent belief or blossoming humiliation? Who could know?

The laughter became scornful, the friends of the family feeling I breached good taste.

"That is really insensitive," whispered one.

"How about some respect for the family?" asked another.

Ridicule gradually translated to smoldering rage.

"Everyone out!" I commanded.

The objections continued.

"I said everybody out!" I screamed from my own frustration.

The room fell silent as the gathered stared at Jairus for confirmation.

"I said everybody out of here. Everybody except the mother and father," I said more calmly, looking to Jairus-- his time to decide.

Jairus raised his head and said, "Do as he says."

"But Jairus, he thinks the child is sleeping," said the one who had suggested respect.

"We know she is dead. Do you think we would say she were dead if she were asleep?" pronounced a grandmotherly type from across the room.

"I know the difference between sleep and death!" added another.

More confusion. I waited for Jairus. I wasn't playing games. There is nothing wrong with questioning the validity of your circumstances until God has confirmed it to be your reality.

"As I said," he stated with some additional spunk, "I would like you all to leave. Perhaps the Master can awaken my slumbering lady." It was carefully phrased, quietly delivered, nevertheless forceful enough to dismiss the aggravated assembly of mourners and comforters, simply not needed at this time. There would be doubt aplenty in the room with Mama, Papa and myself without the accumulated questioning of the confused.

When they were all gone we went into the small room where the little girl lay still. She was so peaceful it almost seemed a sacrilege to interrupt her journey to paradise. By this time her soul must be shedding the fantasy of this earthly entanglement, and grasping with glee the revelation of all beauty, in a breathless whisk to Glory.

I knelt by her bed. "My sweet one, you must come back. It is not time to fly. You are needed here. Young maid, arise."

I lifted her hand.

Nothing.

Jairus winced, trying to disguise his disappointment. The mother bowed her head and cried.

Then. . .the young maid's eyes rolled beneath her closed lids. A finger jiggled, as her chest gently rose. Mama and Papa stopped in the midst of their tears and anguish, he falling to his knees and she leaping upon her awakening daughter, as I stumbled back, astonished.

(Surprise over God's intervention of blessing is not a lack of faith.)

Smiling, chuckling, laughing--just too beautiful.

Jairus rose to his feet and embraced me. "You are the temple boy!"

"I was twelve years old."

"My daughter is twelve."

"The woman healed on the road today had been sick for twelve years," I said, hugging my brother.

To us it was significant; the cleverness of a most ingenious Father

I pulled him back and looked into his eyes. "You saved me from all those crotchety old priests."

"You were doing all right."

"I should be glad Annas was high priest, and a Jew, or I think he might have eaten me alive right there in front of all those brethren."

Sweet, tension-relieving, grateful laughter.

"Thank you."

Emotion so rich you are tempted to look away.

"You did good, Papa. You saved your daughter's life," I managed.

He surrendered, composure set aside, allowing himself to crumple to his knees in joyous tears.

Turning to the mother, I said, "Give the girl something to eat. The journey back to life drains the body of energy."

Jairus wept great wells in gratitude to the God whom he had honored in years of service.

This day the servant was graced with homage from his Master.

****

Salome had spent a peaceful visit with her grandfather. Now the messenger brought the news Herodias requested her return. There would be a birthday celebration for Herod at Machaerus, his palace high in the mountains near the Arabian border, which he had acquired from his former father-in-law, Aretis--appropriate in Herodias' thinking. What better place to revel than at the home of Herod's previous wife? Conveniently sinister.

Salome, having nearly blotted Herod's advances from her mind, did not want to leave the safe haven of her grandparent's home, where she was perceived as a little girl instead of having her blooming feminine qualities eyed with a devious leer. After all, she was just a girl no matter what her body was portraying.

Returning to Herod, she would again become the tantalizing morsel of his insatiable appetite.

Worse was the uncertainty about her mother. What was being devised in the chambers between Herodias and Jartanza? Knowing her mother, something would be avenged. Herodias had always been enamored by the ways of the conniving Italian women. What she learned from them she mingled with her own arsenal of deception to create a separate breed of viciousness spawned from her ravenous heart.

There was precedent. Salome recalled one ambitious eunuch who had tried to extort favor and funds from the presumedly satisfied queen. He believed her appreciation over his prowess proved him to be indispensable. He demanded outlandish payment in exchange for his noble efforts.

She plotted her revenge. She invited him to dinner, drugged him, and in the morning he awoke in his chambers in intense pain, looking down to discover a bandaged stub where his right leg used to be; a servant displaying his dismembered part on a golden platter.

"The queen," the servant said, "wishes me to return this to you as a fresh reminder of her acknowledgement over services rendered, with the aim you will not choose to run away from your courtly duties."

All grumbling from the corps of eunuches desisted.

Salome was fully aware of her mother's fiendish ways. She reluctantly made the journey to Herod's court, escorted into the queen's chambers under the cover of darkness--Herodias and Jartanza morose and inebriated.

Herodias pointed to the bed. "That is what you will wear," she said as she poured a fresh goblet of wine.

"It should be quite beautiful," said Jartanza with a slight bow.

"Well, hello to you, mother," said Salome, disgusted, lifting the garment for viewing.

"Herod is beside himself," Herodias spurted. "He has sent soldiers searching for you."

"I am not going to wear this." Salome dropped the costume on the floor.

"Why is that, princess?" asked Jartanza.

"First of all, the top is too small and secondly, the bottom is too big. Thirdly, it is an outfit for a court whore," she said, glaring at her mother.

"It is the finest silk and laces of the East, from the dancing girls. It is an outfit for frolic, my sweet," Herodias cooed.

"Dancing girl? Just another name for prostitute." Salome plopped on the bed, defiantly.

"Try it on. I would love to see you in it," Jartanza cajoled.

"I am sure you would, little man. It's been awhile for you, hasn't it?"

"Try it on. I want to check the fit," demanded Herodias.

"I can tell it won't fit. I told you, the top is too small and the bottom too large."

"It was made that way. I want Herod to see your bulging breasts and I want that skirt to slide down very low on your hips." Herodias began to undress her daughter.

"Not in front of that man."

"He's as harmless as your grandmother. I don't think he has any sexual thoughts or even any ability, do you, Jartanza?"

"No, my Queen."

"Why am I dressing like this for Herod?" She squirmed to escape her mother's attempts to disrobe her.

"It is a plan, a brilliant plan. It will solve everything. Why must you always resist my efforts to improve our lives?"

"I will try it on, but he must leave."

"Sorry, Jartanza. No thrill today."

"I will await your bidding," he said, backing out the door.

Jartanza gone, Salome pleaded deliberately. "I'll try it on, mother, but I will not dance for Herod."

"Well, try it on. The urge to dance may come later."

****

The feast had gone well.

All the dignitaries of Galilee had gathered in subservient propriety to the bidding of Herod Antipas. The dark, shadowy palace was buzzing with conversation, increasing in volume with the sampling of each new bottle of intoxicant.

Herod was giddy with self-indulgence, flushed, as perspiration beaded all over his double-jowled face, awash in men's praises, surrounded by their gifts, awaiting the disclosure of a final present.

It would have to be very impressive to surpass the luxury already bestowed from the obligatory generosity of the fawning guests.

The door opened as a gentle stream of melody flowed into the room. Herod, drunken, squirmed to determine the source of the tune.

Eureka the subject of his most intense fantasy, the daughter of his queen. He sat upright. She began to dance, moving in and out of the reclining guests with the grace of a deer. Her breasts bulged from the tiny top, bronzed, glistening with oil. The loosened belt on the skirt glided up and down on her hips, giving brief glimpses of the womanly wonder beneath. She moved toward the throne, Herod emitting an audible gasp, reaching out to grab her as she twirled away, prancing past an array of fevered menfolk. Herod tried to stand but his knees shook, leaving his legs limp, as he crumpled back into his plush divan.

She leaped, the skirt slipping lower and lower and her breasts gleaming with oil and sweat. Her lips were dark and ruddy, and full of youthful promise, her black curls flying through the air.

Herod tried to speak but his throat yielded no sound.

She came before him and bent low, allowing her breasts to dangle and gyrate less than a cubit from his yearning grasp.

"Salome, you are more beautiful . . ." Herod stopped as she cavorted about the room, toward the throne, coming so close to him the fragrance of her perfumed oils permeated his nostrils.

He drew a deep breath and said, "I will give you whatever you want."
The words were drowned by a cheer raised in glee over the latest contortion by the fluttering young butterfly.

"Salome!" Herod screamed.

She continued to dance as the skirt slid lower on her hips.

"I will give you whatever you want!" he squalled.

The room was vibrant with furious passion as brazened men groped at slave girls serving drinks, stripping away their clothes.

"Salome, I want you," moaned Herod.

Her tight bodice tore from the strain, breasts jiggling precariously within the tiny confines.

Herod squealed in delight as his men cheered.

"I will give you everything you want . . . up to half of my kingdom!"

Blastus, sitting nearby, chuckled and said, "My king, as you well know, you have nothing to give without Caesar's permission."

"Silence, you common servant. I will give that beauty anything. Up unto half of it all."

Salome swept out of the banquet hall through the open door. Was the dance over? The men sat stunned; those indulging in violence stopped in mid-rape. Where was the delight? Where was the panting princess?

Salome ran down the hallway looking for her mother, gasping for air from her exertion.

Suddenly her mother grabbed her and pulled her into a dark corner.

"He said he would give me anything," Salome whispered.

"He said it so all could hear?" Herodias asked, squeezing Salome's arms tightly.

"Yes . . . what shall we ask? We can have what we want."

"You must hurry back before he cools in his loins. Tell him we want the head of John the Baptist on a serving platter."

Salome shivered. Had she heard right? She knew the consequences of questioning her mother. The woman was capable of turning her violent vengeance in any direction. Salome drew a deep breath.

"Run! Dance! Tell him . . . hurry!" ranted Herodias.

Terrified, Salome pivoted on her heel and raced back to the hall, entering the door, resuming her dance. The men roared their approval. Herod stepped forward, tripping on his robe.

She danced and shimmied to his throne, her top exposing her fleshy, purple, hardened nipples.

Herod fell backwards as if struck by lightening.

"I want," she screamed.

The man-infested room hushed.

"I want," she said more softly, waiting for total quiet.

"Yes, what is it you want?" Herod inquired eagerly, his eyes fixed on her dripping thighs.

"I want the head of John the Baptist served to me on a platter."

"What?" Herod cried, catapulted back to reality.

Salome remained silent, panting and staring at the stumbling, drooling monarch.

Herod looked around at an arena of horrified faces, men hardened by treacherous deeds, quelled as the request stilled the air.

Salome stood, chest heaving.

Herod looked to Blastus, who probed the girl for motive. "What if we make it just a platter of pure gold?" Blastus asked Salome. The cohorts grunted their approval.

Salome declined, shaking her head.

Herod sank back onto his throne, peering at the beautiful maiden, who still shimmered in the firelight but had lost some of her sheen.

"Why?" he supplicated.

She gazed over his head, transfixed.

The conclave turned to see if Herod would honor his word, or would he prove himself to be the royal mite of his reputation? Each moment of indecision would diminish respect from the throng of luminaries. A loss of face could mean dispatches to Rome.

He turned to his personal guard and waved his hand. "Of course," he said casually. "Give her as she asks, and be quick about it."

The guard ran from the hall as the slave girls slipped out of the grasp of stunned assaulters.

Salome turned to walk away.

"You should remain, my dear. You have gotten your request. I may have a request or two of my own," he said, holding out his hand to incline her to a position near his throne.

She glanced up at the sordid King of the Jews.

She would pay a price for her vile request.

****

Samuel was finally ready for sleep after spending hours talking with John, trying to drown the noise of the boisterous celebration, so different than the peaceful climate of their exchange.

Herod had decided to move the Baptist to the prison chambers near the palace at Machaerus, and Samuel had requested to come along with John, having become more friend than jailer.

So the royal escapades were well within earshot of the humble, straw-strewn cell.

They had conversed into the night, until the fatigue of the previous day's journey commanded rest from the two mismatched brothers.

John had dozed off first, most unusual. Samuel was normally the one who snoozed, leaving the Baptist awake, contemplating. But on this night, Samuel watched as John stretched out and slipped away into a motionless solitude of sleep.

Samuel remained alert, wrestling with ideas and reasoning over the illogical, such as his friendship with this imprisoned prophet. What had drawn him to this fellow? Was it merely the proximity effect, loneliness dictating relationship, or was he searching for some intangible in his own experience? The Baptist embodied a soul-peace that seemed to saturate every fiber of his being. John just seemed to know. It wasn't an arrogant display of knowledge; just content without the customary smugness. For example: tonight, while the raucous festivities trickled into the cell, John sat unmoved. Where other men would yearn for the party, free of chains, John appeared the free man devising an escape for those imprisoned by the debauchery of the gala event.

Bizarre, and a bit unsettling. If John were not such a solid fellow, Samuel might deem him as having dispatched his wits to areas of lesser pursuit.

But. . . John was solid, simple, with a sober wit that would appease the most somber Essene.

Finally Samuel slept--an achy, dreamy sleep, luring him deeper and deeper, when suddenly he was shaken to attention.

"Wake up, man! How dare you sleep on your post!"

"I always sleep on this detail," Samuel said before his brain connected with his disciplined training.

"You have a prisoner. What if he escaped?"

"He has no will to escape," said Samuel, trying to focus on the form before him.

"His will shall soon no longer matter," said the shape as he unsheathed his sword.

"What do you mean?" Samuel leaped to his feet, rubbing his eyes.

"Orders from Herod. One head to go."

Samuel stared at the burly soldier clad in the finest armor from the king's guard. "From Herod? What's going on? Herod respects John."

"I have orders. Here is Herod's seal. I need to bring back a head on a serving tray."

"Serving tray? Is this some sort of sick joke?"

"Does sound that way, doesn't it?"

"It must be a trick."

"No, my friend. Our noble King got quite a rise out of a dance by a breasty young maiden. He made some rash promises. She took him up on it," said the guard, moving toward the cell.

Samuel stepped in the way. "Wait, he's asleep. Keep your voice down."

"He will sleep long and hard after he receives my treatment."

"Wait! Are you saying John is to die because of Herod's lust?"

"John?" asked the soldier, pointing at the sleeping prisoner.

"Yes. John the Baptist. A prophet."

"I have heard of him. Some men from my brigade were baptized at his outpost on the Jordan."

"Why should he die?"

"You didn't see the dance. More than one man lost his head," said the guard with a snorting laugh.

"Please be quiet."

"Why? We are not going to wake the dead. At least, not yet."

What should Samuel do? If he challenged the order they both would be killed. If he fought off the guard and released the prisoner, the Baptist would be tracked down and many innocent people could die. What would John want him to do? He wished he could wake him to secure his counsel on the matter, like he had done so many times over the months. Ludicrous. How could you stir a man to ask him advice on his own execution? How cruel would it be to alert him to the coming blow of the sword of death?

Samuel stood, weighing the options, until the guard became impatient and started pushing past him to fulfill the order.

"Wait," whispered Samuel. "He is my friend. I will do it."

"No way in hell. You are too close to him. I can tell. You'd lose your nerve. Anyway, I am Herod's man and he committed this killing to my care."

"Listen, you can tell Herod you did it. I seek no reward for the deed. Any remuneration for the action can go your way. I just want to make sure this man receives a quick completion to this wretched sentence."

The executioner eyed the most common guard. "Then let it be your hand. As long as you never tell anyone you did it."

"Trust me, my comrade. No one would ever hear from me I was the Baptist's beheader."

He sorrowfully took the double-edged sword from the soldier, who was still deliberating the decision. "Could I be alone?" requested Samuel.

The envoy rubbed his chin and considered the matter deeply.

I will bring the head out in a few moments," added Samuel. The harsh reality of his own words crushed his heart.

The brash palace guard reluctantly agreed and stepped outside the enclosure. After all, there would be no possibility for deception--a head as evidence of their agreement.

Samuel hesitated, trembling, mustering the courage for the dastardly deed.

Was it really better for him to do it, or just false bravado in the presence of a raging wave of lunacy?

What would John want? Easy! John would want to live. He truly was a vessel of God, still nonetheless, a man; a young one at that.

Samuel could hear the rustling feet of the nervous, duty-wrought courier of death. The larger man would soon overcome him and commit the atrocity. Maybe the struggle-in-progress would alert John. How horrible to be awakened for your own beheading.

Samuel raised the sword high above his head. John lay flat on his back, his neck protruding, lending itself to a clean and even blow. "Forgive me, dear soul," said Samuel as the tears came to his eyes. "You went to sleep speaking to a lowly prison guard. You shall arise to the voice of angels."

He drew back the sword, arms locked, knees quivering . . . then. . . froze--his body unable to perform a murder so abhorrent to his mind. He stood taut, twitching and recoiling, sweat bursting on every inch of his skin. He couldn't strike the blow. The sword would be taken from his hand. My God, what would John want? He lifted the sword, but his body once again repelled the command.

"Strike well, Samuel," came the gentle demand from the man beneath.

Samuel glanced down. The Baptist's eyes were still closed but a smile was on his face.

"God has given you a mission. Strike well and surely, and give me the mercy of death by one falling of your sword," said John quietly, lying very still.

Samuel faltered.

"If you are my friend, send me to a better place," said John with greater fire.

Samuel reared back, and with an agonizing scream, brought the sword down on the vulnerable, exposed throat of the great prophet of God.

The severed head rolled gently to the side on the hay as a brief gusher of blood sprayed a warm unction of his final sprinkle of life in all directions; splattering in Samuel's eyes, burning, blinding him for a moment.

The guard heard Samuel's scream and ran inside. "He raised quite a mess and fuss," observed the guard as he grabbed the head.

"The blood is his, but the scream was mine," said Samuel, sinking to his knees.

"Wish me luck. I don't know where I'm going to find a platter this time of night." The soldier scurried out of the cell, dribbling the last life's blood of the wilderness preacher all over the moldy hay.

The Voice would cry no more.

"I must go tell Alphaeus," said Samuel, laying his head on the bloodied breast of his Galilean friend.

****

Chusa had been most fortunate. Blastus had been called away to attend to plans at Machaerus before the deadline on the accounting of palace finances. Chusa, having taken the time to secure loans and favors to establish a solid financial base, felt confident he could handle any questioning and scrutiny from the chamberlain.

Joanna saw very little of Chusa during Blastus' absence. Chusa seemed preoccupied, busying himself with court affairs. When Blastus returned, Chusa decided to wait to be summoned rather than bring undo focus, hoping the whole investigation might be forgotten; especially plausible given the foul, dark mood of the regal caravan upon their return from the birthday celebration.

Joanna, on the other hand, wanted to seize the advantage and see Blastus before he had the opportunity to discuss business with her husband. Although she did not regret her generosity to Jesus, and also did not condone her husband's highbrowed thievery, she felt responsible for the crisis; feeling obligated to input the problem before Chusa was output from his position.

Giving Blastus a day to recover from his journey, she requested an audience--immediately granted. Blastus liked Joanna. As is the case in many friendships, there was a seed of romantic affection beneath the surface; a sensation purposefully thwarted by the temperance of prudent souls.

Blastus tolerated the enigmatic Chusa while quietly doting on his radiant wife.

Joanna prepared herself for the meeting. She rehearsed her speech and corrected details. She was baffled, though, by her own attention to personal hygiene and fashion, amused as she watched herself preening, adding fragrance to her already doubly-cleansed self. What kind of meeting did she think this was going to be? She shook off her maiden's musings and concentrated on the redemption of her husband.

In all her fastidious preparation, she totally forgot Blastus had no idea of her miracle. To him, she was the resoundingly optimistic, beautiful cripple, who was about to present herself as a whole woman.

What was she thinking?

Did she really forget?

Or did she secretly hope to be discovered, so the sacrilegious charade could once and for all be unmasked? Too late, for she had already knocked and gained entrance.

Blastus was staring down at some most pressing work, his way to appear too involved to spend much time with any visiting guest, controlling the tempo of the meeting and determining the extent of the intrusion.

Joanna stood quietly, waiting to be observed.

Blastus spoke without raising his eyes. "It is good to see you, Joanna."

"And you, my Lord," she said with a sweetness and charm causing the austere manager to glance up. "I have come on behalf of Chusa."

"Chusa?"

"Yes, I have made a grave error, my Lord," Joanna said as she inched closer.

Blastus inhaled her fragrance and smiled, wondering why she had selected such an aromatic approach. Did she she share his suppressed feelings? Perhaps there was a chance for a meaningful rendezvous.

Joanna pre-empted his thoughts. "Chusa had saved money from court expenses."

Blastus interrupted. "I will talk finance with your husband. Why has he sent you here?"

"He didn't send me. I came on my own. He does not know I am here," she said, as she now moved to his side.

Blastus drank in the full magnitude of her beauty; a sweeping, elegant simplicity. A tear came to his eye. What a lucky man this Chusa was to have this vessel of perfection at his bidding for conversation and pleasure. If he were the little accountant he would never leave the bed chambers of this sanctuary of ecstasy. He would have food and drink delivered, only taking time between massive eruptions of love to receive the nourishment necessary to energize the next flurry of passion. Yes, truly, this beauty was being wasted on the minuscule attributes of some court accountant.

Joanna looked at Blastus with pleading, moist eyes, desiring a reprieve for her husband.

Blastus could sense the sheer pulsing energy of an underused lover.

Joanna quickly turned to walk away, as if suddenly aware of Blastus' thoughts.

He heaved a gasp as if suddenly struck in the chest. "You're walking! Weren't you crippled?"

Joanna awoke from her self-deception. What was she doing here? She had disobeyed Chusa. Whatever she said would determine the future of their lives at the palace.

"I distinctly remember you as being incapacitated," challenged Blastus.

"I was."

"Was? What do you mean, was?"

"I can walk now."

"I can see that."

"I couldn't before."

"I know that."

"I met someone."

Blastus scratched his beard.

Joanna continued with fervor. "I have been healed. It was a touch from God, the most magnificent experience of my life."

Blastus squinted, disappointed he was not the source of the touch and her outpouring of appreciation.

"He helped me have the faith to believe," she said, turning and moving back to his side.

"So, it was a man," he said, wincing. What man had the sensual intensity to create healing in a woman's body? This truly must be the ultimate lover.

"I had given up on ever being whole," Joanna continued. "He saw the tiny speck in my heart that still dreamed of completeness." She knelt at his feet.

Blastus had never been this close to the source of his desire. Breathing in slowly, he spoke. "So you have fallen in love with this man and wish to be rid of Chusa?"

"No," she answered, rising to her feet. "I love Chusa. This man is my Lord."

Lord? Did she mean god? "Who is this man?"

Joanna remained silent, suspicious of his tone.

Blastus sensed her reluctance. "No, really. Tell me. I mean no harm. I just would like to know more. Anyone with the power to free the body of such a beautiful woman should not be relegated to obscurity."

Joanna blushed. Was it good to tell more? A man like Blastus might help Jesus. He might be able to give Jesus opportunity to spread his good work to more people. Blastus might even secure an audience with King Herod. Joanna could not contain her joy any longer. She was tired of pretending; angered by her sequestered profile. It was time to proclaim the goodness of God. She poured her heart out. He listened as she told of her baptism, her healing by Jesus, Mary of Magdala, who walked with her and became her new friend, returning to the palace, and the decision to keep her miracle a secret. "Chusa was afraid people would not understand. But you do understand, don't you, Blastus, my lord?" She reached out and touched his hand.

She had called him lord. There was another she really deemed Lord. He was overcome with jealousy for this man with the healing touch. Herod must be told. Herod would eliminate the competition, just as he had done with John. "This is so wonderful," he pandered.

Joanna knew something was wrong. Blastus was too easily impressed. He didn't ask questions.

"You go back to Chusa," Blastus added, taking her arm and walking her toward the door. "Everything will be fine. Don't worry. We will take care of him and this Jesus fellow."

Joanna had made a severe blunder, sharing too much with this one who, unfortunately, had so little capacity for understanding. "What are you going to do, Blastus?"

"I said don't worry! There is a beginning to all things. There shall be an end." He opened the door and softly shoved Joanna through it.

"You cannot find your answers without faith," she protested as he shut the door, her objection barely sliding through.

****

Blastus stood for a moment, considering his options. He knew Joanna saw right through his insincerity and she was not a woman to sit idly by and wait for the turn of events. She would act in some capacity. It was essential he move first.

Even though he had not requested an audience with the king, he must inform Herod of the state of affairs.

He hurried to the throne room and burst in on a meeting in progress, the participants involved in a heated discussion. They stopped in mid-steam to gaze at the presumptuous steward.

"Did I ask for you?" inquired a bewildered Herod.

"No, but it couldn't wait, my Lord," Blastus insisted.

"Have you lost your ever-peasant mind?" demanded the astonished queen.

"We are busy now," Jartanza stated..

"Shut up, sorcerer. I will correct my own servants," jabbed Herodias.

"He is my servant, queen," Herod corrected with his accustomed pout.

"I will prove I serve you all well," said Blastus, bowing. "You know, my king, I would never intrude on the sacred trust unless it was of major concern to the domain."

"So what is it?" fumed Herodias.

"I will handle this, my dear," Herod said, pompously. "Tell me, Blastus, what brings you here to my chambers, uninvited, tempting me to remove your insolent head?" he said, casting a smile towards Jartanza, who straightened to his tallest, grateful to be bequeathed a knowing glance from the king.

"Joanna can walk."

"Joanna, now who is Joanna?"

"Chusa's crippled wife," explained Herodias, disdainfully.

"Have I met her?"

"She's crippled, for God's sake," Herodias spat.

"He says she can walk," retorted Herod, trying to gain the upper hand.

"He wouldn't announce she could walk if that was normal."

"She has been healed," said Blastus, clarifying the point.

"By whom?" Jartanza cross-examined.

"My throne, Jartanza. My question."

Jartanza nodded, mumbling a plethora of nearly inaudible excuses and apologies.

"His name is Jesus," said Blastus, anticipating the king's question.

Jartanza, knowing the name, fathomed the meaning, and remained silent.

"It is John," said Herod, rising from his throne. "It is as you said, Jartanza."

"I don't understand," queried Blastus. .

"I didn't get it all," Herodias outlined.

"Herodias got his head but not his body." Jartanza attempted to enlighten.

Blastus remained confused.

"It's the entrails, man.   Don't you understand? Must you remain ignorant in all your ways?" screamed Herod at the befuddled chamberlain.

"May I, your majesty?" Jartanza requested, with a full bow.

"Proceed," said Herod,   pleased someone had finally shown a measure of etiquette.

"Herodias has John's head, but his entrails were stolen by his followers. They came and took the body before we could disembowel it and burn the insides in the traditional ceremony of cleansing."

"Forgive my denseness. Entrails?" posed Blastus with a hint of smile.

"It's soul displacement. The life of man is in his bowels. If the head is severed the bowels can be removed and the spirit lives on." Jartanza paused, viewing Blastus' blank stare. Sighing, he continued, "If the entrails can be transferred into another living being, through the spell of soul displacement, then the man can live on through the flesh of this new body. Do you understand?"

Blastus looked to Herodias and then to Herod, hoping to find an ally against this rhetoric of absurdity. They both nodded their agreement, looking pitifully on the perplexed pragmatist.

The King presented, "Because we only had John's head and not his body, his disciples were obviously able to perform the ritual of soul displacement and recreate John in another form--apparently a mightier entity."

"How was I to know that we needed to gut the prophet?" defended Herodias.

Blastus gazed at the alleged regal duo, with accompanying stooge, in total disbelief.

"John the Baptist is alive?" Blastus questioned.

"And using the name Jesus," mused Herodias.

"We need his entrails," Herod determined.

"We need to stop this soul displacement before he uses his miracle power to gain your throne," accented Jartanza.

"How would he do that?"   cross-examined Herodias, tensely.

"How does he heal the cripple?" Jartanza raised a brow to punctuate his point, as the King and Queen whispered and mumbled.

"So, it seems I do get to kill an intruder. My sword is sharpened, peasant." He ran his finger across the blade and pulled his hand back, exposing a fresh cut, the blood dribbling down his arm.

"Bandi, I said no!" Anisa tried to rise, but was restrained by the maid.

"Is it your plan to kill me?"

"Not yet. First I want you to feel the strength of my body. I do not want your torture impersonal. Death by my sword would make you feel that I did not care enough to involve myself. I want you to feel the muscle of my might as I destroy you stroke by stroke."

"Why is this so important to you? " I asked, still scanning for an exit.

"You would like me to talk until help arrives. I am not as stupid as you anticipated." He leaped into the air and kicked me in the head with his heavily armored sandal. I flew through the air and landed against the side of the tent.

"Bandi, no!" Anisa screamed.

"He was trying to take advantage of you, Princess," Bandi said, as he raced over and kicked me in the side. My rib cracked, and a sharp pain pierced to my heart.

"He didn't touch me," Anisa protested.

"Oh, yes, I saw," testified the maid.

Bandi lifted me to my feet and drove the hilt of his sword into my face, breaking my nose, the blood streaming into my throat. I fell in a heap at the pugilist's feet. He drew his sword and ran the blade across my shoulder, opening a cut, squirting blood onto my torn robe.

I was being killed. I was about to die before I got a chance to save Anisa. My death would mean her death. I must stay alive. I passed out, hearing Anisa's screams mingled with memories of her laugh, and the maid prodding Bandi to kill me. I shook myself back awake, and saw the face of Bandi, bent over me with the sword drawn back for the final thrust.

"Drop your blade!" came an angry command from the rear. Bandi twirled to see who had arrived, and as he did I rolled away. "Drop the sword!" I recognized the voice-- Tabuli Manta.

"Not this time, old man," said Bandi as he turned to locate me for the kill.

"What are you doing?" Tabuli demanded of the warrior.

"The boy was trying to rape the Princess," Bandi sneered as he thrust his sword into the sand near my head.

I approached her bed. She looked bad, the radiance snuffed from her face, her skin speckled with a rash from the fever, and her lips dry and crusty.

"Now that you have seen me at my cursed state, will you marry me?" She attempted a laugh, which turned into a dry, coarse cough.

"Are you alright?"

"No, I don't think so. I might just have to die to recover from this infestation." She meant to be humorous, but given the sight before me, the words rang with more prophecy than comedy.

I struck a dramatic pose with arms extended. "Look at my hands. I am better."

"I am glad. Is that why you have come?"

"No, you don't understand. As soon as I left you and this camp, my condition improved."

"So you are allergic to me and have come to my tent in the middle of the night to tell me how I make you sick and you don't want to see me anymore?"

"You don't make me sick."

"Well, there is a relief. Jesus, you have a gift for the turn of a phrase."

I took a deep breath. "Something placed on your skin has infected me."

"Not this again." She fell into another coughing fit, her face blanched and I thought she would be unable to catch her next breath. "Answer me this," she gasped, taking in much needed air. "Why haven't I broken out in the same rash you have?"

A good question, one I had considered and dismissed due to the sheer magnitude of the preponderance of evidence. Her reaction was just different from mine.

"Touch me with your hands," she wheezed, groping in my direction. I stepped forward, knelt down, and gently stroked the clammy brow of the ailing princess. Her labored breathing eased, and I felt the closeness again.

Suddenly, a hand on my shoulder, I turned, and was eyeball to eyeball with Anisa's startled maid.

"You must go," she hissed, trying to push me to the side.

Anisa held on to my hands.

"You not be here," the maid insisted.

"What is going on in here?" Bandi entered the tent, saw me and slowly drew his sword, smiling.

"No, Bandi!" Anisa pleaded.

I stood, looking for a way of escape.

alone, sat awake, staring into the fire as if trying to absorb its heat. I looked up, hearing the sound of a crackling branch. "So you walk back into my life," I said to the lady arriving in the camp. It was Joanna.

"You have lost more weight," she said softly as she eased to my side.

"I think of eating. I want to eat. The work takes the eating time."

"What would mama say?"

"What does mama ever say? Eat up, Jesus, so you can become a strong carpenter."

"But you aren't a carpenter," she said with a grin.

"To the betterment of Nazareth."

A gentle pause, and then she spoke sweetly but seriously. "What are you, Jesus?"

"Cold."

"Not enough flesh to protect the bones."

"Not enough robe to protect the flesh."

We laughed, as she gazed at my "holey" robe.

"There is the consolation," I added, "that as I shrink, the holes in my robe also diminish."

"I suppose that would only be logical to an itinerant optimist."

"I would not call myself an optimist. I am more a pessimist that just hasn't received the bad news yet."

She giggled--clean and pure. She ceased her laughter and continued, solemnly. "John is dead."

"I know."

"Beheaded."

"I heard."

"They know about you."

"They?"

"Herod."

"The fox will now search out the mother hen."

"I don't understand."

"Why have you come?"

"Chusa is gone."

"I'm sorry."

"He took money from Herod."

"I see."

"I gave it to you."

"My ministry funded by Herod Antipas. I am not so sure I like that."

"It is too late to change and I don't recommend you express your thanks in person."

"So you would anticipate a cool reception at the palace?"

"I think we both may wish to decline any future invitations," she said as she squeezed my hand.

Sitting, neither of us feeling compelled to speak. Fellowship has a certain depth when unencumbered by words. We warmed ourselves in the glow of fire and reunion; a sacred passage between hearts joined in satisfying purposes.

"Will you marry?" she asked so quietly I barely heard.

"It would be wonderful to have children."

"How flattering for some woman to be your child bearer and suckler for your squalling offspring," she retorted, miffed by my answer.

"No."

"Because you are too busy?"

"The end will come before she would understand."

"Do you fear Herod?"

"Herod is not my nemesis. Jerusalem awaits my coming. It would not be proper for any prophet to be killed anywhere else," I said with a short, tight laugh.

"You will die?"

"Not tonight. The fire is too warm. The friend is too precious. The truth requires a bit more journey," I said, putting my arm around her.

"That's nice."

"Don't get used to it. The first twinge of muscle cramp and you're on your own."

"It's a deal," she said, snuggling a bit closer to kiss my cheek.

I leaned down, nestling my lips into her soft hair. She looked up at me and I kissed her forehead, lingering, longingly, relishing the intimacy from this cherished lady.

Another place. . .

She caressed my hand and asked,"Why do you think God let me walk?"

"So you could get up and fix me food in the morning."

She jabbed me in the side with a punch which, though playful, made me gasp for air.

"Seriously," she said, with a slight crack in her voice.

"I don't know."

"Good. I would hate to believe it had some tremendous religious explanation and too many heavenly implications." She stopped abruptly.

I waited.

She continued. "I just want to believe He got just as tired seeing my anguish as I did experiencing it."

"Possibly. Or maybe He just likes where you choose to do your walking."

More wonderful silence.

"Jerusalem, huh?" she asked tentatively.

"Eventually."

"What will happen?"

"I'm still learning."

SITTING 32
Three Meetings

It had taken weeks to organize the meeting, difficult times promoting stubborn demands, where egos are mingled with scheduling squabbles, leaving the necessary undone.

(The human race would be extinct if conception were not pleasurable and birthing a foregone, natural conclusion.)

Veshioli had labored long to bring about this conference, one he hoped would be a joining of common wills. He traveled the countryside of Judea and Galilee tracing the footsteps of the Nazarene prophet, struggled to gain favor with Lord Caiaphas, diligently courted the backing of the Herodians, spoken to representatives from Governor Pilate, endured deeply religious conversations with the Essenes, gorged himself on meat and drink in the camp of the Zealots, and deliberated the destiny of man in the inner sanctum of the aristocratic Sadducees--a veteran of many conflicts; a verbal warrior adept at all negotiation.

The preparation was complete. The convocation would be in Ephraim Having appealed to the nationalism of each faction, he prayed for willing and insightful souls, poised for the restoration of Israel.

He arrived a day before the gathering, desiring time to think. He established a respectable camp for the comfort and leisure of his guests. Sitting quietly under a fig tree, he remembered one fateful day in Nazareth, not so long ago when the Jesus problem was nearly resolved. The enraged hometown mob came within a cubit of throwing the carpenter's son over the cliff and dashing the mastermind of this renegade kingdom movement onto the rocks below. How much easier it would have been if Nazareth would have handled their own wayward son; a community decision. Alas.

Veshioli stared into the distance, considering the plight of his race. Why was an uneducated Nazarene able to enliven the imagination of this captive people? Was there anything really new here? Truly, Jesus' ideas had a universal quality, including slave and free in his ranks. He ministered to women, allowing them in his camp. Yet he encouraged respect to the most bitter of enemies--Caesar--a serious problem. The kingdom doctrine discouraged the patriotism of the twelve tribes. If all men were brothers, how would the Chosen people ever gain the singular purpose to take back their lands? There was no room for conciliation with the Gentile dog. Jesus must be controlled! If plausible, he must be guided to a locale where he could remain harmless and ineffective. The ideal? Exile him in a land where ignorance stalls the progress and frustrates his genius. So, what Nazareth had failed to accomplish became the responsibility of clever men of vision--deter the Carpenter's Curse.

The day of the meeting dawned. Barabbas was the first to arrive, with a consort of two warriors and two women. Veshioli had never met the burly leader. All of his correspondence had been through the aide, Jaakobah, who accompanied Barabbas to the meeting along with a slighter fellow named Kreble.

"And who are these lovely ladies?" asked Veshioli, as he nodded in the direction of the females.

Barabbas grunted. "You know, I don't know their given names. I call one "Now" and the other "Later" and sometimes I get that confused."

All five of the unkempt zealots burst into a coarse peal of billowing laughter. Diplomacy demanding participation, Veshioli quietly joined in at his own permissible volume level, but was lost in the abundance of barbaric hilarity.

"Where is everyone else?" quizzed Barabbas, surveying the site with a frown.

"The Sadducees declined to join us on the basis of spiritual differences. They said they already were dealing with the Nazarene question in their own way," replied Veshioli.

"Gonna bore him to death?" hissed Barabbas, disdainfully.

Veshioli smiled as the others looked on, not certain what to do, absent instruction.

"The Essenes," continued Veshioli tentatively, "have decided not to join us because of the make-up of the conclave."

"They heard I was coming." Barabbas' huge head was quickly engulfed in an equally large grin.

"They did."

"They still don't like me."

"Don't approve would be more accurate."

"What is their objection?" queried Kreble.

"I will answer that one and save our priestly friend the twitch and squirm," replied Barabbas.

"Thank you," nodded Veshioli.

Barabbas stalked about, obviously selecting the right moment to present his explanation in the most grandiose style. "Do you see this?" he said, pointing to his mouth. "There are three things a man can do with this great opening to his head. He can drink and eat. He can speak. And, he can kiss a women, deep and long. The Essenes use the mouth only to speak, and ignore the two better uses." Barabbas strutted as his admirers chuckled. "Do you see this?" He grabbed his crotch. The men laughed and the women giggled. Veshioli modestly cast his eyes earthward. "There are two uses for what God dangles between a man's legs. The Essenes permit the practical use and shun the more enjoyable," Barabbas concluded, pinching "Now". (Or was it "Later"?) The buffoonery erupted, ebbing and flowing like a seaside tide.

The next visitor arrived in the midst of the shameless, saucy showcase. He stood back, dumbfounded by the outlandish characterization and collective outburst. He waited, and finally, seeing no end to the gaiety, walked up and greeted Veshioli. "I am Malchus, servant to the chief priest, Lord Caiaphas."

"And when may we expect Caiaphas?" Barabbas dabbed at the gleeful sprinkle in his eyes.

"He cannot attend but sent me to represent him." He stood tall, deepening his voice to disguise his youth.

"Can't or won't?" jabbed Barabbas as he threw a fist of sand into the fire.

Veshioli came to the young courier's aid. "Welcome, Malchus. We are glad to have you. Am I to understand Lord Caiaphas has given you full range of approval, or must you confirm your findings and return with conclusions?" Veshioli shared the zealot leader's disappointment, but opted to maintain control.

"I have the chief priest's ear and authorization to give general approval to worthwhile aspirations," said Malchus properly.

"Look at this! We have been here less than an hour and we are already talking in circles like Roman senators with lily-white hands," fumed Barabbas.

"I guarantee you," stormed Veshioli, "that there will be no indecisive sideways conversations here at Ephraim." He stared at Malchus. We are prepared to make the plans that set the mark for the restoration of Israel." He finished, glaring at the encircled assemblage, not about to have the fruit of his labors bungled by the general inefficiency of priests and soldiers. Having achieved respect, he continued. "Then we are fine. We can proceed. Let me begin by saying I have a letter from the court of Herod and the Herodians pledging their support for the pursuit and full discovery in the matter of the Nazarene and this kingdom movement." Veshioli's voice rang with exuberance.

"Wonderful," affirmed Malchus.

"I hear Herod thinks Jesus is the spook of John the Baptist sent back to claim the king's head," Barabbas guzzled a bit of wine.

"Whatever the reason, the results are the same." A sharpness had entered Veshioli's tone, mannerisms accentuated with a frosty edge.

"I have brought a letter from Caiaphas stating much the same thing," said Malchus, proudly displaying the document and carefully avoiding the stern countenance of his icy host.

"Now, ain't that sweet," chided Barabbas. "Everybody has got a parchment. Excuse me, Jaakobah, did you bring that letter from my Mama, you know, the one giving me permission to attend this meeting of manliness?" Jaakobah simulated a frantic search for the nonexistent letter. The Zealots all chuckled, spit, and snorted, as Veshioli and Malchus looked on in an aggravated pity.

"I think we can dispense with further endorsement and get to the real course of our discussion," said Veshioli.

"Fine with me," replied Malchus.

Barabbas nodded with a smile, eyes twinkling, content he had won the first grappling of wills.

"We have found several witnesses willing to testify against Jesus," said Veshioli, glancing about the assembly.

"Witnesses?" Malchus displayed some surprise.

"Yes, one in particular, a former cripple Jesus healed at the Pool of Bethesda in Jerusalem."

"He healed him?" Barabbas questioned with a chuckle.

Malchus seized the opportunity to become involved. "What he means is, for whatever reason, the man had chosen to be incapacitated and this Nazarene motivated him to walk."

"Why is he testifying against Jesus? I would kiss the Nazarene full on the lips." Barabbas puckered and performed for the amusement of his bored followers.

"The council questioned the man about carrying his bed on the Sabbath, and when the man saw Jesus again, he came back and reported to the fathers," replied Veshioli.

"Reported what?" examined Barabbas.

"Jesus had been rude to the man. I remember the incident well," inserted Malchus. "Jesus told the man--in a very threatening way, mind you--that if he did not repent something much worse would happen to him."

"I would have caused a much worse thing to happen to the little slimy, sniveling runt. I would have run him through with my sword," stomped Barabbas, winning applause from his friends.

"Well, whatever may be our opinions, this witness is willing to testify Jesus broke the Sabbath laws." Veshioli tried to restore focus.

"Where do you dump your dung on the Sabbath, Lord Malchus?" Barabbas sneered.

"I am not a Lord, General. I am a servant, and as a servant of the Most High, I would try to relieve myself before or after the Sabbath," Malchus proclaimed proudly.

Veshioli rolled his eyes.

Barabbas smirked, adding, Then pray that the runs be far away until God is satisfied the day has been made holy."

"Gentlemen, let us proceed in more productive ways," reasoned Veshioli. "Let it be sufficient to say that there are witnesses around to deliver an incriminating charge or two against the Nazarene." Veshioli was frustrated with the bantering of childish ingrates. "Now, if you will permit me, without interruption, to lay out the plan?"

Approving nods.

"We need unity of purpose to reestablish Israel. We do not need Jesus coming in and out of Jerusalem with his troop of rejects opening his bag of uncertainties. Disruptions must cease."

Once again, Veshioli was interrupted, this time by Malchus. "This Nazarene seems to arrive in Jerusalem during the feasts when the city is crowded with people, all dangerously susceptible to the power of suggestion."

Veshioli, ignoring the intrusion, proceeded, We need you, General Barabbas! We need Barabbas in power! We need King Barabbas in full battle array to help us establish . . ." he paused.

Barabbas sat up straighter and taller with each mention of his name.

"To establish . . ." Veshioli was determined to give great place and honor to the resolution of his plan. He concluded, ". . . a Zealot nation--free in Israel."

"How?" demanded Barabbas. "We have battled the Romans for years. The fathers are all dead or disabled. I am leading the sons of broken and despaired friends."

"This is where the unity comes in," said Veshioli with a smile. "We can stake a claim on an area. We do our fighting there, in that concentrated space, and force Rome to come to us. Meanwhile, Caiaphas can reason with the

Romans that one small independent territory will not diminish their authority. The price of defeating the determined Zealots on one sanctified piece of ground, is not worth the good will and diplomacy that could be achieved by allowing it to be governed by the people."

"Rome will not tolerate this," snorted Barabbas.

"Not unless it is in their best interest," Veshioli contradicted. "If we concentrate our efforts into the acquisition of a smaller state instead of trying to claim the entire promised land, then we can defeat the Romans with pesky raids. Even the ever-present fly can pester the ox and make him move to less annoying ground. Do you see? Once we have established our domain, we can buy ourselves time to arm the people for a greater conflict."

Barabbas listened, frowning and fidgeting. He enjoyed killing Romans in mass quantities. Organization was unfulfilling to the spontaneous rogue.

Malchus jumped in. "Caiaphas should be the mediator and gain great respect and power amongst the Roman dignitaries. It would help us reinstitute all the practices of Mosaic law into the mainstream of the lives of the people once again."

"Herod would be in Galilee bound to his token throne," added Veshioli. "Once the Romans discovered the wisdom of isolating their problem subjects into one specific area for self-rule, we could build an army quietly within the borders of this autonomous state."

"So even if Rome changed its mind, we would be prepared to defend ourselves against her legions," Barabbas spoke, dreamily.

"Or perhaps build an army that could, let's say, within one generation, drive the wolf from the sheep altogether," presented Veshioli with a wink.

"What about the Nazarene?" asked Malchus.

"There is our problem. We cannot allow Jesus to split the conscience of the male Israelites between their hearts and their spirits. Barabbas must have full support."

"So what we do with him?" interrogated Barabbas.

"He will be tried for petty crimes against the Oral law and exiled back to Galilee where he can do no harm. The Galileans are cynical enough to keep this kingdom movement in check, and ignorant enough to never impact anyone of quality or bearing."

"This can all be done?" Barabbas winced and blinked.

"Yes, of a surety."

Malchus stood to object. "Wait a moment! Jesus is not oblivious! How can you convict him and dictate his future movements?"

"That is where I need your help," agreed Veshioli "We need someone on the inside of the kingdom movement who can coordinate our efforts with his moves."

"You want a traitor?" Barabbas surmised.

"Is it traitorous to save our nation at the mere inconvenience of some imbalanced itinerant preacher?" Malchus retorted.

"Men have become heroes doing much less for their nation," presented Veshioli.

"I know a man," said Barabbas slowly, rubbing his overly-bearded chin.

"Who?" Veshioli rose to his haunches. .

"His name is Judas of the tribe of Judah. We called him "the Assassin". He was sympathetic to our cause. He was with the Baptist for a time. Then I lost contact with him. Now I heard he has cast his lot with this Nazarene."

"He is not from Galilee?" probed Malchus.

"No--Kerioth."

"A Judean traveling with Galileans could create its own conflicts," mused Veshioli.

"He is unpredictable. He was a killer. I feared him with all the others," said Barabbas, cautiously.

"Perhaps he has mellowed under the tutelage of the Nazarene," suggested Malchus.

"Wait a minute. I don't understand you." The previously silent Jaakobah spoke out his objection. "A man who can turn a vicious murderer into a useful creature demands our respect. Perhaps his message does not need to be relegated to the hills of Galilee."

"You are a fool," said Barabbas, rebuking his cohort. "What should we do--inscribe slogans of peace on the shields of the Roman legions? Shall we graciously die on the point of their spears to demonstrate our tenacity? You must be mad. Give me a man who can change a "proverb-spouting" Essene into a blood-thirsty Jewish tribesman, and then we can rule and reign." His voice became like a roaring lion. The air seemed to pulsate with the anger generated by the crimson-faced warrior.

A prudent moment of reflection, honored by all.

Finally,Veshioli returned to the topic. "Can Judas be contacted?"

"I can arrange it," said Malchus, still eyeing the enraged Barabbas.

"Be careful," warned Barabbas as he took a deep breath. "The Iscariot has one mouth but many voices."

"He is Judean. We are a breed that differentiate between sense and whim." Malchus boasted.

"Can we organize all this by Passover?" Veshioli examined.

"Too sacred of a time," piped Malchus.

"The feast of Tabernacles?"

"Too long," cautioned Barabbas. "We are assuming Jesus has no ambition or plan for his own movement. He will be at Passover at the peak of his power. If the people return home with visions of Jesus' kingdom instead of dreams of a Zealot state, we may lose the moment."

Wise words.

Judas barSimon, of Kerioth--the key to the campaign. He could inform them of details their spies had been unable to uncover.

"What shall we offer this Iscariot?" posed Veshioli.

"If he is a patriot, the promise of a freed Israel should stir his soul," insisted Malchus.

"The promise of power would be a more effective lure." Veshioli gave an all-knowing look at Barabbas.

The Zealot grinned and suggested, "Let him be the emissary between the exiled Jesus and the San Hedrin. It would be the best of both worlds. He could slum with the Galileans for a season, feasting on pork, and then escape to rub shoulders with the empowered ones." Barabbas, an enigma-- manners of a goat and insight of a scholar.

"Very wise, General," said Veshioli. "Do we agree? Pesky details can be nailed down later."

Agreement.

Even Now and Later gave their assent.

"A toast!" shouted Barabbas, as he leaped to his feet.

Each one seized a cup or flask of wine.

"To Israel! May all her enemies be scattered, burned, and slaughtered in the strength of such a magnificent people!"

Five men and two women in the wilderness. A holy seven, drinking agreeably, contemplating the mission fate had bequeathed to them--dreaming of the reward.

****

A definition for total exhaustion--falling asleep while eating.

I was there, simultaneously feeling depleted and a sense of urgency to finish my task; a job description never fully defined.

Chasing time, catching up to being late. I thought I was busy as a carpenter back in Nazareth. Now, trying to sleep, I forget to eat, which leaves me so weak I don't want to move. My bones feel achy and crowded. My mind dulls, head spins, and throat aches so I can barely speak. My vessel crashes.

I decided to take Simon Peter and Zebedee's sons and get away for a few days, heading for the mountains--my favorite retreat. I like them-- mountains, that is. The disciples are fine, too, but mountains are so high.   You can see so much.   Mountains dwarf our egos, feelings of self-importance, problems, and also the crowds. After all, who wants to climb a really big hill just to hear a parable or two?

We sat around a fire in the morning chill talking until silliness replaced discussion, speech became slurred, ideas deserted words, and   sleep overtook.

Except me. I don't know, maybe I did sleep; perhaps what I experienced was a dream. It could have been a vision. Are you awake for those?   All I know is it was a vivid, tangible, palatable experience. Enough background, onto the story.

Unable to sleep, I walked from the fire and my snoring companions. Looking into the morning light, I saw a glistening, shimmering presence, brighter than the burgeoning sunlight, like a golden chariot emblazoned by the desert sun. I moved forward. As I neared the sight, two beings separated and emerged from the gleaming mass, the radiance so intense I could not discern features.   No heat, nor fire; a warmth, not to my skin, but rather a reassurance in my heart. Absent threat, I proceeded toward the brilliance without trepidation.

The beings I believed to be men--not of common stock or lineage--within the family.

"Who are you?" I requested, while still at a respectable distance.

A pulsating light illuminated the silence, an aura shadowing the mysterious brothers.

"It is an honor, my Lord," boomed one of the forms, with a voice mingling the ferocity of a storm at sea with the sweet, gentle dribble of honey.

"Yes, indeed, my Lord," chimed in the other form, with equally robust enthusiastic tenderness.

I fell to the earth, overwhelmed. "Might you tone down so I can see you?"

A giggling chuckle, more the style of children at play than the cataclysmic thunder of heavenly revelation.

"Forgive us," said the first form as he dimmed.

Gradually, the golden essence of two men stepped out of the liquid iridescence, most assuredly of our house, though enraptured with eternal distinction.

"You are angels?"

"No, we are men," replied the second, whose hair fluttered with the fluid glitter of refined silver.

"Once men," added the first.

"When you were men, what were your names?"

"I was Moses."

"And I, Elijah. We have come to talk with you."

"If you would grant us audience," inserted my Moses.

"Am I awake?"

"You are experiencing as much as that human body can assimilate," Elijah articulated graciously.

"Shall we sit?" I groped for meaning.

"We shall," echoed the Moses before me.

"Would you consider me rude if I asked you to shine, still, a bit less?" I was determined to enjoy my visitation. No need to be uncomfortable in the presence of a god.

"Of course, my Lord," said Elijah.

Further diminishing of stinging light, and I was permitted to converse with men instead of talking stars. "Assuming you are here and I am also here, and this is really happening, what is it you need of me?"

"We have come to prepare you, my Lord."

"Slowly, Elijah. Give the gentleman a moment. You must reflect on how confounding human life can be. We are here to serve, my Lord."

"I do not think much about being served. I spend my day distributing to others the portion of life granted to me."

"We have observed the work," Elijah noted.

"There are days," I continued "so many come I am sure God's grace will be exhausted and the heavens left bankrupt of blessing."

"I felt much the same way with the manna distribution in the wilderness. I was always sure this would be the day we would run short. It never happened."

"I know what you mean," I blurted. "It is an amazing sight, but there is always enough to go around. Actually, a little extra to ease my mind and allow a peaceful night's sleep."

The glow gone, separation dissolved, and we were equals.

"So much like his father," smiled Elijah.

"So much," beamed Moses.

"Why are you here?"

"Your Father sent us," said Moses.

"To prepare and explain," included Elijah.

Energized by the notion of a visitation from my Father, whom I had talked about, prayed to, believed in, sensed a oneness with, and now who had sent to--me-- messengers, who were confirming my plunges in faith.

"What must I prepare for?" I asked slowly.

"Jerusalem," said Moses.

"The plan has changed." Elijah hung his head sadly, like a boy losing a playmate.

"Not really changed. We knew man was as prickly as the wilderness bush. There was always a possibility reason would be snuffed by man's impudence."

"Jerusalem," I spoke deliberately. "What will happen there?"

"Forces are at work to produce the greatest fiasco ever perpetrated in the history of human stupidity," Elijah punctuated.

"I believe I am doing well," I objected. "I see progress. I see growth. My brethren are a redeemable sort. They have qualities both endearing and fruitful."

"You have done well, my Lord. But they will not be regained until they are totally convinced of what they have lost." Moses tried to be soothing but the words pierced my heart with a searing conviction. I wanted this strange vision to end. These words were useless to me. They provided no support for my work; just darkened conclusions of scholarly patriarchs, offering no insight into reaching a generation of ravaged souls. Beware the common knowledge of weary prophets. "If you are Moses, you must know the anguish of leading a faithless people, while having your heart broken into pieces over the loss of one rebellious soul."

He crinkled his chin, raised his eyebrows and gave a little nod. I continued, "And if you are Elijah, you must know the thrill of demonstrating the power of God, only to find yourself alone in a cold, dark cave." He frowned, causing a wave of wrinkles to sprout across his bald head.

"I still remember the joys of my humanity," Moses assented.

"The victories and defeats pepper my memories also," said Elijah with a shrug.

"Then you know the prophet who ceases to believe in the quality   he preaches is damned. If he does not see potential for those who have gathered to hear, then he is better suited for duty in the whale's belly."

"It is good Jonah did not come," laughed Moses.

"You will be tried, convicted and murdered," said Elijah, flatly.

"I have always known this was possible."

"You will need to rest and savor your strength," cautioned Moses.

"Why, so I can pour it out in one final, bloody lump at the whim of the Jerusalem officials?"

"No, so you can die at the right time and place instead of from exposure and fatigue in some ditch in Galilee," said Elijah tersely.

"Is there a right time to die?"

"I died short of my promised land," mused Moses.

"I died on cue with the reins of a fiery chariot clutched in my hands," postured Elijah.

"Yes," said Moses, reflectively, "there are better times to die and more noble ambitions achieved."

"If what you say is true, then so be it. But I cannot give up on this work. Certainly I am not oblivious to the human frailty. I see the treachery of mankind everyday. But I must continue to plead their cause as the son of man I am. As Abraham begged for the cities of Sodom and Gomorrah, I, too, am in search of one righteous soul who has not surrendered and given in to the blandness around him.   I must believe this cup of rejection will be dumped on the ground. I do not want to down the dregs from this bitter wine. If it is in my daily bread to do so, then I will consume the foul poison. Elijah, I must take my people to a promised land without benefit of heavenly chariot. I must continue to believe sanity will win, or I will merely become a defeated, bludgeoned, insipid martyr."

The two messengers stared at me, respectfully bewildered.

"You will go to Jerusalem," stated Moses.

"As I had planned."

"You will be energized and enlightened by our encounter," noted Elijah.

"As I need to be."

"When it comes . . ." began Elijah.

"I will die as I have lived. As His son."

Simon Peter awoke, startled, heart racing, sat upright, sweat beading on his forehead, trying to remember where he was. What had alarmed him? He panted, gazing off into the distance, as the rustling of the breeze and the atonal snoring of his two comrades, James and John, provided a gentle interlude to an otherwise still surroundings. Something was strange, an eerie sense of emptiness, leaving a cramping in his belly.

Where was Jesus?

Gone, and not unusual, Simon accustomed to waking up alone.

Jesus was often departed by the time he relented to rising. Today it was different. Was there a frigid edge to the wind? He recalled words-- two days before. Jesus had informed them he was going to be betrayed; a stunning announcement vacant emotion, a calm observation--peaceful. It left Simon reeling. How could this be? Was Jesus wrong? Simon often thought so, feeling great liberty and puffy pride to challenge Jesus. He still believed him to be the son of the living God. But after all, Simon often questioned God. Jesus usually welcomed the dispute, though Simon was not sure about God's response.

This just had to be wrong. How could such a heinous deed be accomplished? Who? The Nazarene seemed invincible to outside interference--the winds and waves obeying his command.

"I wonder where he is this time?"

John.

Simon shivered.

"Out there. Up there. Somewhere we aren't, as usual," said James, rubbing his eyes.

Simon hadn't even noticed the snoring had ceased. "We should find him."

"Come now, Simon. He can take care of himself," chuckled James.

"Remember, dear brother. He is not Simon. Now he is Peter," chided John.

"That's right," smiled James. "From a stone to a rock. Quite a promotion, with no money to show for it."

They all laughed--especially Simon. To acquire this name change all he had done was confirm the obvious, calling Jesus the Son of God. Who else could He be? Most men want to be gods and then try to do mighty works to prove themselves to skeptical followers. Jesus, on the other hand, did the miraculous and told those benefited to remain silent.

"He must be the Messiah," said James.

"I believe so," Peter agreed.

"I know so," John mouthed, in a breathy whisper.

"So where does that put us? I mean, where do we go from here?" James was grumpy before his morning figs.

"Jerusalem," replied John softly.

"I know that. Where else could you levy a campaign to overthrow the Romans, but in Jerusalem?" bickered James.

"Yeah, it's hard to be King of the Jews from Capernaum." Peter joined in on the humiliation of the younger brother.

"It's hard to be king of your own house in Capernaum, right, Peter?" scoffed James, throwing a playful punch at the fisherman's arm.

"What does that mean?" shouted Peter, rising to his knees.

"He didn't mean anything--just about your wife and all," said John sheepishly.

"What about my wife?"

"Just that traveling with Jesus is the best thing that ever happened to your marriage." James continued his testy assault.

"My wife and I have our disagreements," conceded Peter.

"Disagreements don't make holes in the walls and leave a trail of broken clay pots." John finished his point, peering at the darkening features of his business partner. "Oh, boy, here we go."

"Strong disagreements, then, you fishing failures," railed Peter.

"Fishing failures?" fumed James, leaping up.

Peter joined him and the two men went nose to nose in mock fury and battle. "Remember where you were when Jesus called you? Sitting in your boat mending your nets because you were too drunk or too lazy to cast them into the water."

"At least we had a boat that would float," retorted John, jumping to his feet. "You and Andrew were trying to cast your net from the seashore because your ship was full of holes."

"That's when I knew Jesus was a great prophet," ranted James. "When he cast off to teach in your boat and didn't drown, I knew the heavens were with him." James laughed in the middle of his outburst.

"This isn't fair," objected Peter. "Andrew isn't here to defend his lack of talent and devilish sluggardness."

They all fell down on their backsides and laughed. Jesus had made a difference, this they knew. Peter and his wife actually talked now and enjoyed precious moments together. His mother-in-law (healed by the master) found it difficult to lodge many complaints and fester much resistance. Unfortunately, Zebedee had broken all ties with James and John. Life with Jesus had been a mixture of discovery and loss. All of them were a little less sure of themselves, a little more in wonder of the world around them, and a little suspicious of predictable answers.

"I make no apologies. I want to be in power with Him."

James' rolling thunder.

"We all do. We have spent a lifetime rubbing our hands raw with fish scales and rope. It would be nice to enjoy some of the finer things."

Peter's dreamy defiance.

"I just want to be with Him."

John's simpler path.

"Come on, brother. Have an idea. Dream a dream. Stop trying to say the right thing all the time. Jesus doesn't expect us to serve the rest of our lives, especially not Herod and the Romans. He is just biding his time, exploring the soft underbelly of this depraved system, so he may discern the vulnerable spot to thrust the sword of God's vengeance." James paused, standing, tears in his eyes, his head held high, posing for posterity.

"Maybe," said John tentatively. "But I never hear him talk about conquering the Romans."

"Jesus is a doer, not a talker," said Simon.

"I wonder where He is?" James squinted into the morning sun.

"Praying," answered John, knowingly.

"I wonder if that is what he does. He comes back from those solitude times so confident and energized. I should ask him to teach me to pray so I can get that power." Peter smirked.

"No. I get to ask him. You already got a new name. It is my turn to be the smart and spiritual one," said James, imitating the voice of a petulant child.

"I'm going to look for him." Peter rarely felt the need for confirmation.

"I'm going with you," joined John.

"Not without me. I don't want to look like the uncaring one," declared James as he hustled to catch up.

The men walked with no particular destination.

"He will take authority in Jerusalem," said James confidently.

"He has been there before," John cautioned.

"And tore the hell out of the temple," asserted Peter with a clap of approval.

"This time he will whip more than money changers," James predicted.

"I don't think he meant to hurt them." John had a concern for accuracy.

"You kiss to console. You whip to hurt. I didn't see him doing any puckering up to those Pharisees," Peter punctuated, with a rush of manly glee.

"Yes, we are going to see the manifestation of his full power in Jerusalem. We are going to take over." James pounded his hand against his chest.

"How do you know he will use us? I mean, maybe we were just kept around for the Galilee phase," worried John.

"One thing I know about Jesus," Peter concluded. "Whatever he gets in Jerusalem he will gladly share with us."

"Here, here, my man.   Finally you speak some sense," James said as he slapped Peter on the back.

They embraced. Once competitors over the catch from the Sea of Galilee--now brothers.

There had been many dusty roads.

It would be worth it all in Jerusalem.

It was time for fulfillment.

"Look!" John was pointing towards a sudden burst of light.

They had found Jesus.

****

The fishermen had stumbled upon my meeting with the Law Giver of Sinai and Terror of Mt. Carmel. Actually, the conference was over; the two prophets heading back to their reward, and I was off to find my future.

Peter, James, and John stared at the unearthly sight, mouths agape, awestruck by the newest spectacle in what had become quite a marketplace of wonders.

I walked toward them, trailed by Moses and Elijah. All at once my two spectacular glowing companions lifted and ascended, one veering right and the other left, evaporating into the bright blue air.

My three friends sprouted the giddy countenances of boyhood chums on a summer lark. I hustled the remaining distance.

"Your robe!" gasped Peter, tripping and falling backward. "It shines like the sun."

John eased to his knees.

"How do you do that?" cross-examined James, reaching for my robe and then pulling away.

My garment radiated a residue of the glow which had just vanished.

"It's on his face, too," exclaimed John from his kneeling position.

"What was that?" asked Peter breathlessly.

I moved forward. The brothers stepped back. "So you saw it too," I responded. "Must not be a typical vision." I glanced back in the direction of the phenomenon.

"I saw it, too," said James, gazing.

"If it is all right, I did too," John added meekly.

"It's all right," I replied, chuckling. "Gentlemen, I think we were just honored with a visit from Moses and Elijah."

"Moses," repeated James.

"And Elijah," Peter and John sang in unison.

"That's it. I thought I was dreaming, but now that we all saw it, I guess they were really here."

"They are here to take over," trumpeted James.

"The Romans have had it now," Peter squealed in delight.

"As you can see," I pointed out, "they are gone."

"That's right, gone." John was numb.

"We've got to do something." James confirmed his insistence with an unusual leap-dance.

"How about some food?" suggested a famished John.

"No, I mean something about this," James protested, circling us.

"We should build three booths. One for Moses and one for Elijah . . ." began Peter.

"And one for you, lord," finished James, pounding me on the back.

"Do you think they would come back from heaven to live in a confining tent?" inquired John uncertainly.

"What? At the prospect of a small enclosure built by fishermen? They would be crazy not to," I said, hoping my humor would bring them back to reality.

The three looked at me with huge eyes and nodded, grateful for my support for the tabernacle project. A roll of thunder and the sky darkened.

A voice came from all directions vibrating in our chests. "This is my beloved son, listen to him."

A small pinpoint of light trickled through the blackness, giving promise of the return of day.

We were there together--four Galileans.

"We all did hear that?" panted James, glancing back and forth across the sky.

"I did," John deadpanned.

"It was the *Name that should not be Spoken.* First Moses. Then Elijah. Now, well, you know. . . What next?" Peter spread his arms and gazed into the sky.

"I think that's probably the pinnacle, Brother Simon," said James, sucking in breath to soothe his dry throat.

"Did you hear it, Lord?"

John spoke, suddenly aware I was walking away. "Hear what?"

"The voice!" screamed James.

"I can certainly hear yours."

"What now?" Peter demanded, still staring skyward.

"Food," I answered, continuing my descent.

The others followed, reluctantly. Another unexplained event, glorious, culminating in little. They were quiet.

"Oh, by the way," I said, coming to a stop. "I wouldn't go talking about this . . . a. . . . vision to anyone else."

They all agreed, heads bobbing vigorously.

Tell somebody? Where would you begin?

I warned with a greater degree of clarity. "Don't say anything until all has been accomplished."

"You mean Jerusalem," stated James, winking at Peter and John.

"Yes, Jerusalem, or thereafter."

"That will be it, won't it, Lord?"

James was excited.

James was positive.

James was. . . a fisherman from Galilee.

"Then we will have the power to say or do anything we want," cheered Peter.

"Are they right, Lord?" queried John, a little confounded.

"Let's just say Jerusalem is the crossroads to mankind's future." I looked through John, visualizing.

"When will we know?" James hadn't heard.

"Know what?"

"Know when to tell the common people we saw Moses and Elijah," postured Peter with his predictable, provincial pride.

"The place is being determined. The time, you will know . . . you will know."

Blood on the Sandals

" **W**ould you join hands?"

A pause as the man and his lady exchanged a bashful glance in a nervous attempt to choreograph the request. He stretched out his hand, and she tenderly placed her fingertips on his perspiring palm. I watched their united effort, especially fascinated by his hand, once mangled, tiny and withered, now whole.

I met him as a boy playing in the outer court of the temple. I gawked at the feeble appendage, so shriveled and ugly; a piece of human flesh hanging with no purpose--truly an indignity, so misplaced, attached to such a lively, energetic, young boy.

Madez never complained, oblivious to his plight.

Six months ago, our paths crossed again in the synagogue at Bethany. I spotted him sitting next to his father, Nicodemus. The room was filled with Jerusalem's finest who had gathered to remember Sabbath, and, as I discovered later, scrutinize my doings.

Scriptures were read. My attention was constantly drawn back to my boyhood pal, who sat quietly--patiently-- as if anticipating a visitation.

The prayers continued in a drone of repetition. I re-positioned myself so I could see his face better. He looked up at me. I wondered if he would remember? Had I maintained any of my boyish charm? Perhaps Nicodemus had told him about our midnight conversation two years earlier.

The ritual trudged onward.

I became agitated. Here we were in the presence of our Creator, mouthing prayers and psalms, pronouncing ourselves fathered children. Yet precious time was being wasted discussing God's disposition and idiosyncrasies instead of receiving His full, loving embrace.

I stood to my feet, not wishing to interrupt, definitely lacking a plan. Gradually everyone turned and looked my way, eyes dulled with the drowsiness of mental fatigue, some yawning to regain a sense of reason. They were expecting another translation of some overworked piece of law.

I was now the center of attention--such as it was. There was no sense wasting the moment on meaningless dialogue.

"Stand up!" I shouted, extending my hand and pointing at a startled Madez, who, though alarmed, leaped to his feet in obedient expectation.

The room was struck silent.

"Do you think it is proper to do a good deed on the Sabbath?" I inquired of my former playmate.

"Please elaborate, rabbi," interrupted one of the numerous priests scattered about the congregation.

I turned to him. "Which word gave you trouble, brother? Was it good or do?" There was an uneasy growl of laughter which quickly subsided.

"We have six days to do good," said the presiding rabbi.

"But what if we forget? Or, God forbid, what if the need to do good falls on the Sabbath?" I looked around the room. There was no response. I seized the lull and continued. "What if a needed action is found to be in the flow and timing of our Sabbath ritual?"

Madez stood still before me.

"Stretch forth your hand," I commanded. Madez lifted the hand--a miniature, crusty, graying piece of human degradation. There was no surprise, gasps, or concern from the assembled faithful. Madez was well-known, his infirmity a matter of record.

Nicodemus bowed his head. Was it reverence, humiliation over his son's affliction, or embarrassment about my intrusion into Sabbath services?

It made no difference. It was the season for change. I stepped closer to Madez. "Do you remember me?" I whispered in his ear.

He pulled back and squinted into my face. A little smile sprouted at the corners of his mouth. "You look like a tired young man who has stolen the mischievous eyes of a boy I once knew." I laughed. It was very funny. People began to fidget and grumble over the outburst of levity in the House of God. (I enjoyed the laugh. As I said, it was very funny.)

"What do you wish to share with us, rabbi?" interrupted the priest. "We welcome new ideas that would enrich our values and worship."

I peered at his inflexible countenance. This also struck me as funny, so I renewed my laughter. "Is it a good thing to do good on the Sabbath?" I whirled around, trying to make eye contact with each worshiper in the room. A hush fell once again. I stopped laughing. A cowardly silence. The heat of rage surged through my body. I glared at Nicodemus, who was wiggling into a retreated profile, casting his eyes to the synagogue floor.

I was infuriated by the apathy. "What price will you pay for your indecision? How long will you continue to let your committees dictate the mercy of God in tiny increments of scriptural understanding? How long will you allow suffering on the Sabbath day under the illusion God wants to inflict some lesson? Have you asked the Father if he has chosen to cheat this man of his full usage? Could it be there is a better portion of life available to him?" I turned back to Madez. "Stretch forth your hand!"

He had dropped his arm in the climate of uncertainty. Moving to obey, his hand appeared from the surplus of robe--whole, clean and adult. Gone was the minuscule, diseased grasp of a soul assumed cursed.

It was my turn to gasp, followed by the collective astonishment of the congregation. Nicodemus slowly lifted his face and beheld the wonder of God's intervention. Tears welled in his eyes. Madez shivered, wept, repeatedly displaying the phenomenon before his own amazed eyes.

I cried loudly, "The Sabbath wasn't made for God. The time of rest was created for man. Behold, therefore, I am the lord of the Sabbath!"

I exited, hastily, no time to debate propriety, and not necessary to remain for a critique of the healing or my unusual benediction.

These were the memories flooding my mind as I looked upon the hand, joined with my dear friend, Mary of Bethany. I had been asked to preside over their wedding. Mary, too, had seen her share of heavenly intervention. A little more than a Sabbath ago, her brother Lazarus walked away from his own tomb--remarkable events.

Now we are gathered to celebrate an even greater wonder, one that mystifies the heavens. God creates and restores, but man is his selected caretaker. God watches in awe when two members of His creation join wills in an act of united love.

Ceasing my daydreaming, I noticed Mary and Madez were perturbed over my unexplained delay.

"Lord?" said Madez, trying to coax me back.

"Don't worry, Madez, I'm here. Just trying to figure out a way to be eloquent."

I patted his shoulder, as Mary smiled, a concession of politeness. "By the way," I whispered. "No Lord stuff today. I am just Jesus, a friend you have given the honor of presiding over your wedding. And, I do expect to be paid."

Madez stared and Mary frowned.

"Just joking," I quickly retracted.

They smirked, but their impatience was clear. After all, I was the final obstacle standing in the way of consummating their desires.

"Let's proceed."

They nodded in eager agreement, as Mary glanced up at Madez and gave a large audible gulp.

"There are many unions we celebrate on this day; many purposes fulfilled--many hearts entwined. All of God's Universe is poised to commemorate this recognition of the real meaning of life. This is that meaning, a mystery baffling the skeptic and intriguing the gathering of the heavenly host. It is love, without apology or explanation; a joining of man and woman in an unprecedented human action of blending wills. Both souls are complete in themselves. Yet they unite and entangle their hearts, souls, minds and strengths—this union multiplying possibility. It also unearths mounds of challenge, helping to cultivate the adventure that salts their human experience with the true essence of purpose.

My son, place your hand upon the breast wherein beats the heart of your love. My daughter, please let your hand find resting place on the chest that holds the beating pulse of the man you cherish. Father, we link our hearts in the furious and often frightful storm of emotional unity. May his heart commune with her heart all feelings that arise. May there never be a fear to share a temporary misgiving to attain lasting understanding. May their hearts be the door which allows life to enter; an existence filled with twists and turns. Help them to discuss and sift through these passing feelings until all can be shaken down, removing the useless and cherishing the eternal. Repeat with me: We are heart creatures who now gain our completion in linking ourselves together. We are readied to discover the power revealed through this common act of sharing. Hearts united we celebrate with an embrace."

Mary and Madez embraced.

"Embraced in heart, we now congeal our living souls, the portion of us given essence by the very Breath of God. For truly, once the heart is opened, the soul is exposed to experience. We grow. Heavenly Father, forge these two travelers into a spiritual oneness, energizing the beauty of their creation and the glory of their ongoing completion. For you see, little children, in time flesh will fade away into shadowy memories. Your

mutual effort has gained spirit to confirm the love in your hearts. This will radiate new confidence to your joining, enlivening all the discoveries awaiting you in every new day. You may now kiss your mate of spirit. In so doing you combine the will of your spirits to perform earthly work, producing heavenly results.

Madez and Mary kissed again; a sweet, soft kiss where the lips caress and linger. Tears filled the eyes of all gathered

"Now please, lay gentle hands upon the brow containing the mind of this soul you love with all your heart. We celebrate—love birthed in the heart, purified in the soul, to be renewed daily in the mind. We sanctify our thoughts. May they continue to bring honor to this noble mission. The mind, where the greatest concepts of passion can be nurtured to bring the sensitivity enhancing all pleasure. The mind—we rejuvenate this covenant daily with notions of consideration and inspired ideas to welcome newness to our nurturing. Repeat after me: I grant you the key to my mind, accessed from my heart through my spirit, to generate fresh convictions of my love for you each day."

They spoke the words with a warmth causing the small earthen house to gain the glow and glory of supernal splendor.

"You may kneel together as a symbol of your reverence to such an awesome gift your love has conceived and birthed into being.

Finally, it is in your strength and bodies you will actuate the heart, spirit, and mind of your love. Each movement will gain new purpose. Each glance, meaningful. You possess the secret key to the treasure house of this one you love. Your actions will either open each other to greater communion or shatter the confidence of this fragile balance. You may kneel. You shall embrace.

Repeat after me: Oh, brief candle of fire I am, I cleave to your warmth and enjoin my melting wax with yours to form one light of spiritual unity and physical ecstasy."

The heart of each hearer was dissolved into a holy agreement.

"Heavenly Father, this is not defiled and let no man put it asunder. This is the mystery of love, how you selected to maintain the dignity of the creative process, while igniting the fires of human conflict and passion.

Please rise, my children, and as you do, lean on
one another and seal this holy testament with the finest
of kisses."

*They rose, leaned and kissed. The small assembly
erupted into cheers--truly an Eden moment.*

****

Lazarus planned a supper. I guess given the
wedding, having friends in from Galilee, and a recent
resurrection from death, a celebration seemed in order.

After dining, Mary scurried out of the room, with
Madez smiling at the retreating form of his new mate. "She
has a surprise," he winked as he whispered in my direction.

This concerned me. Mary was the more volatile of
the Bethany sisters. Last week when I arrived, she was
furious because she didn't understand why I had not come
sooner to help her brother. She wouldn't even come out and
talk to me, at first. Sister Martha took it upon herself to tell
Mary 'I wanted to see her', and she eventually made her way
out to greet me--toting questions and comments. Mainly,
Mary couldn't comprehend my delay. I was sympathetic.
Facts are, I did stay two days in Galilee before I came. The
disciples needed the rest, so I trusted the Father to handle
the details. Suffice it to say my tarrying led to Lazarus'
burying. Given her nature, she was the most angry when I
arrived, and the most jubilant when Lazarus made his "re-
arrival".

So, of course, a surprise from Mary could have
many sharp corners.

"Close your eyes and keep them shut," cautioned
Madez with a grin.

More danger. I would have to face this "Mary
surprise" blinded. I submitted.

"My Lord," she began. "I know you want us to
call you Jesus, but right now 'Lord' is more appropriate."

I opened one eye and she reached up softly and
closed the flickering lid.

"I have been saving something for the day of our
family's burial. But it is you who have brought life to our
house. You have restored a second chance to my brother,
and you have taken this wonderful man and changed him
from a resolute cripple to the love of my life."

"It was his faith . . ." I began.

"I know it was his faith, but it was your
compassion that allowed the belief to succeed," she said
with finality.

I sat quietly with my eyes closed.

"I now believe this spikenard was never meant to fragrance our deaths. It is aromatic with the fluid of life. So, I anoint you with this, my Lord and giver of Life." She poured the soothing liquid on my feet and then my head. I felt the gentle flow trickle down my face. The sweet odor filled the room. I wept. Being so involved, I had not granted myself time to reflect on the victories--always more to do. The multitudes were like a flock having no shepherd. Now, one of my precious lambs was soothing the weary feet and brow of her shepherd. I was humbled and broken by such a gracious outpouring.

"Woman, do you have any idea how much that costs?" The indignant voice interrupted the stillness. I didn't need to open my eyes. I knew who it was--Judas barSimon. "That could have been better celebrated by selling it and giving the proceeds to the poor."

Tension filled the room, and I wished I could keep my eyes closed. Mary continued her vigil, driven by a mission superseding all opinion.

"Did you hear me?" demanded Judas. He was always a bit edgy when we came into Judea. I think he felt our kingdom movement was better suited for the hills of Galilee, sensing failure for our cause amongst the Judean upper crust.

"Doesn't anyone else have a conscience for the poor?" he howled at the assembled.

"Judas," I said softly as I opened my eyes. "Leave her alone. It is a moment to be treasured, not analyzed. The poor will never go away. You should take what you can and share, giving liberally to the need. But you should never mar the beauty of a tender exchange shared amongst friends. She brings her spikenard of life to prepare me for my death."

Mary stopped in the midst of her pouring. "That was not my intention."

"Your intention will be remembered by generations to come. Its significance will be further revealed by the passage of time."

"I know money! For God's sake, Master, you made me treasurer," squawked the offended Kerioth.

"And I know the heart, dear son. Mary has done a good thing. Tomorrow you may devise your plans for solving the poverty question. Tonight, let us enjoy each other."

"I'm not angry," he said, recoiling. "Sometimes I just don't understand."

"Then come and learn with me."

He shook his head. "Excuse me," he said, backing up, turning and walking to the door.

"Judas."

"Later, Master. I need some time." His voice was distant as he disappeared into the darkness.

I stood to follow him but Madez grabbed my shoulder. "His ears are not tuned to counsel. Your words will sting instead of heal. He must wrestle with his own demons." He maintained his firm grasp on my arm.

"Anyway," inserted Martha as she entered the room, "you can't leave until you have received all of your presents."

I looked around. My surprised expression amused my comrades. They giggled and chuckled, the good cheer greatly relieving the strain of Judas' exit.

Joanna came and sat by my side.

"And what are you up to?" I asked.

"Nothing. I was just drawing close to see the gift."

"What gift?" I chortled as the occupants of the room burst into laughter.

"This," announced Martha. She held a beautiful robe. Joanna rushed to her side and held up a matching cloak.

"This is for me?"

"Yes," said Peter, smiling. "And none too soon. Your backside was beginning to shine through the rear end of that frayed frock."

I quickly stood up and tried to twist around to see if what he said was true. This brought renewed laughter.

"Not even you, Lord, can see from whence you came," said John, giggling.

More laughter.

"I wove it myself," said Martha with that unassuming tone so often masking a heart of gold.

I held it up, looked at it, turning it around in every direction. "It is a robe for a king," I said, smiling at the brothers and sisters in the room.

"We hope so," said Thomas.

"I don't know what to say."

"Now there's a first," quipped Phillip.

"A man who can teach all day in the boat until my skin is burned by the flaming sun. Now he says he doesn't know what to say?" Andrew's remark further fueled the frivolity.

"Say you will wear it," pleaded a sparkling-eyed Joanna.

"I will. I don't know if anybody will recognize me, but I will wear it," I said, holding the garment up for size.

"Wear it when we march into Jerusalem," blasted Simon.

This brought grunts of approval from the admirers.

"Jerusalem it shall be," I said quietly.

"Now that is all the pay you get," said Mary.

The cadre was enlivened again.

"To Madez and Mary," I said, holding up a cup of wine. "And to Martha for her great act of love and kindness."

Martha blushed and waved her hand, feigning disapproval over my over-appreciation. "It's a robe, for God's sake," she said. "It's not a suit of armor, so watch out for Roman spears!"

"And," I continued, "to Judas, who is not here. May we all thank him for his concern and help him feel a part of this glorious work the Father has given us."

Cups were raised and backs were slapped. There was a hum of jubilation continuing on as I slowly sipped my wine, contemplating what demons my friend was wrestling with tonight.

****

"They tell me you wanted to see me," said Malchus as he entered a small side chamber of the temple, dressed formally, anticipating the need to establish a climate of superiority.

"I must discuss some things with you," entreated Judas. The cold night air had left his throat raspy and the wind had disheveled his garments and hair. Malchus had definitely achieved his desired pre-eminence.

"What do you mean, discuss? Judas, you must understand the timing of endeavors. Therein lies the power of accomplishment. We of the order are students of calculation. We anticipate results and require fruit from our investment." Judas stared at his sandals. "Are you listening to me, brother?"

"I need to talk about Jesus."

"And which escapade shall we discuss? Shall it be the unlawful, shameful display entering into Jerusalem? He was on an ass! Am I right? What was the meaning of that?"

"I don't understand what needs to be done . . . "

"What is going on? When we met in Jericho you were unwilling to participate in our noble cause."

"Things were going well."

"You call Jesus eating at the home of that tax collecting bastard, Zaccheus, going well?"

"I saw promise.   Perhaps Jesus could breach the factions."

"Sinners are not a faction. They are a whoredom to the purity of the virgin Israel."

Judas paused and studied Malchus. At length he proceeded, "I need to know what it is you propose."

"I went over this. Lord Caiaphas wants this foolishness to stop.   Prophets on donkeys do not sanctify the people to holiness and pride in their nation. Our king will not ride an ass. Our king will rule with the authority of David."

"What harm?"

"How about yesterday's temple fiasco?   Are you trying to tell me when he rampaged through there he wasn't sending a message? Why did he target the money changers with his whip? He knows those kiosks of animal sacrifice are owned by the high priest.   For God's sakes, they call them the Booths of Annas. Are you trying to make me believe all of this is innocent Galilean naivet ?   He knew who he was attacking. He has devised a plan and if we don't channel his fervor, he will have the whole Jewish world entranced in his simplistic, anemic doctrine."

"He must not be hurt," Judas declared, clasping Malchus's arm.

"The way he is behaving? I cannot control that! You have nothing to fear from the council. They are sane and just men who deliberate the consequences of their actions. On the other hand, the city is filled with pilgrims with causes less, shall we say, refined. These renegades might find the assassination of your master a particularly worthy stepping stone to promote their agenda."

"He can't be hurt.   He has done no wrong. Ignorance of cultural differences is not a crime."

"Not to me or you! Still, there are those who more fervently attend to the letter of the law.   They find such variance blasphemous and worthy of punishment."

"I want to help."

"Then do something!" Malchus grabbed him by the shoulders, whirling him around. "Don't wait for Jesus to be stabbed on the street by some zealot who is half the man."

"Then you do see he has truth and power?"

"I see he has a place in our cause. I personally believe it to be back in Galilee amongst the peasants, who lack the sophistication to devour the deeper oral interpretations of the Mosaic Rule. His little parables and tales will gain their ear, and can be used to draw their tender hearts closer to the Most High."

"He is good in Galilee. He seems happy there. We are all happy there.   There are many miracles there." Malchus waited. He knew Judas was balancing great burdens in his mind.   Such a delicate process must never be disturbed. "You just want him in Galilee?"

"Why would we hurt him?   What is our reward? Are we Herod, lopping   off the head of every possible competitor? Yet, I warn you! We shall not tolerate his interference in our religion. We cannot permit him to defile the temple and mock the traditions. Do you understand my meaning?" Malchus did not trust this son of Simon; a deceit in his manner conjured the sniff of brimstone.

"Tell me, what is it I must do?   What is my involvement?"

"As I told you in Jericho. . .".

"Don't be condescending to me. What you are asking is very confusing. Just because you see the wisdom of your own way does not mean it translates so well to my heart. This is my master. You are asking me to betray my friend."

"I am asking you," interrupted Malchus, "to gather Jesus' flock into safer and more fruitful pastures. Obviously, he feels the compulsion to share his message with all hearers. Still, most movements worthy of note are stymied by a failure to gain the right audience. Galilee of the Gentiles is His people and therefore where his fruit can be borne out in greater effectiveness. Think, Judas. You cannot expect a man of destiny to walk away from his charge. Jesus wants to save the entire world. It is up to his generals to guide him into campaigns which will rally more realistic support and therefore richer conquest."

Judas was spellbound by the logic. "So we are trying to help Jesus gain a following by placing him amongst the Galileans?"

"As you would trim back a tree to gain fruitfulness, so must Jesus be pruned to his greater good."

"I need time."

"I need a man."

"Don't try to insult me into performing your will."

"No intimidation intended. Israel is peppered with men who dream and then complain. We must be men of action, careful and purposeful action, I grant you. We can debate until opportunity has slipped away. Judas, it is in our power to transform our own legacy."

Judas stood, benighted. Malchus' words soothed a wounded, bitter place in his mind. He thought back to the incident in Bethany. Why did Jesus allow such useless wasting of goods to satisfy a quirk? Didn't he care for the poor? Didn't he trust his own accountant to give sound financial counsel? Had Jesus lost faith in his abilities? There had been accusations by some that Judas had pilfered funds. Did Jesus believe the rumors? This hurt. After all, he was fastidious to select the projects that would garner credibility for the Kingdom movement. Moving in and out of prestigious circles, his robes, which were acceptable in Galilee, now appeared dowdy and drab. Is not the purchase of a garment to help promote a cause to a sophisticate a worthwhile investment? Is not bringing a special flask of wine to a rabbi's home a consideration worthy of a few shekels?

They didn't comprehend the stakes. He was a foreigner, a Judean, stifled by ruffian Galileans--softer features, mannerisms subtler. In this troop, his ambition was mocked as an attribute of flawed character, instead of the driving thrust of a determined patriot. Truly, Jesus was gifted, but inept in the arena of diplomacy. Judas could cushion the severity of statements like "Take up your cross and follow me." Perhaps better worded, "A moment of inconvenience can bring a lifetime of riches." Slight changes, not a dilution, but rather a freshening to create a larger mass appeal. If only he could speak to Jesus the way he had bantered with Malchus. Would Jesus allow his personal philosophy to be scrutinized to fashion a more expansive presentation? Jesus was always the teacher and Judas the student. There were never times of compromise. Wouldn't Jesus prosper by greater understanding of Jewish custom? What harm in washing hands before the meal? Why must he always refer to the Holy Writ as "your law?" Wouldn't he fare better if he were more zealous of his people and less willing to "render unto Caesar the things that are Caesar's"?

Questions promoting aggravation, lacking resolve.

Judas was exhausted with reasoning; so much easier when he was younger and enemies were easily identified, rooted out, and exposed--punishments, swift and deliberate. But ever since Bethabarra, his baptism, and his time with Rabbi Jesus, the complexity of intention had fuddled his power of decision. Weren't there enemies that eeded to be destroyed? Weren't there causes demanding e brandishing of the sword? Was it all parables and *blessing children? Was there not a man's message which could emerge from the timid concepts of this Kingdom cult?*

Judas paced around the room. Malchus patiently waited, choosing not to interfere with one so close to the edge; for the slightest intimidation might cause a reversal-- never to regain the same station of willingness.

"He must not be hurt. I can't imagine that soul in pain," said Judas from an aching spirit.

"Are we going to go over this again?"

"It's important. The man has never given grief to anyone or anything. Hell, he tells us to consider the lily."

"Interesting, I suppose. You call him a man; others deem him a god. At least this is what I hear," Malchus said, eyeing Judas carefully.

"I met him as a man and love him as a man. I don't need to talk with God. I don't need God to sup with me. He can remain in the heavens and allow men with drive and purpose to do the work. Jesus is my master . . ."

"But not your Lord?" interrupted Malchus.

"We already have one God we don't know what to do with. If the great *I Am* is in the heavens He certainly can't be dining on the Mount of Olives. "

"Is that where you are camping?"

"What do you need?"

Malchus retreated, sensing a tactical error. "We need him alone, where we can take him into custody without the shedding of blood."

"Sensible."

"I am talking to a man of sense."

Judas stared at Malchus, trying to appear unmoved by the flattery, but the words soothed his tattered self-vision. "I will deliver him to you whole. You make sure he stays that way."

"I have no grudge against your rabbi. If he weren't such an annoyance to our plan, he might be a welcome diversion."

"When?"

"This week."

"Idiotic."

"I know it is soon, but the haste will create focus. We dare not dawdle. The price must be paid."

Judas squinted, frightened of his own next words. Malchus was annoyed with all the posturing, but decided tolerance could assure full cooperation from this volatile ally.

"Passover feast." Judas spoke from a dark closet in his soul.

"Does he plan to commemorate with his admirers?"

"Please, not during the Seder. I will lead you to Him afterwards."

"As you wish," said Malchus, gratified the negotiations were finally complete.

"And you will not hurt him?" Judas persisted, clutching the robe of the departing dignitary.

Malchus removed the disciple's hand from its anxious clutch. "My dear brother, what would we have to gain?"

Barabbas was bored, all the novelty extracted from his storehouse of amusements. Pleasures had been overworked in varying degrees of perversion and misuse, so he sat pouting in his assigned campsite in the wilderness near Jerusalem, awaiting the consummation of the plan empowering him to reign over unsuspecting souls. The possibility was glorious, but the inconvenience, intolerable.

Great men are not suited to a patient vigil, he brooded. After all, did Caesar sit for days and languish in the melancholy of indecision? When did Alexander delay the latest conquest? Barabbas possessed the ambitious itch of these conquering titans; an aching, frustrated military genius relegated to pulling up grass and snapping twigs as Sister Now stroked and untangled his clumps of thigh hair, and Maiden Later massaged a particularly bulbous corn on his gigantic, aromatic left foot.

"I thirst," he thundered pathetically, Jaakobah's eyes darted toward Kreble, who scrambled to his feet, sparking a smirk.

"We have wine," Jaakobah said nervously.

"I know its taste," growled Barabbas, executing a huge stretch.

"You need new wine," said Kreble, as he stumbled to get closer to his leader.

Barabbas eased to his feet to a chorus of creaks and crackles, weaving a step or two as his legs attempted to support his frame. "I need fresh new wine that I do not presently have and I did not purchase!"

The meaning was clear. The ladies rose to prepare the horses as Kreble rushed to obtain his sword.

"General," said Jaakobah carefully, "We have orders . . ."

"Orders?" roared Barabbas, whirling to square off on his timid cohort. "No one orders Barabbas. I have agreed to the terms of their plan, but my personal comings and goings remain my affair."

Jaakobah, realizing the error of his approach, tried again. "Why don't you let Kreble and myself secure the provision? It could be a surprise."

"I like to create my own diversions. We are going to rehearse our skills. We cannot sit here like tentmakers considering a length of cloth. We are warriors and thrive on the grind of the challenge. We yearn to conquer. Jaakobah, can't you hear the cry of the wilderness wild? There is something we lack, pleading we come and liberate it to better use."

Kreble bobbed his head enthusiastically. The women continued to gather the necessary implements.

"There is so much at stake," reasoned Jaakobah.

"Are we little children on our first romp? A pillaging raid is hardly an obstacle to a warrior. We will be out and back, slurping delicious wine before you can even think of another silly excuse why we shouldn't do it."

Jaakobah shrugged in submission to his superior. He was out--numbered, witted, stated, and ranked.

The men mounted the horses, the female workers making their usual appeal to go on the rampage.

"You ladies stay here," said Barabbas decisively. "We may meet up with danger." He winked at Kreble, as the young zealot dreamed of how fragrant, soft and satisfying that "danger" might truly be.

They were off.

The trio rode several miles into the countryside before they spotted a small house nestled into the Judean hillside.

"Looks like we have found our new home," chuckled Barabbas. Kreble laughed, and Jaakobah was greatly relieved. The location was deserted and unimposing; a thatched enclosure with a light shimmering from within. Riding up, they realized the hut was larger than they first thought, probably an inn to house weary strangers; a covered roof wherein was the makings of a loft.

Barabbas did not knock to seek entry, slamming his fist as the door surrendered its moorings. He entered the abode, ducking his head to avoid the frame.

"What is it you want?" whispered an old man holding a flask of wine, desperately trying to hide his trembling woman.

"That should do well, at least to start," said Barabbas as he yanked the flask from the startled man.

Kreble was busying himself probing and poking through the meager contents of the country cottage.

"I cannot give this to you," rasped the man, still trying to maintain his hushed profile. He grabbed back his wine.

Barabbas stepped back and drew his sword, shocked by such a rebellious display. Kreble tried to wrestle the container from the determined houseman.

Maintaining his firm grip, he warned in a wheeze, "You don't understand, I have guests." He glanced up at the loft above their heads.

"I don't care if you are entertaining Caesar," said Barabbas, brandishing his sword. "You will not be serving him this wine."

Kreble threw the man on the ground, but he leaped to his feet and lunged at Barabbas, who was exiting, toting his prize.

"Barabbas, watch out!" warned Kreble. Barabbas wheeled about as the man leaped,.the sword thrusting deeply into his belly. He slumped, gasped, fell over a table, onto the floor--blade upright.

Barabbas looked at Jaakobah, as if seeking affirmation of his innocence in the matter. Jaakobah lurched back in horror, affixing himself to the wall. Kreble diverted his attention to the robust woman, whose shattered countenance mirrored the insanity of the bloody encounter.

Barabbas, fearing to appear tentative before his underlings, pulled the sword from the bleeding midsection, shoving it deep into the heart of the mortally wounded fellow. "Then die, you damn bastard. All for a flask of wine."

Kreble stroked the cheek of the widow. He grabbed her hair and jerked her head back, her eyes frozen. He forced his hand down her robe and fumbled with her breasts. She didn't resist.

"She is terrified, leave her alone," bellowed Jaakobah, pulling at Kreble's robe.

"How am I to satisfy a wench who will not blink?"

Barabbas frowned at the lifeless form at his feet.

"Wake up, you bitch!" Kreble snarled, slapping the woman across the face. She recoiled but maintained her silence.

Suddenly, a rustling from the ceiling above.

"Did you hear that?" whispered Jaakobah.

"Curious rodents," declared Barabbas, peering toward the loft.

"I want this woman," screeched Kreble. "I love her breasts and I can smell her virtue!" He pawed and pinched, trying to gain entrance to her body and soul.

"We've got to get out of here," Jaakobah whimpered.

"I will not run like some synagogue boy caught nibbling at the shewbread," said Barabbas, casting a piercing glance at the retreating soldier.

"If she won't wriggle or cry out I cannot do this." Kreble threw her on the ground, kicking her in the head. She sobbed but lay as motionless as her destroyed spouse.

"We will leave, but not in terror," cautioned Barabbas. "Grab some provisions for our cause and let us make our exit as men of power."

"Shall I check the loft, General?" asked Jaakobah, trying to gird his mind from the mounting fear.

"We have killed enough rats. No need to seek out more," answered Barabbas, ducking to exit the murder scene.

"I want to get inside this bitch."

"Then do it or don't. But be quick about it," spat Barabbas from his new position outside the hut.

"I am going," announced Jaakobah, looking down on the shivering mass of wounded womanhood.

"I like to work alone," Kreble exclaimed.

Barabbas and Jaakobah waited outside in silence as Kreble grumbled, groaned, cursed, and lamented over the battered lady. "I can't get my weapon to do war," he complained.

"I would never admit that," sneered Barabbas.

More slapping. The lady whimpered but did not scream.

Kreble appeared in the doorway. "The woman is as dry as the desert."

"Maybe she finds you unattractive," suggested Barabbas.

"Can we go?" shuddered Jaakobah.

"Not until we can leave as men; when you have lost that young maiden squeak in your voice we will depart."

Silent, standing--shivering tears from behind, creaks from the roof above, Kreble panting. "There must be a thousand of them up there." Kreble lifted his eyes toward the top of the house.

Barabbas stood peering into the distance. Jaakobah knew he was waiting for some obvious sign of the return of order and manliness. Though petrified, he knew they would never leave until Barabbas was convinced it was a noble exit by conquering men. "I just wish I could have busted the whore open myself," said Jaakobah, with all the strength of speech his trembling voice could muster.

A pause, then a tense moment, culminating in an awkward, humiliating silence. "It is time to go." Barabbas was satisfied dignity was intact.

They mounted their horses and galloped into the night, journeying a mile or two, before Barabbas pulled on the reins and halted the escape. "I thirst. Let us enjoy the fruit of our labors," he said, dismounting from his snorting beast. The other two joined Barabbas under a nearby tree. "Kreble, build a fire while Jaakobah and I begin the celebration."

Kreble understood--a rebuke. He had done poorly on the raid, his inability to derive shrieks of terror or moans of pleasure from the vanquished vixen.

Kreble stomped away, shuffling his sandals to stir clouds of dust, so they would know the degree of his frustration and disgust.

The fire was lit, the wine was consumed, and soon the threesome became drunk on the plunder provided from their brazen debacle.

Kreble sang and Jaakobah moped.

Barabbas garbled of glory. "I will rule Israel. I will be the King of the Jews. I will be lifted high for all to see. God will grant me the first fruits of worship so He might retain the rest."

All at once, there was a swishing in the night, first from one direction and then from several.

"The rats have followed us," slurred Kreble. This made the sullen Jaakobah laugh, Barabbas joining in.

Their laughter covered the sound of louder crackling.

"I shall draw my sword and slay all the mice that would dare to infest the Promised Land." Kreble struggled to his feet.

"Stand still," commanded a voice from the deep blackness.

"Talking rodents?" came the bewildered observation of a stumbling Jaakobah.

"Stand away from your weapons," shouted the voice, now nearly upon the surprised revelers.

"Those are no pests. Those are human." Barabbas tried to gain footing, slipped, landing on his seat of power.

Suddenly the grass gained life and the surrounding hills were clad in armor and issued sword.

The zealots were surrounded by Roman leather and crimson.

"Romans?" gasped Barabbas.

"Shall we fight?" panted Kreble.

"That is why we waited until you were drunk," laughed the Roman commander.

The raiders were too intoxicated to respond, a quick head count confirming they were hopelessly outnumbered.

"How did you find us?" managed Kreble from his haze.

"You stupid fools! We were lodged in the loft where you killed that gracious innkeeper," scoffed the commander. "The rest of my men were camping near the trail you rode enroute to your little celebration."

The Roman guards busied themselves removing weapons and all the clothing from the dazed zealots. In no time at all the three men stood, naked and shivering, in the damp chill of the wilderness night.

"You cannot do this. I am Barabbas, King of the Jews. There is a plan."

"Yes, he is a great warrior and so are we," wailed Kreble.

Jaakobah stood, gazing down at his circumcised self.

"Well, Barabbas, King of the Jews. You are under arrest for murder and thievery, and if what you say is true, we might just throw in sedition as well."

"Does this mean the plan has changed?" queried Kreble, blinking and stumbling to the side.

"Shut up, you ass," retorted Barabbas, as the efficient and clever Roman patrol led the culprits away.

****

A tattered garment hung as a barricade over her door; no obvious point of entry and no place to knock. The air was still and cool in the Bethany street. I listened for evidence of life beyond the cloth. A light, a single candle, speckled some gleam through the frayed portions of the fabric.

I stood, evaluating the merit of my mission. "Mother," I whispered softly, positioning myself near the opening.

No reply.

"Mother?" I pursued again, with a bit more vigor. The scraping of sandals. The candle was lifted, moving toward the entrance.

"What is it?" she spoke through a rattle. Clearing her throat, she pursued, "Yes, who is it?"

"I wish to see you, Mother."

"Who are you?"

"My name is Jesus."

"I know no Jesus from town."

"I am from Nazareth of Galilee."

A pause. The silence continued.

I spoke again. "I would like to speak with you."

"Are you the young man that stirs our tombs?"

I assumed she was speaking of Lazarus and the recent resurrection. Her tone expressed disfavor. "I was there."

"I heard you speak once."

"Where?"

"From here. I could hear your talk. You have a fine voice."

"I am enjoying hearing yours." A misplaced pleasantry.

"What is it you want?" she challenged, regaining her suspicious profile.

"I am from Nazareth."

"So you said."

"I know." More delay, as she shuffled her feet, perhaps contemplating a needful retreat.

"I know you," I said softly.

"You know my name and the stories that attach themselves to it."

"I know your pain."

"You may know pain, but you are not acquainted with mine."

"I believe I understand."

"Understanding is very useless to me. Many understand but few are chosen to survive."

"You can."

"Can what?"

"Survive."

"I have survived. I have lived. I have found a place. Jesus, some people search their whole lives to find a spot where they can inhale a peaceful breath. I have found such a haven. I need never wonder what offense I may bring to the tender conscience of some self-righteous soul. In here, I deal with my own complaints and any thoughts God may will my way."

"Hagabus is alive and as well as he will permit himself to be."

"That is a name associated to a time I barely recall, a flicker of youth; a time when feeling was too fluid to have any lasting effect. He is not a problem to me--a faint memory, along with my beloved Trinius. Son, do not try to enter the darkened corridors of my heart to enlighten some memory you feel will bring redemption. I am at peace. I am just alone."

"May I come in?"

"And what will you see? Are you looking for confirmation to your fears concerning my well being? Do you wish to view my poverty first hand? If being poor were a sin, then all of Judea might well be damned."

Aggravated, and I didn't know why. Could it be I was miffed because she had found a purpose free of outside influence?

She interrupted my introspection. "Have you ever climbed a mountain, Jesus of Nazareth? Well, of course you have. Sometimes, you reach a place where both feet are planted on two pieces of rock that start to crumble at the same instant. You glance to the path ahead. You are uncertain of gaining a new foothold before the pieces of stone break apart beneath your feet. Then you might slip and tumble into an uncontrollable fall. So you ease down. You slowly turn and allow yourself to slide to some resting point on a plateau where you regain a sense of control. You look below--there is nothing you have not already experienced. You look above--there is the terrifying apprehension of more crumbling rock and humiliating pratfalls. So you settle in on your cliff of safety. You make a life and hang on. Jesus, do you understand? Everyone finds their best fallen position and they build a future there, if they are smart. If not, they continue to tumble. They land far beneath their privilege in the depths below. Have I made myself clear? I have found my station. Some people may view it as inadequate. I do not care. They haven't stood on my crumbling path. Let them muse their own decline. Let them find their own plateau; a habitat to live and to heal."

I stared at a mended spot in the shredded robe. A meeting with a voice. No eyes to give insight to the heart. "I understand your parable but I must reject any decision to be lonely."

"Must solitude be loneliness? Is standing alone self-pity? It needn't be."

I listened intently, trying to fathom her selected choice.

She continued, patiently. "My life has purpose and direction. I do not mourn nor do I need comfort. I have retired from the cycle of idle curiosity and gossip. I refuse to be the ongoing target of nosy, morally-minded neighbors that contemplate my plight, condemn my decisions, and confuse my happiness."

"It seems you have constructed an answer."

"I have chosen an existence which has both blessing and restraints. Are we really different?"

It was time for me to go. "Thank you for your time. I just wanted to let you know you can come forth. If this is your home, then God bless the sanctuary. But if it is a tomb, my dear lady, you have entered prematurely."

Quiet, so still you could hear the air humming in your ears. Perhaps she had walked away.

"I have a daughter." The crackling voice split the silence.

" Hagabus?"

"She belongs to God."

"Her name?"

"You will see her. Just look for a woman who still climbs, though she hears the rocks failing beneath her."

"I will."

I saw the light gradually move away.

Complete.

I turned to walk away, considering Shira. Was there more I could do? It seemed to be a crime to disturb contentment in progress. Hers was a strong will with some lament in the voice. Truly, not so bad.

I walked into the deserted street. I had come this night to minister to a soul I presumed lost. Instead I met a woman who had found her portion.

****

"I normally do not allow visitors to my home," protested Caiaphas, with an air of propriety befitting the chief of priests.

"Forgive me, my Lord Caiaphas, but the gravity of the situation did not permit me to access proper channels. I needed to speak with you directly." Veshioli was out of breath, shuddering.

"I see." Caiaphas was a tall man, dark features, soft boyish eyes resembling the ripened fig, with a portly growth in his mid-section and a well-fed jowl, giving him the appearance of the prosperous craftsman.

"Pardon me, my lady," added Veshioli, bowing to the feminine presence at the priest's side.

"Oh, yes. This is my wife, Veronica. Veronica, this is . . . a. . . . Rabbi Veshioli. You are a teacher, am I right?"

"Yes, my Lord, the title rings true."

"I am pleased to make your acquaintance," breathed Veronica, with a sweet, melodic resonance.

"There is trouble, my Lord," Veshioli began.

"If you will excuse us, my dear, we have business of a more private nature," said Caiaphas, moving to escort her from the room.

"How remarkable," smirked Veronica. "You do not know the purpose of the visit and already you assume it is too sensitive for my ears."

"She may stay. It is fine with me," said Veshioli, already enraptured by her charm.

"It is not fine with me. She has her own busy routine to attend to," Caiaphas snarled.

"And what is the news all about?" queried Veronica, ignoring her husband and taking the arm of the visiting rabbi. Veshioli was trapped in the midst of a family squabble.

"The news from Veshioli, my dear, is of national security," said Caiaphas, taking her hand.

"Are you afraid I will send my messengers to the Romans to gain price for my knowledge? I am your wife and have heard many secrets divulged in our bed chambers." She stood immovable, as Caiaphas twitched and Veshioli fidgeted.

"Proceed," surrendered Caiaphas. Veronica kissed his hand. "But since I do not know the specifics of the message, I reserve the right to terminate your involvement at any time if I feel it to be for the good of the Law, or our people."

"Done," Veronica acquiesced.

Veshioli stared at the dueling pair, not sure where to start. "You are familiar with the plan?"

"I do not know the plan." Veronica awaited an explanation.

"I am warning you. Listen, but do not interrupt," snapped Caiaphas. Veronica reposed.

"Barabbas has been arrested," Veshioli stated.

"Arrested? Where?"

"In the wilderness outside Jerusalem."

"This does not change your plan."

"Oh, but it does. It totally alters all the inner structure."

"No. The Galilean and the Kingdom movement are at the heart of the project."

Veronica perked to attention. She had often heard her husband mention the Kingdom movement and the actions of a rogue rabbi from Nazareth. It had become the source of her greatest curiosity. She had heard the outlaw speak once through the walls of a neighbor's home;

enraptured by his tales. Yet she had never ventured a peek, perhaps in respect to her husband's wishes, or because she suspected her interest was just another passing fancy of her often fickle delights.

"Without Barabbas," continued Veshioli, "we do not have our ruler for the new independent state."

"Every plan has weak spots. Yours was Barabbas. Why do we care who rules this proposed territory? This puppet prince will answer to the San Hedrin anyway. It might be better to have a weaker man on the throne. Perhaps one who is less likely to develop his own visions of grandeur."

"Barabbas needs no time to develop such dreams. He comes fully equipped with mythical delusions."

They both laughed at Veshioli's pronouncement as Veronica smiled politely.

"The difficulty is not in the actual arrest but rather in the perception of this event," said Caiaphas, rising to his feet.

"I don't quite follow," Veshioli inquired cautiously.

"It is the whole manna syndrome. Our people are fine at beginning an idea, but soon lose their excitement when confronted by any form of change or sacrifice required to accomplish the end to their means."

"I think I see your point. For instance, they grumbled against Moses for the lack of bread in the wilderness."

"Exactly. There is no victory in the faithful execution of a flawed plan. Success is how we evolve with the subtle changes that would attempt to taint the purity of our cause." Caiaphas, in full philosophical spin, paused, glancing at their confused faces. "It is not meant to be simple. If you desire simplicity, join the merry ignorant of the Nazarene brothel. Knowledge should never be accessible. Then, there would be a danger the common laborer would attach himself to a workable idea and propel his mediocrity to greatness."

"And what is wrong with bringing truth to the minds of the common man?" Veronica interrupted.

"Then, where are the exceptional men who can rise to the occasion to unravel the deeper questions of life? Are carpenters to be our guides? Are we to be sufficiently motivated by the intellect of the shepherd? God made wood and sheep for such men--their distractions. This is my real difficulty with this Kingdom Movement. The Nazarene removes the mystery of Godliness and touts tales of 'God the farmer who goes forth to sow seed'. We shall be damned by such inanity." Caiaphas paused, satisfied he had foiled the objection. "The key to our success is to neutralize the Galilean. Then we will find the time to groom, if necessary, a new Barabbas to fill the chair of our independent realm."

"I don't understand. Are you talking about Jesus?" demanded a bewildered Veronica.

"Don't use that name!" Caiaphas sneered. "When you place a name upon an enemy then the planning becomes much too personal. It is not a man but a heresy we decry. This whole trouble-making Galilean faction standing in the way of the institution of a holy compromise with our Roman captors."

"As you said in council," piped Veshioli, "it is better one man perish than a whole nation be destroyed."

Veronica retaliated. "And this is not personal? One man perishing?"

"His ideals, my dear," cushioned Caiaphas. "They are harmful to the structure carefully woven by the Abraham lineage. This heritage grants our people a will and purpose to survive a myriad of conquerors. Without that girding of holy beams, the whole integrity of our cause collapses in the winds of change. The Galileans are a diversion that shake the firm foundation of the fathers."

Veronica was not comforted by the clarification. "Speeches--that is all you ever give--speeches about the holiness of your institution."

"It is not mine. The tablets, prophets and oral law have survived the test of time."

"What if we do need change?"

"Perhaps it would be good if I leave," said Veshioli, backing towards the door.

"Why?" shouted Caiaphas.

"I was just making my departure, to give you time to get your house in order."

"My house is in order. My wife loves to cloud the purity of sound judgment with her emotional rumblings. That is all. As I was saying," he continued, "Barabbas is a setback that gently prods us into the necessity of revising our plan."

"I understand," said Veshioli.

Caiaphas pursued his line of reason. "The heart is still in the body. Do you understand my meaning? We have not lost the blood of our mission. We must divert the Nazarene."

"Divert?" Veronica cross-examined.

Veshioli intercepted the challenge. "We feel the Nazarene is most effective in Nazareth and its surrounding hills, even those remote fishing villages. He seems to have drawn his personnel from the docks. If his efforts of charity and faith could converge in that area, then he would be of greater value to his own cause, and much more productive to the nation."

Veronica frowned, sensing the speech had been delivered many times, more than likely to console intimidated rabbis who had no stomach for treachery. "Are you jealous of this man?"

The two holy men burst into laughter. "Jealous? No!" Caiaphas pouted through his chuckle. "That is foolish, my dear, and a bit insulting. I am the chief priest of Jerusalem. I need no further boost to my ego. I have the attention and ear of all I wish to receive. My concern is the nation and maintaining the holy order for a beleaguered people. It is an awesome responsibility, to carry the Ark of God's purpose without disturbing the contents."

Caiaphas turned to Veshioli, who commenced his own denial. "I feel no jealousy for these misguided Galileans or their unpredictable leader. It is pity I invoke for my people. Why? Because they cannot storm the gates of Rome, they have selected to follow this latest rustling reed."

"Well said, rabbi. You are a teacher after all. A good turn of the phrase," said Caiaphas, patting Veshioli on the shoulder.

Veshioli beamed. "And I was inspired by your parable of the Ark."

"Well, you both can preen and flex all you want, but I think that if Jesus . . ."

"Not the name," warned Caiaphas with a little grin. "We don't want it to be personal."

" . . . If the Galileans," continued Veronica, taking a deep breath, "wanted to be in Galilee, they would be there."

"They always come to the feasts," said Veshioli, matter-of-factly.

Caiaphas nodded in agreement. "Good crowds. Shows respect to tradition. If I were leading their troop I would do the same."

"He has been here other times," Veronica inserted flatly.

"How would you know?" Suspicion entered the tone of the high priest.

Veronica paused. What should she say? It was forbidden to give any allegiance to this kingdom movement. Many of the leaders held sympathy to the cause, but remained silent under the threat of the edict.

The two men peered at her, deemed her silence a lacking of intelligent response, so continued on, whispering to each other.

Remaining silent--what Joseph and Nicodemus had done, hoping to buy time for the movement to gain credibility amongst the hierarchy. Veronica nibbled on her finger, considering the plight of a man. The time for compromise was being plotted away. Would there be a better hour to stir the ashes? She must speak or never know what power her words might have carried. "I know he has been here before," she said, interrupting their mumbling conversation, "because I have heard him speak."

"That is forbidden," pronounced Veshioli, eyes narrowing.

Caiaphas patted the shoulder of his alarmed comrade. "It is not forbidden to hear him. We do, or should I say, must. We have members who spy on him. We all stood back, helplessly, as he made his presumptuous entry into Jerusalem. It seemed the whole world went after him. Truthfully, he might have gained position if he had acted. Instead he slipped away into the wilderness where he finds his sanctum. No, there is nothing wrong with hearing."

"How about believing?" rejoined Veronica, trembling.

Caiaphas studied his mate, allowing himself a space for contemplation. She was the love of his life, though a bit tempestuous. Perhaps just a womanly time, he decided. "What is it you are trying to say, my dear?"

"I am saying you underestimate the power of a needed idea." She restrained any hint of whine from entering her inflection, knowing it would get her dismissed. Caiaphas despised emotional outbursts, unless they were his own.

"Needed? I see. And if that is so, what guidelines should we place on this movement, because God knows, they place none on themselves! We might grant them seat on the council. Perhaps allow them a rotation at the high priest's office?"

"Or entrance to the Holy of Holies?" chortled Veshioli.

"No need for sacrilege, my brother. The point has been made."

"I am not trying to do your job." Veronica was wary. She could never win an argument with her tenacious husband.

He sensed her dilemma; on the verge of overwhelming her once again. "Well that is good to know.

Veshioli, my wife does not desire to control my life and determine my destiny," shouted Caiaphas in mock appreciation.

Veronica bowed her head, the signal of her ongoing surrender to her nemesis and love.

"We have talked in generalities but now we need some specifics," said Veshioli, pushing past the discord before him.

"What is yet needed?"

"We have one of the inner circle of the Galileans who is willing to lead us to him."

"A traitor?" spewed Veronica, regaining her spunk.

"No, a trader," Caiaphas corrected with a smirk. "One of their flock who has enough sense to encourage his shepherd to lead them into greener pastures."

"Where they will hopefully lie down," added Veshioli, smirking.

"What else?" Caiaphas cocked his head and winked at his compatriot. "We have the ear of Pilate at the Atonement. We can secure Barabbas' release. It might do the Zealot good to humble himself awhile in prison."

"Prison? His humility will be accomplished on a cross and therefore have little benefit to either of us," Veshioli objected.

"Really? What are the charges against him?"

"Thievery, murder, and, I believe, sedition."

"Oh, I see. Yes, those will get you fitted to wood any time."

"What then?" Veshioli was attempting to discover the balance of servitude and independence known to please the priest.

"May I be granted exit, my Lord?" Veronica stood, chin raised.

"Now she desires to leave, Rabbi. So much like a woman. Ever present to offer the forbidden fruit and quickly absent to wipe the sweat from your brow as you labor · beneath the responsibility."

Veronica stood quietly as her husband assessed the sincerity of the request. "You may go, love. I will join you soon. My business will not be much longer. Please wait for me in our chambers. Some aloes would be stimulating."

She turned and hurriedly exited the scene of her latest humiliation.

Caiaphas, waiting for her departure, smiled at Veshioli. Assured she was gone, he observed, "My house is in order."

"So I see," Veshioli gushed in excessive admiration.

"Now let us put this affair in order. We must not allow a small distress to encompass the beauty of a relaxing night."

Veshioli nodded. He had great respect for the savvy of Caiaphas. He was hoping this meeting had created a mutual cohesion.

"Actually, I guess all affairs are in order." Caiaphas shrugged his shoulders. "I do not think we need to inform the others of the arrest of Barabbas. The minor details can be handled as they arise. We are on our way to a plausible resolution. Such is always the case," he said raising a cup of wine for scrutiny before consumption. "We are reasonable men. The unfolding of events will grant us the opportunity to use the abundance of wisdom God has provided to us."

"Forgive my insolence, if it appears so, my Lord, but are you suggesting we just leave all the specifics to time and chance?"

"Time and chance and, of course, the wisdom of Solomon."

"What will happen to Jesus?" posed Veshioli, forgetting the household rule.

"The Galilean," the priest answered, clearing his throat, "will be handled and judged by just men, in pious chambers, arriving at temporal decisions with eternal conclusions. I have faith in our system. We shall hear him and judge. God will tell us what to do next."

Some slurping of wine, a quick story, a hug, agreement, and Veshioli slipped into the night, as Caiaphas climbed the stairs to his lady in waiting.

****

I was being watched.

Paranoia? Possible. Still. . .

Trailed--a set of eyes fastened on my every move. When I turned to discover the source, my companions glanced away.

Perhaps. . .

Judas barSimon, a constant source of wonder to me since he cast his lot with our band. I was never quite sure where he fit into the configuration. At times I sensed he was growing weary of our expedition and would leave us. Then he would burst forth with spirited wisdom, ringing with clarity and brilliance.

Now, just watching--an eerie mingling of peer and leer,   scrutinizing for evidence to confirm a foregone assumption. This is the look in the eye of Kerioth.

I tried to include him but he distanced himself in a chosen alienation.   Conversation was stifled and limited to subjects avoiding closeness.

It had always been his way to come and go at will. He was the treasurer for the fellowship, primarily because he could calculate gain and loss without requiring the entire day--educated, and never bashful to remind us all.   Good with people.   When I sent the men out on ministry the townsmen would often comment to me what a fine representative Judas was for the Kingdom movement.   Then again, a brooder--entering a room, he would cause the gathered to feel ill at ease if they were enjoying themselves without his assent. Remaining, he intimidated the congregated, making them uncertain of what profile to take. Laugh and he might frown.   Be sober and he became offended. A friend who seems more amiable and valuable in our minds as he journeys.

Now, an egregious, maddening silence.

All of this on the heels of a rash of tribulation.   We were under constant attack by Pharisees, Sadducees and Herodians, factions who have never agreed on anything, but now have formed their first alliance--against the Kingdom Movement.

Holy things had been given to the dogs.   The religious leaders had stopped barking. There was the growl of conspiracy in the air.

A reckoning.   I knew I would need to time my remaining endeavors to coincide with their waning patience.

One of those was to eat the Passover supper with my friends, an opportunity to regain a freshness with Judas. My dreams were tormented by tragic images, often including him. On the mountain, Moses and Elijah warned of betrayal--haunting words. Still, my heart remained stronger than my apprehension, believing in the work the Father had given me, and cherishing the time with each living soul.

Embraces lengthen.

Tears, present.

My mind, dreams.

Spirit prepares. For what? Its hour--death. No fear, just a dread of leaving any morsel of humanity trapped in my decaying form.

Yes, to be emptied of all creativity, and then to die. This is the greatest gift to a human pilgrim--finishing the course.

Anyway, back to the feast, where arrangements were made, an upper room prepared, dinner served, precious feelings communed, while sitting and basking in the tenderness of a fulfilling moment.

I rose and disrobed--taking a towel and wrapping it around my waist--filled a basin with water, and knelt at the feet of John, the closest friend to me. He looked down at me, eyes bulging in disbelief.   Perhaps frantic questions filled his mind, but he sat quietly as I washed his feet. Likewise, Andrew and James each, though totally perplexed, permitted the execution of the duty, normally relegated to the lowliest body slave.

Thomas wept.

Bartholomew smiled. He was the one who often understood the parables before explanation.

Simon struggled with the intimacy, folding his arms across his chest, as people often do when guarding the entrance to their heart.

James and Jude joined hands and gazed toward the ceiling.

Phillip patted my head and said, "My Lord, I do love you."

Matthew sat in deep contemplation, collecting his thoughts with the same intensity as he had once garnered the Roman tax.

Then, there was Simon Peter.

"You will not wash my feet," insisted the man as he curled his toes and rammed his feet under his buttocks. (Another gentle interlude interrupted by the false bravado of the terror of Capernaum.)

"The purpose of washing feet is to get them clean," I noted simply.

"I know that," Peter replied, glaring at the other disciples.

"If you will not let me reach deep into your life I cannot be part of you."

He paused, looking around the assemblage for an ally. All understood his misgiving, but were unwilling to participate in his revolt.

"Then wash me all over," he demanded, flinging feet in all directions.

I bowed and began to scour each extended toe. "It is where we walk that dirties the sole. Clean up your steps and the whole man will follow," I said, busying myself at a particularly crusty spot of foot.

Peter relaxed and relented to the cleansing, placing his face in his hands, weeping softly.

The others joined him with bowed heads, each finding their sanctuary in thoughtfulness.

Peter completed, there was one friend to serve; one who had drawn away from the others, discovering a corner to himself; a berth granting no further withdrawal.

"What is it you want from me?" Judas implored, with mortified eyes.

I scooted to his side. "This world's leaders rule by ripping the will from the hearts of noble men and inserting control in its place. It will not be that way with us. You call me Master. And if I am your leader, and I wash your feet, you surely shall do it to each other and to all wounded children you shall encounter." I removed his sandal.

"I will need my sandals," he said, pulling away.

"We all will need our shoes when it is time to move. Until then, let your feet rest." I removed the other sandal.

"You once called me Kerioth. Why?"

I surveyed his reddened, twitching eyes. "We had met," I said, beginning to wash.

He pulled back as if the water had stung him. "I do not remember."

"I know you, my friend. I knew you when you did not wish to be known. I stood back and watched you escape the disaster that nearly entrapped your soul. I was there when you began the freshness of a new life."

"These are words of a soothsayer, not suited to a true prophet."

"Is that your problem? Are you trying to determine my title? Is Jesus of Nazareth a true prophet? How have you found me as a man?"

"True. Honest. Caring. These attributes can come through flesh without the aid of divine intervention."

He attempted to escape, but I held firmly to his foot. "How would you describe yourself?" I asked, pouring some cool water over the cracked and flaky skin of his toes.

"I am tired of analyzing myself. You don't leave me enough flesh and blood to live out a decent existence."

"What have you planned, Judas barSimon?"

"You are a prophet. Why do you ask me what you already know?"

I paused my labor, drying his feet, and looked into his eyes. "Is your plot so dastardly you must hate me to gain justification?"

"Why can't we find our place? Why must we wander? Why must we challenge the forces proven to have the power?"

He stood to leave. I held his arm. "Not all are clean. It isn't always as easy as water and a towel. Sometimes we have to come again and again to expose our stained soul to deeper healing and more tenacious cleansing."

"What do you want?" he cried, pulling away.

"What do you plan, Iscariot?"

Judas froze as if struck by lightening. "Who are you?"

"You are about to unleash the fury of your plan without knowing who I am. How wise is it to betray the unknown? Where is your reasonable nature? Do you side with the present power out of respect, or fear? Have you taken the time to assess the value of what you are about to lose?" In his face, I fired my questions in a flurry of billowing rage. This was my brother human whom I would not allow to be sacrificed to chance. There must be no accidental denouncement. He must decide to be villainous, and be willing to live or die with his choice.

"Would you explain what you want me to do. Please, no more stories."

I turned and shouted at the room. "You are clean now, my friends. But not all." Heads lifted, alarmed. "One of you," I continued, "will betray me this night. You may have other names for it. You may find a counsel who will condone your actions. But when it is accomplished, you will be left in the solitary role as the son of perdition."

The room erupted in gasps followed by garbled conversation. Two began arguing, pushing, shoving, and accusing each other of the deed.

"Is it me?" squalled John, with uncharacteristic volume.

"It will be the child so unconcerned with my words, he will dip his bread in this pot of gravy to avoid hearing any more."

At that precise moment, Judas, who had decided to ignore the admonishment, reached into the sop.

Our eyes met. No one had heard my pronouncement, all too busy determining their involvement.

"Do it quickly," I said to Iscariot.

He glanced around to see if he had been revealed, then stuffed the moistened bread into his mouth and scurried out the door.

Unfortunately, I had been correct.

I had been watched, judged without the benefit of defense.

Judas had made his decision.

The plan was in motion.

****

A haze shrouded the street in an eerie darkness as Judas stumbled into his normally familiar surroundings, suddenly baffled as to his whereabouts, peering in all directions. Which path was the right one? What was he going to do?

As he deliberated, a figure emerged from the thickened mist, draped in the garments of the tombs, moving to pass by him. "Judas, why are you afraid?" questioned the presence in a matronly tone. "I named you Judas in honor of the Maccabees." She swept by him, as if jettisoned by the wind.

"Mother is that you?" Judas turned and shuffled along to catch up with the linen-clad form.

From the rising fog another figure appeared, also adorned in burial trappings. "Why don't you save our people as the Maccabees did?" wavered his hollow voice as he scurried on his way.

"Father? Simon, is that you?" Judas stalled, aghast, shuddering, unsettled as to which image to pursue. "I cannot follow you both!" he screamed, flailing his arms with a childish impudence.

"Follow your destiny," replied the motherly spirit.

The night visitors faded into the covering.

Judas panted, heart racing, throat dry, refusing to swallow, and gazed into the expansive gloom. He chased after the woman, calling, "Mother, please! I don't know what to do!" He ran back the other way, whimpering, "Father! I am confused. Grant me reason. My God, explain this." Encompassed by the thickening murk. Was it a sign? Had God resurrected these specters to bring confirmation for Judas' work, or was it doom they foretold?

"Why do you perspire when the night air is frigid to the brow?" A third voice resonating from a particularly dark crevice in a mostly invisible wall.

"Who's there?"

"Be still. You're going to hurt yourself." A form eased from the shadows, in a cloak masking all features.

"Did you see the man and woman who just passed?"

"Many things will pass tonight," said the stranger, stepping back into deeper darkness.

"No more damn parables," moaned Judas as he beat his palms upon his head. "Speak plainly, man, or leave me!"

"Give me your heart and all will be obvious." A robed arm stretched from the bleak environs.

Hands joined.

"You seek Malchus and he waits for you," chimed the stranger.

Judas did not question the source of his knowledge or consider the motive of this undisclosed visitor. He breathed a sigh of defeat, no longer intent to maintain the integrity of his own will.

Heart, surrendered.

Mind, ceased conflict.

Spirit, abandoned, yielded to the counsel of the ghostly.

"I have heard the voice of a god. Who am I to question the prudence? I must see Malchus." He ran off, having regained his purpose, recalling his destination.

Clear, at last.

"Stay here, watch, and please pray." I was ill at ease, my peace invaded. I had been in this garden so many times, yet tonight, the backdrop of the hanging fog and gnarled trees fostered a sinister atmosphere.

Peter, James and John settled in next to a tree, tired--worse, weary. The wine, hour, and the melancholy resulting from my revelations had emptied them of strength, struggling to remain alert. Fresh in their minds was my announcement concerning a traitor in our midst.

"I will be back. I just need some time." I finished my sentence and hurried away, finding little comfort amongst usually supportive brethren.

This Mount of Olives had been our refuge from the insanity of propriety, policy, and religiosity in the city below. Tonight, it held little safety. We were not all here. One of our number roamed the streets below, alone, bewildered--worse, embroiled in a conflict; a mortal pressed between the mill wheel of immortal ragings. What was his plan? Was he counted amongst the plotters of the Jerusalem hierarchy? Judas knew our location. How would he use this knowledge?

No, we were not safe tonight.

I was alone, too, my freedom in jeopardy, my future being determined by men who held me no goodwill.

Liberty, the life of my love; nothing greater than to live and be led by spirit.

I walked a few feet, found a small clearing, and fell on the spot as if dead. "Dear Father, where have you brought me? Is this the sign? Has it all deteriorated to this one useless act of tyranny? Can't you influence the heart of one stray lamb? He has known so much of the power of your love."

I stopped. Was I praying, or merely venting the frustration and doubt in my soul? I hated prayers of pretense, lengthy speeches delivered to fearfully exorcise inner need. "Let this cup pass from me." This was honest-- words I did believe, wanting the bitter dregs to be poured out. I had no stomach to down all of this sour uselessness. I prayed my heart to let God reveal my soul. Circumstance must never dictate conviction; no time to conjure superstitious reverence in an attempt to gain greater hearing. What madness religion! Is the Father aging and deaf? Can't He distinguish my whisper from a thousand breaths?

I considered Galilee; faces of my family passed through my thoughts, to be replaced by a head-throbbing nothingness, focus gone. Judas. I tried to pray for him, but visions of Beskel's head rolling in the fire at the Camp of Deliverance flashed across my mind, sweat bursting on my brow as my heart palpitated.

"Father, let this cup pass from me." Hard to breathe, needing to settle down, fear creeping through my body, generating little prickly pins against my skin, I sat, as my stomach cramped and my bowels tingled, threatening to release.

A new realm of anxiety--frightened, feeling guilty for the weakness. Did the Father demand both devotion and courage? Too much.

Why hadn't I prepared more? I dreamed the horrors. Now it was here--so unexpected, so lacking in promise.

"Father, I do not know what you want of me."

I stopped the prayer--the same words Judas had spoken to me. "Why do I sit here and question what is deemed necessary by Him in whom I have placed my trust?" I prayed to the rocks.

"Because you do not believe it to be necessary." The voice came from behind me. I didn't need to look, remembering the depth, lilt, and condescending inflection-- Mekel. "You know me so well that you do not turn to see?"

"Maybe I feel my faculties are suspect. I do not wish to turn and discover nothing."

"Then how do you know I won't harm you? Perhaps I clutch a sword which I will plunge into your scrawny hide."

"Not you, Mekel. You enjoy watching the atrocities performed by others, but have no drive for enacting your own violent conclusions." I turned, slowly.

"I told you we would meet again."

"So a season has passed."

"I've been busy."

"I imagine so."

"And so have you."

"I'm sure you know."

"Be quite sure. I have watched each miracle and heard each sermon. Very impressive for three years."

"I know you didn't come here to compliment me or commend my efforts."

"Of that you can be sure."

"You are an interrupter of prayer by nature, aren't you?"

"Prayer does not concern me--usually the flustered voicings of a determined loser, or the base greed of fearful humans filtered through a thin membrane of piety."

"Perhaps. But not tonight." I turned away and resumed my supplication. "Father, let this cup pass from me. Not my will but Yours be done."

"Now there is the grist from the grind, am I right? You are just not sure. You find yourself at the mercy of lethargic and ignorant men. Could the clumsy plotting of some archaic council be God's will? What an unfortunate plight. Do you enjoy being thwarted by men with less than half your intellect? Would that sum up your situation?"

"I have my questions. I have never been rebuked for asking. You are the one who feels the heavens disdain human inquiry."

I knelt for prayer, Mekel joining me on his knees.

"Why does God wish His servants to always appear so short?" he chortled. "Does it make Him feel taller when we are crunched to our knees?"

"And when have you ever knelt?"

"Now. It feels very strange."

"You should get used to it."

"I will leave that position for the untalented and defeated."

Suddenly there was a cool breeze sweeping across the garden and a gentle wash of rain settled above me, dropping a soothing drizzle on my fevered brow--the special anointing shower I had experienced before in the desert and at the Jordan. I giggled and rolled on the ground like a man deranged.

"You view this as an outpouring for you alone?" chided Mekel in disgust.

"I see no moisture on you."

"Do you really think this kind of childish trust will gain credence amongst the cynical masses?"

"I don't know."

"An admission of ignorance by a messenger of the divine. How refreshing."

"What do you mean?"

"You know how to escape this garden. You have done it countless times. You know the curves and twists not privy to the arresting party."

"Arresting party?"

"I saw Judas," he practically sang.

"As did I."

"But I saw him last."

"So there is a plan."

"They never have a plan, not even when they are organized. Whatever they accomplish for my father is generally a result of their abstract stupidity or the violence of their lusts."

"Not always."

"Jesus, you are an idealist."

"No, Mekel. An idealist is just a pessimist lacking travel."

Mekel leaned back and laughed.

I prayed through the dark son's roarings. "Father, shall I not drink this cup you have given me? It is for this reason I apparently have come. If there is need of my life then take me. I have given heart and soul and mind. All that remains is my strength."

"So useless." Mekel shook his head as he dabbed at his brow with a piece of cloak.

"Value can rarely be assessed when pressing toward the prize."

"You will not like the outcome."

"I will live it! I don't need to hear it from you."

"No, I mean the way your little movement ends up. I could show you a vision of the future. . ."

"I don't need to see the future. The present is intimidating enough."

"Your followers will be the terror of the earth. The acts of insane violence they will perpetrate in your name would stagger even your well-developed consciousness."

"Forget the flattery, and forego the lesson."

"They will divide, manipulate, control, and devour the finance of innocent poverty-stricken souls. They will preach for profit and deny pulpit to the true prophets who manifest inspiration."

I sat quietly. My thoughts turned to Joanna, then Madez, Mary, Martha, Lazarus. . .

"So you feel the acquisition of a handful of souls to the elimination of thousands is a worthy exchange?" railed Mekel, probing to determine the source of my silence.

"Nevertheless, Father," I prayed, ignoring him, "As I said, not my will, yours be done."

The words hung in the air, finally spoken, the choice accomplished.

I opened my eyes. Mekel was gone. He had simply grown weary in ill-doing, losing faith in my potential. Until evil ceases to find us penetrable, we will never ease into our destined quality.

I sat, no more words to pray. Then the sound of rustling in the grounds nearby--the urge to run. I was ready to escape and make my own way. Instead, I stood and slowly walked down to where my three companions lay asleep. "Get up, my brothers. We are about to find out how great is our God."

A band of about fifty men with torches, swords shimmering, voices deliberate and angry, headed by a priestly gentleman in overstated robe, in a stumbling, awkward march, came upon us, led by a reluctant vessel of entrapment--Judas. Or was it Kerioth? Perhaps, Iscariot? I did not know the man.

He came forward and tried to kiss my cheek. "Wait a minute. Are you going to betray me with the tenderness of a kiss? I don't think so." I pushed him away, and when I did ten men fell on me with ropes and chains. Peter leaped to his feet and drew a sword. In his sleepy daze, he swung at the head of the distinguished leader. The sword fell askew of a lethal blow, but severed his whole ear and right cheek, the blood splattering onto Judas. The band of ruffians stepped back in terror.

"Malchus, my God, your face!" screamed a soldier.

While the men were reeling from the blow, I said to Peter, "Put up your sword and get out of here. I will drink the cup."

My three friends ran off in different directions like schoolboys caught stealing honey from the hive. One soldier grabbed John, but the spry Galilean made his escape by shedding his clothes in the grasp of the surprised soldier.

I stepped forward to intercept further attempts to detain the fleeing fishermen. Malchus had slumped to his knees, his very life's blood pouring out onto the sandals of the petrified disciple of betrayal.

"See, Judas. I told you that where you walk can dirty the cleanest of feet," I said, staring at his bloodied ankles. Judas looked down, turned in horror and ran into the night. Two soldiers chased after him, assuming he was another one of the escaping criminals.

I leaned down toward Malchus. "Not what you had planned, is it, son?" I said tenderly.

He sucked in, swallowing a lump of painful grief.

"Forget everything that has happened before and everything that will happen later. Just remember what the Father is about to do for you now." I reached out, gathering the soft, dangling tissue and ear of the damaged man. I placed it back to its former position. "Father, not this way. Let the memories of pain be mine." I closed my eyes and felt the constriction of his face in my hand. I don't know how to describe it, but I was part of the healing. I could feel the molding and re-creation of this wounded being--like touching Adam as he formed from the dust.

The men were silent, then gasps of astonishment leaked from those nearest to the wounded plotter. I opened my eyes and there before me stood the young man. He was really not much older than a boy. Tears were in his eyes.

"I am sorry," he simpered.

"So am I," I replied, as three of the men drug me along by a rope they had fastened to my waist. Once again a prisoner, rage surging through me as I was handled and mauled like a common thief.

"Where are we taking him?" asked one of the handlers..

"I don't know."

(Captured by "the brethren incompetent".)

"I think he is to go to the chief priest."

"Lord Caiaphas," agreed another.

"No, the other one!" shouted someone from the front of the entourage.

"There are not two chief priests!" complained a soldier next to me.

"Well, he acts like he's one," said the voice of the first handler.

"Then we will take him to Master Annas."

As prophesied and foretold, I would indeed meet Annas again.

****

It was always difficult to secure lodging during the feast days, especially trying to locate quarters for a party of thirteen. Yet she was no stranger to acquiring unusual accommodations at difficult seasons of time.

She had made the journey from Nazareth with all sons, wives, and children in tow, except for Jude's wife, who fell ill at the last minute and remained at home in the care of friends. Even little Joseph came along; the trip too important for the young boy to miss. After all, it was Passover and the Feast of Atonement; the heart and soul of their belief, and, he might get to see his big brother, Jesus.

She might see him, too.

The separation from Jesus had been bittersweet. First, sweet in the sense she had used the time to marry off all the older sons and daughters. She had counseled and cajoled during nights filled with family squabbles when she would deliver prudent wisdom, even at times threatening the young newlyweds into righteous reconciliation. The family was her life. She had retired her youthful aspirations to chase the dreams of her children.

She had recently attended the funeral of her old rival, Chiolita, weeping for a woman she would have been willing to learn to love.

She nursed the ailing Hagabus, afflicted with memory lapses, who had voluntarily surrendered his synagogue duties after once offering a psalm of thanksgiving to Baal.

She never married again, feeling if there was to be a union of lovers in the life to come she would want the connection to be with her beloved Joseph.

But without a doubt, the bitter part had been her alienation from her first-born, Jesus. There was no replacement for him. No one spouted off like him. No one gave the same message of tenderness in a hug. No one else could gauge her moods like he did. They shared memories the other children knew only as tales.

Time to reunite, not that there had ever been a severing of the love and affection, which flourished, though their wills engaged in mortal combat.

She loved him. He desired her respect.

He was her firstborn. She was his connection to family.

She had many children, but only one Jesus.

She could never have imagined the twists and turns her life had taken, her last child born nearly thirty years after the stable in Bethlehem. Little Joseph--born on the celebration of her forty-third year.

Now nearing fifty, it was time to negate trivial feuds and give place to the overwhelming bulk of loving sentiment--restore her firstborn to his rightful place of prominence.

She sat back in the chair and breathed deeply, content, wanting only one thing. She yearned to regain a place in the life of her itinerant oldest.

Word of his deeds had trickled into the Nazareth hub with greater and greater frequency. There was even a small group of "Kingdomers" that met to discuss his teachings. She never missed, actually beginning to understand and comprehend his outreach.

Many refused to listen to the message, calling it the Carpenter's Curse. Storm clouds usually produced rain. She just wanted him to know she believed.

Mary laid her head back and dozed off into a sweet sleep, rarely able to achieve such total relaxation.

All at once the door of the inn was thrust open and slammed against the wall. She was awakened, jolted to a rigid attention. A young girl with a bleached countenance stood panting, gazing about the tiny room, terrified. The little lady had evidently run some distance.

A misty fog trailed behind her in puffs which resembled the smoke of a dying fire. "They have him," announced the wide-eyed girl without preamble. "They have the Nazarene. Jesus of Nazareth is prisoner to Lord Caiaphas." Her voice rose, screeching and cracking.

She turned and ran back into the night, apparently satisfied her mission had been completed.

Mary looked about the dimly lit room. No one else had stirred through the activity, continuing their slumber. She sat quietly, considering the message, eyes filling with tears.

She pondered. 'Jesus of Nazareth is a prisoner of Lord Caiaphas.' She had heard this before, except this time, she was awake.

"Well, young man, it seems you are in quite a spot of trouble," said Annas, groggily attempting to muster some righteous bearing.

There was nothing about him remotely resembling the authoritative holy warrior I had encountered some twenty years before. His face was a fuzzy, graying visage of eroding human flesh deposited into a delta of a permanent frown.

"I will need my seeing stone, the one the Procurator gave me, so that I can review the documents and charges against this lad." Annas fumbled for the tools of his trade.

"There are no formal documents, Master Annas. At least, not as yet," said a Roman soldier.

"Your name, Commander?"

"I am a centurion, Master, overseer to the arrest. My name is Silvedius."

"No charges . . . lacks propriety."

"Your son-in-law, Lord Caiaphas, is still amassing the evidence and gathering all the witnesses."

"In the middle of the night? A bit irregular."

"Lord Caiaphas determined it a national emergency."

"Oh, well, then we must spruce up a bit and be about the business. Now, what is required of me?"

A servant ran up and handed the aged priest an object. "Here you are, Master Annas, your seeing stone."

Annas held the clear stone up to one of his bulbous, whitened eyes. "They say you can see better with this, but I have never had any fortune. You try it, Silvedius, is that your name?"

Silvedius obediently glanced through the rather large circular stone. "It makes the objects a trifle larger, master."

"Maybe to your young eyes. I can barely see the stone."

Silvedius whispered something in the fussing holy man's ear. Annas looked up and tried to focus on me.

"Step closer, boy," he commanded.

Before I could respond I was shoved from the rear. I wanted to protest, but chose to   remain calm.   Words would be the gold of this hour. I had better save mine for the right rate of exchange.

"Are you Jewish?" examined Annas, squinting at my face. "Well, tell me about your crimes. What is the charge again?"

Silvedius hesitated, hoping Annas would forget the question.

Annas snorted, squinted and turned back to me. "Tell me about yourself, young man."

I was back in school with Hagabus quizzing me on a point of study.

"His name is Jesus of Nazareth and he claims to be the King of the Jews," said one of the nearby participants, dressed in the phylacteries of the contemporary religious.

"Oh, that is not good. King of the Jews, eh? That won't do. Where did you arrive at this doctrine, my lad?"

"I have been in your temples where everyone seems to conglomerate. They have all heard me speak. They know my words. I am surprised you are unaware of the teaching," I said slowly, pacing the tension in my voice.

Silvedius reached across and slapped me in the face. "Watch the way you answer the high priest. Use respect."

Angry reactions flooded my mind. The insanity was wearing me down. Still, I chose to dam my mouth instead of being prematurely damned by it.

"You look familiar to me." Annas peered into my face.

I wondered if his aging mind might retrieve the memory of a young boy's confrontation so many years ago.

"I have a niece in Herodium that bears some of your features," he mused absentmindedly.

"Jesus is a man, Master," said a servant sitting nearby.

"I know that. Women often resemble men, at least in my family." He shifted his gaze away from my face. "I wonder what else Caiaphas wants me to do?"

A silence fell upon the room, eternity crawling on its knees to an unknown destination.

"I think we need a prayer," Annas finally announced, rising to his feet.

Everyone bowed their heads, gauging the situation from half-open eyelids.

The old priest prayed, more a discourse on tribes of Israel, prophets and the traditional interpretation of Mosaic law.

I redeemed the time to pray my own prayer.

The visit to the house of Annas had been a jaunt through the courtyard of the absurd.

Caiaphas's chambers would be a different story.

****

"I hear you met my father-in-law. Is he well?" posed Caiaphas as he pranced about his raised platform.

I did not answer, reserving my words.

"I have called for a gathering of the council to hear and judge your movement."

The meeting was rather spontaneous--many members were arriving, dressing as they rushed along. Other disoriented folk, potential witnesses I assumed, were being herded into the enclosure on my right.

"Do you have any opening comments, Nazarene?" Caiaphas asked, trying to simulate decorum amongst the upheaval.

"Point, Lord Caiaphas," called a distinguished man entering the room.

"Yes, Joseph of Arimethea." Caiaphas responded cautiously.

"Why were we not informed of this meeting?"

"You're here, are you not? I don't understand your objection."

"We heard of the meeting from Joanna, a follower of the Nazarene,"

(So, Joanna had been her usual busy self.)

"An oversight, my friend."

"Like this meeting itself," protested another arriving fellow.

I recognized this one--Nicodemus.

"Your problem?" queried Caiaphas, rubbing his forehead.

"To start with," said Nicodemus, "we do not join in debate or review evidence at night."

"It is a national emergency."

"What emergency?" challenged Joseph.

"Sit and see. All will be made evident. Intentions will become crystalline. I would never defy our tradition if it were not of gravest concern to the welfare of our people."

A brief pause followed as Joseph and Nicodemus consorted.

"We will hear," announced Joseph.

"As I stated in one of our earlier meetings, I believe we should hear this man's thoughts," said Nicodemus as both men moved to their seats.

"First witness," bellowed Caiaphas.

One after another they came before the council. One claimed this and the other one contradicted. The discrepancies became so outlandish the listening dignitaries chuckled. For instance: one man insisted I had ruined his life by healing him, totally eliminating his livelihood of begging. Caiaphas grimaced. Then, came a witness testifying I had said I could tear down the temple and restore it in three days. This time I rolled my eyes. Never try to be be clever in the earshot of a dull generation of literalists.

The San Hedrin was stunned by this witness, a serious charge and a threat to the sanctity of the religion and security of the nation. Still, they needed a second witness to confirm the same. Thus reads their law.

A second man took the stand and said, "I agree. But, I think he said three years instead of three days."

A unison of groans rose from the congregated.

Caiaphas leaped from his chair. "What do you have to say to these witnesses, Galilean?"

"Point," Nicodemus objected.

"Not now, Master. You said you wanted to hear him. Well, let's hear him."

"He is under no obligation to testify against himself if no witnesses have been brought," inserted Joseph.

"Witnesses were brought," Caiaphas insisted.

"These witnesses were his greatest defense," piped a small voice from the rear.

Everyone laughed. Everyone but Caiaphas. He stared at me and I at him. I was looking for any resemblance of the kind boy who had befriended me in the temple. The lad was gone, apparently sacrificed to achieve authority and power over weaker men's wills.

"Fine," stated Caiaphas, turning towards the amused council. "But for my information, Nazarene, are you truly the son of the living God?"

A sweeping murmur hissed its way through the conclave.

"He doesn't need to answer."

"My understanding," Caiaphas rejoined, "was that this man was proud of his alleged equality with God. If he chooses silence, he is just confirming his status; another Galilean braggart who claims great power under the influence of wine and the protection of the rolling hills. But when confronted by men of merit, the claims are renounced by scared little boys in weepy puddles of repentance."

Caiaphas was not of interest to me. I was trying to discover the Father's will. Was I supposed to be released on lack of evidence? Or was this the hour the Father had chosen to reveal the power of his truth?

I glanced at Nicodemus, who frowned and shook his head. Joseph did the same.

The council fell still.

"You needn't answer," Joseph counseled.

Caiaphas lifted a hand, demanding silence, then walked around me like a lion stalking its prey. He had no power over me, but there was no revelation for the others if I denied the relationship I had with the Father.

"Yes, I am the Son." As I confessed, my voice gained a rejoicing cheer. "And, it will be my great joy to return to this council someday with my Father in the clouds of glory."

A mingling of despaired gasps, and mumbling cries of anguished surprise rang out in the hall. Joseph slumped back in his seat, and Nicodemus bowed his head.

Caiaphas grabbed his robe, stomped about, ripping at his garment, expressing his horror over such blasphemy.

His cheap theatrics could not rob the glory of the moment. My life was back in the Father's hands, where I always found my solace.

"What more do you need to hear?" pleaded Caiaphas to the astounded fraternity. "He claims to be God; to even be in the clouds with God." Caiaphas fainted, as a servant ran to catch him before he tumbled to earth. Breathless, he pleaded from his prone position. "What do you say to this?"

"He is guilty of death," said a black-bearded member in the front.

The verdicts were offered.

Guilty.

Nicodemus insisted the confession was inadmissible due to the nature of its acquisition. The council would not listen.

"We will take him to Pilate," concluded Caiaphas wearily, with a hint of a smile.

****

"What is going on?"

Enraged, Judas stormed into the room, escorted by a very nervous servant.

"Judas, just the man I wanted to see," said Malchus, trailing on his heels.

Judas lurched back, astonished. "Impossible. I have your blood on my sandals."

"My apologies for startling you. This should help. The council has voted to give you thirty pieces of silver for your intervention."

"Intervention? Thirty pieces of silver?"

"I know it is not much, but it is what we agreed upon."

"I agreed to nothing."

"Oh, I do hope you will not be greedy about this."

"You were dead."

"I was injured."

"I saw you. Half your head was gone."

"Half? You do exaggerate."

"How can you do this when we made plans?"

"Plans change. Grow up, Kerioth. Barabbas was arrested."

"Did you know this in the garden?"

"No, they didn't tell me. But it wouldn't have changed our part. That is all we're responsible for--our part."

"They want to kill him. You said he would be sent to Galilee, you bastard." Judas grabbed the smaller man and shook him.

"They don't ask me," squealed Malchus, struggling to free himself. "It was not the first time they have plotted his death. I felt we could save him. They were determined to come out of this in control. Judas, don't play ignorant. You know these men. They are beaten down so much by the Romans they need some holy ground to call their own."

"They are going to kill him."

"Pilate will stop them. He views them as puffed up wineskins filled with alter smoke."

"And if he doesn't?"

"What can we do?"

"How can you stand by and watch them do this after his mercy to you in the garden? He did heal you, didn't he?"

"Of course. What did you think, it was some efficient Greek physician? Look, there is no sign! Clean, beautiful skin," Malchus panted, pounding his face.

"How can you do this to him?" Judas fell to his knees.

"How can you betray him? He would be safely on his way back to Galilee if you had been exposed and destroyed," he retorted, slapping Judas in the head.

"I was exposed. He knew. He warned me. He let me go."

Malchus stepped back from his attack, shaking. "My God, who is this man?"

"I should have known who he was." Judas headed toward the door, pausing to grab the money.

"Where are you going?"

"I am going to trade back my money for my Lord."

Malchus considered stopping him. He knew he should do something. They had lied to him, withheld information. He should make a stand. It was time to speak out about the raging hypocrisies of this archaic system; time for him to join Judas in railing against this plan, unfolding to dubious, if not ominous, ends.

Now.

He must decide whether to intervene, or spend the rest of his life wondering what could have been done. Judas departed, the room still, he stared at the space once occupied by the traitor and thought about the ramifications of a careless, poorly-timed, misunderstood outburst. Cocking his head, taking a deep breath, he remembered Veshioli had asked him to arrange some provision and lodging for Barabbas' release.

Malchus squinted, softly touched his ear, and slipped away to perform his duties.

****

Chusa had spent months as a fugitive, a profile he had selected after his harried departure from Herod's palace, never quite sure if Blastus was searching for him, conducting all transactions with the outside world in disguise, as time slipped away and money became scarce.

Finance had always been a problem for the little accountant. When he had it, he fretted over its loss, or worse, that some opportunity might arise and he would be shekels short of his greatest investment and windfall.

On the other hand, when he lacked money, he was in a catatonic state of paranoid depression, causing him to resort to some form of thievery. Alas, he was an inept thief, the kind that always got caught, and usually by his own bumbling design.

But now he had devised a plan, a most ingenious one, by his own evaluation. He had requested a meeting with Rabbi Veshioli, the gentleman he was referred to when he mentioned he had information on "the Jesus fellow, from Galilee something or other".

"They said you wanted to see someone about the Galilean question," Veshioli said briskly as he entered the room.

"Yes . . . it's about this Jesus preacher," replied Chusa, already fidgeting with his robe. It always aggravated him when his propensity for nervous energy made him appear guilty, even on those rare occasions when he was not.

"We do not use that name in these holy chambers."

"You mean Jesus?"

Veshioli frowned, his dark eyebrows forming deep furrows in his dried and wrinkled, bald pate. "What is it you want?"

"I think I know what you want." Chusa smirked.

"Oh, I seriously doubt that."

"You want this Je...a . . . I mean Galilean," gloated Chusa, groping for a place to sit.

"No need to get relaxed. You won't be staying long."

"I can deliver him to you. You see, my wife is with him." Tension sweat burst on his brow, initiated by the prospect of the latest failure.

"Oh, I see," nodded Veshioli with a smile.

"No, you've got it wrong. Not with him, together, just with him, like listening."

"Well, thank you for your consideration," said Veshioli as he walked toward the door.

"Did I come too early?"

"I have been involved for hours."

"Don't you want him? I mean, I could trick my wife and probably get him there, too."

"Well, much as I admire a man who can deceive his spouse, I must decline."

"What did I do wrong?"

"You have done nothing because I need nothing from you."

"Why?"

"Because we already have him."

"No, you're joking."

"Nothing funny about it."

"Did he have any money when you took him? The reason I ask is, you see, my wife took some money that was mine and gave it as a donation to Jesus . . . oh . . . I'm sorry, the name again."

"I am assuming there must be an end to this. You do have a life outside of annoying me?" Veshioli advanced toward the door, fully intending to knock over the sweaty, conniving whelp.

"Yeah, I have a life! I just need my money. And my wife too, while you're at it!" he shouted, falling backwards over the unused chair.

"Well, if you want to see this Galilean, I would suggest you go over to where Herod is lodging in Jerusalem and find him there. Pilate has sent him to the Tetrarch to be tried."

"Herod?"

"You have heard of him, I presume?"

"Yes, and he of me. The man is a lunatic."

"That would be King Lunatic to you and me."

"Why Herod?"

"Pilate passed on the responsibility."

"Can you get my money for me?"

"My dear sir, you are persistent, I will give you that. Unfortunately, you are also ignorant. And when you mingle the two you hatch a creature that makes a buzzing housefly seem congenial."

"I don't understand. Are you looking for a recovery fee?"

"Listen, I could have you arrested. Yet that would involve my testimony at a trial where I would have to see you again. So, please reward my kindness by departing my chambers."

"This did not go well.   Please, I am learning. Where did I lose you?"

"Shortly after my arrival."

"That soon?"

"Maybe sooner."   With this, Veshioli forged the remaining steps to the door, determined to make good his retreat.

"Thanks for your time. If you see my wife, tell her I love her. Wait, just say I care. I don't want to get chained down to more financial pressure with another mouth to feed. By the way, if you get my money, there can be a reward." Chusa was wasting breath.   Veshioli was gone and the fugitive from Blastus and Herod's kitchen was left, alone.

****

Pontius had sent for his wife. She was more than a spouse--both a confidante and trusted pair of ears and eyes as he sorted through the many entanglements associated with his assignment.   Judea--a cursed realm, the Jews always complaining. They wished no graven images. They further rejected the value of the aqueducts he proposed to improve the Jerusalem water supply.

He offended their collective tender conscience with every move he viewed culturally or politically significant.

Claudia was his rock.   She had the timing and touch to soothe his tender, bruised ego.   Being Caesar's representative in an occupied land, he was constantly resented and perpetually unappreciated.   Claudia filled the vacuum. She was his breath of social grace during his many conflicts with this provincial religion; a belief structure which he doffed as a catacombs of reason descending to an oblivion of superstition.

Today, yet another excursion into the underworld. It fell the lot of Pontius to evaluate the latest King of the Jews, Jesus of Nazareth. Claudia had warned him to avoid pronouncing judgment on the case. She had been haunted by a recurring dream.   Claudia was not given to such revelations, so Pontius was mindful of her warning. If Claudia had a vision, then he knew he must listen to her counsel.

There had been a beneficial turn of events. The prisoner was Galilean, which placed him under Herod's jurisdiction.   The case was passed--dilemma resolved, a refreshing, unexpected reprieve from the normal gnashing of teeth required to negotiate with the locals.

But Herod had returned the defendant. His interest in the Nazarene had been purely personal, only agreeing to hear the accused in order to settle a private matter. For Herod believed this Nazarene to be the reincarnation of John the Baptist. When he was unable to establish the connection, he sent him back to Pontius. Caiaphas and the council were clamoring for an answer--additional pressure. All must be decided before their festival resumed. There was no time to consult with the legal experts from both cultures. They wanted a decision.

And so, Pontius Pilate sought Claudia. She would be his only counselor before he went out and faced the madness.

"He is back?" asked Claudia, as she scurried into the room, visibly unnerved.

"Herod loves his title but refuses to honor his responsibility."

"I can't blame him. Matters of spirit should be judged by gods."

"I am not a god . . ."

"Much as I love you, I never envisioned your homeland to be Mount Olympus." She giggled. Her laugh sounded so sweet, a welcome interlude. Pilate smiled, and considered continuing the playful banter, but given the circumstances, passed. "What was your dream?"

"He was my dream--he and he alone and the presence that is him."

Pontius was perplexed. "You are usually not one given to talk in this manner."

"I have never had this dream."

"What did you specifically see?"

"Romans. Always what you see and never what you feel. But in this dream it wasn't what I saw, it was what I sensed. I had a strange foreknowledge this man's whole person superseded our tiny reign. We were like ants regarding the camel--unable to see all the hair and humps, we conclude the creature is a hoof."

Pilate chuckled, sipping some wine. He loved Claudia's way of expounding, making the complex simple. "So, Ant Claudia, how shall we swallow this camel?"

"We shouldn't. Use your gift of political procrastination to dismiss the ignorant riffraff."

"They have mentioned the prisoner release."

"Release the Nazarene."

"There is talk of Barabbas."

"My God, no! The man is a pagan to any civilized people."

"He is a prize to our administration. As far as I can determine, he is the most popular and highly organized of the zealots."

"Most organized zealot? Husband, what could that mean? Does he know where to steal two swords?"

"Never underestimate the hate and passion of a proud and oppressed people."

Claudia submitted to her husband's apprehension. She personally found the Jews to be grossly overrated and determined it just a matter of time before Caesar wearied of their insidious dogma and sent legions to wipe them out.

"Caiaphas heads the council," he continued. "Annas was with them too."

"That is not good."

"The old man is wealthy and has loaned money to many local Roman citizens."

"Money tends to disembowel mercy."

Pilate nodded his agreement. "So, do we heed your vision or throw olive branches to the mob?"

"I know what I felt. This Nazarene is transcendent of the authority of this court."

"I have another problem. I can't get him to place a reasonable defense. If I had any justification from him, I could twist it to my advantage. He seems intelligent, capable of understanding his predicament. Yet like a bird soaring above our heads, mocking our inability to rise."

"He is silent?"

"No, he speaks. Statements are brief. He just refuses to answer my personal inquiries. He speaks of Truth. Truth--what is truth? To a Jew, it is just another excuse to maintain their arrogance."

"Is he guilty of any crime?"

"You mean besides lousy selection of enemies?"

"I would say he has done well in finding a friend."

"I don't know if he is my friend, but I can't find any fault in him."

"Then he should not be convicted."

"It isn't that easy. These religious relics are jealous of him. They want Barabbas."

"So? Do you care what they want?"

"You don't understand. The Nazarene could inherit Barabbas' sentence by the sheer brutish demand of a screaming mob."

"There is the whip," she suggested sadly.

"Yes, perhaps a scourging would satisfy their need to see the troublemaker humiliated."

"It could kill him."

"Or cripple him, and he has done nothing worthy of the beating."

"Then what will you do?" She tenderly stroked his hand and kissed each wrinkled and callused knuckle.

"I will scourge him if I feel it will save his life."

"Why didn't they just exile him?"

"The Jews think it rude to ignore their prophets. They must first massacre them so they can later revere their words and deeds."

"The gods be with you, my love," she said, as she rose and kissed his lips.

He softly stroked her cheek. "I fear one already is."

****

On the ninth lash of the whip I felt my heart stop, chest cramping, sending an angry heat of pain the length of my body. My face seemed cold and blanched and I wondered if I would be able to take my next breath.

Then the whip fell again. I was certain this would be my last conscious moment, but my heart leaped in my chest and continued its drudgery of beat.

Alive, tied to a column, helplessly awaiting the next furious blow, trying to steady myself to cushion the impact, but my arms would not squeeze the pillar. The thrust of each strike forced me to loosen my grip and I slumped to the ground, as the sadistic ritual proceeded.

On the twelfth blow I passed out, not to regain presence of mind until I heard the crowd scream a blood-curdling, "TWENTY-SEVEN". I had been granted merciful amnesty from the full raging awareness of fifteen stripes.

Someone came and grabbed my hair, yanking back my head, and peered into my face, I assume to confirm I was still with them. Confident of my participation, the flogging continued. I attempted to form my thoughts into some semblance of reason, not wishing to slip away again. This time I might not return. Focusing, trying to remember how I got to be the victim of this public thrashing.

Barabbas--released, the will of the crowd, my friends shouted down by the well-organized throng.

Pilate decided to beat me, to save my life.

Everyone so angry. Was appeasement possible? Could I suffer enough? Would the sight of my blood satisfy their insatiable appetite for derision?

More strokes--more stinging, ripping pain.

Difficult to remain rational, wanting to plead for mercy and cease the anguish. What did they want to hear?

The next blow rattled me to a new station, my skin lay open, exposing the full bone and marrow of my spine. My legs cramped in jerking, contorting fits of pain.

Preparing to die, I thought of loved ones, I gave my heart release from its labor.

Suddenly it stopped--the lashing ceased.

Thirty-one. Pilate grabbed the arm of the exhausted flailer.

"Why do you stop?" one cried.

"Take it to thirty-nine," pleaded another.

Pilate ignored the rabble.

I seized the moment to take inventory of my faculties. My mind was still sharp. Good. I wanted to be an intelligent presence at my own death.

Feeling was gone in my legs. As the soldier pulled me to my feet, they collapsed beneath me. I searched my mind for connection. I needed my legs, if I was to remain viable. Then a slight tingle, accompanied by a throbbing in my left foot--concentrated on that feeling. I needed that foot to stand. Lifted my head; it fell straight back.

A soldier rammed the handle of the whip into my groin and lifted me to my feet again. My body shuddered, regurgitating the contents of my belly, stumbling and hobbling to gain a stance--aah, bent and twisted, but erect.

Giggles and laughter came from the surrounding audience, finding me funny.

Unoffended, just determined to stand. Then feeling returned to my right leg. Simultaneously my left foot and thigh grew numb, useless.

Thank God for my right leg! I never regained use of the left; dying in pieces. My neck was unable to support my head. My eyes stinging from the sweat and blood. I blinked to gain vision. Not much to see. Encompassed by angry stares and arrogant sneers from condemning accusers, Nazareth all over again. Except this time there would be no help from Simon--no escape.

Pilate positioned his face in front of my dimming eyes. "You survived your scourging," he bellowed over the din. "That, Nazarene, places you in a distinguished minority."

"You should have finished him off," screamed a detractor.

"Eight more woulda done it," squawked an older woman.

Pilate disappeared from my sight. I struggled to turn and follow his movement. Quickly he returned and whispered in my ear, "Do you understand? I have power

over you. This is not Galilee. You are under my control."
He stepped back to look at me.

I contemplated his plight. He was probing to discover some human quality in the mangled features before him.

It was my moment to speak. "It is time," I huffed. I could still speak. God was merciful. "You must understand--you have no power unless my Father grants it." I finished, fainted, awaking to a chant.

"Crucify him. Crucify him!"

Crucifixion. My mind generated images of the heinous act, an execution conceived in the darkest caverns of hell.

Who did they want to crucify?

Him.

Him was . . . me.

I blinked my eyes, searching for Pilate, who stood by a basin of water washing his hands. He glanced at me, shook his head, turned and led his entourage away.

I was alone with my enemies.

Drug to a room to prepare me for death, they washed my wounds. Then, my personal cleanser threw a handful of salt onto my bloodied back.
"Keep you clean so you don't get disease." He laughed.

I passed out, awoke, standing on my crippled legs, wearing a purple robe, reed in my hand, and fresh blood trickling down my face, dribbling into my gaping mouth. They had placed a headdress of thorns on me, mashing it down into my skull, one of the thorns piercing my eye, filling the socket with blood.

My chest was constricted and heavy, like two men sitting on each side. I was not sure I could make it to the place to die. A rope around my neck, they pulled me forward--the humiliated oxen at the command of blinded masters. I stumbled, dragging my paralyzed leg.

They determined I could not carry my beam, so a stranger was compelled to shoulder my burden. I could not see him. I wanted to thank him. I don't know if I ever did.

Others accompanying me on the road to death, one, perhaps two, toting their own beams.

I felt an aching sense of failure. "Dear Father, am I so weak in this hour I cannot bear my own cross? Have I traveled so long, to be defeated now?"

No response.

What did I expect?

Shuffling, even without the weight of the cross, I fell again, yearning to die right there against the cold, cobble-stone path.

My body slid down the hill. I offered no resistance.

All at once, I felt the tender hands of a woman lifting my head, placing a soft cloth against my bleeding, bruised face.

And then she was gone.

I was hoisted back to my feet. The woman's act of mercy bolstered my depleted will.

I would make it the rest of the way. I ascended the hill.

At the top, my right leg began to throb and felt as though it had swollen to twice its normal size. I eased myself to one knee, expecting to be whipped for such a liberty. No one bothered me, busy nailing the first man to his cross. I heard his trebled scream. As horrific as it sounded, weary of the struggle, ready to find a place to die, I yearned for the wooden splinter of rest.

I was next. They drove the spike into my ankles: no feeling in the left, but the right leg erupted in a searing agony, causing my bowels to release and dribble down my leg to the ground beneath. The guard cursed me and complained to his cohort about the foul odor of the discharge.

I closed my eyes to escape the degradation.

Then I was nailed in the arms. My breathing, shallow.

"Don't die yet!" I exhorted myself. Only one blessing left to me--I would be able to decide when to give my spirit release.

I was lifted into the air and dropped into my place, every movement bringing a re-living of each injury.

"Where is Barabbas?" An anguished and wretched demand from my left. Was he talking to me?

"Free." An equally tortured reply from my right.

"Damn that bastard." A curse from the left cross.

"Kreble, it is over." Resigning words from the right.

"Jaakobah, the son of a bitch deserted us."

"He never said he wouldn't."

I squinted at the gathered souls, an assembly of bearded men of stony countenance, arms folded, appearing impatient for my death.

"Father, would you please forgive them, because they have no idea what they are doing." I tried to lift my head and it fell aimlessly to the side. My arms had settled into a permanent cramp, while my chest heaved a gasping sigh.   The blurring vision was worse.   I blinked and flickered.   Mary of Nazareth, once again attendant to my latest rejection.

"My God, My God, why have you left me here alone?" I pleaded through aching sobs.   Why did Mary have to witness the atrocity?   I pushed down on the nail, trying to rise for air.   Urine spurted from my body in reaction to the fresh burst of pain.   Dignity lost--humiliation punctuating the torment.

"You are a miracle man.   Save yourself and us," Kreble implored through his misery.

Yes, Kreble, you have spoken my heart.   I have considered the idea--a wondrous possibility.   To be rescued by angels, to be lifted from this travesty by the hand of God.   "I am thirsty."   They lifted a sponge to my lip; I tasted it--bitter.   Obviously, laced with drugs.   I turned away, needing to be alert, wanting total mastery of my final moments.

Mary sat quietly, looking up at me.   No pity--a silent watch, as always, vigilant to the hour.

John knelt beside her.

"Woman, behold your son," I said, motioning with my head toward the faithful young man.   "John, take her home.   Now she is your mother."   I barely managed to complete the words.   My head began to spin, heart racing.   I pushed down on the spike in my feet, so I could rise to regain breath.

"Master,"   wheezed the one called Jaakobah. "Would you please, remember me in your Kingdom.   I. . . . was . . . a fool.   Another chance. . . . I would do. . . ."

He was unable to finish.   I understood the price he was paying to convey his dying plea.

"This day, you shall be with me in Paradise."

My breathing was now mere puffs of air.   My heart was threatening to disintegrate in my chest.   Nearly over.   I thought about life.   How I loved being alive--so useless to die.   My heart was encompassed by a caustic vexation. Emotion and pain were colliding, to create a vicious offensive of destruction.

I lifted one last time.   "Father I do not understand, yet, into your hands I commit my spirit."

As the last word fell from my lips, my heart jolted and the impact of one hundred spears jabbed across every speckle of skin on my fractured frame.

It was finished.

"He is dead," announced a soldier.

Silvedius gathered the belongings of the executed souls. "If there is a god, we have just killed his son," he spoke to the darkening skies.

The crowd had lessened as the time crept by. The tiny remnant gawked, disappointed. There was not much more to see. One by one, they turned and walked away.

It was time for everyone to go home.

****

No peace of mind could be found in her comfortable home nestled in the hillside above Jerusalem. Caiaphas had been gone all night. His safety did not concern her, knowing he was capable of handling himself in every situation. Something was amiss, the man was hatching a new scheme. Her domesticated role was growing wearisome. He never shared and when he did, it was only brief, terse explanations of his life and work. To be more to him was her greatest desire. Even though he insisted he valued her counsel, and treasured the times of privacy and intimacy spent with her in their prosperous escape, her real function was wife and amusement. Her life revolved around the man, as his lover, his friend, his cook, and his escort--a memorized, unchanging list of duties; nothing separate from this man; no personal pursuit of her own.

Well, perhaps one.

There was her ongoing fascination with this Nazarene named Jesus. Caiaphas had no real interest in the man; his a mercenary intrigue as investigator and spy. He seemed satisfied with the spiritual in his life, feeling no need for further inspiration. God had been relegated a space with the same proficiency with which he retained the names of each member of the San Hedrin and the ages of their offspring. Caiaphas was content with a discussion of the divine, which brought heated moments of debate, followed by a cup of fine wine, a pat on the back, and a well-prepared dinner. He had found his purpose pursuing projects, endeavors which he meticulously molded into his image.

Not her. Exhausted with the procession and pretense of Mosaic law, dozing and dreaming in synagogue, awakening in startled quivers of self-condemnation and guilt--this was her profile in righteousness. Her whole being was tired of feeling guilty and thirsted for intervals of emotion, free of unquestioning subservience.

Then again, there were her personal rebellious times listening to Jesus. Hearing a man talk of the greatness of a most common God caused her to grin like a young girl at play, swinging her feet and giggling as he shared a funny story. Freedom. Yet, how silly--never having seen him. For it would not do for a lady to be found in attendance at a meeting of her husband's enemy. Hiding behind walls, her ears were commissioned to convey the message to her heart; totally entranced by the voice of another man.

His was a musical speech, laced with fluctuating tones and comical change. He would soften his voice almost to a whisper, the gentle comfort reaching deeply into her soul, the compassion stroking the aching need of a festering wound.

How bizarre to have fallen in love with the soothing speech of this special man. Could a wife be unfaithful by just desiring to hear the sweet sounds of hope from another man instead of the dirge of sameness from her selected? Her quest--to attach a face and body to this oratory of wondrous manliness.

Jesus spoke of God as "The Father". How different from her comprehension. The Most High had no tangible personage, just a mass accumulation of force, will, and ideas, culminating in a consuming fire of judgment. Chuckling, thinking of her husband's god of Sinai assuming the role of "father". Good to laugh. There was not enough simple laughter in the home of a holy man.

Jesus was her retreat. Or was he the embodiment of her desire? His words radiated the love every woman needed and so few found in hearth and home. He touched a place in her Caiaphas would not even believe existed, a soul connection.

Could this be what caused the delay? Was it something about Jesus? Were plans being made? Was her commission to remain insulated in this castle and await the return of the master benefactor?

Jesus' words--"Where you store the real valuables in your life, your heart and passion will find its sanctuary." He was right. Her tiny treasure chest was crammed with meaningless baubles. Could you become a new creature by repeating a daily schedule of mediocrity? It was time to move out and discover life beyond the walls.

Veronica donned a common garment and wrapped her head in a veil, not to avoid recognition, because Veronica seldom emerged from the temple of solitude. Veronica just did not want to be perceived as one of the elite ladies from the wealthy sections.

Veronica hurried toward Jerusalem--nearly midday and the streets were bulging with the mass of humanity gathered for the feast. Veronica sought Caiaphas at the temple. He was not there.

"Have you seen Lord Caiaphas?" Veronica asked a nearby scribe.

"Not here," he replied gruffly.

"I know that. Where is he?"

"Pontius Pilate, at the trial," he said as he scurried away.

Trial? Veronica raced from the outer court and headed into the streets. All the faces were stern, plodding to their destinations.

"Did you hear of a trial?" Veronica inquired of a passing gent. He shrugged his shoulders and begged alms. Apparently Veronica still carried the presence of a fortunate woman.

"Who is on trial?" Veronica demanded, stopping a Pharisee.

"The trial is over," he huffed as he moved on. Veronica chased after him, determined to know, weary of constant dismissals.   "Who is on trial?"   Veronica demanded, tugging on the holy man's robe.

"I told you, the trial is over. The Galileans have been defeated and their cursed leader is on his way to Golgotha to be licked by the dogs," he spat, with such rage and venom Veronica lurched back in fear.

He stomped away, and Veronica stood motionless. Could this be true? Caiaphas was dedicated, but no murderer.

Golgotha, a steep climb, just outside the gate. Veronica had never gone there. There were many stories of ghosts, skulls and birds circling above, large enough to carry a man away.

As she ran, she heard the rumble of a crowd. The voices were raging and angry. She pushed and shoved in desperation, trying to climb higher and nearer to the source of the clamor, heart beating faster and faster, tears falling. She shoved at a well-fattened man, who grabbed and squeezed the breasts protruding from the loosened frock. His comrades moved forward to join in the amusement. She pulled and twisted away, continuing to climb. The rumbling roar was closer, just ahead. She poured all remaining strength into a final burst. Ducking low, she wiggled and pushed through the legs of a milling crowd of onlookers. It was all so loud, impossible to distinguish words. She looked up--nothing. Then she looked down the way and saw a small procession of men with armor and swords, trudging the lowly condemned up the hill.

"Is Jesus of Nazareth one of them?" she asked a woman in the crowd.

The lady just stared, apparently from another country.

The parade of death climbed slowly, three men bearing their beams and one man, bloodied, dragging his leg and inching upward. Was Jesus among them? How would she know? She knew a voice, not a man.

"Daughters of Jerusalem, do not weep for me. Weep for yourselves and your children."

The voice--no doubt, flowing from the shell of a broken and beaten man, but . . . his voice.

She wept, turned away--too much. She forced herself to look again, ashamed of the timidity, and saw the crown of thorns on his head. She had heard Caiaphas speak of this little game the soldiers played with condemned men to further denigrate them before butchering them at Calvary.

The procession pushed on, so near, perhaps ten cubits.

Suddenly, he fell to the ground, his chin bouncing twice on the stony path, body sliding down the hill. He didn't have the strength to offer resistance, helpless as a lamb at the slaughter.

She screamed in horror, the din of the crowd so intense she could not hear the cry.

She removed the veil and ran into the street. One of the soldiers poked Jesus with a spear. She heard him gasp for air.

"My God, they're killing him!" She must do something. She crawled and slid across the street, scraping knees and arms on the sharpened edges of the stones, maneuvering closer. She could see his face--cheeks purple with bruises and his nose lay limp to the side. His eye was pierced and his chin covered with fresh blood. He tried to look, but fell back to the ground. She reached out, gently lifting his head, and placed the veil over his devastated features, pressing lightly to absorb the sweat and blood.

Then they hauled him to his feet. She pulled back and quickly crawled away, nearly trampled by the soldier's feet.

Floundering and groping, she regained balance.

The crowd moved along the path to the execution.

She heaved and panted, as the blood trickled down cuts, arms and legs.

Thoughts.

Caiaphas had shown a part of himself hidden during the love encounters on their mount of bliss.

This was murder and she was a witness.

How could she go on?

She would never forget this day. She would still love the man, but always question the ambiguous. She had lived with a stranger all these years. She would continue being his wife, but she would never forget.

She glanced down at the veil in her hands and carefully opened it with the delicacy of a scribe unrolling a most precious scroll.

She wept again, drawing in a tormented breath.

Veronica stared at the veil. There was the image of his battered features, indelibly imprinted on the head covering.

Once again, Jesus had left his impression on **her** life.

****

Pushing and cajoling his way into places before people who, short days before, had clamored to be granted the honor of his presence. This had become the lot of Judas bar Simon of Kerioth.

News from the secretive council meeting, difficult to acquire, had finally trickled out. Jesus was before Pilate, the plot unfolding with deadly accuracy.

The religious leaders had double-crossed Judas, the conclusion unmistakable.

He demanded an audience, waited--time passed-- growing impatient, seized an opportunity, forcing himself past the guards, and raced into the private chambers, frantic, carrying in his extended hand the small pouch of coins, as if trying to keep some hideous disease from infecting his body.

Stopped.

Caiaphas, in all his regal garb, stood before the agitated former disciple, eyes dark and puffy from lack of sleep.

"You damn bastard." Judas glared at the priest.

"Guards!" screamed Caiaphas.

"You were supposed to exile him to Galilee."

"Do you know who you're talking to, little man? I am your high priest. I enter the Holy of Holies for you and the entire nation to offer the sacrifice of atonement for the sins of the people. Do you think I have time to listen to your deranged moaning?"

"What about your sins, lord Caiaphas?"

"Covered by the same blood, but certainly not open to the scrutiny of a sniveling traitor."

Judas lunged at him and was intercepted by an arriving guard.

Caiaphas smiled at the constrained assailant. "What do you want, Judas? You have money. You have your place in our history. You have gained more notoriety in one night than your feeble talent could scrounge in a lifetime."

"I-I want," he stammered, "to trade my money for my master."

Caiaphas' eyes widened in disbelief. "You can't buy back the Nazarene. His execution is worth much more than thirty pieces of silver! His death will save Israel." Judas, distraught, one by one dropped the coins onto the ground.

"Watch him," Caiaphas instructed the guard.

"I have betrayed innocent blood," Judas garbled, expression etched with bewilderment.

"Keep the money, you sorry mongrel." Caiaphas motioned for the second guard to gather the coins.

"It was innocent blood! He is not guilty. He never gave grief to a soul."

The guard handed the collection of silver back to Judas, who seized the coins and flung them at the alarmed priest. "Innocent!" he shrieked.

"Throw him out," Caiaphas erupted.

The two guards grabbed Judas. He struggled free, spitting at Caiaphas. The rabbi drew back, but Judas continued to rain spittle.

"Stop him!" demanded Caiaphas, imperiously.

They chased the frothing traitor up and down the corridor, ducking the baptism of human fluid.

"I want my rabbi back!" Judas paused to shake his fist at the holy one. The guards grabbed him, propelling him to the door.

"You have not heard the last of this. There is more to come! You don't know Jesus!"

"Don't use the name!"

"Jesus, Jesus, Jesus, Jesus," sang Iscariot at the top of his lungs.

Dumped into the street, he immediately leaped to his feet and bit the arm of the closer sentinel.

"He's mad!" gasped the soldier The other man tried to pull Judas off, but the enraged Iscariot kicked him. Terrified, they freed themselves from the attacks and jumped back into the hallway, slamming the door behind them, as Judas threw himself against it.

"I am Judas barSimon," he yelled. "Innocent blood! I didn't know the plan! I want my master back!"

Standing, wailing, the sky began to darken, the wind whipping up little twirls of dust. The earth shook, casting the befuddled betrayer to the ground; carefully sitting up and rubbing his head, trying to regain his senses.

A shrouded form bustled by, the same he had seen the night before.

"Did I raise you to be a murderer?" A craggy, eerie, matronly voice with an ethereal echo.

A second figure passed the other way.

"Judas, study your law and prophets." A deep, accusing, manly rasp with a thunderous timbre.

"You were prophesied," the old woman called across the expanse.

"You are quite dead," rejoined the ghostly male, swallowed by the aggregating darkness.

A ferocious wind blew directly into Judas' face, making it difficult to breathe.

"I must leave you now." A new speaker, shrill tenor from the shadows.

Judas spun around, trying to peer into the dimness..

"I don't need you anymore," the strident new arriver taunted.

"Where are you? Do you have my master?"

"My boy, you are quite mad." A discordant laugh.

"What shall I do? What do you want from me? What does he want from me?" Tears fell from his eyes like great drops of blood. He shivered in the growing cold, mind loosening from the moorings of reason.

"You are due for a meeting. Beskel, Exodusat and many children await your arrival."

He stumbled down the street, the condemning presence following, joined by others, everywhere mumbles, audible yet incomprehensible; a chorus of male and female demons railing, accusatory, mocking, surrounding him, nonsense ringing in his ears.

"Didn't I teach you to sing when you were afraid?"

"Remember the law and the prophets!"

"I am finished with you now!"

Running, falling, rising, flailing, in the grips of hidden horror, the earth trembling as a roll of thunder growled from the sky.

"The Lord is my shepherd," Judas whispered, whirling, looking for the source of his torment. He continued his psalm. "I shall not want." Closing his eyes, trying to restore images of beauty to his fomenting mind.

"Run and you will be healthy!" admonished the motherly chastiser.

"Stop and you are dead!" A high-pitched ghastly utterance.

"My name is Judas, son of Simon. My Mama loves me much," he chanted.

"You remember the song?" solicited the lady heckler.

"I will always do what I can to gain her loving touch."

"He makes you lie down in green pastures!" chimed a phantom.

"He restoreth my soul!" Judas raced into the fading light, glancing ahead--the edge of a cliff.

The chorale of apparitions burst into a frightening peal of disheartening laughter.

"He leadeth you to the edge of hell for His name's sake," howled the prince of tormentors.

"Get your papa a length of cord."

"I don't have any, Papa. I'm sorry. Don't be angry!" Judas collapsed, sobbing, staring at the bark of a twisted tree.

"Never the right tool will make you a fool."

"I know, Mother." His voice was thin and hollow, eyes vacant, unable to focus.

"Why don't you use what you have?"

"My girdle? Of course."

The race was over, no more need to struggle.

"Continue your Psalm." The hoarse orator attempted to speak in more soothing tones.

"I have forgotten it." Judas recoiled like a prankster anticipating the rod.

"No, you haven't. You know everything!" A teasing tone from a treacherous trio of troublers.

"Surely . . . sure . . ." He threw his belt over the limb of the ancient tree.

"Why do you stop? Have you forgotten the law and the prophets?" chided Papa.

"They prophesied about you!" Mother giggled.

"Surely . . . surely . . ." Judas fumbled with a loose piece of leather on his girdle.

"Put it on! You always look so nice."

Judas slipped it over his head and let it dangle around his neck.

"Though you walk through the valley of the shadow of death," boomed a persecutor.

"Sh-h-hadow," hissed the woman.

"Death-th-th," resounded the man.

"Surely . . . surely. . . ." Repeated, panting, staring at the horizon; darkness had nearly covered the face of the deep.

"Your master is dead!" announced a quartet of specters.

"Surely . . . surely . . . I have betrayed innocent blood!" The son of perdition squalled in agony. "What do you want from me?"

Leaping into the air, leather girdle jerked, tightening around his throat, dangling from the limb-- suspended, twitching, as life slowly was snuffed from his body; sandals loosened, floating aimlessly to the ground. The tree limb cracked and snapped. Iscariot tumbled into the valley of death.

AS--

The last glimmer was swallowed by the permeating night.

The wind howled its refrain.

The earth ceased its tremors.

The lightening chased the thunder away.

The voices were silenced.

PARADISE

Fragmented--body splintered into thousands of tiny pieces as my mind continued a harried pace, refusing to comprehend life had ceased--thoughts still vying for purpose, a chance to be enacted, as memories dangled precariously, threatening to leap from my treasure; my soul journeyed on, trying to create distance from the devastation, once my life.

The events on a small hill of dying men seemed alien, a blurring nightmare of frantic activity.

Centurion Silvedius thrust the spear in my side. A hazy image of loved ones lowering my body from the cross, Mary assisting with grim proficiency.

Catapulted to Eternity, clinging tenaciously to my last fading memory of Earth. Like seeing through a pool of chilly, still water, I watched my beaten and bloodied body wrapped in linen. Tried to speak but my mouth wouldn't move, no longer lips teeming with the moisture of life. Mine were cracked and purple, lying motionless on the brutalized features of the corpse below.

My spirit tried to soothe the rebellious uprising in my warring members. Finally, the mind succumbed to the evidence at hand and the heart grew weary of futile emotional rejection. Blackness settled gently, an icy cloak over me--not cold--numbing pain and easing struggle. Voices faded and the light was extinguished like a candle blown by a brief gust of wind. I surrendered to the uncertainty of death.

Sleep. Yes, sleep such as I had never known, granted to me like alms to the beggar; water to the parched. I relented--a cushioned realm of total peace, not merely mortal relaxation, more the healing relief of a ravaging exhaustion.

Tension, ceased.

Striving--irrelevant.

Fear dispelled.

Everything previous, merely an illusion of tranquillity. Now suspended in a fresh awareness granting me personage but demanding no participation. Was I to be eternally coddled in this wispy, intoxicating presence of nothingness, dreaming without image, revelation without the turmoil of discovery or the pressure of decision.? Would I grow weary of such undemanding languishing? (Yet, truthfully, such concerns did not arise; not one moment was sullied by my fussy need to discern.)

My human journey. There, I had learned to imitate peacefulness, often deluded with a deceptive contentment--a satisfaction quickly dissipating in the wake of uninvited, unwanted, or undesirable circumstance. My placid smile could change to a grimace, further evidenced by the nervous, tightened jaw and the grinding of teeth.

Now, the charade was unmasked. Here, only the mastery of relinquishment.

I floated on in bliss, the permeating darkness replaced by a golden glow with a texture of sweet butter. Granted sight, a few creamy images. A field of vision not limited by the periphery of human eyes. Completed view-- sight without movement, attention, or focus. A gossamer shimmering in my spectrum, like sunlight dancing on the water, a picture mingled with sensation. Gleam became light, and the glistening light, image.

Then, a familiar face--my papa, Joseph, looking much the same as I remembered him (if you allow some measure for incandescence). He grabbed my arm, lifted me up. We embraced; not the touching of bodies, but rather, an engulfing and inclusion of one soul inside another.

"I had to plead a fine case to be the one to welcome you. Everyone wanted to be here." He was a sparkle personifying a man. "You can speak," he said, sensing my dilemma.

"Where am I?"

"Always the first question, and by the way, your voice will gain depth as you adjust to the surroundings."

It had seemed puny, so I attempted what I hoped was a smile. "What do I look like?"

"You are not yet distinguished, your essence trapped and warped between two worlds."

Joseph had acquired a brighter vocabulary to match his appearance. He proceeded. "Explanations are always tedious. You are no longer in need of verbal instruction. You are now in a place where you can experience and know. Let me guide you on to Paradise."

He lifted his arm and I moved to his side. "That's the way," he approved.

"I didn't feel myself rise!"

"Most refreshing, don't you think?"

I agreed, realizing how achy and cumbersome joints and bones could be.

"Look," he said.

I did. There before us was a construction of pure light, a wall of congealing glow, perhaps two hundred cubits tall and one thousand cubits wide (although I was sure my measurements would prove minuscule to the actual size.)

The barrier possessed life and will--glittering, emitting liquid firelight in all directions, as it glistened with silver and reddish hues; then, transported back to a whitened clarity of fiery crystal, as if all the silver, gold, emeralds, and precious jewels on earth were melted by the heat of the sun and swept across the sky in a wave of pulsating, churning fury.

"It is the cherubim. Beyond, lies Eden." Joseph pointed and I was given a brief, fleeting glance into the glory within. Then it was gone.

"Eden?" I whispered.

"Where man was conceived and where he returns to await the Promise."

"What shall I do?"

"There is more than doing. Do you remember how inadequate effort appeared to be on Earth? Here, you give, and your gift is energized instead of resisted. Pass on through," Joseph said as he walked toward the jostling, frothing mass.

"How?"

"And you will have a companion joining you on your quest." He pointed to my right side. Puzzled, I turned, anticipating another glimmering revelation.

Jaakobah, my dying companion.

Joseph explained. "It has never been tried before. But this is your destiny. You will lead a sea of souls through this wall of flames."

"Flames?"

"Yes, not in the sense of a heated inferno--a passage that more or less burns away the useless residue."

I mustered a frown.

"We were all flesh. Carnality tainted even our purest motives, clinging to the heart, soul, and mind of earthen pilgrims."

I motioned toward Jaakobah. "Is he dead?"

"Most assuredly," Joseph chuckled.

Jaakobah looked very dead. His body bore the scars of torture, and he lay in a limp, weakened, lump of defeat.

"He is dead, yet he lives. Remember? You invited him. The problem is, he didn't spend his earthly time in the pursuit of many worthwhile ventures. So death robbed him of his greatest asset--strength. The cherubim will not be gentle to the lad. He is only salvaged by his last action of faith in you, and by your word of grace. He will go through only because the Son gave him permission. I am afraid there will not be much left after this excursion. Hold him tightly. His only right of passage is his faith in you."

"Are you saying our time as humans was meaningless?"

"No, the life we led is our most valuable commodity. Still, we were often determined to destroy the competition, in the process damaging our own souls."

"So, there is a good self?"

"There is a self that includes others in the vision. You will see. You will understand it all very soon."

With this, Joseph leaped into the air and disappeared into the vibrating glow.

I grabbed Jaakobah's hand. He offered no resistance nor did he emote any semblance of assistance. I tightened my grip on the decimated brother. "Come on. I don't want to lose my guide."

I lifted my comrade and we were both absorbed into the molten melee. I don't know what I anticipated, but it was not anything like what I experienced. There was no heat at all, but rather a honey-like thickness tugging at my flesh, distorting my features and shape. I was being moved and jolted in some sort of purging and cleansing action, as if my enlarged form was being peeled away, unveiling a fresh, lean lightness.

I pushed on, holding tightly to Jaakobah's hand. He seemed to bog down, slipping into the quagmire, faltering, then sliding away. I tried to gain a foothold, but the surrounding effervescence took control and pulled me on, like swimming through clear liquid sand. My companion faded into the billowing torrent. I attempted to turn back-- no retreat. On and on I careened through the glassy sea, each scouring moment releasing an inner explosion of joy; a revelation dormant beneath my heavy-laden exterior.

All at once the tumultuous tide ebbed and I eased myself out into the warm breeze of a springtime morn, caressed by a fragrance, not merely aromatic, leaving me with a sweet assurance and a giddy expectation--weakened, refreshed, startled, rejuvenated, stripped but reborn beyond all realms of expression.

"What took you so long?" Joseph asked, laughing.

"It was my first time. I got lost."

"What was lost in there was never really needed."

"Lost. Jaakobah! I loosened my grip on him." I turned back to re-enter, gazing into the wall--no sign of him.

Joseph peered into the formidable barrier. "As I said, it has never been tried before. Till now the passage was based upon the destruction of the earth skin. Then, the heart and spirit can glide through to survive and grow," he said, nervously.

"What do you mean? Will he be all right?"

"I really don't know. You see, when we live in flesh we only see flesh. Even our hearts and spirits are aggravated by encumbering short-sighted earthly demands. The cherubim purges the heart, soul, and mind of all the worrisome conflicts. What emerges is who we really are when devoid of muscle, tissue and form."

Most informative, but not very comforting. "What if there is not enough valuable to push through?"

"As far as we know, the vanquished souls remain within, awaiting a champion."

"Champion?"

"You are the Son of Man."

"I don't understand."

"And here is your first rescue!" He pointed triumphantly towards the teeming froth.

Amazing. A decrepit palm, barely extending from the raging light, dark and crusty, bones poking through skin. Was it worth saving? Yet this much had survived, a determined remnant punching a hole to the other side.

I reached down and grabbed the devastated hand, and felt the flesh crackle as I gained a firmer grip. I pulled. Resistance from the flames. Tugged again. Progress. Slowly the skeletal remains slithered out onto the ground below, ablaze with the shimmering golden fluid, and lay twitching on the landing. Jaakobah, I presumed, in no pain, but no force of life to muster movement. Eyes bulged from shrunken sockets, skin gray, cracked and split, his arms weak and useless at his side, legs conforming to the position of his fall. I looked to Joseph. Before he could speak, I beheld a sea of hands protruding from the cherubim, in varying degrees of decay and brokenness, all reaching their bony fingers to gain a gracious grasp of exit.

Joseph stood in wonder. "These are the travelers that dreamed of a hope fulfilled in your coming. You were their promise. Now you must be their Savior."

I needed no further encouragement. I raced up and down the glistening edifice, yanking hands and pulling on anything daring to break through. One after another the writhing prisoners were dislodged from their position of delay, falling in piles, wallowing like fish snatched from the water, retrieved, but unsuited to the atmosphere. I continued the joyful liberation until all hands piercing the tide were freed to collapse in the world beyond. Thousands--no, more--yes, many more, a hurting horde huddled in heaving heaps. The confidence they had invested in their own abilities had debilitated their hearts and starved their souls.

"They cannot journey," I protested to Joseph. "What good have I done?" 'Twas an illusion of salvation, the remains incapable of survival.

"Wait." Joseph was staring off into the distance.

The scenery was stunning, land rich and green. As I watched, the landscape came alive. A twitching twig, a creeping in the grass, a bustling in the bush, a bed of flowers craning their stems--movement, inching forward. The forest of Eden was crawling, groping, and stretching, coming our way. Bushes and trees sprouted torso and limbs tumbling down the hillside, as the grass and leaves were swept and congealed into beings possessing body and motion, emanating shrieks of glee, a wilderness of children at play, making their descent upon the brittle souls, not actually plants, rather burgeoning, intelligent, fellows of bearing, speaking a language of purified silliness, rich in nobility and graced with speed. They somersaulted with shouts of triumph, gliding toward the broken sons of men.

I laughed, overcome by the vision. Joseph joined my festive giggle. The descent of emancipated greenery encompassed the incapacitated army, lifting, carrying, tickling, absorbing, like bouncing balls of youthful energy granted the grace and muscle of a legion of men. Somehow, they transfused their jubilation into the debilitated beings, a miracle, as these formerly imprisoned friends gained the strength to move; some even to stand. The rest were surrounded and toted away by rejoicing forms, communicating in a language of giggles and gurgles faster and faster, spinning, swirling. Soon, all the work was done and the horizon settled back into a vision of sparkling light and glorious shrubbery. .

"Where did they go? What will happen next? Who are the creatures? Will I see them again?" I burst with a flurry of questions.

"Seraphims--the same luminated bushes Moses saw, though he was careful to his reputation not to mention they also dance. They will take these weary friends to experience what they failed to discover during their journey on earth. They will have the chance to grow a heart and birth a soul." Joseph finished, turned, gliding away like a graceful deer, as I followed him into the heart of this Eden of man's desire.

****

Joseph disappeared.

I scanned my surroundings. Odd. Gone was the blossoming over-growth, and the sweet odor's reassurance. A sweltering heat beat upon my head, a humid furnace, the same oppressive, burning sunlight from Nazareth days.

I panted, perspiration streaming into my eyes. "There is no sweat in Eden." I spoke aloud.

I was moving in a full gallop across desert sand; late afternoon, the sun was low in the sky. My destination-- a small pit of mortar. How did I know that?

"Mortar?" I gasped.

Was I back in Nazareth on that horrible day? It all felt the same--same heat, eyes burning and twitching.

What was going on? I continued to race toward the pit, tears mingling with my sweat. Maybe I could just stop. Why should I relive this meaningless disaster? On I ran, driven by an aching, inquisitive dread.

Nearing the trench, I slowed, and then stopped, refusing to look. This was not Eden, rather a contrivance of hell. No God with style and grace would put me through this again!

I inched my way forward, while simultaneously wanting to retreat from the living grave. Then, an inspired notion. Perhaps I was being given an opportunity to change the outcome, my chance to right an inconceivable wrong. God brought me back to rescue my little brother. After all, I had saved the souls trapped in the cherubim's fire. What had Joseph said? "My destiny"--that was it. Maybe what we considered good fortune on Earth was the completion of successful retribution in the world beyond.

Seizing the moment, I jumped into the hole, digging, throwing giant handfuls of clay into the air. No Jomar, not even the small impression left in the sand. And where was Joseph? I had not labored alone. Joseph had broken his leg in the pit, undoubtedly, along with the death of his youngest son, leading to his early demise. I halted, shaken, realizing I had lost two loved ones in this narrow trench.

I resumed digging, driven to correct nature's error. Pulling, scraping, wheezing, laboring to exhaustion, gasping for air. "My God, my God! Why have you. . ." I paused. What was I asking? Did I believe my Father was the source of this destruction? I knelt down in the crusty surface of the clay. The sun's heat lessened and a cool breeze dried the sweat on my brow.

"I am not in there. I never was in there."

I looked up through tears, to see the little soul. "Jomar."

"Jesus!" he replied, grinning, displaying boyish vitality. "There are no answers in the clay, dear brother. There never were. This event became your root of bitterness. You held it in memory. At times, it nearly suffocated your faith, causing an unanswered question of heart, from which sprang all of the fears tormenting your journey. As you can see, you have blamed a small pit in the desert sand for taking a precious gift in your life. But I was never there. I was in Eden before one grain of sand sullied my homespun robe, celebrating my fifth birthday beyond the Cherubim in the beauty of Paradise."

"But it was so real, so tragic."

"It was not so real. And certainly no lasting tragedy."

"But when I think of what you could have become, the life you could have lived."

"Behold, what I have become. Consider the life I now live. When you blessed the children in Galilee, it was also for me. But, as you can see, I am blessed. You must let the root die, dry up, and be blown away."

As he spoke, my heart exploded, scattering triflets of anguish in all directions, as the tears liberated an avalanche of ideas lying dormant in my mind.

Jomar, joined by Joseph, offered his hand.

I reached up, touched him, and was lifted into the air, deposited exhilarated, on the ground above. "What was that?"

Jomar giggled.

"But a brush with the Glory," Joseph said.

"I forgot you haven't ascended," said Jomar, chuckling.

"If that's a brush, take me where I may immerse myself."

The three of us erupted in unbridled revelry. (We shall all know the cleanness of that one day very soon.) "I am ready," I said, as I stood to join my kindred.

"There is more for you to absorb," said Jomar, racing toward the golden beams sparkling in the distance.

"I must join him," said Joseph. He, too, sprinted away. I decided eternity must be a running place; souls seeming to gain energy through the chase. Joseph scampered along, his legs bulging with the dance of youth, in full power of his faculties, speeding off to new dreams.

A gorgeous tapestry of sky and the sweet, empowering fragrance of blooming life encompassed me in a whirl of dizzy delight.

"Walk with me."   A voice; gentle, but commanding.

I turned around, but no one was there.

"If you were to see an angel, son of man, what should be his appearance?" The voice again.

I pivoted, still nothing. "Forgive me, but I am a bit leery of angelic visitors."

"Oh, really, and why might that be?"

"The last angel I spoke to had fallen somewhat from my lofty ideal."

"Too bad, perhaps I should have stayed around at the well, but you were in over your head, and when you finally surfaced, too exhausted to converse."

He began to take shape, skin bronze, like the glint of fine armor. His smile, polished pearl.

"So you're the one who pulled me from the well outside the Camp of Deliverance."

"I did with your help."

"It is wisdom to climb toward a rescue."

"Then walk with me, and see what you might discover."

"You mean there's more to see?"

"We never lack adventure."

And so, we rushed into the beauty before us, like young pals at play,   stallions itching with springtime madness, beckoned to a festive romp.   The essence of budding excellence within our grasp--glimmering greens and lustrous yellows, glossy with the richness of hue.

"Come and plant your gift of life here amongst the rest." My comrade pointed to an open spot I thought, seconds before, had been engulfed with rapturous foliage.

"What is your name, dear angel?"

"What name would you like? Wait! I think I know. You wish my name to be that of a commonly revered virtue."

"How did you know that?"

He smiled at me. "Eden is a land of surprise, not secret.   I know your whims and choose to remain uninformed, until you desire to share. Still grasping the idea?"

I nodded, bowing my head.

"My name is. . .Longsuffering."

I crinkled my face, contemplating.

He burst into laughter. "Longsuffering!" he roared. "You mortals really must think heaven is a dull place. Do you suppose we sit around and talk about God all day?"

"I didn't know. . . "

"Actually, we sit around and let God talk about Himself!"

I huffed a laugh and the more I thought, the more I chuckled, until both of us were clapping our hands and slapping our thighs in a gleeful outburst.

"My name is Sandiel," he said through the levity.

I frowned, not sure he was serious.

"I think they chose it because it rhymes with Gabriel."

We both found this inexplicably funny and were once again overcome with sheer silliness.

"What should I plant?" I inquired, as the fit subsided.

"You have in your mind a treasure chest of memories, fruitful pearls from your earthly stay. It is here in this garden the spiritually and emotionally destitute can come and be nourished to health so as to continue their journey to the Glory."

"You mean each one of these areas is a garden of one human soul?"

"It is their tale, filled with the joys and lessons of the heart. Each soul garners so much personal treasure during habitation. Now, you can enter their garden and become one with their dreams, victories, and conflicts. Unfortunately, some souls learned very little because they risked nothing, or squandered their passions on deception. For them, this Garden of Souls is a place of rekindling; here they can come, dwell, and regain their innocence, the essence of their true humanity, and comprehend the place prepared for them."

Such a splendid explanation. "What shall I place in my garden?"

"Walk amongst the beauty of your fellows. I'm sure a righteous notion will come your way."

He ambled away, giving me place to enjoy the spectacle.

I stepped into the brisk flow of a tiny brook and was transported in a breath, entering the garden life of a woman, surrounded by a gentle flow of emoting memories. At first, I watched the scenes played out before me, then, gaining courage, I became a part of the unfolding; my spirit entwined with the heroine of the tale, feeling the rush of girlish joy when she became betrothed to the loving man of her dreams, and permeated with the sensations of their union and the bliss released in their pleasure. I joined her through childbirth and the relief and unabashed exuberance over the great human reward derived from her effort. Mother and wife--I was privy and portion to the mixed emotion; there as she grew older, attaining the status of matron with great honor, wisdom, and purpose.

Entering the garden of another living soul, I found myself in total darkness, yet surrounded by powerful sounds and odors--the memory-life of a man-child born blind, an experience rich with texture and taste, a manly passage, attune to the subtle nuance of voice.

I moved forward. On and on I foraged into this forest of rich human emotion, with spiritual wanderlust. What had Sandiel called it? A garden, yes, THE GARDEN OF SOULS, truly a harvest of the finest of human seed.

My heart was joined with the royalty of kings deciding the fate of nations, celebrated the outpouring of gratitude from the pauper given bread at his greatest moment of need, memories of children in gregarious play, the intrigue of diplomacy, and the thrill of mutual love shared in deep moments of committed sexual exchange. Trivialities stood side by side with deep lasting interchange, equally sensed, equally valuable. It was a sanctuary where the spiritually famished could enter a feeding frenzy of experiential delight.

I merged with dynamic people who never gained much earthly prominence, but possessed a wealth of yield.

Unaware of the passage of time, deeper and deeper I traversed into the conservatory. Colors conceived in dreams flashed in brilliance before my thirsty eyes, as I plumped on the blessing shared by those who had planted their memories; deep and tender interludes of God's involvement in their earthly span. Other inhabitants, mostly bruised and ancient, were dragging their feeble remains through the gardens, and emerging with ruddy cheeks and a renewed spark of life.

The conclusion was intoxicating. Mortality was not a brief vapor of puff and smoke, but rather living bread to the starving seekers--our dreams immortal. Those rescued from the Cherubim's judgment will be delivered to this Paradise, to gorge themselves until the heart-life of others can trickle into their emptied insides.

Now, it was my time. I searched and found the place Sandiel had set aside for my planting, sat in the middle of my space, closed my eyes and let the memories flow, rich with family and friends. Egypt, Xantrippe, Anisa, Joseph, Mary--each face spurred a feeling which lit a fire, igniting fresh recollection. The events of my life were still enriching to me, like a warm cloak which has served well and can be graciously placed upon the shoulders of a shivering friend.

My mind journeyed faster than I could ever assimilate on my own, a sound vessel, steering my recollections, discovering my place of harbor   for those children yet to come. I slowly opened my eyes, surrounded by burgeoning greenery and wide-petaled flowers, tree limbs hanging down, heavy-laden with fruit dripping with juice. My garden. I was giddy with the satisfaction of a farmer granted a bumper crop.

"Ahh. . ." Sandiel, admiring the results. "This is the first soul to visit your garden, Son of Man." Nestled in his bosom was a broken waif of a man I recognized-- Jaakobah. "You told him he would be with you in Paradise," Sandiel continued, gently passing Jaakobah into my open arms.

"I have given my life to you," I whispered. "Come, my friend, and eat your fill. I enjoyed my time while living. Come and feast, so you might really find your life."

I hugged his frail frame. With great effort, he looked up at me, his eyes moist with tears. A small shudder rattled his body, as he fell on his knees and crawled into my space, soon hidden from view by a fine cool mist.

"He'll be fine now," said Sandiel.

I was flabbergasted, thrilled by hope. Sometimes it appeared that life on earth had been ransacked of value. Now I was seeing the reason emerging from the rout, far more elevating than any concept of eternal life conjured in hallowed halls by the spiritual clerics of the day.

"Walk with me." Sandiel launched in his customary brisk pace. We glided deeper into the awe-inspiring caverns imprinted with the handiwork of a most creative God. "Here is the center of the garden," Sandiel declared, finally slowing to a stop--simply a small clearing inhabited by two trees. "You will choose."

"Are you assuming I know what you're talking about?"

"It is for you to choose."

"Adam was given the benefit of further revelation."

Before me were the two trees in the middle of the garden--the Tree of Life and the Tree of the Knowledge of Good and Evil. "Tell me, Sandiel, what would be the fault of choosing knowledge over life?"

"With one you get both. With the other you achieve neither."

"Well said, especially considering you lack the temptation necessary to rejoice over good judgment."

"It is the duty of angels to proclaim without benefit to refrain."

We exchanged smiles.

I considered the two trees, one large and billowing with leaves literally sprouting from other leaves, no barren space, full and lush,   gnarled at the trunk, adding further evidence of maturity.

The other was smaller, perhaps at one time bloomed with colors, but leaves had fallen, drying in piles on the ground below. As I stood and watched, this lesser tree changed colors three times in a matter of four breaths. First green, then blue, followed by red. Finally it settled on a most common brown.

"It is for you to choose," repeated Sandiel.

I chuckled. "It is a most serious choice, dear angel. Mankind has always deemed the accumulation of information as the first step to achieving maturity and inner peace. Of course, this has always proven to be erroneous. The problem is, all knowledge is ultimately filtered through human desire, stripped of all its sacrificial nature. What is left? Self-gratification." I paused. Sandiel stifled a grin. "Life, on the other hand, is a variable, demanding our full attention to detail, without any guarantee of reward.   I choose this one," I said, walking over to the ever-changing, but presently dull and brown, smaller tree.   "This tree is confused and unpredictable, yet sometimes colorful enough to represent the uncertainty of life."

I picked a piece of the fruit and bit a large juicy hunk from the purple and yellow pod.

My head began to spin, like I was going to faint. I was being pulled away, the sensation very similar to the whirlwind that had brought me to Paradise. Yet this time I was spiraling down. The visions returned, cascading before me--my friends, gathered in an upper room, heads bowed, and prayers offered. I saw women collecting flasks and bottles in preparation for a burial. Mekel at a banquet, lying in a drunken daze, surrounded by the lords and ladies of Judean royalty.

Onward I twirled, leaving the light of Eden to fall into a deeper and deeper pit of darkness. Was this hell? Had I chosen my tree poorly? The descent continued. I saw soldiers gathered around a fire in the chilly night, and Caiaphas in full priestly garb, a rope tied around his ankle, incense burning in his hands. Peter, weeping by a tree.

All at once, breath returned to my lungs, and a sense of the normal   aches, pains, and creaking associated with mortality.

I fell, pleading for purpose, when suddenly I plopped into a soft pillow-like form, immediately feeling cramped and confined. I had achieved body. I struggled and wriggled, the jolt of earthly life rushed through my limbs and erupted in a throbbing quiver from the top of my grimy head to the bottom of my dried and crusty feet.

I jerked straight up and screamed, "I said, it is finished!"

A snicker from a corner of the black enclosure. This was no longer Eden. I peered through the darkness, seeking the invisible jovial chuckler.

"Welcome back, Jesus, Son of the Most High." Sandiel. I knew his voice but could not see him.

"Am I blind?"

"No, just needing enlightened." He lifted his arms and a glow of light gradually lit the room.

"Where am I?"

"You chose well. You selected the unpredictability of life over the religion of knowing."

"So, I am rewarded by descending into this dark cave of Hades?"

"You are rewarded with glorious resurrection. How does the body feel?"

"It appears to all be here. A bit bruised and cut."

"Crucifixion tends to damage property without recourse."

"It's a tight fit," I said ruefully.

"You have grown in Paradise, both in spirit and heart."

"So. . . I am alive again?"

"Just as you said."

"What now?"

"You will go and tell them they can have this fullness of life, too."

"I can do that."

"There are limitations."

"I assumed."

"Just forty days. You mustn't overuse this body. It has been shattered by the Calvary atrocity. Be careful. Make it last." Sandiel was like a father warning a youngster on points of etiquette. "You will have the power to move in spirit, but also eat and fellowship with them."

"I see. And exactly what do you expect them to believe?"

"Those who already believe will feel justified. Those who never did will just double their efforts to remain in doubt. Lord, many will see you but not all will believe." Sandiel, a good friend, trying to ease the pain of a pending blow.

Being human, I knew all of this. Proof does not guarantee action. Fortunately, though, it does not take hundreds to propel a good idea. "I am ready."

"Let me take care of the stone." A streak of golden lightening thrust from his hands and rolled the stone away. A beam of yellow light flooded the cave.

"I am risen!" I started through the opening, paused, gazing down at the slab of stone where I had been laid, grave clothes in disarray. "Better stop and fold these up. Someone will notice a sloppy job. Anyway, there is no hurry now."

I completed the task, placing them neatly on the slab.

"Mary would be proud," said Sandiel dryly.

"Mary would be shocked," I laughed. "Are you coming?"

"No, I have an appointment with some ladies who have chosen to be early risers."

I shrugged and bounded toward the opening.

"Lord?"

"Yes, Sandiel." I said, pausing at the entrance.

"Happy Easter!"

Epilogue

A field of blood, potter's turf, occupied by one shallow grave, the width and length of a man, unmarked, with a small tuft of robe poking through the shifting sand. The dogs from the hills would soon visit by night.

"You are the last. I have met with the rest. I promised to come back. I am here." I stood bracing myself against a stiff wind blowing from north to south, spraying sand in my eyes; a howl of disapproval raised from the chilling breeze.

"Where was the change, Judas? When did I lose contact with your heart?" There was no answer, as well should be. For Kerioth was quite dead and the opportunity for life long gone. I stood for a moment searching for some semblance of reason--an intangible yet uncovered. Were there answers? Certainly not on a frigid Judean hillside at the grave of a comrade turned traitor. I knelt and scooped some sandy soil in my hands, attempting to cover the exposed piece of robe.

A decent burial. What does that mean?

"Good-bye, dear friend. I asked the Father to forgive you, because you certainly did not know what you did." I walked away, a dog yelping in the near distance.

****

Forty days, newly human. In Paradise I had no real yearning to return to the puzzle. Now earthbound, no real pining for the beyond. A great gift from God--blessing to find purpose in each stopover.

I was left with just three days, making my plans to go to Bethlehem and spend time remembering the joys of the journey. I had seen everyone except James. I had just about resigned myself I would leave this Earth a second time without seeing him, when suddenly he was there, standing in front of me, on a deserted stretch of road near Jericho. His face was thoughtful and stained with the furrows of tears, eyes scrunched as if bursting with questions leaping over one another to gain precedence.

I was going to Bethlehem, I said, taking a step toward him.

He remained still so I halted my advance. I wanted to speak but submitted to the wisdom of silence. This was his time. Too many moments had been robbed from him and given to my charge.

I am sorry I was not at. . . the. . . a. . . cross, he said, choking back the tears. I tried to be. I just couldn t." He paused as his eyelids flickered with the overflow of tears, easing himself to a seated position in the middle of the well-worn path. "You know, that is something Papa always refused to build. I nodded and smiled, remembering Joseph s aversion to the construction of crosses. I couldn t believe they were killing you, he said, dabbing his eyes with huge, soiled hands.

I stood still, afraid to breathe.

I can t believe you are alive. The statement lacked affirming joy. I always knew you were special. God knows, Mary made that clear. For years I thought your name was special. He smirked and I carefully mirrored his grin. Do you know what drove me craziest? If you were so damn special, then how come I could do everything better than you? I could run faster, jump higher, work longer, eat more, and laugh louder than you ever could. He stopped and probed my eyes.

No contest.

. She never thought what I did was important. You were precious by being born but I couldn t get to be special no matter how I tried. An explosion of raging tears. I moved to draw close but he pulled away. He didn t need my arms, just my ears.

He continued, weeping unashamedly. She was wrong to do that! I see, now, you are special, because of your work. But I can be valuable in my life just like you. James sobbed, as I watched quietly. This is going to change my life, he said, chuckling, crying, and coughing all at the same time.

It s changed mine.

He glanced up as if shocked to hear my voice, then released a sprite of boyish laughter. I suppose it has. He took a step toward me and then hesitated.

I didn t plan this. . . I held out a hand.

I know. . ." He observed the invitation.

No, you don t know. I didn't plan this, but I didn't resist, so God was able to do His will and mine in all my dealings.

Religion never meant to me what it means to you, he said flippantly.

You're right. It means nothing to me. It bores me so much I want to jump off the Nazareth cliffs in despair.

Me, too, he sighed, greatly relieved.

The air grew still. He stood quietly. What am I going to do, Jesus? He fell in my arms, and wept like a little brother should be able to do in the security of his elder brother s embrace.

Live on! But remember to use your life to enrich your own soul. Then open your heart to share this wealth with those who have folded their tent to dry up and die.   .

I love you, big brother.

I never doubted it.

I will honor your memory by keeping the dream alive.

Just say yes and really mean yes. And when you say no, back it up to mean no.

He hugged me again, turned, and sauntered down the road. I thought about following but decided this was the perfect farewell for two brothers who dwelt in the same house, shared little in common, but always knew they loved each other.

****

My voyage to the past is over, back in Bethlehem in the manger, time to go. Climbing the stairs I pause to look across the darkened cave. A dubious place to begin, yet a fine place to end.

Opening the door, I'm engulfed by the light of the fading day. Relah and her brother Gretoon sit quietly at a table, eating. She makes no greeting.

Thank you, I said, handing her my small pouch of coins.

You paid me already. She stares straight ahead, munching a morsel.

I will not need this provision. I dropped the leather purse on the table. Without blinking an eye, she snatches the coinage and buries it deeply in her bosom. The retrieval is comical. I want to laugh but opt for a neutral smile.

Thank you, she says demurely.

Thank you." I walked toward Gretoon, who sat still, wide-eyed, with his right hand seemingly stuck in a bowl of soup, dinner dribbling down his chin.

Gretoon is busy eating, she said, stepping between her brother and my approach. Something's very wrong. I mentioned your name to some townsfolk.

I see.

Just then Peter walked through the door, without knocking.

Who are you? Relah whirled and spat at him Don't they knock in your cave in the hills?

Peter looked at me with that helpless look men get when women wax maternal.

He is my friend. I try to retrieve Peter from his wounded state.

Is he dead, too? That is what I was told--Jesus of Nazareth is dead.

I ll wait outside. Peter exits nervously.

Coward, I yelled after him.

It is just another hoax, Relah jabbed furiously, tear in her eye hinting of disappointment.

Hoax? No.

Then explain."

Explain? No, again.

She stares, confused, ready for a verbal warfare that would never commence.

I walk to Gretoon, stroking his head and removing the soaked hand from its dipping place in the food pool, washing it off with a soft cloth.

Here, my dear friend. I placed a rock in his hand, about the size of a rabbi s nose, which seemed dwarfed in the massive paw of this silent giant. Remember. Grrr...ooot. This is the stone we tossed in the stable. Grr....ooot is Gretoon.

I said it again, and a third time.

Relah stands in silence. I avoided her glance, ignoring her disap-proval.

Grrr...ooot is Gretoon, I whispered in his ear for the fourth time.

Are you dead? demanded Relah, interrupting.

Not now, I spoke over my shoulder, continuing my conversation with Gretoon.

Squeeze the stone, dear brother. Believe. You are Gretoon. Grr......ooot is Gretoon. Just squeeze this stone and believe. You are Gretoon.

Grr...ooot, he blurts forth, just like he had done in the stable.

Squeeze it and believe Grrr....ooot is Gretoon, I repeated as I stepped away, maintaining my gaze into those bulging eyes.

What is this? Magical potions and mystical stones? Relah asked defiantly.

Maybe. But it is the only magic your brother has granted us. I can not explain my reasons to you today, Relah." I said, turning her toward me. "Just let this gentlemen have his stone, and if you desire, encourage him to squeeze it, pray, sit back and note his progress.

And if there is no progress?

Take the stone, throw it away, wash his hand, give him dinner, and love him as you have so many days before."

Grr....ooot, came the basal grunt from behind us.
She whirled around and said, I heard it!
He remembers.
Grr...oooot, Relah shrieked.
Grr...ooot, comes the monotone reply from her stony-faced brother.

On and on they go until they are so involved in the treatment they no longer need the doctor.

I say goodbye, but the frenzied siblings don't hear me, so I step outside into the late afternoon sun, Peter pacing a few feet away.

That woman scares me," he says, his eyes shifting in terror.

Me, too. Let s get out of here before she thinks of more things to say. We ran off in mock horror, chuckling as we stepped. After a furlong or two we slowed our pace, walking in silence; so much to say, no place to start.

"I followed you to the grave. . . Judas."
"It was cold."
"Windy and cold. Why did you go?"
"Why did you follow?"
"Curious."
"Me, too."
"What did you find?"
"Memories and feelings cluttered with confusing realities."
"I think I understand."
"You probably do."
"It could have been me."
"You think?"
"A traitor is a man who lives too long in denial."
"Saved in time."
"You knew I would do it."
"Deny?"
"Yes, deny you."
"That's why I told you, so you wouldn't be shocked by your own action and would know I already had forgiven you."
"You forgive me?" Peter choked.
"I forgive Judas, and he's gone. You have your whole life to be faithful."
"Thanks to you."
"Your faith, my patience, God's grace."
Peter glanced into the distance. Your mother.
Mary, silhouetted in the gleam of the setting sun.
I will meet you at the mount, said Peter, giving a quick embrace, excusing himself; running ahead, but

stopping briefly to touch the face of the descending matron of honor.

I walked toward her and she to me.

If we had done this earlier, we could have breached our differences in half the time, I said, getting within earshot. .

Differences? Son, you know I am incapable of being difficult, she feigned offense and then burst into laughter. You saw James?

Yes, I did. We embraced each other's causes. I was beginning to wonder if any of my family was ever going to hug me.

We were afraid to, explained Mary. After Magdalene told us how fussy you were in the garden after your resurrection about being touched, well. . . we couldn t risk the rebuke.

Mary Magdalene does not embrace. She possesses. We laughed and then stood silently looking into the fading light.

I saw him, I said to her.

She smiled. I knew if there was any way, Joseph would be there to greet you.

He was. He was my guide.

She chuckled. I almost asked you if he was well. Quite a question.

He's very human.

Compliment or insult?

Compliment. Paradise is a place where humanity is revered.

Don t tell me anymore. I will find out soon enough and I don t need to have my mind on the heavens when the earth screams for my involvement. Once again, Mary of Nazareth chose the prudence of the practical--her precious way.

Dear woman, do you know God rejected all the lineage of David to bestow his hope in your body?

She didn't respond.

I am not the Son of David! It is my joy to be the son of man, birthed and nourished by his dear servant, Mary!

She turned and ascended the mount, finished with conversation; she would ponder these things in her heart.

I remained, desiring a final glimpse. Soon I would see THE GLORY. But here, I experienced the kingdom through His power.

Paradise. I wondered if many souls ever returned from THE GLORY to spend time at the Garden of Souls in Eden.

I supposed not. Once enraptured in the victory, the memories of the struggle do seem to lack much promise.

I believed, though, I would return on occasion, more or less to trace the roots begetting me such an offspring of life.

I was wrong at Golgotha.

It is not finished.

Rather, a beginning; where God creates a new realm of heart so our redeemed souls can receive the consummate joys of Eternal Bliss.

THE END

Acknowledgments

Cover Model: Jerrod Micah Cring
Cover Photo: Tim Cope
Cover Design: Janethan
Editor: Janet Scott
Logo Design: Dolly Cring
Research: Steve Kimbrell, Angela Cring
Investors: Jerrod and Angela Cring, Bruce Crower, Steve and Sharon Kimbrell, Troy and Melody Scott, Alan and Nadine Fitzpatrick, Russ Cring, Brian Roles, Janet Scott

Special thanks to 18:1,2

****

I hope you enjoyed the book and the story told from the perspective of our protagonist, Jesus. Being human, as he was, you have approximately 41 hours to relate your enthusiasm about this book to a friend or family member before the normal pressures of life and the duties of the trail place the experience on file. If you would like to write to the author and share your discoveries or order additional copies of the work you may address all correspondence to:

> **I'M. . . the legend of the son of man**
> **LWS Publishers**
> **227 Bayshore Drive**
> **Hendersonville, Tennessee 37075**
> **(615)826-3871**
> **1-800-643-4718 Access code 74**
> **www.imsonofman.com**

Thanks for your time and may the legend live on!

Glossary of Characters

Alphaeus *(Al-fee-us)*: Friend of John the Baptist
Andrew *(An-drew)*: Disciple and Simon Peter's brother
Anisa *(Ah-knee-sa)*: Princess of Treoli
Annas *(An-is)*: Chief priest and father-in-law of Caiaphas
Bandi *(Ban-dee)*: Guard of Princess Anisa
Bantar *(Ban-tar)*: Stonemason, employer of Joseph in Egypt
Barabbas *(Bar-ab-bus):* Zealot leader--Camp of Deliverance
Beloit *(Ba-loytt)*: Dwarf, wise one from the East
Benjamin *(Ben-jah-men)*: Co-prisoner, Camp of Deliverance
Berkiel *(Burr-key-ell)*: Original innkeeper
Beskel *(Bes-kell):* Giant chief of guards, Camp of Deliverance
Blastus *(Blast-us)*: Chamberlain to King Herod
Caiaphas *(Kay-a-phis)*: Chief priest
Chenaul *(Sha-nawl)*: Female wise one from the East
Chiolita *(She-oh-lee-tah:* Matriarch of Nazareth
Chusa *(Chew-zah)*: Steward to King Herod--Joanna's husband
Claudia *(Claw-dee-ah)*: Pilot's wife
Elijah *(Ee-lie-jah)*: Prophet on Mount
Elizabeth *(Ee-liz-a-beth:* Mother of John the Baptist
Exodusat *(X-odd-oh-sat):* Commander at Camp of Deliverance
Gen. Rasuti *(Rah-suit-ee):* Rival for Triolian throne
Gretoon *(Gra-tune)*: Relah's brain-damaged brother
Hagabus *(Hag-ah-bus)*: Priest and patriarch of Nazareth
Herod *(herr-odd)*
...**(the Great)**: Infanticide of Bethlehem
...**(Antipas)** *(An-tah-pus)*: Beheader of John
Herodias *(Hair-oh-dee-us):* Wife of Antipas, mother of Salome
Jaakobah *(Jay-coe-baah):* Emissary to Barabbas
Jacob *(Jay-cob)*: Also known as Jude, brother of Jesus
Jairus *(Jay-I-russ)*: Temple friend to boy Jesus
James
...**(brother)**: 2nd oldest son of Joseph
...**(fisherman)**: Disciple, brother of John
...**(disciple)**: Son of Alphaeus
Jamon *(Jay-mawn)*: Little Jeremiah's father
Jartanza *(Jarr-tan-zah):* Chaldean mystic
Jehu *(Jay-who)*: Zealot warrior-thief
Jeremiah *(Jer-ah-my-ah)*: Little friend of boy Jesus
Jesus *(Jee-sus)*: Son of man, protagonist
Joanna *(Joe-ann-ah)*: Chusa's wife, Jesus' companion
John
...**(the Baptist)**: Cousin to Jesus
...**(the fishernman)**: Son of Zebedee
Jomar *(Joe-mar)*: Jesus' little brother
Jona *(Joe-nah)*: Father to Simon and Andrew
Joseph *(Joe-sef)*: Father to Jesus, husband to Mary
Joseph (little): Last child born to carpenter family
Judas *(Jew-dus)*: Son of Simon, Iscariot
Jude *(Jew-d)*

...(brother): Other name for Jacob
...(disciple): Brother of James, son of Alphaeus
Justin *(Just-in)*: Comrade of Alphaeus
Kerioth *(Keer-ee-oth)*: City and nickname of Judas
Krebel *(Kree-bell)*: Barabbas' raiding partner
Lazarus *(Laz-ah-russ)*: Brother to Mary and Martha
Madez *(May-dez)*: Nicodemus' son--withered hand
Malchus *(Mal-kus)*: Chief servant to Caiaphas
Marius *(Marry-us)*: Spy from Bethabarra
Martha *(Marr-thah)*: Sister of Mary of Bethany
Mary
...(mother): Wife of Joseph, mother of Jesus
...(Magdalene): Former possessed- supporter of Jesus
...(of Bethany): Lazarus' sister Madez's wife
Matthan *(May-thin)*: Old man in stable
Matthew *(Math-you)*: Tax collector, disciple
Mekel *(Mee-kel)*: Incarnate of Satan
Michael *(My-cull)*: Companion to Alphaeus
Moses *(Moe-sus)*: Law-giver, visits Jesus on Mount
Naomi *(Nay-oh-me)*: Little girl from Nazareth
Nathaniel *(Nah-than-yell)*: Disciple of Jesus
Nicodemus *(Nick-oh-dee-mus)*: Brother to Hagabus
Philip *(Fill-up)*: Of the Essenes, disciple
Pilate *(pie-lit)*: Procurator of Judea
Praella *(Pray-ell-ah)*: Mother to Anisa
Rachel *(Ray-chel)*: Mother to Jeremiah
Ratheal *(Raw-thee-ell)*: Mary of Nazareth's suitor
Relah *(Ray-lah)*: Granddaughter of innkeeper
Ruth *(Rooth)*: Sister of Jesus
Salome *(Sal-oh-may)*: Dancing daughter to Herodias
Samuel *(Sam-you-ell)*: Guard to John the Baptist
Sandiel *(San-dee-ell)*: Angel in Paradise
Santere *(San-tarry)*: Chief of the wise ones from the East
Sariola *(Sar-ee-oh-lah)*: Exodusat's woman
Shira *(Shy-rah)*: Trinius' wife
Silvedius *(Sil-vay-dee-us)*: Centurian at the cross
Simon *(Si-man)*
...(boy zealot): Son of Jehu
...(of the zealots): Disciple
...(the leper): Witness against Hagabus
...(Peter): Disciple of Jesus
Susannah *(Sue-zan-ah)*: Ex-prostitute
Tabuli Manta *(Tah-boo-lee Mon-tah)*: Sage for Triolian caravan
Thomas *(Tom-us)*: Disciple at Cana
Trinius *(Trin-ee-us)*: Husband to Shira
Veronica *(Ver-on-ih-cah)*: Wife to Caiaphas
Veshioli *(Vesh-ee-oh-lee)*: Chief of the spies
Xantrippe *(Zan-trip-ee)*: Mentor for Jesus in Egypt
Zebedee *(Zeb-ah-dee)*: Fisherman from tavern